AN ILLUSION OF LOVE

SCHOOL OF MAGIC, BOOK 3

PATRICIA RICE

Book View Café

An Illusion of Love

Patricia Rice

Published by Rice Enterprises, Dana Point, CA, an affiliate of Book View Café Publishing Cooperative P.O. Box 1624, Cedar Crest, NM 87008-1624
http://bookviewcafe.com
Cover design by Kim Killion
ISBN 978-1-61138-886-2 e-book
ISBN 978-1-61138-887-9 print

ONE

SPRING, *1871*

THE CORONER'S DAMP DUNGEON STANK OF FORMALDEHYDE AND WORSE.
Azmin Malcolm Dougall turned up the oil lamps to drive the eerie
shadows into the corners. She chose to call the underlying scent *mold*—
not decay.

She'd seen decomposing corpses before. Calcutta had unfortunately
been littered with them after the cyclone. She accepted that the corporeal shell housing the human spirit was a natural element that returned
to the earth just as dying leaves did. The spirit was what mattered.

To that end—she set up her tripod, slipped her experimental dry
plate into her camera, and perched the box on the stand. The chemicals
she was using to produce the dry process plates were cutting into her
budget, but she'd created some exciting results that gave her hope she
might have discovered her gift.

Tonight, she added to the experiment with her new—and dangerous
—magnesium reflector.

The oil lamps flickered in an unexpected draft, and she frowned. The
cellar shouldn't allow air currents. That was the reason she had set her

first experiment here. Light was the key to success and flickering would ruin the image.

She set up her new reflector to illuminate the corpse on the slab. Thankfully, for her purpose, the body needn't be uncovered.

Lighting the last lamp, Azmin held her breath, positioned herself behind the box, lit the magnesium coil—and uncovered the lens to catch the flaring light.

The door swung in with a rush of spring wind, extinguishing half the lamps, and plunging the cellar into gloom except for the bright explosion of the magnesium.

"Bloody hell!" the uncivilized intruder shouted in fury.

Muttering an unladylike curse under her breath, Azmin covered the lens. The shot was ruined, and so were her chances of catching the corpse's spirit.

The wretch entering practically electrified the chamber with a furious energy that might terrify both living and dead into fleeing. Azmin, however, wasn't of the fearful sort. She studied the rude apparition in the remaining dim light.

Tall, lean, wearing a white lab coat that failed to conceal menacingly broad shoulders, the intruder visibly calmed himself by shoving a long-fingered hand into his mop of thick dark hair. Swinging to her, he glared. His unfashionably clean-shaven jaw and sharp cheekbones exposed centuries of intimidatingly aristocratic ancestry. In the dim light of the one overhead light, his eyes gleamed silver as they narrowed.

Azmin glowered back. Despite his white lab coat, Azmin recognized the professor, and her insides lurched. She'd once traveled halfway around the world to avoid the rake. He was even more magnificent now than he had been as a student.

"What the. . . Hades. . . are you doing?" he demanded, amending his intended obscenity.

"Packing my equipment," Azmin replied in her brightest, most insouciant manner. She had always liked to irritate Dr. Alexander Dare the same way he irritated her.

Irritation might not be quite the correct word. But despite appearances, she was a lady, and she did not use carnal words. Or even think them. The frustration he caused had always been of a physical nature.

"Who gave you permission to be in here?" Recovering from his momentary shock, the good doctor proceeded to the slab and threw back a corner of the sheet, revealing a man's bare chest. "I haven't much time. You need to remove yourself forthwith."

The man still had the world's longest lashes, concealing stone-cold eyes—iron gray at times like this.

"Forthwith," she mocked. "Who stuck that stick up your rump? You used to be fun."

"Children have fun. Men work. And you haven't answered me. What are you doing here and who gave you permission? This is no place for a lady." Setting down his leather bag, he produced a small tool case and laid it open on a table.

Azmin packed her far less expensive carpet valise. "The coroner's wife is interested in spiritualism. I have permission to photograph the spirits of the recently deceased, not that it's any of your business, but it is thoughtful of you to remember that I *am* a lady."

"Spiritualism," he snorted. "Do you rattle bones and raise sheets? The dead are dead."

"Their bodies are, agreed. And if a spiritualist would allow me into a séance, I might learn whether or not she was actually raising spirits. But for some reason, they won't allow photographic equipment." She snapped her valise closed and shouldered the long handle of her reflector.

"And what good would it do you to photograph a spirit, even if they existed? They can't talk." He drew a mark over the corpse's chest. "You're better off learning something useful, like knitting."

He hit on a sore point. She *wanted* to be useful. She was a Malcolm. Malcolms had psychical talents that helped others. She should have more useful gifts than knitting—if only she could discover them.

If glass plates didn't cost so much, she'd throw one at the professor's head.

She didn't want his attention, she reminded herself. Ten years ago, she'd traveled halfway around the world to India to avoid having anything to do with the man. It was just her rotten luck that when she chose to return to the most remote outpost she could visit—Edinburgh —he was here too.

She let herself out of the cellar. He didn't even notice.

~

ZANE NOTICED THE INSTANT AZMIN DOUGALL DEPARTED. THE SUBTLE scent of exotic flowers disappeared with her, leaving only the stench of formaldehyde and decay.

He hadn't known she was in Edinburgh until they'd both been invited to the same country estate over Christmas. He thought she was in India, where Hindu princesses belonged.

He cracked the corpse's rib cage and pried open a path to the man's heart and lungs. The coroner's notes said the deceased smoked cigars, and the evidence of that was in his lungs. But had that caused the weakened state of his heart?

Absorbed in his work, Zane managed to forget the irritating female and her flashing lamp until he'd snipped out the organ he intended to examine in his lab. Sewing up the incision, he winced as he remembered telling the lady to learn knitting. The Azmin he'd once known would have heaved heavy objects at his head. She'd only been about sixteen then. She'd grown up.

She'd *definitely* grown up. Tightening the lid on the jar containing his specimen, Zane tried to block out memories of the skinny, rebellious adolescent garbed in colorful gossamer that illuminated her dusky skin and made her stand out like a peacock among pigeons.

These days, she appeared to be wearing widow's weeds. He supposed she was old enough to have been married. He should probably tell his niece that one of the marquess's relations was in town. Louisa was lonely for company. . .

Have Azmin flitting around his house? Squash that idea. He should find company more Louisa's age. He'd been meaning to speak to the ladies at the School of Malcolms. Louisa couldn't attend, but perhaps they had students who might visit. He should have done that months ago, after he'd heaved out the last governess.

He'd been more intent on the research that might save Louisa's life.

After donning his coat and locking up, he stepped into the unlit lane smelling of urine and spring flowers. Only then did he wonder what transport Miss Dougall had used—he had to keep thinking of her as a woman and not an adolescent brat. This wasn't exactly the safest area of Old Town for a lady. His social training really had deteriorated these last years to have let her go without asking.

He scanned the medieval alley between towering stone buildings, but only shadows beckoned. Carrying his physician's satchel, he strode down to the main road where wind cleared the air. He shouldn't be worrying about the damned female. She probably had servants and a carriage. Her father had made a fortune in India, and she had too many aristocratic connections to have married into poverty.

Accustomed to walking the ancient streets of the university and hospital sector at all hours, Zane strode past gaslights toward the Georgian mansion he currently called home. He'd like to return to his laboratory, but he neglected Louisa enough as it was. The whole point of paying the outrageous lease in George Square was so that he could go home occasionally to let the household know he was alive.

A rumble of male voices from the tavern ahead warned of trouble. The tavern attracted students. They wouldn't dare bother him, and he could hope his presence might quell the dispute.

"I'm going after the bugger," one of the men shouted, hunting for a handhold on a wall. The street was a mixture of commercial and obscure businesses, some with enclosed work yards designed to keep out trespassers.

"That damned light nearly blinded me!" another drunkard shouted, waving a fist and nearly staggering backward. "What in hell was that?"

"Photographic equipment," a vaguely familiar male voice suggested.

Zane slowed his stride, recognizing one of his lazier students. Septimus Jenkins leaned against the tavern, drinking from a flask and not joining his inebriated companions in attempting to scale a wall. Perhaps he wasn't as stupid as he seemed.

Photographic equipment? Remembering the bright light Azmin. . . Miss Dougall. . . had been using in the cellar, Zane quelled his instinctive reaction and approached as professor to student. "I'd suggest one not risk head surgery by climbing a wall in your current state, gentlemen, especially a wall into a private yard."

"We were assaulted," the one with his hand on top of the wall cried. "We can't let him escape."

"I will have to report you to the authorities if you continue," Zane said in a bored tone. "As far as I'm aware, there are no laws against bright lights, but there are penalties for trespassing."

The bulkiest, drunkest of the trio raised his fists. "I say we go after the bugger and don't let this toff stop us."

"I wouldn't do that if I were you, Mickey," the lounger said. "He's a prof."

Ignoring this wise advice, Mickey swung.

Prepared, Zane blocked his attacker's fist with his bag. With a shove, he pushed the inebriate backward, into the vine-covered wall. When the lad gave every evidence of coming after him with two fists—and because he wanted to prevent anyone from going after a *photographer*— Zane released his vexation by ramming his free fist into a broad jaw. The drunkard slumped to the ground.

"Warned you," the lounger said laconically. "Come away, Bill, we'll have another round."

"The light near blinded me," the wall-climbing Bill complained, giving up his handhold and dropping down to weave toward the tavern.

"I'd suggest the lot of you return to your rooms and sleep it off," Zane said in disgust, continuing on his way.

Again, they ignored his painfully, shamefully accumulated wisdom. Leaving their companion to sleep it off, they returned to the noisy tavern.

For a childish moment, Zane savored the punch. Once upon a time, he'd been free to unleash his primitive urges. His current part-time status at the university didn't allow such behavior any longer.

Suppressing further vulgar triumph, he pondered the anomaly here.

Photographic equipment. The lady wouldn't be so insane as to try to take night pictures outside a tavern, would she?

The Azmin Dougall he remembered had been a quiet mouse in public—with flashes of rebelliousness in private. She'd always been too clever for her own good. And he'd been an immature idiot.

Because of his juvenile urges, he now owed his sixteen-year-old niece a life, a life Louisa would never have again—

He couldn't risk his position for a long-ago acquaintance who wasn't his problem.

TWO

"I'VE PREPARED LAST NIGHT'S PLATES," AZMIN SAID, SETTING OUT THE negative frames needing printing. "But the one from the coroner's appears to be ruined because the auxiliary lighting blew out."

Just add one more sin to Dr. Dare's oversized head.

Keya examined them to see that the frame and paper were properly positioned. "I'll print these out today. Perhaps we should stay with images taken during daylight."

"Living people move," Azmin complained, shrugging on her coat. "It's easier to experiment with light on corpses, although I've yet to prove the spirit lingers."

Keya reluctantly nodded. "If this will teach you night photography, it might be useful for the police or newspapers. That could potentially lead you to the women who need our help. Perhaps you can try the coroner shot again."

And risk running into Dr. Dare? Probably not. But Azmin kept last night's encounter to herself. Keya was an excellent companion, but she harbored harsh opinions of men, for good reason.

"The spirits of the dead are only good for practice," Azmin said with a shrug. "They can't tell us anything. I wish it were easier to experiment with living spirits. I'm not sure how I will determine if there is such a thing as recognizable evil."

Surely knowing which people were evil would be a useful gift. She shook out her dull brown skirt, then checked the mirror to pin her hat.

"Or recognize a sick spirit," Keya responded absently, settling in to work on their paying projects.

"Reading auras would be simpler," Azmin complained, gathering her art supplies. "I envy my more gifted relations. I'll end up a spinster teacher, painting watercolors in the attic and remembering that one remarkable photograph. Maybe what I need is more subjects like you."

"That *is* the point," Keya said dryly. "To find other women hiding abuse and their abusers."

"I need a proper studio for that. Candid photography is much too difficult, and I won't know who the camera is capturing." Azmin left the workshop, lifting a hand in greeting to Mr. Morgan in his office. Their landlord's bespectacled partner nodded but continued working at his desk. An investor and accountant, Mr. Morgan didn't talk much.

Azmin's distant cousin Lady Phoebe Blair and her inventor husband owned this unusual collection of rooms over the Blairs' workshop and animal shelter. She was grateful they were willing to lease them for offices. It saved a great deal of traipsing about or calling for a carriage as she ran from her teaching chores to her university classes, leaving a few hours for developing her photography. She had even upon occasion slept here, although Keya heartily disapproved.

Azmin inhaled the first scents of spring as she strode down High Street, in the direction of Holyrood and the School of Malcolms, where she taught young relations of her father's multitudinous British family. She enjoyed teaching eager minds, but she was a trifle jealous of the more gifted students. Even ten-year-old Anna had painted a lovely portrait of a princess doll—which exactly resembled the gift her parents had sent from France, *months later*. Prescience wasn't quite so scary when one was ten.

Her father possessed none of the gifts of his Malcolm family, so Azmin assumed her lack was due to him. That one odd portrait she'd taken of Keya and Keya's husband had been the first mysterious occurrence she'd ever produced. She'd probably not used enough silver nitrate, but the fact that her reading of that image had been correct kept her trying to reproduce it.

She'd translated the photographic images of a ghostly white Keya next to her shadowy dark husband as reflecting Keya's loss of spirit and her husband's brutality. And she'd been right.

Maybe she was just good at guessing. She hadn't been able to duplicate a ghostly image since, but just knowing that others in the family had what once had been called *magical* gifts kept her trying. Their family's odd abilities were why the School of Malcolms was so often called the School of Magic.

Azmin turned off the wide thoroughfare with its less than century-old structures and down a narrower lane of storefronts and towering, ancient stone edifices. Stepping into a narrow aperture between two shops, she climbed the exterior steps to the first floor above the storefronts and entered the school. Off the foyer, Lady Agatha and Lady Gertrude lurked in the parlor, sipping tea. They gestured at Azmin to enter. No one knew for certain if the old ladies were prescient or just observant, but any encounter was always edifying.

"Good morning, Miss Dougall," Lady Agatha, the younger, rounder of the sisters, chirruped. "A word, if we may?"

Come into my parlor said the spider to the fly. . . Azmin enjoyed the company of her students, but she didn't rely on the school's income for support of anything except her expensive hobby. So she felt no fear as she entered the spiderweb.

"Good morning, ladies. You are looking refreshed this lovely spring morn. How may I help you?"

"It is nearly noon and most people have been up for hours," Lady Gertrude said with a sniff, raising her pince-nez glasses to examine Azmin's attire. "You know we do not require our teachers to look like wrens. That puce is most unsuitable with your coloring."

Azmin beamed and took the full skirt in hand to sashay it about. "I am taking lessons in disguise from Lady Phoebe. She advises plain colors for invisibility."

Lady Gertrude rolled her eyes at the mention of her irrepressible niece.

Lady Agatha pressed onward. "We have a request from Professor Dare."

Of course, they did, Azmin thought in resignation. Coincidences did not abound in her life. Did the old manipulators know she'd seen him last night? Had they written him first?

Lady Agatha persevered. "Dare's young niece is an invalid and much alone. He has asked if we have a governess or companion for the poor girl. We don't, but we thought a few art lessons might do her good."

Dare had very definitely not requested *Azmin*. He might have asked for a governess, but he had not in a million years requested a photographer. This was all about the ladies and their so-called prescience.

Azmin mentally consigned Dare to the gates of hell but blithely continued smiling. "Which niece is that? He has only the two sisters, and last I knew, they were in London."

"Oh, dear, I quite forgot that you've been away these last years and have not been apprised of all the news. Men are quite dreadful that way," Lady Agatha said with a pained sigh.

From that, Azmin deduced that her father had not bothered communicating with his many relations—no surprise there. He was a military man through and through and openly scorned the eccentricities of his mother's extended family. Still, he'd chosen her Hindu name in honor of a favorite Malcolm aunt and sent Azmin to stay with her once she was school age, so he had some understanding.

"I shall dutifully update Papa," Azmin suggested, waiting for the answer to her question. Dare had been the late baby in his family, a much-wanted son and thoroughly spoiled, in her honest opinion.

"It's a tragic tale. A terrible fever afflicted Louisa when she was quite young, and Dare's sister insisted on tending to her. And then his sister contracted the fever. Louisa survived. His sister did not. Professor Dare was only just setting up his practice at the time. He was devastated by the loss." Lady Gertrude set down her teacup, frowning as she gathered her thoughts.

"This was after I left for India," Azmin suggested, filling in the timeline. When she'd left, Dare had been planning on marrying a wealthy debutante whose family would set him up in said practice. "He had a niece about five or six at the time." Dare had been a dashing twenty-four with little interest in young nieces or lovesick adolescents. "I am extremely sorry for his loss. His family must have been devastated."

Agatha nodded and patted her nose with a delicate handkerchief. "And his mother a healer—she couldn't reach London in time. The fever that almost killed her left Louisa's heart weak, so even a healer cannot cure her. A very sad story. London is such a pit of disease and pestilence."

Old Town Edinburgh's medieval slums were no better. Azmin refrained from commenting. "And why are Dr. Dare and his wife caring for Louisa?"

Lady Gertrude waved a dismissive hand. "He is not married."

Dare wasn't married? All these years and he didn't marry? Azmin's knees went weak. She forced herself to remember her employer was still talking.

"He has dedicated his life to finding a cure for his niece," Lady Gertrude continued. "Louisa's father has remarried and left her with the Dares in hopes they might provide her with a proper come-out. But from all reports, she's simply not well enough. Dare's parents have gone to the Americas in search of a cure."

Azmin thought her head might start rattling like her employers' tongues if she did not bring this to an end. "So Dare's world-famous herbalist mother cannot cure Louisa and has left her with a bachelor? Why? I know for a fact that our family has enormous resources for raising children, as they raised me. Your school being another of many possibilities."

"Yes, dear, but Dare feels culpable, you see. He is the one who introduced the fever to his sister's household. And despite his training, he could not save them." Agatha sat back, crossed her hands in her lap, and looked satisfied that this was sufficient explanation.

Azmin started to argue with the ridiculousness of their assumptions, but the clock chimed eleven. "I am late. If you think I should teach Louisa, then make the arrangements, please. I shall see what I can do."

Trying not to reveal the turmoil raised by her insane acceptance to have anything to do with Zane Dare, Azmin ran upstairs to her classroom. For the next hour, she concentrated online and form. She'd been trained in all the skills of a lady since she had shown no other useful aptitude. She had a good eye and a competent hand and had been provided excellent art teachers. Should she ever marry, she could cover the walls with her puttering—a very useful skill, indeed.

Surely Dare didn't realize who the ladies meant to send to his niece. Maybe he'd throw her out and ask for someone else. Azmin didn't think she could tolerate being under the same roof with him for long, but perhaps she could time lessons for when he was not there.

Because Louisa's tale caused an ache in Azmin's heart—she knew what it was like to be young and left out, banished from society for reasons not of her own making.

~

ZANE FROWNED AT THE MATERIAL UNDER HIS MICROSCOPE, JOTTED NOTES, and sat back on his work stool, exhausted. Straightening his back, he tried to remember when he'd eaten last and couldn't.

The heart he'd dissected had not revealed the secrets of the universe but only contributed to his small store of knowledge. He understood that scars could cripple the arteries and veins and weaken the heart muscle. He did not know how the fever caused those scars or how to correct them.

Prevention seemed the only cure—and that was much too late for Louisa. And he did not dare experiment with Lister's germ theory for fear of introducing the fever to his family again.

He packed up and called it a night. It was no doubt too late for dinner but Cook usually left the remains for him to scavenge. And Louisa would still be up. He'd ask her if the school had sent anyone over. He didn't know what else to discuss with a child.

Louisa wasn't as precocious as sixteen-year-old Azmin had been. He shut out that foolish memory. Princess Azmin had been an undisciplined brat. Louisa was a young lady.

The spring evening was chilly, but he walked quickly down gas-lit thoroughfares of respectable shops into his more sedate neighborhood of century-old townhouses. Even the private park was quiet. When she was feeling well enough, Louisa liked to sit on a park bench and feed the birds. He should drive her over to the Meadows where she could see more. It was a short walk for him, but she lost breath before she reached the end of the block.

Louisa greeted him cheerfully the moment he walked through the front door. "Thank you, thank you, dear uncle!"

He shrugged off his hat and coat and hung them in the closet, then entered the velvet-draped front drawing room where his niece had evidently been waiting for him. "And for what do I deserve your generous gratitude?"

"For Miss Dougall, of course! She is brilliant! She has traveled the world, and she sketches the most delightful scenes in just minutes. She says she will teach me as best as she can, but that I must practice and practice. She's so funny!"

Frail, her golden hair falling to her shoulders, his niece sat near the fire, buried under shawls various family members had sent over the years. She was holding a sketch pad and pencil and beamed as if he'd given her a box of chocolates.

He crossed the room to admire her drawing. Instead, she handed him a collection of pages containing vividly colored bird sketches. "These aren't watercolors. How is this done?"

"Wax pastels," she said triumphantly. "Miss Dougall says they are a little costly, and I would do better to learn watercolor because the colors can be mixed. But she entertained me while she talked by sketching these. Can you imagine being so talented?"

Dougall. Zane tried not to roll his eyes. Of course, the meddling old ladies had sent the annoying Hindu princess. Her father was a Malcolm, so of course the school knew of her, although why she was teaching was puzzling.

Perhaps she'd matured, as he had. He shouldn't be awash with dread at a *schoolteacher*. And *photography hobbyist*, he recalled with a little more apprehension. Azmin in the morgue was more like the fearless child he remembered. "Did she name the birds? They look like parrots of some sort."

"Don't be silly." Louisa took back the sketches. "They don't have parrots in India. One is a sunbird, and this is a kingfisher and of course, here's a peafowl. You remember those monstrous noisy birds at Ashford's estate?"

He did, indeed. It had probably been Miss Dougall's father who had sent them. "She has captured the colors very nicely," he admitted. "I had thought the school might send over a student or someone more your own age."

"Miss Dougall said she might bring a few of her students so we could all practice together. She's lived in India!" Louisa cried in excitement. "Her mother was *Hindu*. She is a more exotic creature than the birds!"

Yes, Azmin was that, or used to be. The mocking crow he'd encountered last night hadn't been very colorful. "I'll call up some dinner, and we'll discuss your lessons. I'm glad your teacher is enthusiastic."

"Let me call Mary," Louisa said, unraveling herself from her nest. "I need to learn to be lady of the house."

Zane's heart tugged. It was highly unlikely that his niece would ever be more than a dependent spinster, but how could one make an eager child understand her limitations? He couldn't.

He let Louisa call for his dinner and escorted her into the dining room on his arm, sitting her at his right-hand side. The maid produced a pot of tea and a meat pie for his niece, who seldom ate much and had to be encouraged with tempting tidbits.

She chattered about her lessons and the teacher's promise to bring a few oil pastels as well as watercolors. Zane wondered how much this was costing him, but mostly, his thoughts drifted to the child he'd known a decade ago. Azmin had been staying at Iveston Hall that summer, as had been an assortment of the marquess's relations.

His mother's eccentric family believed in tradition, and family gathered for all the usual festivities of weddings and births, or just because one had a prescient notion that it would be safer to leave the city. It hadn't been prescient to know that fever raged through London that summer.

Bored by the dearth of entertainment in London after everyone fled the unhealthy humors, Zane had allowed himself to be dragged from his student revelries. His parents had insisted that he make useful connections at Ashford's country house party. He had, engaging himself to an heiress invited to the festivities.

His connection to the quiet, non-English child garbed in gauzy saris, wearing enough gold and silver on her arms and throat to sink a ship, had not been useful, not in the way his family had meant. Azmin had thrown a book at him for an insult. He'd challenged her knowledge of the book. They'd formed an intellectual alliance of boredom and amusement and competed over the number of books they could read while the others were out swimming and playing at Robin Hood.

She'd been a child, like Louisa. He'd just earned his medical degree. They'd only been reacting to ennui, nothing more. He'd realized academic stimulation was healthier than the drunken revelries of the city—while still managing to annoy his hovering family by developing an inappropriate rapport with an adolescent too young to be courted.

That had been a decade ago, and he still recalled Azmin's laughter and the flash of her unusual Malcolm-blue eyes when he challenged her. As a scientist, he'd known blue eyes were unlikely in someone of her coloring. Having grown up with Malcolms, Zane knew blue eyes were dominant in women with odd *abilities*, like his mother's. His own gray eyes indicated that like most males, he had no magic. Maybe Louisa needed a little Malcolm weirdness in her life.

"You'll have to let me know Miss Dougall's schedule so I can send a carriage to fetch her," he said as Louisa wound down.

That way, he'd know when not to come home.

THREE

"THE LADIES AT THE SCHOOL SENT ME A NOTE THIS MORNING. DARE thinks I need a carriage," Azmin said in amusement, washing paper through egg white. "I wonder if it might be that chickens in India lay a different kind of egg?"

Keya chuckled and took the paper for drying. "I am not certain I follow carriages with eggs."

"I've been spending too much time with the aunts." Azmin dried her hands and picked up the photographic plate containing the tavern scene. "They rattle and hop from one subject to the other, and it's like watching a tennis match."

Lady Agatha and Gertrude were not her aunts, not any more than Dr. Dare was her cousin. It was just simpler to refer to them in family terms. Adding "in-law" and "great-great aunt" or "second-cousin to the third degree" only complicated life.

She took out one of the previously dried albumen sheets, set it against the glass plate, and fastened the frame around it. "If printing doesn't bring out the weird shadows, we may have to send for Indian chickens. Or maybe use peafowl eggs."

"Or it could be that *you* need to mix the solution and not me. If we are dealing in magic, then scientific experimentation does not apply." Keya set the frame with others to open in sunlight.

"It's not magic," Azmin complained. "It's some innate sense that some of the family possesses. I've never had it. My cousins teased me horrifically, trying to determine if my paintings revealed secrets or if I could read their auras or smell their characters or whatever. I was hopeless."

"You are a most excellent artist and photographer. That should be enough," Keya said loyally.

Azmin knew better than to hug her—years of abuse prevented her friend from enjoying easy familiarity. So she focused on what was important—helping others like Keya. There was no money in India to aid in the fight, so they must form the organization here, where great wealth and technology had led to even greater wealth.

"Being an artist is not enough if I can't identify abused women. Once we launch the studio, we'll at least bring in more income, as well as establishing connections with other women. And if I'm to use my time teaching Dare's niece to sketch, he'll pay dearly for it." She wasn't fond of budgeting, but Azmin sat down at her desk to calculate what a few hours a week would cost of studio time.

"I know your mother's family disowned your mother and thus you, but your father's allowance is generous," Keya protested. "You need not be so tight with your purse."

Azmin snorted at mention of her mother's royal family. "My father is newly married and no doubt producing a son and heir as we speak. He will not be so generous once his new wife starts spending his wealth. I am being practical. He gifted me his house, since he will not be returning here. If I can save most of my allowance and subsist on my own income, I will have funds for my old age."

"He will not forget you!" Keya protested.

"Your future as much as mine depends on him," Azmin reminded her. "Do you want to take the risk of returning to India?"

Keya wrinkled her long nose and changed the subject. "Why would Dr. Dare wish to send a carriage for you?"

"Because he is a gentleman who doesn't believe ladies should be wandering the streets alone. I told the ladies we don't need his help. It's good that you found Wilson and his hackney or we would have frozen this winter." Azmin set her pen aside.

She hoped and prayed that Keya was safe here. Scotland was the other end of the world from India, and the only place Azmin knew to run. But it wouldn't be difficult to find two brown-skinned women in mostly-white Edinburgh if Keya's husband came searching. "Perhaps we should start using hired carriages more often. We are too visible."

"We are wrapped in hoods and cloaks and scarves! Who would notice?" Keya scoffed.

"It's almost spring. I am told Edinburgh's weather is relatively mild, so I surmise that it does eventually become warmer and the need for cloaks, unlikely. How is the studio coming along?"

"I have ordered carpet for the reception. We should visit other studios to see how they decorate. I am quite certain the fashions of Calcutta are outdated."

"Excellent thought." Azmin contemplated her busy schedule and wrinkled her nose much as Keya had earlier. "If you dress in widow's weeds, with a long black veil, you could probably visit on your own. Your English is nearly perfect."

"You are only avoiding doing it yourself," Keya accused.

Azmin grinned. "Indubitably. If you let me loose with wallpaper and carpet, I will choose the most expensive, and then be disappointed that they won't fit our budget. If I don't know what is out there, I'll be quite satisfied with whatever you choose."

"If you started your studio here, near the workshop, it would not require anything fancy. There are more offices available here." Keya gestured at the simple room they worked in.

"I don't think students can afford our fees. No, we need the wealthy ladies who collect *cartes de visite* and mourning photographs and the like." Azmin began gathering up her supplies. "Although I must wonder if it requires the presence of both husband and wife for the oddity to show up."

"If you are good enough, couples will come for family portraits. One step at a time," Keya wisely advised.

"It is just such a slow process!" On that complaining note, Azmin set out for her day of teaching and classes. Her expensive cameras had to wait until she had a few hours to spare.

Although she supposed she could show a camera to her private student. She'd wait to see how much interference Dr. Dare would offer.

Irrationally, she was almost looking forward to any challenge he presented.

~

XANDER—HE READ, HIS FATHER PREFERRING THAT DIMINUTIVE OF Alexander—*I have heard ill news of the earl. Unless you are seeing a definitive breakthrough in your research, it is time, as my only heir, that you take up your responsibilities.*

Zane wished to heave the missive onto his office fire, but Viscount Dare was not a demanding man. His father was simply stating facts. The Dare family was lamentably short on male heirs. His distant great-great-uncle, the earl, who had never been a part of their lives, had to be in his nineties now. He'd outlived two wives, various sons and grandsons, and all his brothers. Zane's father had been the heir for decades. Everyone had always assumed the old man would remarry a third time and reproduce. He hadn't.

As viscount and immediate heir, Zane's father was the one responsible for the earl's affairs these days. But he was currently in the Americas, and even when he was at home, he had half a dozen irons in the fire that kept him traveling.

Zane earned the majority of his income from his teaching position since research paid nothing. But he had a small trust fund, and the family assumed Zane's dabbling in teaching and scientific research could be carried on anywhere, even in Norfolk. He shuddered at his one memory of sheep, pigs, and turnips. The estate was miles from anywhere, isolated as many of the grand homes in the area were. It would be a rural prison.

The only title he'd ever aspired to was doctor, and he'd attained that. He sat down and dashed off a note asking if he should hire a barrister to look into the entailment. Perhaps the land could be sold off.

The *title*, however, could not be so easily shirked and required a residence closer to London. He'd worry about that when he came to it. His father was healthy and likely to live forever.

Of course, if no one found a cure for Louisa. . .

That did not bear thinking and would in no way affect the burden of a title. On his way home, Zane posted the letter, knowing his father would not receive it for weeks, probably longer if he was on the move again.

As he walked up the gas-lit street toward his home, he saw no sign of any carriage. Miss Dougall had not accepted his offer of one. He simply had to assume the dratted female had her own conveyance and would not be foolish enough to be out after dark, which was when he normally returned home. He didn't know why the woman was teaching—just to annoy him, quite probably. She used to wear enough gold jewelry to fund a hospital.

Fortunes changed, he knew. Perhaps he should make a few discreet inquiries. Her late husband may have gambled away her funds. . .

Except Louisa had referred to her as *Miss* Dougall. None of his concern. Letting himself into the house, he set his hat on the shelf in the closet under the stairs and followed the sound of voices. Other than the maid, Mary, Louisa had few people with whom she might talk since he'd booted the governess. He really was a derelict guardian.

The chatter grew louder as he approached the dining room. Peering in, he saw Mary cleaning up a dinner for more than one. His stomach grumbled. Coming home after dark meant he often missed meals. He should stop at a tavern instead of forcing Mary to prepare a late plate. Oddly, the table seemed to be missing most of its chairs.

Puzzled, he continued to the small drawing room at the back of the house. Louisa had called the room grim and refused to use it. He'd simply considered it one less space he had to heat. Every farthing he saved went to his research.

The small room wasn't grim now. The overhead gaslights had been lit. A fire burned in the grate. Lamps had been set on all the tables. And a bevy of colorful skirts billowed over feminine boots standing on. . . chairs?

He tried not to gape as he sought Louisa, who was—thankfully—on the ground holding what appeared to be an assortment of paints and. . . Zane squinted—stencils?

"There you are," Louisa cried, spying him as she turned to catch a protective cloth sliding from the furniture. "We are making your house beautiful!"

Zane had a bad feeling about this. . . He gazed up from the skirts at eye height to the ladies wearing them, who were up near the ceiling. There were three of them wearing white smocks over their bodices— and a fourth wrapped in what appeared to be the remains of a white sari embroidered with rows of tiny stitching.

She didn't even look down as she dabbed color into a stylized stenciled drawing of ribbons and flowers.

Grudgingly, he studied the completed work. It was quite brilliantly done, a classic *trompe l'oeil*, beautifully dimensioned, of sashes, flowers, and fortunately, no cherubs, in shades of ivory and gray.

"You did all this today?" he asked in disbelief.

"I told Miss Dougall that this room would make a lovely garden room if it were not so dismal, so she brought over some stencils and her students." Louisa handed another pot of paint to a female holding out an empty one. "I said you would happily contribute to the school fund in exchange for the work. Do you not think it is brilliant?"

"I was not aware you wished a garden room," Zane said warily. "What exactly is a garden room?"

"Behind those abominable draperies is a lovely bow window overlooking a walled garden. I should like to plant roses and lavender. If it only had French doors, it would be just like home." Louisa sounded more cheerful than wistful.

He should have known she'd be homesick. "We only lease, not own," he reminded her. "I cannot make structural changes."

The female in the old sari turned and flicked paint at him. Zane scowled and wiped at it with his handkerchief. "What was that for?"

"For being an insufferable prig. We have brought beauty to your home, and all you can say is that you're not *allowed to make structural changes*. My word, Zander Dare, what happened to the boy who would have been ripping off those velvet abominations the minute Louisa complained of them?" Miss Dougall had covered her sable hair in the old linen, and black lashes hid her light eyes, but she couldn't conceal laughing ruby lips.

"Removing moldering draperies is likely to pull the screws straight out of the plaster," he grumbled, shoving his handkerchief back into his pocket and fighting his usual reaction to the brat. He recalled now why he'd let her tease him back then—she fascinated him as much as she annoyed him. "If all of you would climb down from there without breaking your necks, I'll have a look at the draperies."

"We're almost done, sir," one of the students cried. "I've just this small corner to finish."

"You cannot have done this in one day," he grumbled. He knew he grumbled, and he almost hated himself for sounding like a dour old professor.

Dour old professors kept their positions and their laboratories. Professors without laboratories couldn't fix Louisa and ended up on pig farms.

"Finish up your stencils, ladies, and let us remove ourselves from the good doctor's presence. I can complete any small bits another day." Miss Dougall climbed down from her chair to stand directly in front of Zane, no longer the shy child but a defiant grown female. "We apologize for being carried away and outstaying our welcome."

"Oh, do not apologize when he is being grouchy," Louisa advised. "He is actually very nice and understanding when we do not pop surprises on him. Uncle Zane, can you really take down the draperies?"

As the students scampered from their chairs, collecting brushes and paint pots, he studied the heavy maroon hangings. "Will you wish to replace them?"

Louisa turned to the teacher who was cleaning up and putting tools away. "What do you think?"

"You need draperies to keep out the cold in winter and as privacy at night," she said. "You simply need to be able to move them to the side during the day."

"Like the doors at home," Louise cried. "Where do we find people who make them?"

Miss Dougall cast Zane a look from beneath her long lashes, then wrapped a brush one of the students handed her and dropped it into the bag. "I'm sure your uncle will know. If not, my assistant can help. She is researching the décor for my new studio."

Damn the female, now he wanted to know more about her studio and her assistant, and he'd have to spend the next days researching draperies.

Zane tried not to look as Miss Dougall unwrapped the linen from her hair and shoulders, but the room was brilliantly lighted, and it was difficult not to notice the gold thread woven into the dull brown cloth she'd garbed herself in. Even in mourning, if mourning it was, she adorned herself in gold.

"I will call for my carriage to take you back to the school," he suggested. "It's quite dark at this hour."

The young students cheerfully accepted his offer. Within the half hour, they'd bundled up and. . . left Miss Dougall blithely walking down the street on her own.

He should let her go. He was hungry and cold, and he needed to speak with Louisa. . .

Yanking his hat and coat back on again, Zane strode after her, convinced this was what a dour old professor should do.

FOUR

"I DO NOT NEED AN ESCORT, DOCTOR," AZMIN PROTESTED AS THE wretched man caught up with her and offered his arm. She was not particularly petite, but Dare's size was intimidating. "Go back and admire your new sitting room, have your dinner, and tell Louisa what a brilliant child she is."

"I cannot in all conscience allow you to wander these streets alone. It's bad enough to have the guilt of one disabled female on my hands. Should anything happen to you. . . I should have to find a monastery and drop out of the world." In impatience, he took her arm and threaded it through his.

Guilt? *Monastery*? She had so many questions. . . She stuck to the pertinent.

"Have you ever been to Calcutta, sir? I have spent these last ten years walking filthy streets mobbed with pickpockets and thieves, stepping over crippled, homeless beggars and unimaginable filth. I am neither helpless nor a child." She should resent his assumption that she needed a man's protection, but apparently she was an idiot. She was inordinately pleased that he'd *noticed* her. She probably should soak her brain and wash it out with lye.

"You were never helpless, although your behavior has always been childish," he said, confusing her brief moment of pleasure. "I at least outgrew impulsiveness. Obviously, you haven't." He halted at an intersection.

"I recommend that monastery," she retorted. "Perhaps once you inter yourself, Louisa could go somewhere with more family around. She's a lovely child, with a cheerful attitude that conceals a great deal of loneliness."

Azmin wasn't certain why she was speaking to him like this. He was older, well-respected, a gentleman, and no doubt heir to fortunes and title. She needed people like him to support her cause. She should just slap herself now.

Except she knew herself well enough to know she was trying to chase Zane away. She didn't want him to know where she kept her workshop. That was ridiculous. Professor High-and-Mighty would never lower himself to come looking for her.

"Which way?" he demanded.

With a sigh, she started down the cross street, heading in the direction of Holyrood.

"With my mother out of the country, I am the only one of the family left with medical training," he replied, apparently in explanation as to why Louisa couldn't go elsewhere.

"Sommersville?" she inquired, remembering the medical duke his mother often consulted, who was somehow related to the Malcolms.

"Isn't in Yorkshire these days. He's in the south battling his own problems. You think we should ask a duke to watch over her?" he asked in derision. "If Louisa overexerts herself, she has weak spells. I am always close at hand. The servants and the neighbors know how to find me at any minute of the day. The rest of our family. . ."

He hesitated at describing the hordes of Malcolms Azmin remembered with such fondness.

"Is rambunctious," she finished for him, understanding his predicament. They would exhaust Louisa beyond measure. "Has she found any gift that might keep her amused? Perhaps she is a librarian. They lead a quiet life."

"Like me, she seems to have been bypassed by the family's eccentricities. Or it could be a side effect of the disease. It leaves her feeling left out," he said with what sounded like sympathy.

"Ah yes, I remember those days. We are the outsiders—unable to cast spells or order dogs to do tricks or anything of use." She said that with a hint of irony. Malcolms kept journals of their various inexplicable gifts, talents, and eccentricities. Spellcasting had never been among them.

His laugh was short. "My sisters were equally untalented, and most of the boys in the group had no interest in playing mind games, so I did not care so much.

Azmin was the one who cared. She wanted to have an extra sense or perception. With no family of her own, she longed to feel a part of her extended one. She'd buried the loneliness by staying busy.

Their path took a turn past the tavern where she'd attempted to catch an image of the drunkards. The stench of gin and vomit polluted the spring air. Dim light barely reached through the filthy tavern windows. This part of town wasn't precisely reputable.

"You are fortunate to not care how others view you." Resigned to showing him her workplace, Azmin turned down a dirt path too small to qualify as an alley between the tavern and a garden wall. "And I am glad that you understand Louisa is not you. But she does need female relations who might notice if she's gifted. We cannot always tell on our own."

"Does that mean you've discovered your talent?" he asked, with what almost sounded like interest.

At this hour, the Blairs had locked up the back gate and gone home. "Nothing of use," she said blithely, hiding both hope and despair as she opened the lock. "You can leave me here. My companion is waiting."

He glanced up at the solid structure which resembled an enormous carriage house more than an office or home. There were lights in the upper story. Keya would be ready to leave. Mr. Morgan had a suite and lived here. There were guest rooms for when the Blairs' household spilled over. Azmin rather liked the eccentric building.

"You don't live *here*?" he asked in incredulity, stepping into the yard, uninvited.

"I work here. I thank you for seeing me—" Azmin gave up. The professor's insatiable curiosity had taken him to the garden wall over-looking the street in front of the noisy tavern.

"You took that photograph the other night that had the rowdies climbing the wall?" he demanded. He'd already found the dog shed and chicken coop she'd used as steps and climbed up to look.

"I had a photographic plate prepared that I couldn't use because you interrupted me. I've been waiting to test my equipment in that spot. The lampposts and the tavern's carriage lights and the window form a pool of illumination. I hoped I could learn how to use artificial light if accompanied by my magnesium reflector."

He climbed back down, shaking his head in disbelief. "You're unnat-ural," he muttered. "No right-minded female in all those furbelows—"

Azmin headed for the back door. "I was appropriately garbed at the time. You simply didn't notice, as always. Good-night, professor."

He caught the door and held it for her. "One of those young thugs attempted to beat me up when I prevented him from climbing over the wall after you. I don't advise any more impromptu photographic experi-ments. I cannot even imagine capturing more than light and shadow, at best."

"And you're a photographic expert as well as a medical one?" she asked caustically, giving up on being rid of him when he followed her into Mr. Blair's workshop. He was a friend of Mr. Blair's, she remem-bered. Her landlord wouldn't mind.

Dare had been beaten up because of her? Azmin winced. She supposed she should apologize, but it wasn't her fault that men were violent animals who reacted to a flash of light.

"I obviously know more about human behavior than you," he replied with equal irritation. "One does not startle drunks. Their reactions tend to be unpredictable."

"Illogical and violent," she concurred. "Like all men, except to an extreme when reinforced by alcohol." She stomped up the stairs without looking back.

～

ZANE KNEW HE HAD NO RIGHT TO FOLLOW THE FEMALE UPSTAIRS. HE HAD exceeded all boundaries already. But if this lofty brick structure was an office, it couldn't be entirely inappropriate to see where his niece's tutor worked. And it simply didn't seem safe to allow an unprotected lady to wander around in this vast, poorly lit structure in an unhealthy part of town.

She would hit him with a brick if he said that aloud. She'd walked the streets of *Calcutta*. The stories emerging from that hellhole. . . He shuddered.

Miss Dougall led him down a corridor lit by only one lamp. "It's just me, Mr. Morgan," she called as she passed a door with light seeping under it.

The occupant grunted a greeting.

She knocked on another door. "Keya, I've brought a guest."

There was a distinct warning in her voice. Zane doffed his hat and held it under his arm, his fascination outweighing his hunger.

A brown-complexioned, older woman opened the door. She looked as if she belonged in the colorful saris Azmin used to flaunt, but she was modestly garbed in servants' attire. A narrow scar ran from her mandible to the zygoma. The wound had damaged the orbicularis oris, distorting her mouth.

"Keya Trivedi, may I present Dr. Dare, the gentleman who hired me to teach his niece?"

The woman was no maid. She carried herself with pride, bobbed no curtsy, and didn't lower her eyes in respect. She also didn't offer her hand. She merely opened the door wider and gestured entrance.

"To what do we owe this honor?" she asked in low, musical tones.

"Dr. Dare is seeing that I arrive safely. Apparently, the tavern's clientele is prone to aggression." Miss Dougall drew off her gloves and glanced around. "The photographs? Did printing help?"

Zane was too intrigued by the workshop to notice the companion's reaction. Neat and orderly, the tools of Miss Dougall's trade lined the walls and benches. A pair of comfortable chairs and stools faced the grate, where a coal fire burned. A low table held the necessities for tea preparation and consumption.

Framed and unframed photographs filled every available space not meant for walking. Not just black and white either. There were tintypes and old-fashioned daguerreotypes and methods he didn't recognize. The lady had experimented with them all, adding rosy colors to cheeks, depth with clarity—even he could recognize her talent.

"Before I say anything, tell me what you see," Miss Dougall said, studying the photos her companion handed her.

Even oblivious as he was, Zane heard her suppressed excitement. He swung around to find out what they were doing.

"I do not have enough knowledge to know if these odd shadows were caused by light conditions or poor dispersion of chemicals," Miss Trivedi said cautiously. "This one—the lighting is very bad, but there does seem to be an odd. . . perhaps a dual image?"

Drawn by curiosity, Zane peered over Miss Dougall's shoulder. He grimaced at the outline of the corpse from the other night. The sheet was recognizable. Most of the rest of the picture was just dark shadows. A lighter. . . shadow?. . . hung above the sheet. "Probably a reflection of your flashing light off the sheet."

Miss Dougall shot him a look of disgust and reached for the second photograph. "Keya? What do you think? The light is better in this one."

Zane felt almost comfortable arguing over foolishness —as if they were still the two young people they'd once been.

He couldn't afford to be that young whelp again. Slapping his hat on, he prepared to leave.

Again, the companion answered cautiously. "There is an odd. . . gloom. . . on the one gentleman's back. Again, it could be a bad wash."

"That's the tavern photo?" Zane asked, unable to resist examining the results of what had caused such a commotion.

The drunkards were clearly depicted. At the time she'd taken it, all three were standing under the lamppost, smoking cigar stumps, from the look of it. Dressed in shabby student attire, coats unfastened, caps covering their shaggy hair, they simply looked disreputable as far as Zane could tell. Jenkins was taller and leaner than his muscled companions. It looked as if he'd thrown a pack over his shoulder, but that part of the image was obscure.

"They're a disreputable lot of drunks. Your experiment shows no more," he said in disgust. "For this, you risked your life?"

"I was perfectly safe behind the wall," she retorted. "And if you don't see the darkness, you are blind."

Zane snatched the photo and tilted it away from the light, but the image didn't change. "He's not by the tavern window. There is no similar shadow in the image. It appears as if he is wearing a pack of some sort on his back, or your photography could just be bad."

Azmin looked as if she wanted to smack him. Zane refused to accept that blots on a piece of paper meant anything at all.

"And what do you see?" the companion asked of Azmin, looking worried.

"Evil," Miss Dougall said distinctly, taking back the photograph and turning it face down on the workbench. "It is as if he has a demon on his back. And in the other photo, I see the corpse's spirit lingering above the body. To me, it is quite distinct. And I understand that no one will believe me when they cannot see what I see or feel what I feel. I feel malevolence."

A demon?

She turned and held out a polite but cool hand to him. "Thank you for escorting me, professor. Our carriage will arrive shortly."

Zane ignored her hand and picked up the photo she'd discarded. He pointed at the so-called demon. "He's one of my students. He is *not* the one who attacked me. Do not let your imagination run away with you."

Azmin offered a brittle smile and retrieved the photograph. "Do not become too attached to that young man. He is a danger to himself as well as others. Good-night, Dr. Dare," she said formally, holding open the door.

Zane slammed his hat on and strode out, not understanding why he was so damned irritated by her dismissal.

FIVE

Excited, and more than terrified, by her perception of *evil* and possibly spirits, Azmin desperately wished to carry her camera with her everywhere and experiment. But even if she only used cheap tintype, she had to be practical. People walking down the street weren't likely to stand still so she could check them for demons.

And it wasn't exactly as if she believed in demons. "A spirit could be corrupted," she said to Keya the next day, continuing an earlier discussion, as she chose supplies for her afternoon lesson.

"You have yet to prove the gentleman is evil or that such a concept exists. In my faith, we believe bad karma is carried with you into your next life, until you learn to be a better person," Keya replied, working the problem through her knowledge. "We believe in moral and natural evil but not *demons*. Perhaps it means he's afflicted with disease."

"That's not what it feels like." But Azmin nibbled at her lower lip. "I have the same ugly feeling as I did with your husband, but perhaps evil is a disease? Or accumulated bad karma?"

"You need to write down exactly which process you used to develop those images." Keya veered off to the helpful rather than continue painful speculation. "At least we now know it isn't the local eggs in the collodion or sunshine causing the distortion."

"That is a relief, I admit. My notes are on the workbench." Relieved not to have to discuss religion, Azmin adjusted her hat and picked up her bag. "How did you fare with the wallpaper?"

"I had them bring the samples to me," Keya replied in triumph. "Mr. Morgan said I might use his office. None dared show disrespect while he was present. They perhaps thought Mr. Morgan might wallpaper his new buildings," she added with a hint of amusement.

"You did not mind leaving your face uncovered? I noticed you did not cover yourself for Dr. Dare."

Keya's husband had required that she hide behind veils after her marriage. She could have abandoned the habit, but she was sensitive about the scar on her jaw.

"Your professor did not even see me," Keya said, with a ripple of laughter. "He was too busy hovering over you. If I had met him without you, I would have thought him terrifying. Such intense eyes! They are like mirrors to the soul. He is not the usual sort one expects of an intellectual."

"There's a usual intellectual?" But Azmin knew what she meant. This new Zane—she had difficulty thinking of him as Dr. Dare—was all tough sinew, controlled power, and scorching intelligence. It had been like having a burning torch at her back—disturbing and titillating.

When she'd known him before, he'd had a reputation for unleashing that raging energy by carousing while earning stellar marks at the university. Having to behave within the confines of family that summer. . . she could see now that he'd been looking for an outlet for his blazing intelligence as well as his physical energy.

Frowning, she suggested, "Perhaps I should ask your hackney driver to pick me up at Dare's house first, so the good doctor will be not be compelled to accompany me again. I'm glad you discovered Wilson."

"Wilson reminds me of an old servant I once had. She was deaf, and blind in one eye, but she was the most loyal, honest, hardworking maid I had. I missed her sorely when she died."

Keya had been raised in wealth. She deserved far more than Azmin could offer under normal circumstances. Keya, however, had accepted escape as a fair trade.

Eager to visit her new student again, Azmin hurried out. If she could turn Louisa's art lessons to photography, she might fit in a few more experiments, and charge his High-and-Mightyship for the expense. From the size of his house, he wasn't hurting for funds, even if he was only renting.

When she arrived at Dare's home, the maid gestured at the small park across the street. "Miss Howard has not yet returned. She likes to sit on the bench and read when the sun is out."

Azmin couldn't help but think Louisa courted pneumonia in the spring wind and weak afternoon light. Carrying her satchel, she crossed to the park.

Louisa was sitting on a wrought iron bench—with the gentleman from the tavern, the *evil* one.

Azmin froze. She had utterly no logical reason to chase the man away. Louisa looked animated as she chatted. Her cheeks were flushed, and her gloved hands gestured excitedly.

The gentleman appeared attentive. He was good-looking in a youthful sort of way. His blond hair was overlong, but his side whiskers were fashionably trimmed. He wore a cap instead of a formal hat, an untailored coat, and a single-breasted waistcoat, but that was common in this part of town. The dark shadows under his eyes and his drawn features hinted at dissolution.

Shadow and light danced over them from the still-barren trees. Azmin couldn't help fearing that she was looking at Keya and her abusive husband all over again.

Dare hadn't mentioned that his student was a family acquaintance.

"Opportunity knocks," Azmin muttered, forcing her feet to continue down the garden path.

"There you are," she cried, approaching the bench. "What a lovely spring portrait you make with the budding tree in the background. May I have the privilege of taking your photograph?"

The gentleman smirked. Louisa almost elevated off her seat. "Would you? Please? This is so exciting." Then remembering herself, she added, "Miss Dougall, may I present Mr. Septimus Dare? He's a cousin of sorts."

Odd, Zane hadn't mentioned that. Hadn't he called the man Jenkins?

"I only brought a few of the dry plates to show you how the camera works, but I think I can use this post to hold my camera steady. You will need to sit still until I tell you I'm done."

The day was bright enough that she shouldn't need more illumination. Azmin situated the couple out of the shade of the trees—and with Mr. Dare's back turned slightly toward her. "Smile for as long as you can!"

As soon as she declared herself satisfied with the shot she'd taken, Azmin packed up her camera again. "You really should come out of the chill, Miss Howard. Would you rather work with watercolors today or learn more about the camera?"

She would feel a thousand times better if she separated the girl from the student.

"Please, call me Louisa! I thought we settled that yesterday." Louisa rose and offered her hand to her admirer. "It was good seeing you, sir. I do hope you will come again soon so I may show you our portrait!"

The child had been raised well. If Azmin had been limited by her health, she would probably be sulking in a library corner and barking at anyone who approached. Louisa, on the other hand, was cheerfully trying to appear normal.

"Isn't he the most handsome man you've ever met?" Louisa whispered as they entered the house.

Well, no, Dr. Dare was a million times more handsome, but Louisa wouldn't see her uncle in the same light. "Does Mr. Dare's family live nearby?"

"No, he is here to study medicine, like Uncle Zane. Will you really show me how to use a camera?"

"I should have had someone build a *camera obscura* so you have an understanding of how the box works. Are you ready to learn the science of photography first?" Azmin followed her student back to the sitting room they'd transformed yesterday. The ugly curtains still hung, but it took time to have new ones made.

"I am willing to learn everything!" Louisa bravely declared. "My last governess said I should not use my intellectual energies to the detriment of my physical energy. She feared too much mental stimulation reduces reproductive abilities so ladies should not exert themselves. I think she was just too lazy to teach me science." Louisa flounced into a chair by the fire.

Azmin snorted inelegantly and unpacked her bag. "And I suppose she believed violent emotion causes fever and that the moon is made of green cheese."

"When she ought to believe we can read minds and auras," Louisa said with glee, bouncing in her chair. "The world is a marvelous place."

"I trust you learned that part from your uncle and that he was not the one to hire the aforementioned governess."

"An agency sent the governess. He sent her packing when he overheard one of our conversations." Louisa wrinkled her nose. "He does not talk to me much. I think he was born an old man."

Azmin laughed. "When we were much younger, your uncle dared me to juggle eggs while I was wearing a new gown. I took the dress off and stood there in my petticoats, juggling, and he rolled on the carpet with laughter, which was very poorly done of him. No, your uncle was not born old. He has grown that way."

"Did you break the eggs?" Louisa asked, grinning.

"I did not. I am exceptionally coordinated. But I threw them at him when I was done, leaving him to strip off his new tailored coat and waistcoat while I donned my gown again. We were very bad influences on each other. Now, let me show you how the camera works." Azmin sat on the floor beside her student and held up her least heavy camera.

Remembering the Zane of her adolescence made her sad for the cautious, stuffy man he'd become. Perhaps she ought to fling a few eggs his way.

"How's the research, Dare?" The dean stepped into the laboratory and glanced around at the collection of equipment Zane and his fellow workers had accumulated. Much of it, Zane had purchased himself out of his salary. The school never had sufficient funding for new apparatus.

He experienced a decided chill at this unannounced visit.

A distinguished gentleman with a magnificent gray beard and mustache compensating for his receding hairline, Dean Reynolds did not normally roam the halls to speak with part-time professors.

"We have learned that scarring of heart tissue has an impact on blood flow, and we are searching for a remedy, sir." Zane set aside his microscope and returned his spectacles to his pocket. "Is there something I can help you with?"

The dean tapped his fingers on the high worktable, still looking around and not at Zane. "The school needs to expand. We need more classroom space. The budget does not have room for new buildings."

Zane's gut clutched. He'd worked in academic environs long enough to grasp the direction of this conversation. "Without medical research, you will not continue to attract the high level of teachers and students we currently enjoy. A university is more than classrooms."

The dean nodded, still tapping his fingers. "I agree, but I am at the mercy of our directors. More classrooms mean more students mean more income to fund new buildings."

"Our research on heart disease is imperative," Zane insisted. "It is connected to the work of Lister and Pasteur in that infectious diseases can cause scarring of the heart. If we could—"

"Yes, yes, I've read your work. I understand and agree. But unless you can produce a definitive breakthrough that cures people, the directors are not interested. They have hired an architect with the idea of converting this entire building to classrooms. You are welcome to take on more students, of course. Your work is known, and your stature in the medical community is exceptional."

Zane felt invisible hands shoving him out the door, in the direction of Norfolk and a pig farm. He wouldn't go without a ruthless fight. "I appreciate the warning, sir. I will explore a new location for my work. It may mean directing my family's funding to a different facility." Fire cannon one.

"Now, now, don't be hasty," the dean said, taken aback. "Ashford and the duke have been generous in their donations, as has your father. Perhaps if they could see fit to fund a new facility for research elsewhere in the city..."

"We're a large family. The funds are spread among many. I can't ask for more. If the university truly wishes to be known as a place that produces ground-breaking research, it will need to find additional funds on its own." So, he was angry. He probably shouldn't take it out on the old man, but people *died* of heart disease. No one died from a dearth of spacious classrooms.

The dean nodded reflectively. "We'll see, sir, we'll see. But producing strong results would go a long way toward convincing the directors."

Strong results. . . It was *research*, not an epiphany. Or even a symphony, a wry imp in his head retorted. Collecting data was little more than musical notes to the uneducated.

"You should socialize more, Dare," the dean added, surprisingly. "When was the last time you attended one of our receptions?"

Probably never, but Zane suspected that wasn't the correct answer. "I have my young niece at home, sir. Hiring a governess to keep her company is difficult."

The dean grunted a decided harrumph. "Marry, boy, marry. Women are useful for that sort of thing. They know which dinners to attend and can play up a fellow to the right people. Some of the directors have eligible daughters with good dowries."

Zane had heard all that before. He was, after all, expected to provide the next heir. Having his lack of wife shoved down his throat by a university dean instead of his family did not make the idea any more palatable.

He left early, after his last class, needing to walk off his ill humor. Yesterday, he hadn't arrived home until well after Miss Dougall had left. *Miss Dougall*—he had a hard time thinking of the defiant brat as a respectable young lady, if one could call an insane camera-wielding female *respectable*.

But Louisa had been practically bouncing with excitement at the notion of learning photography—which involved chemicals that made healthy people ill. He needed to have a word with the irresponsible wench.

Today, Miss Dougall was practically lying in wait for him. The moment Zane hung up his hat, he heard her tell Louisa to practice her sketching, and that she needed a word with Dr. Dare before he hid. He scowled as his niece laughed.

Removing his overcoat, Zane waited in the corridor—not hiding.

The chit appeared already wrapped in a voluminous cloaked redingote in an unbecoming navy and carrying her satchel. At sight of him, she imperiously pointed at the drawing room. While he lit lamps, she removed objects from her bag of magic tricks.

"Did you know Louisa has been seeing a gentleman who calls himself Septimus Dare?" she whispered. "Who very much resembles the tavern drunkard you said was a student named Jenkins?"

"Seeing?" Zane asked in disbelief. "How could she see anyone? Or even meet them?"

She handed him a frame. "I took this today. It hasn't been fixed yet, but it's still clear enough. Louisa was sitting in the park, chatting with this young man. Look, just look! Can you not see the blackness clinging to him? He does not mean her good."

He'd had a wretched day, which she was making even more miserable with these family eccentricities. But he carried the image over to the lamp where he could study it.

There was a smirking Jenkins, who did appear to be carrying a pack on his back again. The pack was amorphous and not in the least normal. And he'd never seen the student so much as lift a book, much less a heavy pack of any sort. Zane scowled. In the print, Louisa looked enrapt.

"I know nothing of photography or shadows, but I do know this young man, and his name is *Jenkins*. How dare he use my name to seduce his way into Louisa's company." Zane flung the picture back to her and started for the door.

"Don't confront her," Azmin warned, catching his arm. "That is the absolute worst thing you can do."

He glared down at her. She'd tilted her veiled hat to conceal most of her face—probably her intent.

"I'm supposed to be protecting her!" he insisted.

"She is old enough to marry! You cannot treat her like a child. And she is no doubt trying to listen right now, so keep your voice down. Can you find out more about this young man? I have told her the image was corrupted, and she's asking if I might do another. We need to speak where she cannot hear."

"When are you available?" he asked, churning with fury and ready for action, any action, preferably one that involved reporting Jenkins to the authorities for fraud and misconduct of some sort.

She released his arm. Without Azmin's stabilizing hold, Zane paced, applying his mind to how Jenkins could be stopped.

"Lady Phoebe and Mr. Blair are having a luncheon at the workshop tomorrow to celebrate some new invention. Perhaps you could come then? Even if you do not have time to stay, we can find a place to talk."

"I could walk you back now," he said impatiently. He doubted she had anything to say of use.

"The hackney will be waiting for me. If you can, find out more about this student, but do not harass Louisa! We don't know anything yet." She tucked the frame back in her bag, straightened her hat, and waited for him to let her pass.

"At least you have the sense to take a carriage." He followed her sweeping skirt to the door. She was wearing a half-hoop today and looking as a lady should, except for the monstrously ugly color, of course. She belonged in gold and copper and emerald—the colors of the jewels she'd once worn. Where were the dangling earrings that had once so fascinated him?

He wanted to know her story. He hadn't even asked if she had married.

"I can't allow Keya to walk the street," she answered dismissively. "So we help the driver. He has difficulty obtaining fares."

Difficulty obtaining fares? What the. . . ?

Zane stepped outside to watch an ancient vehicle with patched wheels totter down the broad street of mansions. The horse looked ready for the glue factory. The carriage could use the glue.

Before he could pry his tongue loose in protest, she climbed in without assistance and the hackney rolled away.

Zane had the urge to rail and shake his fist at the heavens. A large drop of rain hitting his head restored sanity. Growling, he strode back inside, hoping to at least have his supper on time.

A day contemplating a pig farm and a woman who believed in demons had him pounding walls in frustration. But today still wasn't as bad as the day he had seen his six-year-old niece lying lifeless on her bed. He had to fix his goal on taking care of Louisa—which might mean keeping the demon woman around.

SIX

CHAMPAGNE GLASSES IN HAND, LADY PHOEBE AND HER INVENTOR husband, Andrew Blair, studied Azmin's images.

"Why evil?" Phoebe asked, unhelpfully. "That is certainly an odd distortion on his back, but it could just as easily be red or green and mean sorrow or good. But if you're concerned, I could have a dog follow him about. I've been training a stray who knows these streets well."

Phoebe had a gift for reading the minds of animals, as far as those minds could be said to have thoughts.

"Knowing where Jenkins goes may be useful, but it will not tell us if he's evil or even criminal," Azmin said with a frown. "How does one prove evil intentions?"

"By a man's actions," Mr. Blair replied pragmatically. "Here comes Dare now. He's a man of science and won't believe in evil."

"*You* don't believe in evil," Phoebe said, taking her husband's arm. "But you're not a Malcolm. Dare is. He's been steeped in our eccentricities all his life. His mother is famed for her herbal knowledge and psychic healing abilities."

"His father is known for his scientific treatises," Azmin reminded her. "Go back to your guests. I just need to speak to him about his niece."

She hurried off to steer Dare away from the noisy luncheon crowd. She was relieved that Phoebe's aunts— Azmin's employers and the formidable owners of the School of Malcolms—hadn't shown up. But everyone else in the Blairs' circle seemed to be here, including Phoebe's pets. Happily, the barn-like downstairs could hold multitudes, plus the enormous buffet.

Azmin was pretty certain students and Phoebe's former neighbors were coming in off the street to snatch food. The neighbors—and Phoebe—had lost their flats when the façade of their medieval tenement fell off. Lady Phoebe wasn't wealthy, but she had a generous heart.

Raised in aristocracy, Dare looked briefly bewildered by the motley crowd and relieved when Azmin emerged from it. He brought with him a hint of fresh air, a faint whiff of formaldehyde, and an aroma of something male and spicy. She really should not linger in his company like an infatuated infant.

"Would you like a bite from the buffet?" she asked.

He glanced over her shoulder at the crowd and shook his head. "I don't have time to go in there."

"You might never come out again," she agreed, taking his arm and steering him toward a quiet corner by the enormous stone fireplace in the front workshop, away from Phoebe's animal shelter.

"Was that a raven on the hat rack?" he asked.

"Phoebe's pet, along with the dog that looks like a pony. As you would know, if you paid attention, she's an animal-talker." Azmin reluctantly released his arm and stepped away. There was something so. . . elemental. . . about the doctor. "Have you learned anything more about your student?"

"He is registered as Septimus Jenkins and as a first-year medical student, although he seems a little older than most. His home is listed as York, which isn't far from my parents' home. They're well known in the area, so he could be familiar with my family." Dare rubbed his nose as if used to removing spectacles. "I haven't had time to make more inquiries."

"I will be the first to admit that his encounter with Louisa could be perfectly innocent. But I would be lying if I said I believed it." She hesitated, uncertain if she should reveal her experience. It meant telling Keya's painful story.

"Any suitor would be unsuitable," he protested. "Louisa is too young. She's not had a come-out. And she's not healthy enough to entertain notions of courtship and marriage. Any exertion exhausts her. She cannot even walk a few blocks without having to rest. Dancing is out of the question. Beyond that—" He wisely stopped.

"She's a sixteen-year-old wishing to exercise her feminine powers, and this gentleman is the only one she knows. You should be entertaining more promising students in your home. She'll learn the difference between flattery and sincerity soon enough. But that is not the point."

"And the point is?" he asked in frustration.

She had to tell him. He probably wouldn't believe her even then, but he could not understand her fear until he understood her experience.

"I learned photography in India, from a military man who needed an assistant," she said, looking for the shortest possible way to explain. "Many women in India do not uncover their faces in front of men not of their family, but they want portraits just as anyone does. I learned to take their photographs and develop them because as a female, I was acceptable."

"Unusual," Dr. Dare agreed. "But logical."

Azmin tilted her head in acknowledgment. "Keya's husband wanted a portrait of the two of them together for their wedding anniversary." She took a deep breath and continued. "When I developed the plates, I didn't see the healthy couple in my studio. Instead—to me—her husband was distorted and enveloped in shadow, and Keya appeared almost wraithlike. I'd never had anything like that happen before, and I reacted rather strongly. I *knew* it reflected wrongness, and I suspected abuse. Standing there alone in my developing room, I was physically shaken and terrified. It doesn't matter if my reaction was illogical to an anomaly no one else could see. I felt fear."

"And that does not happen often either," he said dryly. "You normally haven't the sense to be afraid."

"I normally do not go into situations over which I have no control," she corrected. "Her husband was a powerful, wealthy man in Calcutta. It was very difficult to go past his servants and speak to Keya alone."

He frowned. "And your intuition was correct? She was being abused?"

"Regularly. She had not produced children. She ran his household, kept his books, her dowry had made him wealthy, but they had no children. At various times over the years, he'd broken her wrist, her nose, her ribs. . . She's a strong woman but she wept when I confronted her."

Azmin rubbed at her eye to push back the tears. It had been a terrible, dreadful moment when she'd realized her intuition had been correct and how awful her potential gift was. She'd been coming to terms with it ever since.

"And you think seeing the darkness around this monster indicated he was abusive? And that whatever you saw on Mrs. Trivedi meant. . . ?" he asked in his professorial voice.

She breathed deeper to steady herself. "I have taken pictures of her since we arrived here. She no longer appears as a ghost. She's regained her life. I really cannot explain better than that. That was the one and only time it has happened, until your student came along."

He frowned and rubbed his nose. "So you think it's possible this Jenkins abuses women?"

Since that seemed more acceptable to him than a demon, Azmin nodded. "At best, he has ulterior motives that are not healthy for Louisa."

"Yes, any real gentleman would know better than to confront a child in the park without introduction, which is why he probably stole my name. Even Louisa would have been wary of him otherwise." Now he looked both angry and impatient, as if wishing for a battleax and a castle to storm.

He believed her.

Sort of. She could work with that. "At least Louisa looks reasonably healthy and not wraithlike in the photo. I need to find out more about your student. Perhaps he has women he's abused or men he's cheated. If I had evidence—"

"What would you do with it? The police won't listen unless you prove he murdered someone. I'll just trounce the lad and tell him to keep away." Dare looked as if he were prepared to do that, right this minute.

She caught his coat sleeve again. "Violence solves nothing. If he has a goal in mind, it will simply make him more determined. My father is a military strategist. He taught me a few things about planning. We need to find who Jenkins' friends are, where he lives, where he goes."

"Which is how you rescued your companion?" Dare asked perceptively.

"Exactly."

Azmin did not explain about battle plans. She rather assumed, in this case, Dare would take that part in hand once they had a strategy. Although, if they were truly battling evil. . . perhaps they should seek a bishop.

Zane knew he needed to be concentrating on his research and looking for another facility to carry out his work, but his brain insisted on buzzing around Jenkins and Miss Dougall's unconventional conclusion.

He was well aware that he could not outright dismiss her inferences from a photograph. His mother's family was ostentatiously weird, but they hit close to the truth enough times that he had to take them seriously.

But Azmin—he really couldn't think of her as *Miss Dougall*—admitted that she had no experience with her abnormal gift. He couldn't ram a student's head through the wall because she said so.

A floppy-eared hound with squat legs raced up behind him and fell in step as he strolled toward his office.

"Hello, old fellow. Do you read minds too and know I'm as hungry as you are? Although you look as if you could lose a few pounds and not miss it." Spying a mutton pie vendor, Zane stopped and bought two, handing one to the hound. The dog barked politely before accepting it, then appeared to bow—front paws flat and back end up, tail wagging—after he scarfed it down.

He knew feeding a stray was a mistake, but he welcomed a mindless companion who didn't talk or take weird photographs. The dog happily trotted after him. Professors could have dogs, couldn't they?

Zane ordered the hound to stay when he entered the building, and the creature flopped down in the brown grass, panting happily. Someone was missing a well-trained animal—Lady Phoebe came to mind.

He gathered the papers he needed for his classroom, checked the roster, and confirmed that this was the class Jenkins was in. He only knew him as a lackluster student who only showed up half the time. Maybe this would be one of those times.

The class was a small one. Zane studied his lecture notes and watched over his reading spectacles as the students ambled in. Jenkins wasn't one of them.

After class, he gestured at one of the brighter students, one who wore turned-over collars and frayed trousers and boots that flapped at the sole.

"Burns, do you know Septimus Jenkins? He's been missing from class for a while." Zane scratched notes on his papers as if the question was one of indifference to him.

"I know him," Burns said warily.

"Would you know where he resides? I'd like to have someone check on him. Classroom space is limited and there's no reason to waste it on someone who doesn't wish to be here."

Burns shook his head regretfully. "He sometimes visits with friends in the rooms above me." The student hesitated, as if holding back.

Zane studied him over his spectacles. "Unsuitable friends?"

Burns nodded. "They experiment with altered states of mind. I can't approve."

Zane understood the need to experiment with drugs, but not outside of laboratory conditions. Heroin and opium were dangerous but the ones most frequently used. He frowned. "You're right to stay away. Addiction is an ugly consequence."

"Should I speak with him, sir?"

"No, no, don't do that. I'd rather you not mention this to anyone. We'll let the dean's office handle it, thank you." Zane wanted to give the lad a five-pound note for his help but feared the boy would be offended. He'd arrange for a monetary award for work well done.

And then Azmin's words came back to him, and he stopped the boy again. "Burns, I'm thinking of holding small dinners for students so they can get to know each other, maybe help each other with their studies. I'm not much in the way of these things, so I'll need to ask around, but would you be interested in such a gathering?"

The lad looked properly startled, then thoughtful. "That might be a good idea, sir. We are a bit scattered about town. If several of us could find a place and time to meet, it could be useful."

"Very well, I'll look into it, thank you again." He dismissed the lad, then wondered how the hell he'd arrange a dinner for all-male students when he only had Louisa for hostess.

The dean's advice returned to haunt him—he needed a wife.

He'd be better off holding a dinner in Lady Phoebe's barn.

SEVEN

"I saw him," Keya said, radiating fear, wringing her hands as she joined Azmin in the hackney that evening. She anxiously studied the winter-dark street as if expecting a monster to leap from the shadows.

"Who?" Azmin demanded. "Someone you recognized?"

"No, but Yedhu would not send someone I know. This person was asking questions, and Wilson heard about it and pointed him out to me. Turban, beard, dark—he does not belong in this city, and he is asking questions about *me*, using my married name. I know it is one of my husband's men. I cannot come back here. I will stay in the flat, hidden."

"You may as well put yourself in prison," Azmin cried in dismay.

"He will have thugs," Keya said in resignation. "I cannot fight them. They will torture and kill me and take my head back to Yedhu."

"Karma doesn't work fast enough." Disgruntled, Azmin sank into thought. She had not imagined Yedhu would bother having his wife followed when he had a newer and younger one.

"I do not think I will come back as a happier person after I stabbed his guards," Keya said with dark humor.

"Your religion is as riddled with misogyny as my father's if karma judges you for saving yourself. Personally, I believe men invented the rules to protect themselves against their weaknesses by keeping women under their thumbs. We are given this life to make the world a better place, and you cannot do it locked up in our flat." Azmin winced as the rattling carriage jounced over the bridge into the new side of town.

"I should learn to stalk my prey and shoot the brute?" Keya asked cynically.

"If being a terrible person qualifies, Yedhu deserves shooting." Azmin mulled the problem. "How could your husband have found you so swiftly? It took us months to sail here. Word of our destination could not have traveled back so fast!"

"The question is why anyone would look for me. There is no one back there who wants me. It can only be Yedhu seeking vengeance." Keya spoke matter-of-factly, but sadness echoed in her words.

"Did you steal his fortune by any chance?" Azmin asked, trying not to believe a man could be so vile as to follow his abused wife halfway around the world.

"I did not have access to his fortune," Keya said bitterly. "Only the few bangles he allowed me to wear. If anyone stole his fortune, it would be his second wife. Nevertheless, I am not safe."

"We need to hire a sturdy footman for the studio anyway. People should know a man is guarding the premises. Until we find the man asking questions, you can oversee the renovations and stay inside. The servants only know you as Miss Trivedi, so if anyone comes looking for you under your husband's name, they'll know nothing. But a properly trained footman can ask questions of strangers." Azmin frowned in concentration as the carriage halted to let them out in front of her father's townhouse.

"We must allow only one workman inside," Keya warned. "We cannot trust entire crews of men."

"I'll start asking around. Lady Phoebe knows everyone, and if she doesn't, her aunts do. You have friends here, Keya. You aren't alone. We'll try to find out who is asking questions and why." Azmin stepped out and verified no one watched from the doorsteps of the neat line of lamp-lit terraced housing.

The constable stepped out of his watch box to check on the carriage and tipped his hat to them. They were safe here. They had to be.

Keya pulled up her hood, and they hurried inside, looking like a widow and her servant. The ground floor public rooms were cold and barren, waiting for their transformation into a studio and reception area. Upstairs on the first floor, the fires were lit and the table was set for dinner. The flat was cozy and brightly decorated in all the colors Azmin and Keya enjoyed. On the second and third floors lived other single women who rented rooms, which covered the household expenses.

"This is a good reminder that we need to look to our safety if we start helping abused women," Azmin said after they discarded their coats and sat down at the table.

The maid delivered their soup, then departed to give them privacy to talk.

"It will be dangerous," Keya agreed. "Men like to control their possessions, and if they cannot, then they destroy them. I have seen Yedhu beat disobedient servants and kill a prized horse because it refused to be trained to the reins."

"I do not believe all men are that evil, but we must be very careful. We do not know for certain what my photography is telling us."

Keya pushed her spoon around in the soup but nodded. "It would be lovely just to take happy pictures of smiling brides and new mothers."

"I will give those clients to you. I'd rather practice with light conditions and spontaneous images. Wouldn't it be wonderful to someday capture sunsets? They're working on color chemicals even as we speak. Let us think happy thoughts."

And tomorrow they would hunt for a six-foot, two-hundred-pound footman who knew how to use a gun.

AT LUNCHTIME ON THE DAY AFTER AZMIN HAD TALKED TO ZANE ABOUT Jenkins, he surprised her by rapping on the door of her workshop.

"I need your help," he told her in a voice that sounded more threat than plea when she let him in. "Where's your assistant?"

She had left Keya in the flat, surrounded by servants and tenants.

Not that the tenants were of much use as security, but they were extra eyes and ears and could run for help if necessary.

"Keya is afraid her husband has sent someone to take her home, so I may need your help as well." Azmin set down the frames she'd been working on. "What can I do?"

She would not feel gratification that the intimidating doctor had sought her out. The old Zane simply knew she was unconventional, so his problem might be insulting.

Looking like an angry god, he paced her workshop. His broad shoulders and furious energy threatened to fill the small space. "You said I should host dinners for students so Louisa might practice her social graces. And the dean said I needed to socialize more, perhaps influence the directors into funding my projects. I have no idea at all how to begin."

Passion looked good on him, better than the dry husk she'd seen lately, but his intensity was a trifle overwhelming.

"You marry and let your wife handle it. What happened to the fiancée?" she asked with amusement, referring to the engagement that had driven her from England in the throes of adolescent despair.

Zane shrugged, not appearing troubled by the memory. "She thought she was marrying the pleasure-seeking son of a viscount who would allow her to live in luxury. A poor professor who refused to go into debt to keep her happy and who spent his hours researching did not meet her exacting standards. After I missed a dinner engagement or two, she threw the ring back at me."

"You used to be a charming layabout living off the family fortune, so I can see how she might have felt misled," Azmin said dryly. "Were you heartbroken?"

He glowered. "Being crushed like an insect was unpleasant, but as I've been told, I have no heart to break."

If she had lingered in England instead of running away, would her life have turned out differently? Probably not. Dare still had his head under a microscope and no time for compassion. And she had grown up and learned a little more about what she wanted since then—starting with respect.

"This is all irrelevant." He gestured impatiently. "I am *not* marrying simply for Louisa's sake. So what I need is someone who can help me host dinners." He stopped pacing long enough to look at her. "Are you married?"

Azmin laughed. "Am not and don't intend to be. I am very serious about my career."

"And the widow's weeds?" he asked, casting today's black gown a look of distaste.

"My shield of invisibility. I am no longer like the peacock, flaunting my lovely feathers to attract attention. I don't know why more women don't follow the wisdom of their animal counterparts. Peahens hide in plain sight. No one plucks their feathers." She began packing her bag for the afternoon's tasks. "Now, again, what can I do for you? I have hosted dinners for officers and their wives, but in presence only. Servants did all the work. Lady Phoebe is probably the person you should consult."

"Phoebe is patently insane. She would arrive on her penny-farthing, encourage the guests to take turns riding it, then entertain us with a parrot and three dogs."

Speaking of dogs—a hound howled from the yard. Giving a decided growl, Zane stalked into the corridor. Out of curiosity, Azmin followed him and strained to see over his broad shoulder to look down at the walled plot of dirt.

"I made the mistake of feeding the beast. Now he follows me everywhere. There's a man spying over the wall." Dare added the last as if it were a natural part of a beast following him.

He started down the stairs leaving Azmin bewildered and staring out the window.

The Blairs kept the back gate locked so no one accidentally let out Phoebe's animals. In a glance, Azmin found what Dare had seen—a bare-headed, brown-skinned man with his hand on the wall. Keya had described the man looking for her as having a turban, but perhaps there was more than one? Men of foreign descent did not often inhabit these streets. Scotland was poor, and the harbor exported more people than imported them. That did not mean a military officer or two might not bring home a foreign servant. . .

But anyone acclimated to society would be wearing a hat and knocking on the door, not spying over a wall.

Lifting her skirt and petticoats, Azmin raced after Zane. She wanted to talk to the intruder, not beat him up.

Instead of opening the gate and scaring the man off, Zane intelligently had hidden behind the ancient pine where Phoebe's marten lived. The unfamiliar hound dog in the yard barked happily instead of howling now that he had company.

Azmin lingered in the shadows of the deep doorway. The intruder's thick black hair appeared above the aging wall again, as if he'd found better footing. She had a brief glimpse of dark eyes, but apparently alarmed by the size and energy of the yapping hound racing back and forth, he dropped out of sight.

Azmin ran for the gate along with Zane. He got there first, racing off down the alley. She knew she couldn't catch up wearing restraining petticoats and skirt. Zane disappeared around the corner. She slammed the gate shut so the dog couldn't escape, glared at the gnarled bare vines covering half the wall, and marched back into the yard to look for secateurs.

Mr. Blair appeared in the doorway as she rattled through the shed. "Did you need something? What was that howling? I expect Phoebe attempting to raise the dead, but she isn't here."

Emerging covered in spider webs, triumphantly bearing a pair of rusty shears, Azmin pointed at the floppy-eared hound she'd prevented from running after Zane. "Phoebe's, I presume?"

The dog lay down, panting happily and looking up at Mr. Blair for a reward. He shrugged and provided a treat from his pocket. "Probably. Why the shears?"

"The vines make it easy for intruders to climb up. Dr. Dare is chasing after one now. I mean to make it more difficult for criminals to enter." She strode for the wall.

Phoebe's husband intercepted her, lifting the heavy shears from her hands. "I'll do that. It's broad daylight. Were you expecting intruders?"

"Possibly. I assume they'll try the tree next. I'm thinking of laying traps."

She was studying the branches and the ground when Zane returned, empty-handed.

"He ran into a crowded tenement. I couldn't barge in and run up and down stairs, demanding that he be turned over." He joined her in studying the tree's branches. "Possibly one of your companion's inquisitive strangers?" he asked, reaching up to test a lower branch.

Before she could reply, he crossed to the vine-covered wall and began tugging the clipped tendrils down as Mr. Blair chopped them. The hound chose one to chew on and contentedly lay there, tail wagging, as the men pruned.

"Don't you need to return to work?" Azmin asked, hunting through the shed for rope and not finding any.

"And leave you alone with scoundrels climbing over the fence?" Zane yanked the vine with more ferocity than required, staggering backward as it ripped from the wall.

"I can handle one scoundrel," she retorted.

She would have said more but Phoebe's husband returned from the other side of the gate, looking satisfied. "I hadn't thought anyone desperate enough to scale the wall, but it doesn't hurt to be cautious. Do we have any idea of what he might want?"

"Your inventions, my photographs, Phoebe's pigeons, Mr. Morgan's plans—" Azmin blithely traipsed across the debris toward the door. "It's cold out here. Who would like a cup of hot tea?"

Zane sent her a sharp look at her uninformative reply but merely responded, "Coffee."

"Man after my own heart. I have the beans in a cabinet up front. One of these days, we'll install a proper kitchen." Mr. Blair traipsed through the open area that should be a kitchen but Phoebe was currently using as an animal hospital. "Dare, you should take some of those biscuits to feed the hound."

"You are not staying here alone," Dare whispered, slipping hard squares of Phoebe's baked dog food into his pocket.

Azmin bit back words of protest as a ripple of fear ran down her spine. He might be right. How many men would Yedhu have hired?

EIGHT

Ascertaining that Azmin had a class at the university next, Zane left the hound locked in Lady Phoebe's yard. Azmin looked annoyed when he insisted on escorting her, but he wasn't done with her.

She wasn't married. She wasn't a widow. He was being as outrageous as the rest of his family to even think what he was thinking. But with pig-farmdom looming in his future, he was desperate.

"You cannot wander these streets alone if thugs think you can lead them to your companion," he insisted, keeping an eye on their surroundings as they walked.

"Really, you underestimate me," she said demurely, which immediately raised suspicion.

He glanced down and only caught her unfashionably large hat brim for his effort. He knew her skin was more a dusky cream than the brown of her assistant's. Still, lacking the usual pale English rose complexion, Azmin stood out in a crowd, and he assumed she preferred not to draw attention. But a man would have to be blind not to notice her even in the damned ugly black she wore today. Unlike her hat, her gown was the latest fashion, conforming to her shape as if designed for her hourglass figure.

With the silly bustle to add emphasis, the sway of her hips had heads swiveling.

Which gave him ideas beyond the one for which he'd approached her. It had been such a long time. . . But he shoved unseemly thoughts aside and stuck to his goal. "I need a hostess. You and your companion need protection. We should join forces."

That caused her to tilt her hat and slay him with those impossibly iridescent aqua eyes. "I cannot imagine how."

Her haughty disdain didn't discourage him, and Zane continued as if she hadn't spoken. "I lease a house large enough to hold a dozen families. You and Mrs. Trivedi—"

"Miss. She considers herself unmarried." She increased her pace, no doubt angrily. "And we will not bring jeopardy to your niece by leading villains to your house. I should probably end our lessons."

Zane quelled a flash of panic. "Don't you dare. I have never seen Louisa happier. Good health often relies on attitude. If you are concerned that someone is looking for Miss Trivedi, then she may stay in your residence. I'll hire more servants. You will be properly chaperoned. Louisa may call you her cousin—"

"I am not abandoning Keya. She is terrified. And I am not abandoning the studio we've worked these last months to establish. She needs to be there to oversee the renovations. You are being ridiculous. Ask Phoebe's aunts for a suitable hostess. You are probably more closely related to any number of their students and teachers than to me. It is a school for Malcolms, after all."

"Louisa likes you. And if you are as strong as you keep telling me, you are better able to protect her from scoundrels like Jenkins." They arrived at the building containing her classroom. He held her arm to prevent her from running off. "I'll escort you to my home after your class."

He couldn't read Azmin's expression. He was bad at reading people, he knew. But just seeing her like this, her eyes glittering, her rosy lips half-parted. . . jolted his insides in ways they hadn't been jolted in a long time. There were moments when he thought she taunted him on purpose.

He was eight years her senior. He refused to let the rebellious wench discourage him.

Stubbornly, Zane met her outside her classroom when she emerged later. His research wouldn't go anywhere without him, but Miss Dougall might.

"I have given your. . . interesting. . . offer considerable thought," Azmin announced before he could say a word. "I still believe you are better off asking for a more appropriate companion for your niece. And Keya would be far better off with a very large footman guarding our door. But I have not had time to inquire about footmen, and I do not wish to abandon Louisa to a villain. We might create a temporary situation until we've put things right."

"I will send my carriage with you so you might pack bags," Zane said in triumph.

"No, you will not. I will go to Louisa's lessons as always. I will take my usual transportation home. Keya and I will pack. I will send word to the ladies that we need someone to occupy our flat and oversee renovations, preferably several of the teachers. The school is overcrowded, and they will be delighted to have room to breathe." Despite the narrow front of her skirt, she marched briskly alongside him. "And I shall have them ask around for an appropriate footman."

"And then what? You will vanish into the night?" As she practically had all those years ago. One day she'd been there, the next she'd been gone, leaving him to the disastrous debacle his life had become. He should have learned his lesson, but he was desperate at this point.

"No, of course not. We do not even know if these so-called thugs are seeking Keya or not. My home is in Edinburgh now, and no one will make me leave. But until we can determine who is in more danger, Keya or your niece, then it does seem as if we should join forces, as you say."

"I should send my carriage at midnight?" he asked dubiously.

"You will not send your carriage at all. I do not want Keya in any way associated with your niece or your residence. Wilson will discreetly deliver our luggage to the alley in the morning. It will be foggy, as usual, and quite possibly raining from the looks of those clouds. Should anyone be watching at that unseemly hour, which I doubt, it will appear as if you simply hired a hack to take you to school."

Zane was beginning to enjoy this precise battle strategy. Her military father had taught her well. "You thought of all this while you were in class?"

"It was an art class. I can paint without thinking of the next line to draw. Anger added some interesting elements to an otherwise boring still life." She slowed down as they turned onto his street.

He understood anger. It bubbled inside him—or maybe that was just frustration over his inability to control life's hurdles.

The shadows were already growing long. Zane surveyed the route ahead, but there were no alleys for hiding in along this street of elegant Georgian mansions. "Perhaps I should take up painting. It might relieve me of my desire to punch people in the snout."

"Probably not," she said in amusement. "I still wish to punch people in the snout."

He chortled, imagining this bundle of fluff and fur swinging a fist.

"Anyway," she continued, "Be ready for the carriage at dawn tomorrow. And have a maid prepared for Keya's arrival through the rear entrance as the day goes on. We have some experience with eluding criminals. Men always underestimate us."

"Louisa will be thrilled at the cloak-and-dagger," he said dryly. "I am not so enthusiastic. Tell me you will not be wandering the street alone in the dark."

"I will not be wandering the street alone in the dark," she answered agreeably. "I have done so without harm, but it is miserably cold and wet this time of year, and neither of us is accustomed to it. But you must be prepared. . . We are independent women. You cannot dictate our lives."

That sharply smacked him into place. He'd not given sufficient thought to what hell a trio of women could create while rearranging his home, his life, and his head.

Perhaps he should join a club like other gentlemen did and hide there in the evenings. For now, knowing his niece had company, his laboratory would suffice.

~

"THIS IS SO EXCITING!" LOUISA DANCED ABOUT THE SITTING ROOM THE next day when Azmin arrived for her lesson. Or what passed for dancing—she performed a little jig before coughing, gasping for breath, and dropping into her chair. "I've always wanted a sister."

"This is only temporary," Azmin warned. "Until the studio is complete and all the strange men have quit running in and out." That was the story she had told after the maid had shown her to her new room. It wasn't a lie. It just wasn't the entire truth. "Perhaps by then, Dr. Dare will have found a more suitable companion for you."

Louisa blithely dismissed this possibility with the wave of a frail hand. "You will find this house much more convenient than one across the bridge and decide to lease rooms here. I will prove so entertaining that you will not wish to leave."

Azmin's heart ached at that brash declaration. She remembered those days when anything was possible. She hated to discourage a child who had so many reasons to never dream. "We shall see about that. I am a very managing sort of person, and you will no doubt wish me to Hades before week's end. Now, let us resume our lessons."

She'd walked over at her usual time. She simply wouldn't be leaving. Wilson would appear on schedule after the lesson, but the student Azmin had invited to join them would enter the carriage instead. Wilson would take the student back to the school, pick up a couple of teachers, and proceed to Azmin's home, where Keya was waiting. She'd exchange cloaks with a teacher, climb in the carriage, and be taken back to the school. From there, she'd make her way through the streets with the escort of Mr. Morgan.

By the time Wilson finished playing musical passengers, anyone attempting to follow would be ripping out hair.

Their biggest challenge would be living under the same roof as Zane.

The implacable doctor arrived as Keya and Mr. Morgan were being introduced to his niece later that evening. Azmin admired Zane's ruddy-cheeked, windblown look, and liked to think he'd hurried home because of her, but she assumed it was his concern for Louisa. With his jaw already darkened with whiskers, he appeared dangerous, until his expression of relief tempered his ferocity.

He smoothed down his ruffled hair, shook Mr. Morgan's hand, and invited him to dinner.

Knowing the accountant's solitary habits, Azmin added encouragement. "I believe Dr. Dare eats when he can, so the kitchen will already be sending up plates. You have to dine sometime, and we will not delay your return to work. It will make for a more balanced table."

Mr. Morgan was in his thirties, much too old for Louisa and perhaps a little too young for Keya, but if Zane needed an influencing power, the bespectacled investor was a good start. Morgan knew everyone in the city with money.

Their blinders-wearing host didn't realize that, but Zane was at least attempting to be hospitable. And having another stranger at the table allowed Keya to relax. Her companion sent Azmin a grateful look when she saw several vegetable dishes served as well as the beef. Azmin had had a word with the cook on the previous day about Keya's preferences. British food was often a struggle for her.

Louisa was the first to notice that Keya did not take meat. "Oh, I've been reading about different religions! Are you a vegetarian? How do you exist without meat?"

Zane attempted to quiet her, but Azmin tapped his hand and shook her head. Keya offered a brief smile, one that did not quite turn up right because of her scar. "We eat many different types of lentils and beans. They are very good cooked with curry and other spices, which are easy to come by in India, not so much here."

"The expense of importing spices traditionally prevented our cooks from learning their use. Now that the spice trade has opened up, they are more available," Mr. Morgan offered, expressing an unusual degree of interest. "Cooks and apothecaries are experimenting with them. Pepper is the biggest commodity, of course, but ginger and cinnamon are popular, and I believe turmeric, cloves, and cardamom are used for medicinal purposes and can be had in the right shops. Are there others you need?"

"Cumin, coriander, and mustard," Keya replied, eyes down. "But your milk is not a good substitute for coconut milk, so I must learn to adjust. I experiment when I can."

Azmin had known that Keya had been instructing their maid on how to prepare the vegetables she found at the market. They had arrived from India in early winter, when the selection was limited. Having only root vegetables to work with was a sore trial for someone who had lived in warmer climes. Azmin had grown up with bland English food. She should have realized Keya was missing home.

"Can you show us how to cook Indian food?" Louisa asked eagerly. "I would love to taste it."

While Keya and Louisa fell into a discussion of menus, Zane asked what Azmin had been wondering. "How do you know so much about the spice trade, Morgan?"

"I grew up in Glasgow. I started out investing in ships and learned which spices brought the most profit. English cooks aren't familiar with the use of Indian spices, but chemists have been incorporating them into a number of compounds. I know nothing of the effects, only profits," Mr. Morgan replied with a shrug of his wide shoulders.

"My grandmother is an herbalist who grows her own medicines," Louisa said, excitedly joining the conversation. "Do you think she might be interested in learning more when she returns home?"

Glad that her host and Louisa were engaged with their guest, Azmin relaxed even more when Keya and Mr. Morgan fell into a discussion of which spices might be more profitable in Scotland. She had feared her companion would be uncomfortable in a strange household, but Keya had grown up in a family accustomed to dealing with the British. Her disastrous marriage had crushed her spirit, but her knowledge and intelligence were still there.

Another problem loomed though. Azmin waited until after dinner, after Mr. Morgan had left, and Louisa and Keya had retired to the sitting room with their respective sewing tasks. Azmin longed for her workshop, just as Zane most likely wished to retreat to his laboratory, but they were both being extra polite. She might as well start the downhill slide into irritating familiarity by invading his study.

He looked up from what appeared to be a report he was writing. She hadn't realized he wore spectacles. Her heart melted a little at the sight of his harsh cheekbones softened by a wire rim and the hank of hair falling across his brow.

"Keya is here as my companion," she began, using caution. "But I am here to help you entertain students."

He continued watching her over his glasses, waiting.

She clasped and unclasped her hands. "People talk. Mr. Morgan knows Keya, and his mentioning her would not be unusual. Besides, he seldom talks. But students. . . Would remark upon your dinners and Keya's exotic presence in the same breath."

He took off the glasses, rubbed the bridge of his nose, and sat back in his chair. "True. I had not thought that far ahead. We would be endangering Miss Trivedi *and* Louisa."

"I will speak with her. I cannot think what to do next. She was willing to hide in our home and willing to hide here, so *I* am the problem. If I sit at your table without her, gossip will follow. Neither of us can afford to ruin our reputations. I know you didn't want Lady Phoebe to hostess, so perhaps we should postpone the dinners until we have solved Keya's problem."

Zane muttered what she assumed were blasphemies under his breath, set down his spectacles, and stood, as he should have from the moment she entered. "Have a seat. Let us discuss this like adults."

"I thought we were discussing like adults," she said with a hint of humor as she settled in a rather musty wing chair.

"Then let us say, let me explain myself." He returned to his seat. "It is not only that Louisa needs company, although that is a very large part of my need to entertain—to save her from the likes of Jenkins. But beyond that—" He rubbed the bridge of his nose and frowned.

Azmin waited, almost holding her breath. Zane was actually communicating with her, taking her seriously. She hoped.

"The school plans to close my laboratory and turn it into classrooms," he admitted with a sigh of exasperation. "The dean has hinted that if I entertain the appropriate people and raise sufficient funding, my research might be saved. If it is not saved, I have no good excuse to remain here. My father wants me to go to Norfolk and learn pig farming."

"What?" Azmin practically rose from her chair in horror.

He waved her back. "My great-great-uncle is an earl. Somewhere in the family tree there was a disagreement and our branch drifted away, but the earl is in his nineties now, and my father is his heir. Since my father is far busier and more productive than I am, he believes I am the one who should take over estate duties. He will not be interested in funding a laboratory if the school throws me out."

"Oh dear, I see." Azmin sat back and pondered the predicament. "You need to entertain the right students, the ones with wealth, whose families might be an influence. And then you need to bring them together with whoever makes the decisions about funding at the university. . ."

Zane chortled unhappily. "The first student I asked is poor as a church mouse."

"You're doomed," she said conclusively.

NINE

PACING UP AND DOWN BECAUSE HE COULDN'T SIT STILL ANY LONGER, Zane ran his hand over his jaw and realized he needed a shave. He gazed morosely at the fire in his grate. Azmin was right. He was doomed. He probably would make a good pig farmer. He could set up a laboratory in the earl's crumbling mansion and never have to socialize again.

Louisa might die if he did not cure her. She'd hate a pig farm. She'd die sooner than she should if he subjected her to their madcap families in London. Banging his head against a wall might feel better than this frustration.

"I am sorry our plan will not work out," Azmin was saying. "I'm sure between us, we can find a better one. I am very good at looking after myself. It's just Keya—"

The prim female had boldly declared that nonsense about being strong and looking after herself one too many times. He didn't know why, but it grated.

Without giving his actions a thought, Zane reverted to an earlier time and a person he hadn't been for years. He leaned over Azmin, hauled her out of the chair, and into his arms.

"You weigh all of a hundred pounds and cannot fight men twice your size," he corrected, furious with her and himself.

She felt damned good in his arms. She was plump where it counted and slender where it didn't. And her fists were too small to do much damage when she whacked his shoulders with both hands. Her small boots, however, connected sharply with his shins, and he winced.

"If you were an assailant, I'd go for your eyes and not your shoulders," she informed him coldly when he set her down. "And another more painful place instead of your shins. And then, if you weren't howling in agony, I'd stab you with my hat pin or the *katar* I keep in my hair."

She yanked out a lethal-looking blade with a highly ornamental hilt that fit over her knuckles. He'd thought it a hair comb, but with the weight of a fist behind it, the blade could rip out a carotid.

Her gorgeous sable hair tumbled in a fall of thick, shiny silk past her shoulders.

He still didn't release her. She glared straight up at him while she refastened her hair with the lethal pin. Without her hat in his way, he could study her more closely. She looked as dazed as he felt and hadn't stepped away, as she ought. He focused on her lush, slightly parted lips.

Her outrageous independence stirred his desire as much as her beauty. Zane didn't know how it happened, but his mouth covered hers, and it was like nectar to a honeybee. He was instantly drunk on sensation. Her tart words vanished, replaced by intoxicating sweetness and heat that stoked banked embers.

Her arms slid over his shoulders, and her fingers tangled in his hair. He deepened the kiss until her tongue met his, and her breasts left indentations in his heart. When lower parts became engaged, he tried to step away and couldn't—not until she yanked his hair and pushed him back.

She threw herself into her chair and crossed her arms over temptation. "*That* is why I need a companion."

"Because you kiss any man who touches you?" he asked, as much in bewilderment as anger. He didn't know who he was anymore. Or who she was, for all that mattered.

"I'd smack you for that remark, but then you'd probably turn all beast again. Most men have so many whiskers it's impossible to kiss them without being mauled. And they taste like whatever they ate last. I don't like kissing." She pouted and looked away from him.

"You liked kissing me," Zane said with certainty, returning to his desk chair to conceal evidence of how much he'd liked kissing her.

"That's irrelevant and only complicates our problems. I will have Keya share my room tonight, and we will remove ourselves in the morning." She started to rise.

Zane pointed at her. "Sit. We're not done here. I apologize if I've offended you. Despite all indication to the contrary, I am a gentleman. I won't do it again unless you ask, and I certainly won't invade your private quarters. And yes, attraction complicates matters. But we're two intelligent people and can figure this out."

Desire damned well complicated everything, but she didn't seem to understand that. Even though he knew she was too clever for her own good, Zane was grateful for Azmin's innocence, or she'd probably stab him with a *katar* for his thoughts.

In his wastrel youth, he'd never lacked for feminine company. He'd paid for his poor habits by burying himself in work these last years. But the taste of Azmin's lips. . . He was simply lonely, he told himself.

She settled down again, frowning. "I don't think what we just did was very intelligent, but thank you for recognizing that I am not an imbecile."

"An imbecile?" Jarred from his melancholy, Zane stared at her in incredulity. "If anything, you have far too much gray matter stuffed into that delicate cranium of yours. It works overtime to complicate things. Your objection is easily resolved. I suggested earlier that Louisa should call you cousin and say you are her companion. You do not need Keya at the table when we entertain students. Why would mere students dispute your status?"

She still refused to look at him but rubbed her elbows unthinkingly as she contemplated the fire in the grate. She wasn't delicate, Zane reminded himself. Her bone structure was slender, but she was of average height, and her little feet packed a considerable wallop—which was probably the reason she'd adopted current fashion for half hoops and bustles, which left her feet close enough to his shins to connect. So, she wasn't completely naïve. Well, the knife proved that.

"There may be villainous thugs out to harm you or Miss Trivedi," he warned her. "No matter how well-prepared you are, you can't fight a man my size, or one with a weapon. The streets you walk are rough. People will not necessarily rush to your rescue even in daylight. If a thug believes you can lead him to Miss Trivedi. . . Is she as prepared to fight as you are?"

"I will consult with the aunts in the morning," she said with resignation. "They were thrilled to send a few teachers to live in my flat, and everyone would be disappointed if we moved back. They did not seem to have any doubts about you or for Louisa's safety. If we assume they have some degree of prescience. . ."

"I assume no such thing," he said flatly. "They're dithering old ladies puffing up their consequence. One assumes they know I'm reputable and will cause you no disrespect—so they've already been proven wrong. They know nothing of Indian thugs or young scoundrels who may mean harm to Louisa. I'll hire a stout butler to guard the door and a hefty footman to accompany you when you go out."

"It's not that simple," she said unhappily, rising from her chair. "I appreciate what you're doing for us, and I will attempt to comply to my best ability. But you truly have no understanding of the freedom I've enjoyed these last years. Giving it up. . . simply isn't possible if I'm to achieve my goals."

Frustrated, he rose with her. "I have just told you I'm the heir to an *earldom*. Most women would be thrilled to take over my household, and after what we just did, be expecting matrimony as well. *You*—you can't wait to escape. Am I that distasteful?"

"Did I behave as if I found you distasteful?" she asked in disgust—or distaste.

But no, Zane knew that kiss had been more mutual than any kiss he'd ever shared. "You found living with *family* stifling and that was why you returned to India?" He still unreasonably thought of her departure as an abandonment when he'd needed her common sense. Finding Azmin gone after his disastrously impulsive betrothal had hurt him far more than his fiancée flinging his ring at him.

"Living within the confines of proper society is stifling," the annoying female said with a dismissive gesture. "I am attempting to accept it, but only on my terms. A husband—any husband—would have no understanding of the things I've seen and would oppose my attempts to correct what's wrong in this world. If more women had experience in traveling beyond their familiar home. . . Men would suffer greatly. Let us not pursue that topic but simply say that marriage is not my goal."

Knowing the unconventionality of her thoughts, Zane really ought to question *that topic*, but Azmin was heading for the door. She was telling him she was still a reckless, rebellious brat who could make his staid life hell. He probably should let her go, but he suffered an irrational alarm at being abandoned again when he needed her help with Louisa.

He tried to pacify her. "Stay here at least until we find Keya's enemies. I will try not to *stifle* you. Consult with the school or Lady Phoebe about a butler and footman to act as guards. I will ask around as well and have the agency send over a few for you to interview."

"A butler?" she asked with an inelegant snort, hand on the door latch. "You want me to interview a *butler*? I'll have Lady Phoebe send over one of her unemployed tenants. He'll happily keep out strangers and beat up anyone who approaches Louisa when she goes out."

Zane pinched the bridge of his nose. "That is not the way to impress wealthy students."

Apparently recovering, she shot him a saucy grin. "You'll not invite the wealthy ones. Unless you really have turned into a stodgy professor, you'll invite the interesting ones. Pigdom is definitely in your future."

Later that evening, Azmin examined the room to which she'd been assigned. Her chamber was all pale blues and silver, with a poster bed made of some light wood and a delicate wardrobe with dark and light inlays. All very sophisticated, very English, and not her at all.

Morosely, she sat in front of the vanity mirror and regarded her decidedly un-English reflection. Her dark lashes only emphasized her elongated eyes and her bronze—not rosy— complexion. Her nose and chin were too pointy to meet standards of English beauty.

Still, Zane had kissed her, and it seemed to have been with enthusiasm. She experienced a thrill simply thinking about his lips on hers. But why had he done it? Had he been without a woman so long that anyone would do?

She had to prevent her silly, impressionable heart from taking his actions seriously. Even though his father seemed healthy, Zane still might be an earl someday. And for now, for his research, he needed the kind of proper wife who would entertain university officials and wealthy financiers to fund his career. Louisa's future might rest on his success.

She could never be the hostess he needed. Once she established her studio, she would be actively looking for abused women to rescue. It was a dangerous and unpredictable occupation, as she'd learned from Keya. Besides, Zane didn't believe in her newly-discovered gift.

And even now, she would rather be out taking photographs and developing techniques to enhance her abilities. She would stink the house up with her new chemical coating if she worked here.

She recognized Keya's light knock on her door and called for her to enter.

"I like your Dr. Dare and his niece very much," Keya said, settling in the chair opposite Azmin's.

"But?" Azmin knew Keya never complained. It had been beaten out of her. But she'd encouraged her to speak up.

"I liked it better when we were in charge," Keya said hesitantly. "I cannot explain. I am so sorry I have brought you to this."

Azmin poured tea from a pot the maid had carried up and handed Keya a cup. "It's an adjustment, like all things in life, I suppose. At least this one is temporary. I think we need to lay a trap for whoever is looking for you. I still think there is some chance he does not mean you harm."

"You said he climbed over a wall! That does not sound innocent to me." Keya huffed and sipped her tea.

"He was afraid of a *dog*. Can you think of anyone at all who might come looking for you? Surely all your family has not cast you out? It is their fault you had to marry the beast."

Keya's sad dark eyes moistened. "Yedhu provided them with official connections they could not have made on their own. They have prospered from my marriage. It is the way things are done. I have younger sisters and brothers who must make successful marriages. I have ruined their chances by running away."

"Shouldn't they all be married already? How young are they?" Azmin knew enough about the culture not to be shocked, but it seemed exceedingly unfair that a woman as valuable as Keya should be sacrificed for others.

"I am the oldest child of my father's first wife. I still have a few younger siblings at home, and he has many more children by his second wife. It is the reason he was willing to give me up when I was fifteen. I was used to doing things the way my mother did. His second wife wanted me out. I have disgraced them." Keya seemed a little angrier now than she had been originally, when she realized she'd have to leave India and all she knew and loved.

"Fifteen! I thought you were older when you married. How old are you? You said you were married for nearly twenty years—"

"I am a runaway at thirty-five," she said with a wry smile.

"You're still young enough to marry again! Is divorce possible? Perhaps my father can help. I can find a way of sending a letter through the diplomatic pouches he receives. Since I haven't heard from him, my first letter may have gone astray."

"Perhaps I should immigrate to America." Keya warmed her hands on the cup. "They have photographers there who might need experienced assistants."

"They will assume you are a wild Indian and ask where you keep your tomahawk," Azmin said in amusement. "It is an alternative we can consider, but I'd rather confront whoever is asking after you first. Let's set a trap at the workshop," Azmin said in determination. "We will be perfectly safe."

Unless the brigand brought an army of sword-swinging fiends prepared for an execution. Azmin would work out that detail later.

TEN

THE NEXT DAY, ZANE SET ASIDE HIS RESEARCH FOR MORE IMMEDIATE concerns. First, he hunted down Lady Phoebe in her rambling animal shelter to ask about finding Jenkins and hiring her unemployed neighbors.

"Stalking a student is not precisely permanent employment," she said with a worried frown. "Although I suppose earning a small sum might help one of our tenants find a better home."

"Miss Dougall suggested you might also know a few people of the more respectable sort we could hire to guard the house. They would perform as butler and footman, but I do not require references. I just want strong, honest men willing to protect women." Zane eyed the owl currently ensconced on a wooden pedestal. The creature's leg wore a splint.

Phoebe gurgled with laughter. "You'll need to provide the men I send with livery and appropriate attire, but I know a couple of rascals you can trust. Just don't let them speak to guests. I don't suppose you could use a housekeeper as well?"

With a sigh, he saw his quiet household turning into a menagerie for Phoebe's human patients. Zane accepted the necessity. "Mary could manage when there was just two of us, but she'll be overwhelmed if I am to start entertaining. I don't think a non-speaking housekeeper, however, would be a good addition. Another maid, perhaps? And do you know where I might hire a cook?"

"Not in my neighborhood. Students might not mind mutton stew and hash, but entertaining adults requires a professional cook. I'll ask my aunts. If you provide rooms for everyone, I can send you entire armies of help." Phoebe fed a tiny kitten with a dropper as she spoke.

Zane knew Lady Phoebe was the daughter of an earl and had been raised as a proper lady, but her work with animals required rough clothes, old dusters and hats, and occasional flits about town on her penny-farthing. She was the most eccentric female he'd ever encountered, but she had her fingers on the pulse of Old Town Edinburgh and its inhabitants. He thought he could rely on her better than an agency.

One didn't tell agencies they needed footpads and thugs.

While he was there, he inquired if Azmin was upstairs, and learned this was her time to teach. He'd been hoping for a bright spot in his otherwise gray day, but he set aside his disappointment. Apparently his life was more boring than he'd realized if he was looking forward to arguing with Azmin—one more bad habit from his wasted youth.

The hound followed him out the back gate in the no-longer vine-covered wall. Zane turned to shoo it off, but Lady Phoebe handed him more of her dog biscuits. "If you see your student, have Dog follow him. He's a good tracker."

Dog? She couldn't come up with a more imaginative name? Taking the lady's advice with a grain of salt, figuring she wanted someone else to feed the creature, he took the alley out to the main thoroughfare. There he found a vendor and bought Dog a meat pie instead of the nasty squares.

Satisfied that he had the search for servants underway, Zane returned to his office, where he made up lists of students to invite to his first dinner. He realized he had no real idea if they were wealthy or not. Azmin was right. He wanted to invite the interesting and engaged ones who might support each other in their studies.

And the dean was also correct—he'd shut himself off from his colleagues by burying himself in the laboratory. The urgency for finding a cure for Louisa, and the dean's pressure to produce, had taken over his life. But having a little help at home—might lessen his burden.

The thought of unconventional Azmin leading the discussion at his dinner table lightened his mood considerably, if not his burden. His life had become criminally boring.

Septimus Jenkins finally put in an appearance in the classroom. The young man's revolting attempt at sideburns and mustache reminded Zane of Azmin's comment about kissing. He had to bite back an inappropriate grin and remember the reprobate might attempt to kiss Louisa.

Jenkins slept through most of the class, but he managed to fumble his required report from his pocket when Zane called for the papers at the end of the session.

He slipped Jenkins' work into his coat pocket before depositing the others in his office. Once outside again, feeling like an utter idiot, Zane gave the paper to Dog to smell, then pointed out Jenkins as his student ambled off with a couple of muscular young ruffians.

The dog sniffed, yipped, and tottered off after the trio.

Now what? Did he believe Phoebe would read the animal's mind and learn where Jenkins went? Absurd. Still, he decided to leave early so he could stop at the animal shelter and warn Phoebe that her dog was on the trail.

Would Azmin be out of class and on her way to teach Louisa at this hour? Zane pulled out his pocket watch. He thought she wasn't due to be at his house for another hour. Maybe she would be at the workshop when he talked to Lady Phoebe—which was a ridiculous thought. Azmin was living in his home now. He'd see her at dinner. Why would it matter if he saw her now?

As he approached the Blairs' peculiar workplace, Zane heard an altercation and Dog's howl before he saw anything. Had Dog actually followed Jenkins to his favorite tavern, the one next to Phoebe's animal shelter? Zane ran toward trouble.

"It's her! It's the colored photographer aping her betters!" a man's voice shouted.

In an instant, Zane's blood pressure spiked to explosive. He dashed around the corner to the side street lined with shabby businesses, gripping his walking stick in the middle. The crowd in front of the tavern confirmed his worst fears. Swinging his stick at the ruffians on the edge of the mob, he cleared a path to the center of the fracas.

Thugs from the tavern had Azmin trapped against the wall Jenkins' friends had attempted to climb a few nights ago. He now knew Lady Phoebe's animals were on the other side. Today, it was Azmin trapped against the stones.

Instead of screaming, the damned woman had one hand buried in a skinny, blond fellow's hair, attempting to ram his head into the stones behind her while lashing out with her deadly boots at a second scoundrel. Connecting boot to shin to unbalance the shorter, sturdier villain, she drove the fingers on her free hand at his eyes. Her equipment rested at her feet, too heavy for her to swing. A valiant fight, but she didn't stand a chance.

Especially since there were *three* of the bastards taunting and shoving at her. Dog howled at one who looked like Jenkins—who appeared to be inching toward Azmin's valise. What the hell?

He'd ask questions later. Grabbing Jenkins' collar, Zane sniffed the sickening-sweet scent of incense that came with opium smoking. Is that what was happening in that den of iniquity? But this lot was just drunk —in the middle of the day—judging by their reeking breaths.

In a fury, Zane hauled Jenkins off his shabby boots and flung him up against the tavern wall, then smashed his fist into his jaw. It felt good to finally lay hands on the bastard, but it wasn't much of a fight. Jenkins slid down the wall, then scrabbled through the tavern's door, out of sight.

Azmin released Stout Villain to turn and knee Blondie's' privates. The skinny thug emitted a high-pitched shriek. While he was off-balance, she rammed his head into the wall again. Zane wanted to cheer, except Stout took her distraction to jump back into the fray.

The bigger villain grabbed her waist and hauled her off the ground. "I like a woman who can hold her own. C'mon, darkie, give us a kiss."

Zane's skin crawled. Furious, he shoved aside the last bystander, breaking through just as Azmin reached for the deadly weapon in her hair.

Before she could stab out her captor's eyes, Zane smashed the dolt's cranium with the knob of his walking stick, bringing him to his knees. He had never derived pleasure from violence, but he did not regret kicking the howling bastard in the kidneys to topple him. The miscreant had the sense to stay in the filthy gutter, groaning.

With every intention of hauling the damned woman out of there, Zane swung around, only to watch with disgust as the cursing blond man recovered sufficiently to raise his fist.

Zane seized his arm and yanked it behind Blondie's back. *Katar* finally in hand, Azmin ripped open the fellow's buttons. The bastard was blamed lucky she didn't take his guts out. Zane twisted the arm he held until he heard a crack, then flung him to join his comrade. The crowd in the street backed away. So it was just the three troublemakers involved and not a mob. Odd.

Tongue lolling, Dog sat down on his haunches and looked up expectantly. The animal had found Jenkins as he'd been told. Gathering Azmin into his arms, Zane fished one of Phoebe's dog biscuits from his pocket and threw it at the hound.

Glaring in disgust at the muttering crowd, he helped Azmin right herself. Her redingote was hanging off her shoulder, she'd lost her hat, and she was trembling, probably with rage, but she seemed otherwise intact.

Zane shouted at the onlookers. "Will one of you dolts please call a constable? What's the matter with you? A lady is attacked and you stand there gawping?"

"Ain't no lady," one wit shouted back.

"Blackies are good for only one thing," another piece of scum shouted.

Fury escalating to red hot, Zane wanted to plow into the crowd with his fists, but he wanted to haul Azmin away more. Did she have to endure these insults regularly?

She pushed him off. "Don't," she murmured. "My driver is here. I need to find him. Let me go, please."

Her driver? Zane glanced at the rickety carriage waiting down the street. Before he could question, he spotted Dean Reynolds' portly figure bearing down on them, full steam ahead.

"Devil take it," he muttered. Now he didn't know whether to tell Azmin to run or to hang on for support.

"What is the meaning of this, Dare?" the dean shouted, gesturing at the crowd and the men on the ground. "I had students running to tell me you were fighting a mob. And who is this. . . this creature? You have a moral obligation—"

The *creature* yanked out of Zane's arms, grabbed her equipment, and marched down the alley between the tavern and Phoebe's garden wall, back straight, steam practically rising from the top of her uncovered head. Dark sable hair spilled like a waterfall down her proud back.

"She is a *lady* who has just been assaulted and insulted," Zane replied, pouring every bit of scorn he possessed into his voice as he picked up her hat. "You would do better to ask the students why they didn't help."

Zane turned his back on the man who held his laboratory in his hand and raced after Azmin, his fury unabated.

"Don't. . . *touch*. . . me," she muttered as he caught up with her at the gate. "Just don't. And you needn't defend me. Go back and apologize to the important-looking man. He's right. I'm no lady."

"You're related to half of British aristocracy! Of course, you're a lady. What you aren't is the names they were calling you." He took the key from her trembling hand and shoved open the gate.

"Oh, well, one can't expect the ignorant to differentiate between Africans and Hindus," she said, sounding nonchalant, even though Zane knew she was no such thing. "And really, it shouldn't matter if I'm a *lady* or not, not any more than it should matter what color anyone is. No *woman* should be mauled simply for walking down the street. Would they have attacked a man? But bigots will be bigots."

She was distancing herself from him. Zane could feel it. He ought to let her go. He ought to go back and try to placate the dean. Perhaps he could explain. . . A stodgy professor would explain. Zane wasn't feeling like a professor right now. He was feeling murderous.

And he wanted to shout some common sense into the fool woman, but she was unfortunately too damned right.

"And bullies will be bullies and punching them in the snout won't change things, I understand. But recklessly walking alone doesn't help either." He tried not to shout, but he wasn't certain he was successful.

"You were brilliant back there, by the way," he added grudgingly, taking the damned heavy valise from her hand. He didn't know how to express how he felt at the way she'd defended herself. Terrified, proud, and appalled that she should have had to learn such street fighting.

Her silence was troublesome. Azmin was only silent when she was plotting. With the gate open, she crossed the yard in determination instead of heading for the safety of the animal shelter.

Zane was desperate to have her in his arms. He wanted to promise nothing like that would ever happen again. But that was the youthful dreamer talking through his hat. Stodgy professor recognized the lie.

Shouts of alarm rose from the street.

Azmin wound up her hair, shoved the katar back into the mass of silk, and climbed the unorthodox steps she'd created for looking over the wall.

So furious she wanted to cry, Azmin cast off her concern for Wilson, and the trap she'd set. First, she needed the identities of the tavern bullies who'd attacked her. Except for Jenkins, they'd been too old to be students. She lifted her skirt and climbed the rocks and animal cages to the top of the wall. She had grown much too comfortable in these streets and had forgotten how evil men can be.

She would not think of gallant Zane standing up to the important official yelling at him—because of *her*. Those were his choices, not hers.

The shouts on the other side grew louder. A primal scream of pain sent shivers crawling up her spine. That could have been her. She clutched the top of the wall and lifted herself to peer into the street she'd just left and gasped.

The blond man lay bleeding in the street. *She hadn't done that!*

He might have deserved murdering, but she couldn't callously let someone die without offering aid.

She held out her hand to Zane. "My camera, quickly. You'd better go back out there. I think he needs medical attention."

Instead of listening, Zane climbed up beside her with the valise. "What the hell happened?"

"I have no idea." Azmin removed her camera, set it on the wall, and slipped in a dry plate. She kept telling herself she'd seen worse, that she could do nothing to help the man who had assaulted her except preserve the moment for authorities.

But her insides roiled with fury and humiliation, and she figured she was going to hell for taking photographs instead of helping.

She balanced the camera on the wall for steadiness, focused on the man in the street, and hoped she could capture some of the people shouting, running, and crowding around. "I didn't have a chance to use my knife. I *know* I didn't do that."

"I know you didn't either." Zane stepped up beside her to study the scene. "He needs surgery and antiseptics, and I'm not even carrying my bag. I'm not about to abandon you to save his unworthy life. The constable just showed up. He'll have him hauled to the hospital. It's not far, and their doctors are more experienced than I am."

Azmin hated that she'd driven him to such a declaration, but she took satisfaction in it anyway. Blondie deserved to suffer.

She'd feel better if a little suffering would teach abusive men not to use violence, but she doubted it would make a difference.

The familiarity of the camera steadied her hands. She thought the day was bright enough not to need further illumination. She found the focus and snapped before the constable figured out how to move the wounded man. If anyone wanted to pin murder on her, she'd at least have tried to capture an image of the victim's spirit. She wondered if it looked black as Jenkins'.

Black, like they'd called her. They needed to learn their colors. Because of her mixed race, she wasn't even brown. Maybe tepid tea, at best.

She still shook when she thought about their cruelty. So, she'd quit thinking about it. Covering the lens to protect the plate, she placed her camera back in the bag. "Climb down. I need to see if Wilson is inside." And if her bait had been bitten. What worried her was that there was no reason for the aging driver to be anywhere but his carriage.

She waited for Zane to remove himself from her path. He was intimidatingly tall and broad and radiating angry intensity. She simply didn't have the strength to fight him right now. She was too utterly, immensely grateful that he'd been there when she'd needed him. And that was foolish, but she still shook with terror and knew his greater strength had saved her. She wanted to spit just remembering the foul smell of the stronger man's mouth as he tried to kiss her.

Zane took her valise and offered his hand to assist her down—as if he hadn't just seen her beat up two men. As if she really were a lady. She was back to wanting to weep all over again.

Telling herself it was just nerves, she accepted the assistance, then dropped his hand, picked up her skirts, and hurried across the yard, wishing he would go away. And hoping he'd stay. If Wilson had left the messages as he'd been told—Keya's stalker might be upstairs now. She wasn't prepared for another physical battle.

She didn't like the coincidence of Wilson possibly arriving with a stalker and the daylight attack. For once, she didn't argue with Zane when he followed her inside.

Neither Lady Phoebe nor Mr. Blair seemed to be inside the large echoing space occupied by assorted animals and tools. But Mr. Morgan was always in his office. This should be safe enough. Drawing in a deep breath, Azmin steeled her shaky nerves, lifted her skirts higher, and ran up the stairs. Only when it occurred to her that Zane was being awfully quiet did she realize how much of her limbs she'd revealed as he politely followed her up.

She was definitely not a lady. And she felt better for acknowledging that, because it gave her a thrill knowing he looked at her ankles. She supposed she ought to like him more for not being a bigot, but that hurt was a little deeper and needed more time to repair.

She held a finger to her lips as they reached her door. It was ajar. She was pretty certain she'd locked it. If Keya hadn't been hiding in Zane's home, Azmin would assume her assistant was here.

Zane set down the valise and held his walking stick like a bludgeon. He stuck out his arm and pushed her back against the wall, then used the stick to nudge the door open.

A knife slammed into the paneling, burying into the wood almost up to its ornate hilt. "Where is she?" a male tenor shouted. "Where is my sister?"

Well, that was enlightening. Azmin eyed the now useless knife. Someone didn't know not to waste weapons.

"Since I don't have a brother, you're in the wrong place," she called from behind Zane's arm.

A slender, brown-skinned youth materialized in the doorway, his eyes blazing with fire and a sword gripped with both hands. "I have come to rescue my sister from slavery."

Ah, so the trap had sprung.

"Oh, that's rich," Zane muttered, eyeing the stripling unsteadily holding a sword almost as big as he was. "All he needs is a lance and a noble steed."

"And flags flying," Azmin reminded him, curiosity spoiling her impending temper tantrum. "Lion-Heart stomped all over other countries in his not-so-gallant Crusades. I suppose it's fair to return the favor."

"I am no Crusader," the boy said, straightening his shoulders. "My sister was sold into slavery by her despicable husband and his second wife. I wish to take her home, where she belongs."

"Do we invite him to dinner?" Zane asked dryly.

"Since he's lying, I think not." Azmin emerged from behind him.

"I am not lying!" the boy shouted. "I am Gopala Trivedi, and I know my sister is hidden here."

Only because Wilson had told him so, the poor gullible idiot.

Azmin tried to find a resemblance between the young man and Keya, but she couldn't. If Keya had left home twenty years ago, this young man couldn't have been more than an infant. He'd have no memory of her.

"Maybe I should take his photograph, see if he's evil." Entertaining the idea of being able to identify evildoers bolstered her flagging morale.

"Can evil be stupid?" Zane asked, his patience wearing thin.

"We can find out, but not right now." Developing negatives required a steady hand, and hers did not qualify at the moment. "But I suppose we should find out more. Tell me of your sister," she demanded.

The slender lad managed to look defiant as well as confused. "She was married to a cruel man who called her an assassin and sold her. She is of good family. We will pay a ransom for her return."

"Her name?" Azmin demanded.

"Her name is Keya Trivedi Yedhu. Where do you keep her?" the youth insisted angrily.

"Does she know you? Will she recognize you?" she asked.

The knife-thrower looked flustered. "I don't know."

At the sound of heavy feet coming up the stairs, Zane sighed in exasperation and brought his walking stick down on the young man's arm. The sword clattered at his feet.

Then all hell broke loose. Again.

ELEVEN

A TOWERING TURBANED BANDIT EXPLODED FROM ONE OF THE EMPTY offices, pistols in hand, shouting blood-curdling, unintelligible curses. Azmin screamed. With no defense against bullets, Zane grabbed her waist and took her down to the floor, covering her with his body.

Bullets hit the wall where their heads had just been.

Zane stretched out his arm and snatched the sword away before the skinny lad could reach it. He could do considerable damage with a blade from this angle—if bullets didn't hit them first.

Hugh Morgan surged out of his office, gun and knife in hand. "What the hell. . . ?"

As Zane swung the sword at the youth's boots, hoping to bring him down, Morgan fired at the bandit, taking off his turban.

Staggering backward into the workshop, the lad shouted incoherent warnings, apparently in Hindi, because Azmin shouted back in the same incomprehensible language.

Another set of feet pounded up the stairs. Hugh turned his pistol toward the sound and Zane raised his sword.

Drew Blair burst into the corridor waving a pistol, just as the bandit rubbed his bare head, pulled back his bloody hand, and crumpled.

"Well, that was boring," Hugh muttered, shoving his smoking pistol into his waistband. "Can't you find tougher villains?"

Blair snorted, took in the scene, and shoved his weapon into his coat pocket. "Someone to see you, Dare. He was pounding on the door, and I had to let him in." With that, he returned to the stairway to yell at whoever he'd left below.

Unamused, Zane rolled off Azmin and tugged off his cravat. He hesitated over whether to use it for binding the shooter's hands or for staunching the bleeding scalp. His oath as a doctor was being tested today.

More familiar with turbans, Azmin unwound the bandit's and began wrapping it around the graze. Zane grunted at this decision and tied his wrists. "You only grazed him, Morgan. We need a place to stash these two until we confirm their identities."

Unarmed, the boy whimpered and looked on, making no attempt to escape.

Accompanied by Blair, Dean Reynolds emerged at the top of the stairs. Zane cursed beneath his breath. The man couldn't leave well enough alone.

Reynolds harrumphed at the sight of Hugh with a pistol in his waistband, Zane tying wrists instead of heads, and Azmin with her skirts hiked up to her knees as she scrambled around on the floor tying a bloody bandage.

"I think I've seen enough, Blair. Females and foreigners are nothing but trouble. I'd advise you to remove the lot." He glared at Zane. "I want to see you in my office in the morning."

"You SHOULD HAVE LET ME KNOCK THE BRAT AROUND A LITTLE," ZANE muttered, feeling frustrated as he and Azmin walked back to George Square to talk with Keya. He was still furious that the dean had seen him brawling like a sailor. The fragile threads holding his laboratory together were unraveling.

He'd sever the last threads if he called the dean the bigot that he was.

It was bad enough that uneducated mobs insulted Azmin—but the dean of a university? In this day and age?

Frustration enhanced his fury. Azmin didn't deserve. . . Hell, no one deserved that treatment. And there was no one in sight to beat up. Even smooth-talking, youthful Zane wouldn't have been able to produce a speech that could make any of this better.

"You should have let me photograph them." She countered his frustrated declaration.

They'd locked Keya's stalkers in a windowless room until Keya could identify them. Zane still wanted to shout and ask where in hell Azmin's head was for letting the hackney driver lead thugs to her.

"Take *photographs*—and give them another chance to attack you? Not on my life," he almost shouted. He never shouted. He had to be the sensible one here.

They were walking respectable streets of busy stores and decent residences, surrounded by normal people in suits and trailing gowns, with horses and carriages clattering alongside them. But they'd just been fighting brigands with swords and guns. The world made no sense.

"I'm sorry," Azmin said, not sounding in the least regretful. "Next time, I'll let them carry me off so you can rescue me."

"Saying things like that only makes my head spin," Zane retorted. "You've been assaulted by thugs who were probably hired by an idiot who thinks you own *slaves*! I'm writhing in frustration here and thinking I need to send you back to the school and Phoebe's aunts. You are even more insane than *Phoebe*!" He didn't seem able to calm down.

They'd almost reached the house and for Louisa's sake, he had to rein in a fury he hadn't unleashed in years.

She sent him what appeared to be a look of admiration as they climbed the front stairs. "Ah, you're not completely dead. Good to know. I've had my doubts."

That did it. He'd probably just lost his position because of her reckless need to do everything herself. Her insult roiled his frustration back to adolescent behavior. Zane opened his front door and practically flung her through it.

He didn't know what he would have done if a six-foot, rotund giant with muttonchops hadn't blocked his path.

"Sir?" the giant asked stiffly, as if Zane were the intruder.

Azmin straightened and dusted off her skirt, unsuccessfully hiding a smirk.

Zane double-checked to verify this was his foyer. There were his umbrella and his old walking stick. He was home all right. He glared at the incongruously garbed giant wearing top hat, suspenders, and tail-coat—over a yellowed starched shirt. "Who the. . . devil are you? Or better yet, what are you?"

"Uncle Zane, is that you?" Louisa called from the back of the house. "Mr. Thomson, are you not supposed to announce visitors?"

"He's not given me his card yet, miss," Thomson bellowed back.

Azmin giggled. That was better than having hysterics, but Zane still wanted to shake her. Shoving past the burly guard, he aimed for the back of his house, his haven of sanity. . .

Azmin shrieked, and he swung around just in time to block a walking stick aimed at his head. Zane yanked it from the fellow's massive fists and broke it in two.

It had been that kind of day.

"You'll have to do better than that if you're the bodyguard the ladies sent." With that growl, he flung the broken stick aside, left the giant blinking in surprise, and marched back to the sitting room.

"Dr. Dare doesn't like changes in his routine," he heard Azmin say apologetically to his new doorman or footman or whatever in hell it was.

"There is a reason for routine," Zane roared back. Composing himself, straightening his coat, he stepped into the sitting room where his new house guest stood on a chair, stripping draperies from the window, while Louisa steadied the impromptu ladder.

"Uncle Zane, did you meet Mr. Thomson?" his niece asked excitedly. "Isn't he a most marvelous butler? Although we might wish to buy him new clothes and persuade him he shouldn't wear a hat inside."

"Mr. Thomson, yes." Zane took off his hat and started to toss it aside, but Azmin slipped up from behind and grabbed it. She handed it to the growling bear who had followed her—and who now backed off when it finally sank in that Zane was his employer.

"I thought I was supposed to interview butlers," Azmin said, as if any of this made sense. "Did the ladies think we weren't capable of choosing properly?"

Keya stepped down from the chair and removed the pins she'd clenched between her teeth. "I believe it is a matter of Mr. Thomson being somewhat of a public nuisance who must be removed from the street. But I could be incorrect."

"That sounds like Lady Phoebe sent him." Azmin patted Zane on his coat sleeve, as if that would relieve his head from spinning. "We'll sort out servants later. We have more urgent matters at hand. Keya, could we speak with you in Dr. Dare's study?"

Louisa looked intrigued but wisely held her tongue. Zane credited his brother-in-law for raising the girl properly—unlike Azmin's negligent father who had allowed her to run wild.

In the streets of Calcutta. He needed a brandy—which was what immature Zane would have done. He refused to let her reduce him to adolescent drunkenness.

"I'll have the new maid carry in a tea tray," Louisa called cheerfully after them.

"New maid? Will she be wearing sackcloth and ashes?" Zane muttered as he escorted his guests back to the study.

"Missing her front teeth and wearing an evening dress," Azmin suggested, unhelpfully, employing the insolent guessing game they'd played that last summer. "What's your wager?"

"The two of you are very amusing," Keya said stiffly. "But I assume this is not because you are in good humors."

Zane shut the door and let the women settle their skirts and petticoats into his ancient chairs before answering that. "Do you, Miss Trivedi, happen to have a younger brother?"

She watched him in puzzlement. "Most likely half a dozen of them."

"This one is in his early twenties, about the same height as you, slender, and calls himself Gopala," Azmin explained.

Zane watched as the infernal women exchanged worried glances.

They knew something he didn't. He rubbed his temple and waited on the new. . . maid. . . to set out the tea tray. The waif with a ragged haircut in the doorway didn't look old enough to be out of school.

"On the desk," Azmin suggested as the girl hovered helplessly. "What may we call you?"

"Me, miss?" At Azmin's nod, the urchin answered warily, "Mary?"

Thin hair and sallow skin from lack of nutrition, Zane noted. Barely reaching five feet—probably due to her mother's poor diet. Definitely one of Lady Phoebe's rescued slum residents. Malcolm women did not think or live within society's boundaries.

How had he survived in Edinburgh all these years without running across any of his mother's eccentric family until now? Maybe it was because Blair had married into them, and Zane had made the fatal mistake of liking the inventor. It was hard to believe a sensible man like Blair would fall for pretty blue eyes. . . Malcolm blue, like Azmin's. That wasn't hard to imagine at all. Zane contemplated pounding his head against the wall.

"We already have a Mary," Azmin was saying as Zane pondered his descent into madness. "Do you have a last name? It's more proper to use that."

He refrained from rolling his eyes at this lecture on propriety from the Queen of Improper.

"Belkin, miss." The maid gingerly set the tray in a narrow cleared space on the far corner of his desk.

Zane grabbed the teetering tray before it tilted off the edge, then shoved books out of the way so it fit. "Thank you, Belkin," he said in a voice that sounded like his father's. When had he grown old? "You may go now."

The girl looked a little confused, forgot to curtsy, and fled.

"Good thing we didn't wager or we'd both lose," Azmin said, appearing considerably less agitated than earlier. "Do we bet whether Belkin has two children at home so Phoebe couldn't cast her into the streets or that she is the sole support of her bedridden mother?"

How could she be amused at a time like this? He was still ready to throttle people. "No bet. You've delayed long enough. What is it you're not telling me?"

AZMIN KNEW ZANE WAS TOO PERCEPTIVE NOT TO QUESTION. SHE HAD hoped he might go away and leave them to figure it out themselves, but he seemed to have become a remarkably domineering sort over the years.

"Keya, this is your story," Azmin told her companion. They both knew the arrival of her brother could not be easily explained away.

Keya anxiously entwined her fingers—not a good sign but understandable. "What does this person who calls himself Gopala say?"

"He claims Yedhu and his new wife called you an assassin and sold you into slavery." Azmin didn't dare look at Zane. He was undoubtedly steaming and looking for an excuse to fling them out—also an understandable reaction.

She was not an easy person to live with. Today had certainly proved that.

Keya's eyes widened in shock. "Why would anyone say such an impossible thing?"

"Who is Yedhu?" Zane asked in frustration.

"My husband. He was the one who *owned* me," Keya spat, breaking her usual stoicism. "I am worthless to him. It is more likely that my family wishes to save face and return me to him."

"So Gopala is your brother?" Azmin asked before Zane could jump in.

Keya's expression softened. "I have a brother called Gopala. He was only three when I married. I raised him after Mama died. He was such a sweet, brave little boy. But I have hardly seen him since then. It does not make sense that he came after me. He should be married by now and raising his own family."

Azmin handed her a cup of tea and kept one eye on Zane, who remained ominously silent. "You should probably speak with this person. Do you think you'd recognize him?"

"If he has not grown a beard, he has a scar on his chin from tumbling off a table." Keya stared glumly at her tea. "I do not want to go back home, ever. Can we not make him go back where he belongs?"

"No one can make you go home," Zane announced unexpectedly, sounding quite firm on the matter.

Azmin almost choked on her surprise.

"We will not allow you to be bullied. But we cannot leave men locked in a closet either. You will have to direct us."

"I cannot believe anyone from my family has come all this way after me," Keya murmured. "It is not reasonable after all these years."

Yedhu would beat Keya to death if he ever got his hands on her. Had he offered a reward for her return? Azmin bit back her anxiety and held out one tendril of hope. "Might your brother rescue you if he truly thought your miserable husband had sold you?" Azmin asked.

"Or better yet, why would your husband tell a young boy such a story?" Zane asked with an air of cynicism.

Azmin and Keya both looked at him in surprise, then exchanged glances. Why *would* Yedhu enlist Keya's family?

"Yedhu would never speak to my family," Keya said firmly. "It is either not Gopala, or it is a trick."

Despite her brave front, she was trembling, as she had every right to do. Azmin couldn't allow her friend to suffer more. "I will photograph him! I will show you the photograph, then you will not have to go near him at all until you're sure it is safe."

"Over my dead body!" Zane roared, apparently losing his last thread of patience.

TWELVE

"Well, it would most likely be my dead body," Azmin pointed out helpfully. "No one else has to go near the prisoners. But they're unarmed. I fail to see why I can't photograph them for Keya."

"And to see if they have black shadows or demons!" Zane tried not to roar, but she had pushed him dangerously near a limit he hadn't known he possessed. "It takes far too long to set up your camera for a meaningful photo. Morgan and I will tie them up and let Keya see them one at a time."

Azmin shot him a glare but quit arguing. Zane hoped it was because she finally saw sense.

Within the hour, they were back at the workshop, a shaky Keya in tow.

With the two women behind him, Zane waited as Hugh Morgan unlocked the closet containing the sword-wielding maniacs. The bearded bandit had awakened and was bellowing what were probably Hindu obscenities. Keeping the women behind him, Morgan gestured for the more harmless younger man. Gripping his walking stick, Zane blocked any attempt by the larger man to escape.

Hands tied, the slender swordsman looked furious as he stepped out of the closet. Morgan relocked the door. Zane took Azmin's arm to prevent her from interfering—and because holding her calmed his temper.

"Gopala?" With a trembling hand, Keya touched the boy's chin, where presumably she recognized the scar.

Azmin practically deflated at this gesture. Zane held her as they watched. He was still dubious about the story the women had told him and wanted to hear this, but Azmin leaning against him was a decided distraction.

"Keya!" the lad shouted joyfully. "I found you. Now, we can go home." He cast a suspicious look at the rest of them. "Unless these people think to stop you."

Having been told his claim that she'd been enslaved, Keya slapped his jaw lightly. "The British do not allow slavery. You would know this if you studied. I came here of my own free will and have no wish to return home. Who sent you and why?"

"Ouch," Zane murmured. "She just reduced the conquering warrior to mouse."

"He's young. He'll recover," Azmin whispered back unsympathetically. "You were a right pain at that age."

He probably had been. Zane didn't question but listened to the boy's angry reply.

"Our family sent me," he cried. "They were told you went unwillingly with the royal princess. I have the means to ransom you if I must."

Royal princess. Zane rolled his eyes. Azmin's mother's family might once have been royal, but India spread royalty thin on the ground much as Europe did purportedly aristocratic *counts*.

Keya patted her brother's jaw and nodded at Morgan to release him. "Who told you that lie?"

"Yedhu's servants," Gopala said in bewilderment. "They adore you and want you home. He is dead now, and you are their new mistress. If you do not go home, they will have to find new positions."

Azmin gasped. She wriggled to escape Zane's embrace. He rather enjoyed keeping her impulsivity in check, but he no longer had a reason to hold her back. This looked like a family misunderstanding, not dire jeopardy—except for the bandit part.

"Yedhu had a second wife," Keya responded bitterly. "Let them work for her."

"She has no money," Gopala cried. "You know the authorities will not recognize a second wife. It is all yours since he left no sons. If you do not claim it, who knows what will become of his household?"

That sounded positive. Zane didn't know why he was here. Family disputes weren't his bailiwick. He should be in his laboratory while it still existed.

"When did you hear Keya was gone?" Azmin demanded.

Startled, everyone turned to her. Zane started calculating shipping times, but he didn't know the date of Keya's arrival.

"When Yedhu was cremated, three months ago," Gopala replied. "We asked for Keya, and we were told she had been taken." He looked proud. "We found a steamship using the new canal. It made good time even in the British winter."

He must have left about December. If Azmin started school in January, she and Keya had to have already been settled in Edinburgh before the lad had left India. Yedhu had died well after they'd sailed here. So Keya hadn't murdered her abuser. Nice to know.

Zane watched with interest as Keya and Azmin hugged each other and exchanged whispers. He glanced to Morgan, the shipping expert, who was frowning but not disagreeing with the timing.

"How did Yedhu die?" Keya asked cautiously.

"He'd been ill for months, the servants said." Gopala shrugged. "He called for you, they said. They think it was karma that he fell ill after selling you off, and he wanted to correct his wrongs."

"Who came with you?" Keya demanded. "Is he the one who filled your head with nonsense?"

"Your majordomo," the lad said in bewilderment. "He said he would help rescue you."

Keya covered her scarred mouth and shook her head. "That man is as cruel as Yedhu. Maybe worse! He filled your head with *evil!*"

Gopala looked even more confused. "He has been very helpful. But if your husband did not sell you, why did you go?"

It took the boy long enough to ask.

"Because Yedhu would have killed me," Keya said flatly.

That didn't seem to faze the oblivious lad who apparently could only keep one goal in his head at a time. "But he is dead now, so you can come home! You will be wealthier than royalty. Our sisters will have the best suitors. . ."

"I suggest you hire a lawyer to verify that." Mr. Morgan broke his usual silence. "I know several good ones here but not in India. A good firm here can send letters through diplomatic channels and find counterparts in India who will investigate the existence of any estate. Without the name of the executor or who is handling the estate, it will take time."

"I'll have my father check with local authorities as well," Azmin said, holding Keya's arm and watching the boy with suspicion. "He might at least verify Yedhu's death."

"Gopala would not lie," Keya said in protest, but she didn't object to their suggestions beyond that.

"Someone lied," Zane reminded her. "They made your family believe you were in danger. Why would they do that?"

"A trap," Azmin murmured. "If they knew she was in England, they could have sent letters to locate us." To Zane's surprise, she turned on the shocked young man. "Did you hire the men who attacked me yesterday?"

The men from the tavern? Zane clenched his fists and recalled that scene in a new light. He'd thought it had been a mob, but on reconsideration, he realized it had only been Jenkins and his cohorts harassing Azmin. The others simply threw insults. Somehow, the fact that they might have been hired made their bigoted attack even filthier.

"We were told her owners would fight," Gopala protested. "Yedhu said if we hired help to keep the princess outside, I could find Keya alone and smuggle her onto a ship."

"You *believed* stupid servants who allowed Yedhu to beat your sister —then compounded the wrong by hiring thugs to hurt *me*?" Azmin asked angrily.

Gopala did not leap to deny it.

"Do I call the authorities?" Morgan asked. "We can have them flung behind bars."

Keya's cry of dismay diverted that thought.

"We can't leave them in the closet," Zane pointed out, logically enough. "A court would settle the matter."

"They are not British," Azmin reminded him. "A judge would look at their color and leave them languishing in our jails. Can they not be sent back where they belong?"

"I did nothing wrong!" the boy shouted. "Keya, don't let them send me to jail."

"We can ship them home," Morgan said abruptly. "I know a few captains."

Zane shook his head in disbelief that the stoic businessman had taken Keya's part so thoroughly.

"But. . . But what about our family?" the boy cried. "Keya, you must go with me!"

Zane clapped him on the shoulder. "If she doesn't want to go with you, that's the end on it. You can use your ransom money to go where you like, as long as it's not here, hurting innocent women."

Azmin threw him a grateful look which almost rewarded him for wasting time on this nonsense.

Keya simply chewed her bottom lip.

"THERE'S A DOG TRACKING US," AZMIN REPORTED AS ZANE ESCORTED them back to his house. Learning she'd been the target of hired thugs had made her nervous.

He glanced over his shoulder and muttered. The stuffy professor had taken to muttering a lot lately, she noted.

He halted so the dog could catch up, then bent to scratch the hound's ears. "One of Lady Phoebe's animals. I had meant to leave her a message about it when I went to the workshop earlier."

A message, about a dog? She would question, but they had reached the house, where the broad giant welcomed the hound as if it were a favored guest. Azmin tried not to snicker at Zane's expression as his new doorman led the hound down to the kitchen, talking to his new best friend.

"I'll send word to Phoebe about the dog," Azmin promised. "I wonder if she has sent a footman or if we have to use your new doorman as messenger. I don't think we can quite call him a butler, but he'll know the workshop."

"Houses don't have doormen," Zane protested.

Ignoring this quibble, Azmin turned her attention to Keya, who had closed herself off in silence. They should talk, but Azmin suspected her friend needed some time alone. Learning that her abusive husband was dead would be an enormous relief, if only they could believe Gopala's tale.

"Keya, why don't you go upstairs and lie down a bit before dinner?" Azmin suggested. "I'll send Belkin up with a tea tray."

"Make sure you have an empty table for the tray," Zane warned. "Belkin only manages one task at a time."

Keya offered a faint smile and drifted upstairs.

"Louisa is being awfully quiet," Azmin said, glancing back at the door. They hadn't come through the park. If the girl was out there, they hadn't noticed.

"She may be napping. She does that frequently." Since the doorman had gone off with the mutt instead of taking their outerwear, Zane had to hang up his own hat and offer to help remove her caped cloak.

After her encounter with the nasty Jenkins fellow yesterday, Azmin was a little anxious about Louisa. "I'd like to see if she's here or out reading in the park." Without removing her redingote, she hurried down the corridor to the sitting room, wishing for a properly trained maid she might ask about Louisa's whereabouts.

She heard the front door open and close. If Zane was checking the park. . . She'd pray the young thug wasn't there. If Louisa had been seeing Jenkins—her host was in no humor for reason.

She found Mary and confirmed that Louisa had gone outside. Azmin rushed back into the late afternoon gloom. It wasn't exactly a pleasant spring day. The wind was so chilly that she wore her gloves. But Louisa was better adapted to the climate, she told herself.

"Is she in the house?" Zane asked in concern, meeting her at the gate.

"Mary said she went to the park. She's not there?" Not waiting for an answer, she strode toward the bench where she'd seen Louisa reading before, a burning sensation searing her heart as she saw the empty seat.

"She cannot walk far." Zane paced alongside her.

"We should have warned the servants not to let her out alone. . ." At the sound of rustling bushes, Azmin swung on her heel.

Looking wan but triumphant, Louisa stepped through a budding hedge. Her cloak was covered in leaves, but she appeared unharmed. "I hope you weren't looking for me. I told Mary where I was."

"You wandered off!" Zane declared, irate.

Azmin placed a calming hand on his arm. "You felt well enough to walk? Or did your young man suggest it?"

"He's my cousin, not my young man." Ignoring her uncle, Louisa aimed for the gate. "He suggested I might grow stronger with regular exercise."

"It is your heart, not your limbs affected!" Zane roared.

Azmin squeezed his arm a little tighter. Gopala had admitted Jenkins had been one of the young thugs he'd hired. That didn't mean anything more than they already knew—Jenkins was not a good person. Telling Louisa that would only encourage her to defend him.

"That was thoughtful of him to think of your health," she said, pinching Zane's arm to keep him quiet. "He really should not meet with you here without a chaperone, though, even if he is your cousin. It must be a distant relationship at best if no one recognizes him."

"I cannot ask Mary to sit with me every time I wish to read in the park," Louisa argued.

Azmin squeezed Zane's hand. He glared. She chuckled, enjoying the familiarity. He took the warning.

"We will try harder to have one of us about so you're not bored," Azmin said sympathetically as they reached the front door. "Your uncle frets that you'll have a bad spell, and there will be no one to run for aid."

Looking like the wary adolescent she was, Louisa pulled off her gloves and hat. "And if my cousin visits? Will you chase him away?"

"He would do better to knock on the door and introduce himself," Azmin said before Zane could explode. "If we knew his address, we could send an invitation to dinner."

Mollified, Louisa nodded. "He says he studies in the park when the weather is fair, so he must live nearby. I'll ask next time."

Azmin took off her hat and hit Zane in the face with her feathers so he spluttered instead of shouting something useless like *There will be no next time!*

Looking interested at this byplay, Louisa continued, "Can you tell me now what the secret meeting was all about?"

"Someone calling himself Keya's brother showed up unexpectedly. We wished to make certain he wasn't—" Azmin stumbled, uncertain how much Keya had imparted. She was badly shaken by this incident to top of all else that had happened and hiding it badly.

"Someone sent by her awful husband? Keya doesn't treat me like a baby." Louisa stuck her tongue out at her uncle.

Azmin managed a smile. Louisa shouldn't be burdened by their fears. "Your uncle does not understand women. We'll teach him, little by little, but you must be patient with him. Go order some tea so you can warm up, and I will be with you directly."

When Louisa vanished into the nether regions of the house, Azmin dragged Zane into his study. "I never want to be a parent if this is what it is like," she said, holding her hand over her still-racing heart. She simply didn't need one more shock to her system or one more person to worry over.

"An army," he agreed with a heartfelt sigh. "We need an army to surround the place. She was blue around the lips and fingers and coughing. That's a bad sign of overexertion."

"Or cold." Azmin held her hands over the burning embers in the grate, letting her nerves calm down. "But yes, an army would be good. I want to find out more about Jenkins. I took his photograph with Louisa. He *knows* who I am! Was that why he only threw insults instead of attacking me as Gopala hired him to do?"

"Ah, he knows about your camera then. Perhaps that explains why he seemed interested in your valise. He probably meant to sell the equipment." Zane paced, looking murderous.

"Write a message to Lady Phoebe," he continued. "I didn't have the chance to let her know the dog was following Jenkins. I assume the animal showed up outside the park because he tracked the cad there. Maybe the lady has a magic trick or two to let us know where else Dog has been."

Before Azmin could reply to that remarkable declaration, Zane wrapped his arms around her from behind and kissed her cheek. He was so very nice and warm and. . .

Desire coursed through her, heating her to the marrow. She *needed* comfort after this day.

THIRTEEN

AZMIN KNEW BETTER THAN TO SUCCUMB TO HER INAPPROPRIATE DESIRE
for Dr. Dare. At the same time, she'd studied the *Kama Sutra* in Hindu
that her father didn't know she could read. She *wanted* to experience the
sublime transcendence of the body. Just not with Zane. He was too
dangerous to her damaged heart.

While she struggled with her warring mind and body, he turned her
around so her bodice crushed his coat, and he could kiss more than her
cheek.

With his questing lips pressing hers, the day's insults vanished, and
she succumbed to pure bliss. His kiss reminded her of yesterday's sensa-
tions and taught her new ones.

His whiskers scratched her upper lip. The touch of his tongue
shocked her. No man had ever kissed her like this before... He tasted of
tea, and every faculty fed her desire, instead of putting her off as with
other men. His musky male scent intoxicated more than the most
potent incense. She quit arguing with herself and melted into his
embrace.

Zane groaned against her mouth, indicating she wasn't the only one
consumed with insanity. His tongue probed, creating a hot river to her
lower parts. She almost jumped out of her skin when he cupped her

bottom with his big hands, despite the interfering contraption beneath her skirt. When he lifted her against him and kissed her throat, she almost expired of desire on the spot.

Only the giant's heavy footsteps jarred them back to the moment.

Zane cursed under his breath. Heart pounding, Azmin shoved away. Having someone hold her after a day like this was—*weak*. She could not allow herself to return to that pathetic adolescent.

Rubbing the bridge of his nose, Zane reluctantly released her. "I used to want to do that when you were barely out of school. I was afraid I was a pervert."

Her jaw dropped, but she didn't have time to speak before Thomson shoved open the door without knocking, excitedly holding out a card.

"It's Lady Phoebe at the door, milord. She came here. Tell her I'm doin' good, please?"

Pulling herself together, Azmin took the card. "You must knock before entering, Thomson." Although his thundering footsteps had worked better than a slamming door. "You're doing fine, but we should find a salver for you to carry visitor cards on so you do not bend them."

Zane had retreated behind his desk and was reaching for his spectacles when Phoebe brushed past the burly giant and cheerfully greeted them. "Thomson, how are you faring?"

"They have a dog, milady." The big man said with an adoring, gap-toothed grin, taking the cloak she handed him.

"It's Dog I have come about. Fetch him, would you, Thomson, please?" Phoebe flapped her hands to usher him out, then shut the door.

Azmin offered a chair by the fire. "You must be chilled. Shall I send for tea?"

Phoebe snorted inelegantly and began pulling off her gloves rather than take a seat. "I am here to prevent my aunts from descending on you. They are seeing so many ominous portents that they are prepared to set up camp in your drawing room—Dare's drawing room," she corrected, sending him a disapproving look, as if she knew what they'd been doing.

Azmin sat so Zane could too, but Phoebe continued pacing.

"Do I owe your aunts for dispatching a guardian doorman?" Zane asked dryly, standing while he waited for Phoebe to perch.

The lady waved her hand in dismissal. She seldom wore hoops and her single petticoat took up little space as she wore out the carpet. "They are still all a-dither choosing teachers to occupy Azmin's home and debating whether to bring their carriage out of mothballs to transport them. *I* sent Thomson and Mary. They're uncle and niece. There's a whole household of the family squeezed into a two-room flat after the tenement's collapse."

Azmin knew Phoebe referred to her own lost home. The medieval walls had buckled, and the whole façade had fallen off. Mr. Blair and Mr. Morgan meant to demolish the block of ancient buildings as soon as homes were found for the hundreds of tenants.

Before either of them could reply, Thomson returned with the hound, which jumped all over Phoebe's skirts—one of the many reasons for her plain dress. She rubbed his ears and head and settled him down, while gesturing at Thomson to depart, this time closing the door after himself.

"Belkin and Thomson are both quite trainable, I think," Phoebe said. "Whether or not you're good teachers is another matter."

"My profession is teaching," Zane irascibly pointed out. "What I need to know is whether that dog actually followed Jenkins and if you have some way of knowing."

"You needn't be resentful just because you have no Malcolm gift," Azmin told him pertly, trying to re-establish her distance. She needed to remember he didn't believe in her spirit photography.

Zane glared at her.

Phoebe finally flopped down in the other wing chair by the fire to continue rubbing the dog's head. "It seems he followed your young man to a tavern—I'm fairly sure I recognize the Green Lion even from a dog's height. The walls still have a trace of green paint on them."

"If that's the tavern near the workshop, then we know that much," Zane said.

"Yes. Tawdry and disreputable, little better than an opium den. After that, Dog tracked him to a tenement with so many distracting smells that Dog forgot his task." Phoebe patted the hound and fed it a biscuit from her pocket.

"Will he be able to find it again?" Zane asked.

Azmin was utterly amazed that he accepted this information as anything but foolishness. Even she had difficulty believing Phoebe could read the hound's mind. Well, she had strong doubts that the fat creature rolling over to have his belly rubbed had a mind to read—except Dog had been at the Lion with Jenkins, and again, near the park with Louisa.

"He'll recognize the scents. You'll just have to take me with you so I know when he reacts. My gift has its limits. Despite his distraction, Dog was smart enough to follow Jenkins after he left the tenement. I believe I recognize the park just outside your door?"

"Yes, that's near where we found him—after Jenkins ran off, abandoning my niece in the shrubbery. I want the man's head on a pike." Zane stabbed his pen at his blotter as if wishing it were a knife.

"He does not seem to be a gentleman, certainly." Phoebe rose. "But one should not judge by the emptiness of a person's pockets. What are your intentions for the gentlemen we're currently feeding in the upstairs cupboard?"

"Undecided. First, we must speak with Keya's brother about where he might stay until we find a ship," Zane suggested.

"Drew was sounding him out, trying to determine if he has any training in anything. He's concluded the boy can work with wood and wants to give him one of our smallest rooms for now."

Azmin breathed a sigh of relief. "Thank you. I'll feel better if Drew is keeping an eye on him. Jenkins, unfortunately, is a different matter. Would it be possible to find a reasonably respectable footman to follow Louisa when she goes out? And who can run messages as needed?"

"A young lad, perhaps?" Phoebe brightened. "I can do that. Give him some new shoes, and he'll worship you forever."

"Send him over, but I was thinking more in terms of a soldier with a bludgeon," Zane said, rising to show her the door.

"Oh, I can provide one of those too," Phoebe said cheerfully. "He has a wooden leg and isn't much good as a messenger, though."

THE INTERVAL WITH LADY PHOEBE HAD GIVEN ZANE TIME TO REGAIN HIS composure after the heated kisses he'd stolen. But watching Azmin thoughtfully scratching the dog's head and not running as she ought disconcerted him all over again.

"I'd thought you beautiful with your cheeks rosy from the wind," he said, closing the study door after Lady Phoebe, as he shouldn't. "But you're even more striking when I can see your mind spinning a dozen wheels."

She gaped at him in shock, as she had every right to do. Zane was pretty certain he was in shock as well. He used to spout those flatteries with the ease of a practiced rake. He hadn't done so in a decade, and this time, he meant his words—which shook him even more. Because he didn't know his intentions now as he had all those years ago. Seducing a *virgin*...? He didn't do that. And he was pretty certain from her kisses that Azmin was inexperienced, at best.

She shook her head and looked back to the hound. "You used to say wicked things like that all the time. You never meant them. My cheeks aren't rosy. They're brown and very un-English. But my mind is spinning, so you're correct on that count."

He used to say things like that to her? No wonder he thought himself depraved at the time.

"Your cheeks do so become rosy when they're cold," he argued, although they had a dozen more intelligent things to discuss. "Do not classify me with the tavern louts. I think your bronze coloring is striking and very appealing. Tell me why you ran away that summer."

She didn't even look surprised at that digression, so her thoughts had traveled there too.

"That's irrelevant." She waved a dismissive hand. "I was a confused child. These days I know enough to understand that kisses are physical urges which belong inside the shelter of marriage, but I am not suited for the confinement of a wife's role. And you must marry someone of your own kind who can aid you in your endeavors instead of riling your employer. So we must stop these unseemly. . . *physical*. . . affections and apply our minds to the problem at hand."

"Of my own *kind*?" Zane knew enough to be outraged but not enough to even know how she arrived at any of those conclusions. "What *kind* am I? A *doctor*? If that's my kind, I'll never marry. Women can't be physicians. Not that I'm considering marrying anyone," he hastily added.

"Exactly," she said in satisfaction, standing up. "And neither am I. Therefore we need to halt any further physical contact. You need to construct a list of students to invite for dinner now that it appears Keya is in no imminent danger. Once we have a student dinner running smoothly, we can collect names for an adult dinner, although I may not be the best choice for hostess, it seems." She headed for the door.

"*Stop right there!*" Zane roared. He couldn't remember any woman so unbalancing him as this one. He was a rational man, but she was driving him to madness.

She crinkled up her lovely dark eyebrows into a quizzical expression. "Do I have it wrong? You wish us to leave instead of staying to help?"

"I wish no such thing!" He was shouting again. Why in the name of all that was holy did she reduce him to a shouting imbecile?

The maddening wench waited, looking delectably fragile and formidably disapproving at the same time. She'd been manhandled as no female should be—and instead of hysterics, she resorted to obstinacy. Strands of her long hair had come loose from her pins and fell in unruly lengths over her gloomy gown. He could imagine running his hands through that thick waterfall of silk. . .

Zane rammed his hand through his hair. "You're running again," he finally said. "This is not how adults converse. You used to do this every time someone else entered the room. You'd get an expression like a trapped rabbit, then flee at the first opportunity."

"Do I look like a trapped rabbit now?" she inquired with interest.

"No. You did earlier, when Thomson barged in. You've learned to hide it better now. Sit. Explain why you think I'm not your kind. Let's start there." He deliberately sat even though she was still in flight.

He needed to sit or his physical response to her presence would be noticeable. Sensible conversation would ease the problem.

"I don't see how this is a topic of any interest or relevance." She perched on the edge of the wing chair. "You are a highly-respected physician, the British heir to an earldom, and I am a half-Hindu photographer of little consequence, one who is insulted simply for walking down the street. You must marry a reputable heiress to produce an heir and secure funding for your research. Your world is one of society and propriety. I, on the other hand, wish to develop my artistic and possibly psychical gifts with the unlawful goal of saving other women like Keya. Our worlds do not mix. What is there to understand?"

"None of that was true that summer when you ran away. I came back from a visit, hoping to hear your sensible advice, or at least your sarcastic opinion, and you were gone. I thought we were friends and you would at least have said farewell." There, he'd expressed some of the misery he'd suffered when the one bright spot in his summer had disappeared.

Admittedly, at the time, he'd been a little relieved as well. She'd been too clever and would have castigated him rightly for his engagement. And she'd been too damned young to be so appealing. But then the disease has struck, disaster had followed disaster, and he'd really needed someone who would listen, heed his anguish, and she hadn't been there. That had been when he'd realized she'd filled an empty place in his life that he hadn't known existed.

He thought he'd overcome that foolishness. Perhaps he was just suffering from nostalgia.

Her expressive features shifted into a thoughtful frown. The firelight danced along her tawny cheek, but her long lashes hid her eyes.

"Sixteen is a difficult age," she finally said. "I was out of school and expected to make a proper introduction to society the next spring. I did not like the restriction of British clothing nor the dreary, heavy fabrics of fashion. The school I attended was international, and no one thought to object to my saris there. They assumed I would be returning to India where my clothing made sense."

"It made sense in a British summer, I remember," Zane said, trying to process what she was saying. What did clothes have to do with anything? "It was especially hot that year. I was wondering if that had anything to do with the outbreak of disease in the city. Your thin fabrics were much admired."

"No, they weren't," she said with a dismissive shrug. "Everyone laughed at me and tried to guess what I wore under my clothes. The boys tried to touch me to find out, until I raked their faces or stabbed them with forks or whatever was at hand. I learned to carry hat pins in my hair."

"I would have thrown them in the lake for you if you had only told me." Zane tried to remember which miscreants had been around that summer, but the family was large and the guests were numerous. And boys would be boys, he had to admit. Iveston had been filled with the younger generation that year, and masculine boisterousness had abounded.

"You were the only one who treated me as if I were a real person and not a doll to be pushed around. You *talked* to me. You made me think maybe all of England wasn't full of beef wits and clodpolls. And I understood that you were simply as bored as I was. I really did." She gestured helplessly. "But you left and found a wife, and I realized I did not want to be presented to society. So I went home, where I belonged."

"You had spent *ten years* in England and only six in India and that as an *infant!*" he protested. "You no more belonged there than I did."

She smiled briefly. "I realized that eventually, but I needed to grow up. So I did. Now I wear clothing to suit the occasion and the weather, just as any adult must. And I know people everywhere can be beef wits and clodpolls, but that there are very many interesting people as well. I became my father's hostess and learned the things one must do to be accepted in any society. And I learned I didn't care about society and I truly enjoyed photography. I am sure there are names for women like me. I've been called names all my life, everything from princess to slut. Names do not define me. But your position can be harmed by insults and gossip. If we are to have a conversation, might I ask questions of you as well?"

"In comparison to you, I am quite boring and an open book. What would you like to know?" But he was already going over her words in his head and knew there was more to them than he'd first heard. He'd gone straight for the part about *belonging* and ignored her childish opinion of the arrogant ass he'd been. And possibly still was.

"Why did you engage yourself to a woman who hadn't a thought in her head beyond the next pretty dress she meant to wear?"

He pinched the bridge of his nose. Louisa's illness and his sister's death had managed to erase most of that humiliating experience, and he preferred it that way. "I want to think I'm a better man than that now."

She waited in silence.

"This is important to you?" he asked, studying her composure. Azmin was not a placid woman. He might not notice most people, but he knew her. His answer was important. So he answered as honestly as he could. "I was trapped. I *let* myself be trapped."

She raised expressive dark eyebrows.

"That was the summer I grew up and realized I needed to take responsibility for my life. I had a medical degree and no practice. My parents are patient people, but as I've said, we're a small family. An heir was expected. The lady's father promised to buy a practice for me. I courted her as expected. One thing led to another, and we were caught in an embrace in the garden. I did what I thought was right. And was grateful when she flung the ring back at me later."

That had been after his sister died, and he started haunting mortuaries in search of answers. Brought to his knees by real life, he'd only been relieved when she'd publicly denounced him. The real humiliation had been realizing what a light-minded fool he'd been to engage himself at all.

Research scientists had no business marrying at all.

FOURTEEN

AZMIN DIDN'T SLEEP WELL THAT NIGHT. LIKE GHOSTS FROM HER PAST, regrets haunted her. She truly had been too young to know her own mind when she'd left England. She didn't have that excuse now. And still, she was confused. She'd left Zane downstairs last night looking as unsatisfied and unhappy as she felt. She wasn't certain what to make of Zane's explanation of his betrothal—but it rang true.

Rather than fret, she joined Keya the next morning in returning to their normal schedule. Azmin had brought the negatives of yesterday's bloodthirsty crowd home with her. Instead of returning to the workshop where Morgan guarded their captives, they traveled over to the new side of town. She could develop the plate and meet the teachers the school had sent to live in her flat. They would check on the studio's progress while they were there.

"Your home is so. . . colorful," one of the teachers cried when she let them in. "I've never seen anything quite so. . ."

"Exotic?" Azmin supplied drily when the young woman hesitated a moment too long.

"It smells heavenly," another teacher added. "I don't recognize all the scents, but they smell of love and nature and. . . protectiveness, I think. I feel safe here." Honey-blond and plump, the young woman held up one of Keya's incense sticks. "These are fascinating. They are nothing like the scents of the Highlands. I recognize sandalwood and cinnamon but what is this one?"

"Frankincense," Keya said with a hint of amusement. "If you light the end, it will fill the room with relaxing aromas suitable for meditation."

Assuming anyone smelling love and protectiveness in incense was a Malcolm with a gift for fragrance, Azmin ignored the meditation discussion. She tried to look at the flat through the eyes of others. Admittedly, peacock feathers did not normally adorn British drawing rooms. The delicate turquoise and gold silks they'd looped over the brown velvet draperies were unusual, but in her mind they lightened the perpetual northern gloom and went well with the Turkish carpets she and her father collected.

She supposed the wicker furniture was lighter than most heavy pieces in fashionable drawing rooms, but wicker wasn't *exotic*. Bassinets and carriages had been made of rattan for years. Perhaps the colorful silk pillows they padded them with were a little foreign. But she had warm childhood memories of an aunt with a colorful room similar to this, so she knew it wasn't utterly outrageous.

The artwork, however. . . reflected much of her mother's Hindu background, definitely exotic to British eyes. The beautiful copper dancing Shiva with its multiple arms, a particularly fine framed, illuminated manuscript page in brilliant oranges and blues, a stylized representation of an ancient temple, and the elephant statues, of course. . . all reminded Azmin of her other home and gave her comfort. They were meaningless to these teachers who had never left this island.

They would never fit into Zane's very British household. He apparently preferred the lighter, cleaner lines of antiques from earlier eras. She needed this reminder that what made her happy disconcerted others.

She had thought herself inured to insults until yesterday. In India, she had been a mongrel, neither white nor brown. She'd worn bustles and frills for her father's military guests, and saris when she went out in the street, never quite belonging in either garb. As the daughter of a royal princess, she had mostly been treated with respect. She'd simply learned to ignore the whispers behind her back.

She had hoped in Edinburgh, her sable hair and tawny coloring might not be noticeable if she wore fashionable clothing. But surrounded by blond, blue-eyed Malcolms, she could see she'd been fooling herself. Even in drab colors, she was as exotic as peacock feathers. She'd simply have to learn to strut—which made her smile again.

Ascertaining that the teachers were settling in and enjoying the freedom of having their own suite, Azmin and Keya returned downstairs to the studio. Keya might never be safe, but since they'd caught the men looking for Keya, they'd cautiously allowed work crews to enter. The refined cream-and gold-wallpaper—so unlike the upstairs décor— was already up. The oak floors had been polished to a gleam. Keya had chosen an English Axminster carpet of maroon and gold for the center of the floor. Cheaper than Brussels and more familiar to the British eye than a Turkish or Persian, the rug gave a good solid feel to the space, one that Azmin hoped would make women feel safe.

"We only need to add the furniture," Azmin cried in delight.

"You might wish to examine the photography room," Keya suggested. "We only have one background screen. More need to be ordered."

"And we need a spare room full of different styles of chairs and tables so all the photographs don't look the same, but that can be done a little at a time. *Cartes de visite* don't require much background. We could advertise those first." Azmin swung around, admiring her former parlor with delight.

"A discreet sign outside the door," Keya reminded her. "You cannot advertise until the house is clearly marked."

"Gossip is already spreading," a young woman pinning draperies at the window said from her ladder. Keya had hired as many experienced women as she could find to do the necessary tasks. "I've had several of the neighbors ask when you will be open."

"I suppose we should have a grand opening reception to introduce ourselves to the neighbors." Azmin jotted a note in her reminder book. "We could have punch and cookies, display some of our work—"

A rap at the front door interrupted that train of thought.

Grey, their only maid, hurried to answer it.

"Footmen," Azmin added to her notes. "I'd rather have someone a little better trained than Phoebe's miscreants. This should be an elegant, welcoming salon, and we need to feel safe here."

Keya was worriedly listening to the low conversation in the foyer, but she relaxed when the maid carried in a card on a salver. Grey bobbed a curtsy. "A Mrs. Balfour to see you, mum."

"Do we know any Balfours?" Azmin murmured, studying the card. It had no photograph.

The draper chimed in, "A neighbor, I believe."

Azmin brightened. "Opportunity! Show her in, Grey, please."

A large woman sporting a fur-trimmed pelisse swirled into the room in an old-fashioned circle of petticoats. "My dear Miss Dougall, how good it is to see you all grown up! When I heard you were opening your father's house, I was all atwitter. Of course, I have been in the south of France these dreadful winter months, but I have returned!"

Azmin bit back a smile at her neighbor's prodigious overconfidence. "Good morning to you, madam. I fear you have me at a disadvantage. If I ever visited this house in my infancy, I do not remember it."

"Of course you do not, dear one. Your rapscallion of a father abandoned these parts for sunnier climes long ago. But you attended the same school as my dear niece, Eleanor. You almost had her convinced that she wished to live in India! Fortunately, she found a nice young professor last fall and married before I left for France."

Azmin recalled no Eleanor from her school days, but that had been almost a decade ago. Who was she to deny her existence? "I am sorry I cannot offer you a proper seat and tea. As you see, we're still under construction."

"I know, and isn't it thrilling!" the woman trilled. "I hear you have taken up photography, and I wish to be your very first client. A woman photographer! Isn't it amazing? And you have brought back an Indian to assist you! How very ingenious. Eleanor will be thrilled."

"Appointment book," Azmin muttered, jotting another note and trying not to wince. Having lived with the British all her life, Keya was accustomed to remarks like this. She was capable of correcting people as she saw fit.

"Perhaps you could try out your new studio, Miss Dougall," Keya suggested formally. "We could offer Mrs. Balfour a discount for being our very first customer."

A woman with this much self-possession would spread the news far and wide. . . Keya was an astute businesswoman.

"I have my four-lens camera here," Azmin said, considering. "I assume the chemicals have been stocked. We might try some *cartes de visite.*"

"Oh, yes, please," Mrs. Balfour said eagerly. "I am wearing my best pelisse. I haven't had new cards made in forever. This is so exciting. Your first customer!"

Mrs. Balfour made a delightful customer. She agreed to sit at an angle that would disguise her sagging jowls and emphasize her formidable figure—and fur pelisse, of course.

"We will develop these and have the cards made up within the week," Keya informed Mrs. Balfour as Azmin retreated toward her dark room with the plates.

"May I bring my niece in?" Mrs. Balfour asked. "She has been ill this winter and is still looking a trifle peaked. Seeing an old friend would be good for her. I have no children of my own, and Eleanor is my favorite of my sisters' children."

"If you will give us a day and time, we will be here," Keya assured her. "As you can see, we're not quite prepared for opening, but for an old friend, Miss Dougall will make exceptions."

Azmin admired her companion's salesmanship. *Old friend,* indeed!

But they had their first customer! After the lady departed, and with the negatives processed, Azmin swung in a happy circle in the middle of the unfurnished parlor.

"Wise decision," the draper said, climbing down from her ladder. "Mrs. Balfour is likely one of those types who boss all the neighborhood ladies. You'll have them at your door soon enough."

Finally, she was on her way! Financially, at least.

For her other purpose—seeking to identify abused women—she needed more evidence.

That part of her scheme wasn't quite so clear as it should be.

~

IN HUGH MORGAN'S OFFICE, ZANE STUDIED THE LIST OF SHIPS SAILING from Leath in the coming week. "How do we know the murderous black beard won't jump ship at the first port?"

"I'll be talking to the captains. The thug can be locked up until the ship's out to sea, and then there's no place to jump. It's a slow cargo. He won't see land for months." Morgan sat at his desk, wearing his wire-rimmed glasses like any mild-mannered accountant.

Zane was learning the big Scot was far from mild anything. "I'll pay for his passage, of course, and happily take your suggestion."

"He'll earn his passage. It won't cost a cent. I'd add the young one if I could, but the ladies would complain. Anyone wishing to harm Miss Trivedi is lucky they aren't dropped into a shark pool."

Zane had that same feeling about the tavern bullies Gopala had hired to hold Azmin outside while he *rescued* Keya, but the bullies were British. Shipping them to India wasn't an option. "Harming ladies should involve transport," he agreed. "But I suppose the Americas object these days."

Hugh snorted and turned to a better subject. "I've consulted with a lawyer, and after he's established credentials of a counterpart in India, he will telegraph about Miss Trivedi's family and any inheritance. But it might take months to establish credentials. Telegrams are not good for delicate matters."

"We can telegraph *India* now?" Zane asked, distracted. "Then her brother didn't even need to come here!"

"Unless he travels in wealthy or diplomatic circles, he may not have known. The lines were only completed in the last year."

"So was the canal, and he knew about it. Modern wonders materialize faster than we can comprehend." Hearing feminine boots on the stairs, Zane set the list down and checked the hall, catching sight of a trailing skirt vanishing into Azmin's workshop. What was she about now?

Leaving Morgan to his machinations, Zane strode down to the workshop, which was unlocked, of course. Because the fool woman could *take care of herself*.

She glanced up from placing a plate in the camera. He'd learned she had several types of cameras, the uses of which were beyond his knowledge.

"What are you doing here?" she asked, closing up the equipment.

"I could ask the same of you. I'm arranging for the transport of Miss Trivedi's would-be kidnapper. And you?"

"I want photographs of the bearded villain. Gopala might be naïve, but my intuition says the other one is guilty as sin. How am I to determine if evil creates a physical shadow on my plates if I don't photograph bad men?" Equipment in hand, she waited for him to back out of the doorway.

He was probably six stone heavier than she was, and she needed to recognize that size counted. He didn't budge. "You are planning to unlock the prison door and ask him to smile?"

"Don't be ridiculous. Keya prepared curry laced with laudanum. He should be reasonably docile by now. I meant to ask Mr. Morgan to stand by me and open the door, and Thomson is on his way upstairs as we speak."

The giant's footsteps thundered louder than the pounding in Zane's head as he contemplated this audacious plan.

"Won't the laudanum corrupt the parameters of your experiment? Perhaps people are only evil when they are awake."

She made a moue of distaste. "Experimentation is complicated. I'll have to take what I can, when I can. Perhaps he won't be entirely asleep."

"In which case, you need someone standing guard with a gun in hand!" He was near shouting again.

"You may have my *katar*, if you like," she offered, pulling the knife from her pompadour. A few dark strands fell loose.

Zane snatched the knife and marched down the corridor to

Morgan's office. "Do you have a pistol? Our resident maniac means to take photographs of the bandit."

The damned accountant looked more intrigued than appalled. He removed a gun from his desk and the knife the Scots called a *sgian dubh* from his sock. "Will these do?"

"Yes, come along before she starts singing hymns and calling on spirits." Zane stomped down the corridor, where the madwoman was waiting outside the locked door.

"I heard that," Azmin said. "I don't sing anything, and I don't perform séances. I simply want to photograph spirits."

She turned to Morgan, eyeing his weaponry with approval. Even though he'd always been a man of peace, Zane decided he would start carrying pistols and knives too. And maybe a whip. It was the only way to be certain she didn't get them both killed.

Handing his weapon to Zane, Morgan unfastened a contraption on the door. "Alarm," he explained. "Door opens in, not good for prisons." He unlocked the door and peered in. Evidently deciding it was safe, he allowed Zane to see inside.

The bandit looked up groggily at their entrance and attempted to stagger to his feet. Zane pointed Morgan's gun at him. The man sat down again.

Zane had spent half his youth on horses. He'd occasionally hunted with hounds. He knew how to shoot, but he'd never used a pistol on a human being. As a physician, his goal was to save lives, not take them. But he could make an exception for a brute who would have murdered them.

"Mr. Morgan, if you will hold the reflector, this will take just a moment." Azmin handed him the light equipment, set up her tripod, and aimed her camera. "I'm using simple wet collodion for this shot, so I must take it back to my darkroom quickly. It would be lovely if I could take several shots with different methods."

"You have other methods?" Zane asked, interested despite his fury.

"Normally, I use wet. The dry gelatin is still experimental." She threw him a knowing look. "I didn't wish to experiment with too many different parameters."

Damn, there was the fascinating mind he so admired.

She pressed a bulb and the magnesium in the reflector exploded into bright light. The thug jerked as if he'd been electrocuted. Morgan slammed the door and locked it.

"One more, please?" she begged, hurrying down the hall with her camera. "I just need a few moments to insert a new plate."

"Do you want us to turn the villain over in case evil lurks on his back?" Zane asked sardonically.

She glanced up at him with hope but must have read his expression. "Sarcasm, very good."

"Evil?" Morgan asked as the lady disappeared into her workshop.

"She believes her development process reveals the evil lurking in men's souls. Best not to inquire," Zane warned. "It will only muddle your mind."

Morgan snorted. "As Phoebe muddled Drew's. That's not happening. *You* may be in danger though."

The taciturn accountant fell silent after this unusual observation. Zane preferred it that way. He'd rather not discuss his muddled mind, because that's damned well what Azmin had done to it. Maybe he should study whether she used a siren spell. The marquess had relations with *compelling* voices. . .

Azmin was back quickly, her gray skirt rustling. Zane wanted to see her in saris again, but he had to admit that—except for the color—the form-fitting fashion suited her. Why on earth she thought she wouldn't fit into society was beyond his comprehension. She'd look gorgeous on any man's arm.

He wanted her on his. But that required marriage, and he'd already proved his unsuitability. If anything, he was worse at bowing to society now than he'd been when his betrothal had been broken. He couldn't walk away from a wife as easily as he had his fiancée.

He and Morgan repeated the earlier procedure of unlocking the door and standing armed while the lady set up her camera and handed over her reflector. Except this time, she caught them by surprise and entered the room with the tripod. The bearded bandit growled and lumbered to his feet. The flash went off again, and he stumbled back-ward, blinded, giving Azmin time to escape.

"Thank you, gentlemen! That was perfect. What are your plans for him?" While Morgan locked the door and set the alarm, she hauled her heavy camera down the corridor.

"Shipping out two nights from now," Morgan called after her, before entering his own office, not to speak again.

Zane thought he ought to learn from the accountant and keep his mouth shut, but he'd never been able to disguise his curiosity. Carrying the rest of her equipment, he followed Azmin into her workspace. "You used the dry formula the night at the coroner's?"

"Yes. I have no good means of carting chemicals. And that did seem to turn out well, you're right. But the gelatin is experimental and expen-sive, and I'm more familiar with the wet process. So I use that when at all possible." She carried the camera to the back room, shutting the door.

He should go back to his laboratory and leave her to her machina-tions. He'd simply wanted a hostess for his dinner table and a companion for Louisa. They could be found anywhere. He didn't need a scheming enigmatic Malcolm who might get them all killed.

That's what he would do. He'd ask the dean if any of the board's daugh-ters would be interested in being hostess for a dinner party for students. He should widen his parameters.

FIFTEEN

Azmin could barely concentrate the next day as she taught her art students and attended classes. She'd stopped at the workshop first thing that morning to see if the varnish had dried on the would-be kidnapper's negative, but she didn't have time to print it out. So many things could go wrong with a glass plate—the fixing solution could be too strong, she could have washed away too much, she could have added too much varnish. . . She needed to see the printed photograph and not the reverse image on the plate.

She'd sent the hackney driver to the studio to retrieve the photograph she'd taken of the stabbed man and the crowd. There had been an interesting light hovering over the bleeding man that she needed to study. The crowd around him, however, was mostly shoes and trousers and of little use for identifying witnesses.

After her art class, she returned to Zane's home and Louisa's lessons as usual.

Giving her wrap to Thomson, she hurried down the corridor. Keya had brought the draper over to measure the sitting-room windows, and the three were discussing fabrics when Azmin entered. Keya had pinned up gauzy cotton ones to let the late afternoon light spill across the faded carpet.

As always, Louisa made an attentive student. Today, Azmin worked on teaching her the simplest camera. She was explaining about negatives when someone entered the front door and Thomson lumbered to greet them.

Zane was home early? Azmin's pulse raced a little faster, even though she mentally cursed. She had meant to run back to the workshop before dinner and print the kidnapper's photographs. The stuffy professor would not approve of her running about in the dark.

She was a free woman, she reminded herself. It didn't matter what Zane thought.

The sound of her uncle's voice distracted Louisa, but Azmin continued their lesson. The world did not revolve around the man— even though the memory of him protecting her with guns, swords, and fists gave her heart palpitations. In his tailored suit and silk ties, Zane did not look like a hero, but she knew the muscular power beneath his waistcoat. She had to remember he used his strength to thwart her when he could.

The rounded tones of a feminine soprano startled her into nearly dropping the camera.

Louisa lost any pretense of studying.

Fine then. She certainly wasn't the only woman in his life. Azmin began packing up her equipment. It was obvious that lessons were done for the day.

A moment later, a blond vision in pink ruffles and rustling petticoats arrived, followed by Zane, looking a little too smug.

"May I introduce Miss White, daughter of one of the school's directors. She is here to help us plan the student dinner." Zane made the introductions.

The vision in pink fluttered her lashes and clung to Zane's arm, all but purring as she examined the lovely little parlor they were creating for Louisa. She whispered something that had him patting the hand on his coat sleeve.

Feeling a foolish twinge of jealousy—most certainly brought on by her crushed adolescent hopes—Azmin curtly acknowledged Miss White. Once everyone had been made known, she picked up her equipment bag. "This is excellent timing. I will leave Louisa in good hands. Since I know nothing of your students, Dr. Dare, I will take my leave now. I have work to finish. I shall be back in time for dinner."

"It's almost dark out there," Zane protested. "I didn't see your driver waiting."

Because they didn't need a carriage while living in his house. Azmin was too confused to explain her reaction. It was like being sixteen and overlooked all over again. And she had utterly no good reason to feel that way, did she? Except she'd thought he had decided to let her handle the student dinner. She should be glad he'd listened to her arguments, right?

"It's not dark yet and it's only a short distance," she called back as she hastened for the foyer.

A quick and eager student, Thomson had her redingote out and ready before she reached him. She offered him a brief smile of appreciation and left Zane arguing with the women in the sitting room.

Why did she have the feeling that for an educated man, the doctor was an idiot? Did he know anything at all about Miss White? Or was he doing it all over again—falling for a flirtatious smile, flapping eyelashes, and the benefit of a respectable, wealthy family.

It was good to know his weakness before she did anything stupid like believing the blasted man when he said he *wanted* her. Obviously, he meant that only in a carnal way. Had she believed anything more? Her fault, if so. She should have learned that lesson.

The lights were on in Mr. Morgan's suite as she entered the back gate of Phoebe's workshop. Mr. Blair must have gone home early, but she knew where the lamps and matches were. Letting herself in, she lit a lantern so she could find her way through the maze of animal cages and tools. Spying a small hatchet on Mr. Blair's work table, she purloined that for the evening.

Despite the precaution, Azmin figured it was early enough that she didn't need to worry about thieves or drunkards breaking in. Everyone should be sitting down to their dinners. *She* had quite lost her appetite, but she had work to do, so that was fine. Eager to print the results of yesterday's photography, she hurried up to her studio.

She set the negative into the frame with the paper she spent so much time preparing and carried it up to the roof. It took forever in the fading light, but finally, she saw the image forming. Holding her breath, praying she'd caught the right moment of development, she ran downstairs with the frame and pried it open.

She exhaled in wonder—there it was, clear even before she finished the process. The evil shadow lurked around the image of the black-bearded thug who'd been sent to kidnap Keya. She had *sensed* that Gopala was innocent and that the large man harbored violence. Perhaps that was how she should describe the shadow instead of *evil*, except she sensed malevolence behind the violence. But how did one trust instinct?

How did her cousins know when what they *felt* was real and not the product of overactive imaginations? Lady Phoebe, at least, saw results when she talked with animals. Azmin would have to talk with Olivia, who saw auras, and ask her how one could have confidence in interpreting colors.

The light over the stabbed man in the other photo was puzzling and caused no instinctive reaction. She thought he was one of the men who had been paid to attack her yesterday. She certainly ought to feel his violence, if so. But if he'd only done it for the money and wasn't actually evil. . .

She eagerly pried at the next frame. A knock at the door interrupted. Zane wouldn't knock. It had to be her neighbor. "Come in, Mr. Morgan. Have a look at the images."

"Miss Dougall?" a tentative male voice asked from the doorway.

She glanced up—Keya's brother. How had she forgotten Mr. Blair had housed the boy here? Well, he was only a few years younger than her, so he wasn't a boy. He just appeared very young with his smooth brown jaw and velvety dark eyes.

"Yes, Mr. Trivedi?" She continued prying at the frame, not wishing to harm the paper beneath.

"I wonder if you would speak to Keya for me? She is very angry, and I do not understand why. I only wished to help." He remained near the doorway.

"It is for Keya to explain her anger." The frame popped off, and

Azmin cautiously lifted the negative plate to reveal the second photograph of the thug beneath.

This one was simply a closer image of the black presence. She had only caught a corner of the prisoner's back, but the shadow did seem thicker there. It should be clearer once she fixed the image.

"Perhaps you can persuade her to at least speak with me. She never came home after she married, so we never had time to know each other. I wondered. . . does she think her place is above us now? Yedhu was a very wealthy man and moved in powerful circles. He adorned her with jewels and gold. Our family is well known, it is true, but we are not wealthy. Our little sister has found a successful man she wishes to marry, but his family will not agree to the match unless we provide a grand wedding and dowry. I have too many sisters for that to happen." He folded his hands together as if to keep from wringing them.

Azmin sighed and showed him the photograph. "See this? See the black shadow around your friend?"

Gopala stepped hesitantly into the room to study the paper. "Yes? I do not know photography. Did you use special lighting to create the shadow?"

"The lighting should *erase* shadows and brighten subjects. Your friend is enveloped in a blackness of his own making. That's what happened when I took Yedhu's photograph. He lived in darkness, as does your friend here. How did you find him?" Feeling a little more confident of her interpretation, Azmin dipped the paper in gold chloride solution to bring out the details.

"He found me after Yedhu was cremated. There was a great mourning feast, but Keya wasn't there, which worried us. We asked questions and Ulf pulled me aside to explain. My family was understandably horrified, and he offered to help us find her."

Azmin hung up the paper to dry and reached for the next. "And he did so out of the goodness of his heart?"

Gopala shrugged. "He did it for the reward, I imagine. He is poor and greedy. That does not make him a bad man."

"I'm pretty sure that shadow hovering over him makes him a bad man, like Yedhu." Azmin dipped the paper of the second image into the solution.

"A shadow makes him bad?" Gopala asked in rightful puzzlement. "And what made Yedhu bad? I did not know him, just *of* him, as one does wealthy men."

Point taken. People put on public faces. "You spent months with this Ulf and never saw him do anything bad?" Perhaps she was wrong about the shadow. Or perhaps evil only emerged when one was thinking malevolent thoughts.

Gopala was uncharacteristically silent. Azmin glanced in his direction. It was hard to see in the light of a single lantern, but a frown appeared to mar his smooth brow.

"He gambled. And sometimes people who won his money became injured. I did not *see* him do anything though. The sailors quit gambling with him after a while. He did nothing to me. And you have not answered me about Yedhu."

"Yedhu was a violent man, much as this Ulf is, just as Keya said. I think the shadows on their photographs reflect that." Azmin looked up at the pounding of footsteps on the stairs.

A loud bell abruptly clamored, and the corridor erupted in shouts.

STOMPING UP THE STAIRS TO AZMIN'S WORKSHOP, ZANE FUMED. HE WAS now making a complete ass of himself in front of a director's daughter. But he'd heard the frost in Azmin's voice, and he had a notion that she was distancing herself again. Last time, she'd run all the way to India. This time. . . she was damned well endangering herself. Morgan had a dangerous prisoner stashed in—

A loud clamor shredded his already ragged temper. He raced up the last few stairs.

Before he reached the top, the easily recognizable bulk of the murderous bandit dashed toward him. Zane had come unarmed—again. He had only his walking stick. It simply never occurred to him to travel with weapons when he had two perfectly good fists.

Hearing Morgan shout, assuming the Scot was right behind the villain, Zane backed against the staircase wall, out of sight. He wasn't about to let a violent criminal loose on the streets to attack the women again. He just had enough time to thrust his stick across the stair as the prisoner reached the top.

Blindly racing down the stairs, the escapee didn't see the stick. It hit right above his knees. He howled and pitched forward, down the narrow flight, landing with a distinct thud. Zane winced. That would have broken a few bones. He knew he should examine the man lying still in the dark at the bottom, but Azmin came first.

To Zane's relief, her door opened and she peered through the gap, appearing startled and wary but unharmed. At seeing Zane, she opened the door a little more, and Keya's brother peered around her. Gopala was a handsome young man, not much taller than Azmin. They made an attractive couple.

Realizing the two weren't far apart in age, with similar interests and backgrounds, Zane suffered an insane flash of possessiveness before common sense prevailed.

"Get back inside," he shouted. "I need to check on the prisoner. He may have had help."

He descended the dark staircase, wishing he'd brought a lantern. Even as he thought it, Gopala appeared on the upper landing carrying a lit one. So much for hoping either of them would obey his command.

He almost wished they had and that he couldn't see. The light illuminated the body below clearly enough to recognize that the bandit's neck was twisted at an angle necks shouldn't twist. He'd been a heavy, muscular man and not an acrobat who knew how to land well.

Zane closed his eyes and fought back a surge of nausea and remorse. Even though he had meant only to stop a dangerous man, he hadn't meant to *kill*. He had always thought of himself as a healer, even if he didn't possess his mother's more magical abilities. Watching helplessly as his sister died had caused him to realize the medical profession lacked sufficient knowledge to save lives. He wanted to save people from dying, not kill them. So he'd given up medicine for research.

Kneeling, Zane tested the fallen man's pulse. Nothing. *Damn.*

Morgan arrived at the top of the stairs. "He pried open the door with a fork. Do we need to tie him up?"

With a heavy heart, Zane stood. "I don't think he'll be going anywhere."

And of course, Azmin hadn't done as told. She watched from the top of the stairs, covering her mouth in shock, before disappearing into her studio. At least he knew she was safe.

The stubborn female reappeared a moment later, camera in hand. "Move over, Zane. You might want to move *far* away. I don't know where spirits go when they depart, but his was evil."

Of all the ridiculous. . . Still in a state of shock, Zane stepped downstairs into the animal shelter, leaving the landing empty so she could set up a tripod. Gopala held her reflector light. Zane was going to strangle her the instant she put that equipment away.

Not before—because he couldn't contain his appalling curiosity at what she might capture. And because he damned bloody well understood. He wanted to cart the body off to the morgue and slice out its heart to see if it was as black as the bandit's soul.

If she was insane, he was equally deranged.

He closed his eyes against the vivid flash, opening them again only after the bubbles of light behind his eyelids dispersed. The moment gave him time to set aside his turmoil and gather his thoughts.

"Blair has some wide planks down here. We can carry the body to the morgue. I'll speak to the coroner, tell him an intruder fell." Zane glanced up at Azmin, who was about to rush off to her studio. "You will return home with Gopala as escort. What the bloody hell were you thinking, coming here where dangerous criminals lurk?"

"My work might be as important as yours. I needed to prove that man had an evil shadow," she called down in exasperation. "And if anything, I'd be protecting Gopala and not the other way around."

Zane almost strangled on the retort he swallowed.

She swept back to her studio, then returned, minus her camera but brandishing a hatchet. "I carry weapons, unlike some people I know."

Morgan snorted. "She's right, you know. Despite the company he keeps and his knife-flinging capacity, Gopala is a pacifist who doesn't even know how to use a weapon. He can help me carry the villain down to the morgue. Take your warrior princess home."

A Hindu pacifist, of course. Why wasn't Azmin a pacifist too?

Because she was a Malcolm, first and foremost. A maddening, insane, thoroughly independent Malcolm sent to make Zane's life. . . much too interesting.

Treading heavily up the stairs on which a man had just lost his life, Zane left Morgan and Gopala to their unpleasant task, while he faced his.

"I didn't have a wet plate prepared. I had to use dry." Azmin was efficiently removing the framed plate from her camera, and Zane could only watch her in wonder.

"You're a ghoul," he said, because that's how he felt about his urge to cut out hearts.

"Only to the British mind," she replied absently. "Look at the photographs I took yesterday, over on the counter. I'll take this to my developing closet."

"What do you mean, only to the *British* mind? Yours is just as British as mine, and wanting to examine a corpse is ghoulish." As she closed the plate in a box, he turned on a gas lamp to study the image of the prisoner in his cell. The big man cast a dark shadow.

"It's not ghoulish if you believe our bodies are merely shells for the soul, and that our spirits move on when the shell expires," she insisted. "It's a Malcolm as well as a Hindu belief, although Malcolms interpret through our Druidic view of spirits and ghosts and whatnot. Every culture has its way of accepting death. Do you see the shadow? Even if we hadn't seen it for ourselves or Keya hadn't warned us, I can tell this man was violent. He would have been a danger to those sailors if he'd sailed with them. I do worry how a soul carrying that much bad karma can be cured in the next life, but I can hope he'll come back as a helpless female so he learns what it's like to suffer."

"Dead is dead," Zane said. "Whether or not there is an afterlife of any sort, it doesn't replace the corporeal needs of this man's family."

Laying down her box, she abruptly turned and flung herself into his arms. "I'm sorry we dragged you into this."

Zane clung to her. The guilt of causing a man's death had frozen his soul. He understood that killing the bandit had ultimately saved lives, quite possibly Keya's and Azmin's, but he couldn't accept that he'd been the one to cause death. In Azmin's vitality and warmth, he let some of his frozen horror dissipate.

"If the black-hearted pirate was like Yedhu, then his family will be glad to hear the end of him," she said into his shoulder. "Had he not set out to capture Keya, he'd be alive now. His greed brought about his end, not yours. Go, put his death to good use. Take out his heart and examine it and let your notes be his memorial. It's more than he deserves."

If anyone could understand his need to study death, Azmin could.

"Women are ruthless." Zane rubbed her back, feeling her shudders. She wasn't as calm as she pretended. "You're like pretty confections with a hard nut inside."

She laughed against his coat. "We're all different, like a box of bonbons. Some of us are sweet and gooey inside. I'm not."

Then she shoved away and smacked the shoulder she'd been leaning against. "And I'm still furious with you. Do not even attempt to walk me home, or I may have to beat you about the head until you learn sense."

"I either walk you home or throw you over my shoulder, because hard nut or not, you're still only a bonbon." Tired of denying his need, Zane encompassed her in his arms again, and this time, he kissed her the way she needed to be kissed.

She smacked him with her puny fists, but she didn't resist. Wrapping her slender arms around his neck, she lifted herself into him as if drowning and needing rescue.

He knew the feeling and was gratified that she returned it.

They needed a bed to take this moment to its natural culmination. He could take her here, but they would both regret it.

A woman's scream shattered the moment.

SIXTEEN

THINKING THEY NEEDED A DESERT ISLAND BEFORE THEY COULD EXPLORE kissing without interruption, Azmin clung to Zane's arms as they both froze at the screams.

She thought she'd done an excellent job of proving she was unshaken by a man's death, but the professor knew her too well. *As she knew him.* Realizing that she understood Zane's shock, dismay, and morbid curiosity—because they were so much like her own—rattled her even more.

She did *not* need a woman screaming to conclude this evening.

Zane released her to peer into the corridor. "Morgan's light is out. I think he and Gopala have left. Stay here. I'll check the street by the tavern."

Instead of smacking the back of his head as he deserved, Azmin grabbed her hatchet, turned off the gaslight, and picked up the lantern. She hadn't taken off her redingote in her haste earlier, so she needed nothing else. "It's probably just an argument, but I'm not staying here alone."

The screams had silenced as quickly as they'd begun.

Zane held his arm across the doorway until he was certain the hall was clear, then led the way down the stairs. The treads were blessedly free of any corpses. No further screams penetrated the thick walls of the stairway. Not until they entered the back garden did a woman's cry of pain resound through the cold night air.

"And all before dinner too," Azmin said with a sigh, shouldering her ax.

Zane held up his deadly walking stick, shot her a glance that was probably angry, and unfastened the back gate. Azmin locked it after them. Morgan had a key and could let himself back in.

Zane was already striding down the alley leading to the street. Azmin scurried to keep up. From here, she could hear punches and grunts.

"A tavern fight," she whispered. "That place should be shut down!"

Zane blocked her path again at the end of the alley. She stood on her toes to peer over his shoulder.

Underneath the street lamp, a woman pulled herself off the street and attempted to stop a tall man from hitting another. He slammed his fist into her jaw instead. Her whimpering protests abruptly halted as she collapsed into the filthy gutter.

Azmin gasped and attempted to duck under Zane's arm. He caught the capes of her redingote. In the street, the vicious brute turned on a man swaying unsteadily. With another blow, he sent the shorter man into the street. Then the animal picked up the woman in the gutter and threw her over his shoulder as if carrying a sack of flour.

The villain was marching off with his burden before Zane would let her pass. He lingered longer, leaning over to examine the unconscious man on the ground. "Drunk, if the stench of gin is any indication. He's alive and coming around."

Azmin didn't care about the drunk. How he could detect gin over the stinking billows of smoke from the tavern was beyond her. Before Zane could stand up again, she raced after the brute heading down the street. She kept her lantern only open enough to see where she placed her feet and her hatchet stashed safely in her pocket.

"Where do you think you're going?" Zane caught her elbow but fell in step beside her. "I'll go after them. You go back inside."

"I'm fairly certain that was Jenkins," she warned. "What is an acceptable punishment for a man who punches women?"

She was furious, as much with herself as the situation. How *could* she stop the abuse? She couldn't.

"Judge and jury," he said implacably. "*You* cannot do anything. *We* can follow and maybe help the woman if she needs it. We can also see where he goes. I've been trying to track him for days. Phoebe's animal isn't helping."

"Then you think it's Jenkins too?"

"From what I could see, yes. But we may have formed erroneous misconceptions and should keep open minds. He may have been stopping an hysterical woman from doing something rash."

Azmin snorted in disbelief. "Because a man who respects a woman knocks her unconscious and flings her over his shoulder."

"He's not a muscular man. An unconscious body is damned heavy, so that's the preferred method of carrying a load. You are acting with prejudice."

"Jenkins is shrouded in black like Ulf. He's at the very least a violent man. I wish I had my camera. I need to know more about those black palls my chemicals form. You will note that I did not speak with prejudice and call the darkness evil." Azmin hurried faster when the man ahead turned a corner.

"Ulf?"

"The man Mr. Morgan is hauling to the morgue. You saw his photograph. It shows the same black shadow as Jenkins has. I just couldn't take a good shot of his back to see if it looks like a demon." Ahead, the man entered one of the overcrowded tenements lining the back streets of the old town. Azmin broke into a run.

Zane wrapped his arm around her waist and hauled her from her feet. "Caution, please. You could be entering a den of thieves."

No matter how much she enjoyed his arms and masculine strength, she didn't have time for this. She elbowed Zane until he set her down. He didn't release her. "The world is so *unfair*," she whispered unhappily. "Why should being bigger make men more powerful?"

He made a disparaging grunt rather than point out the obvious—*big* and *powerful* were essentially the same in this world. Azmin had to appreciate his reticence. Her logic had little to do with her resentment. The world simply did not add up in a reasonable manner.

Zane opened the outer door and entered an area that had been walled off to form a vestibule. The stench of urine and cooking cabbage wafted through the unheated air.

"Shouldn't you go home and escort your guest back where she belongs?" Azmin asked scathingly rather than reveal her terror of this prison-like environment.

"You mean Miss White? She's perfectly capable of telling the carriage driver her address. Or if she suddenly falls comatose, her maid can do the same. I'd rather go home and eat dinner." His stomach growled as if to prove his point.

"We might as well. We've lost him," she pointed out.

Zane took her lantern and opened it further, pointing at the floor. "No, we haven't."

Wet drops of blood led up the stairs.

Zane knew propriety required that he take Azmin straight home, and then he should find a constable. But Azmin was already heading up the stairs, and he'd killed a man tonight. He needed to know he didn't let a woman die because he was adhering to what was *proper*. The *right* action was to save a life. He'd only been living half a life lately and never had to make that distinction. Azmin was forcing him to deal with a wider world outside his laboratory.

Shouting arguments, crying babies, and clanging pots covered the sound of their progress as they hurried up the dark narrow stairs. At the first landing, he heard pounding boots descending. Not wishing either of them to be recognized, Zane leaned against the wall in a shadowed corner and dragged Azmin off her feet, concealing both of them in her enveloping redingote.

Kissing her successfully quelled any protest. He *liked* kissing her. He was grateful she returned the favor. His shins had barely recovered from the last episode when she'd expressed her displeasure.

The pounding boots didn't hesitate but rushed on past and out the street door. Reluctantly abandoning the bliss of heated lips, he peered over Azmin's shoulder. The departing coat looked remarkably like the ratty one Jenkins had worn.

Zane hastily set Azmin down before she could kick. His cock had more interesting desires than continuing this mad chase, but he resisted temptation. "I am starting to appreciate your nondescript garb." He headed up the stairs again.

"I told you, I blend in," she muttered. "And *you* don't," she added, grasping what he hadn't said.

"Exactly." Her billowing, dreary redingote and gray skirts could conceal a maid or a teacher, as long as she kept her fashionable bustle and bodice concealed. Whereas his tailored coat and starched white shirt and collar shouted wealth in these environs.

"Charming. Now I'm your shield of disrespectability."

He heard laughter in her voice, so he didn't argue. He didn't know how she could laugh on a night like this. His stomach growled again. Maybe she'd eaten before she left so she wasn't as irritable as he was.

Or as frustrated. He was beginning to suspect that Miss Azmin Dougall had no notion of where kisses led. He, unfortunately, did.

"That could have been Jenkins leaving to find a physician," he said, trying to return rationality to his roiling emotions.

"Or dumping an unconscious woman and making a run for it," she added with cynicism, halting on the third floor and following the trail of blood down an unlit corridor at the back of the building.

The trail was heavier.

"I'm not sure that your gift, if that is what it is, is making you a better person." Zane knocked at the door where the trail halted.

"Being able to determine which men are truly evil instead of blaming them *all*, as is my wont, must be an improvement." She held an ear to the door. "I think I hear a groan."

He tried the latch. It wasn't even fastened. Pushing the panel open, he called into the dark interior, "Madam, are you well? I'm a physician."

A whimper emanated from a corner of the room.

"That sounded like a cry for help to me." Disdaining caution, Azmin shoved past him and into the room.

And *room* was all it was. Zane opened the lantern to illuminate the darker corners. It revealed a curtained bed in one corner, a commode with a washbasin on top, a rickety table and chair near the door, and a shelf above a dresser used as a pantry. A rat scampered off the shelf, onto the dresser, and out of sight. Hooks on the wall served as a wardrobe.

The stench of cooking cabbage was faint in here. The scent of blood was not.

A moan from the bed drew him after Azmin, who was already pulling back the curtain. Did the woman know no bounds?

Needing to ground himself in healthy, human warmth, Zane caught Azmin's waist while he studied the partially conscious woman moaning and tossing her head. The victim lay on top of threadbare covers, holding one arm tightly to her chest. Her pain was so obvious that he set Azmin to one side and bent to examine the arm. He couldn't quite decipher her fretful mumbles but understood her anguished cry when he touched the arm.

Azmin, on the other hand, apparently interpreted moans. With a gasp, she tugged at the woman's skirt and petticoat, revealing the source of the blood they'd followed. "She's miscarrying! I wish you had your bag with you."

Excrement. Another life lost to this wretched evening.

"I have no modern miracles in my bag to fix what is lost," he declared curtly. "But we might save the woman. Infection is our enemy. See if the dresser contains clean linens. And find soap. I need to scrub my hands." Unable to prevent nature from prevailing, Zane returned to what he could fix.

The humerus was cracked or broken but not splintered and breaking the skin. Cursing under his breath, he glanced around, looking for anything he could use to immobilize her arm. From a dresser drawer, Azmin removed a treasure trove of old rags that appeared to have been bleached with lye so many times, they barely existed as more than threads. "Those might work. Can you bring me the chair too? I may be able to remove a chair leg for a splint."

"What about a wooden spoon?" Azmin pulled open another drawer. "I saw one in here."

"It may be too thin, but I'll give it a try. Soap?" He shrugged off his coat and rolled up his shirt sleeves.

"The fire is almost dead but the water is still a little warm." She filled the basin beside the bed and brought him a sliver of yellowed lye soap. "She keeps what she has clean."

"That may save her life, but I make no promises. We can't move her until the bleeding stops. She's lost too much blood." He scrubbed. "I don't want my hands to touch her dress. It's been in the gutter. Can you tear off her sleeve? It's almost as thin as those rags."

"Will my petticoat be useful? The one is heavy flannel, only I've been wearing it all day."

"I'll surmise that your petticoat is far cleaner than anything in this room, no matter how much she tried to scrub. So, yes, please, flannel is excellent."

Although he did not see patients any longer, he was a physician. He knew what needed to be done. He simply had never performed these tasks outside a hospital staffed with trained nurses. Upon occasion, he'd had to shout and throw tantrums until people learned cleanliness, but at least supplies were on hand. Here, he didn't even have laudanum.

His mother was the one who healed with her gift and herbs. He had no magic to ease the pain.

Azmin gently tore the sleeve off the damaged arm. "Easy," she murmured to their patient. "The doctor can help you. What's your name?"

Zane's gut twisted at that promise. Who had he ever helped?

"My baby," the woman murmured, louder this time. "*Help my baby.*"

Not possible. One more failure of medical science.

"Your arm is broken, madam." Zane examined the painful twist of her humerus. It had taken a serious blow to crack a bone that thick. "I'll need to set this. I'll splint and bandage it so it can't move and cause you pain. Do you have a name we can call you?"

"Jane," she muttered, tossing her head. "Jane Jenkins. Where's Sep? Did he bring you?"

Zane bit his tongue and set to work rather than speak his thoughts.

Azmin stood in for him. "That's a lovely name. Is Sep your husband?"

Jane winced as Zane manipulated the cracked bone, but she managed a nod. "Is he here? I want to see him before he goes to work."

"We sent him on to work," Azmin said reassuringly. "You're in safe hands with us."

Jane screamed as Zane tested the bone's alignment. Men went to war and suffered worse, but women shouldn't have to suffer because of a brute of a husband. If he ever caught up with Jenkins, maybe he'd teach the bastard what broken bones felt like.

"I'm sorry, Mrs. Jenkins, but that should be the worst of the pain." He wrapped the heavy wooden spoon in thin rags and knotted it in place. Then he turned and caught Azmin lifting her outer skirt to untie a red flannel petticoat.

So, that's where she hid her colors. A lacy, embroidered confection of pink and red concealed the practical flannel, and beneath the flannel, she wore white bloomers adorned with a rainbow of embroidery. Once Azmin removed the ugly flannel, she was a confection of colorful, angelic gauze. Had the light been on her, he'd see her limbs.

He'd learned as a student to use humor or lust to distract from grim reality. The old method still worked. Shutting out what he could not heal, he wondered if her calves were as shapely as the rest of her. She dropped her woolen skirt in place and glared.

Back to grim reality. Zane grabbed the flannel and began tearing it into strips. "Thank you. And I apologize for looking, but I'm not sorry to see that you haven't lost your taste for pretty gossamer."

"Fine cotton is not practical in this climate," she said stiffly.

He wrapped a strip of flannel to hold the splint more firmly. "No, I suppose it's not. Is there any coal to throw on the grate? I don't want you freezing."

"My baby?" Mrs. Jenkins whispered through her grimace of pain.

Her baby didn't have a chance. Preventing her from bleeding to death or dying of infection was all he could offer. He had no words to tell her.

After adding coal to the fire, Azmin kneeled beside him at the head of the bed. She took the patient's unencumbered hand between hers. "Sometimes, babies aren't ready to be born," she whispered. "Their spirits need to linger longer in the heavens. When that happens, there is nothing we here on earth can do."

Zane needed an assistant to carry off the messy remains of that *spirit*, but his patient needed Azmin's help more than he did. Mrs. Jenkins was shaking her head in denial, but she wasn't hysterical, yet. He needed her calm, and Azmin was a miracle worker.

So he did the dirty nursing work, massaged the woman's womb, and tried to keep his hands as clean as possible until he was satisfied he could do no more. Then he padded the bleeding with a combination of the remaining thin rags and more flannel.

By the time he was done, his patient was unconscious. He felt her brow for fever, but she was cold as ice. "She needs more blankets. Stay with her, and I'll canvas the neighbors."

He had to knock on several doors before anyone answered, and he despaired at the one who did. In a swirl of opium smoke, a filthy slattern stood in the doorway. Wearing a bedraggled housecoat, with an old briar pipe stuck between her gums, she regarded him with suspicion.

When he explained what he needed, she shrugged. "Men don't care for their doxies. She needs to learn to look for herself."

"She's his *wife*. He's a poor student who works nights. If you have a warm blanket and some coal, I'll pay you for them." Exhausted, hungry, and wishing he were back in his laboratory with microscopes and slides that didn't remind him of how cruel this world was, Zane maintained the politeness he'd been taught from birth.

"That's not what he says when he comes here looking for his dope. I told him I could get a good price for her those nights he ain't about, but he's not hungry enough to share her yet."

A berserker rage swamped him. He wanted to catch Jenkins at the top of a stairway as he had Ulf. Sometimes, men simply deserved to die. . .

In a haze of irrational fury, Zane took the blanket offered and strode back to the room where a woman could have died this night.

He'd damned well save the woman, and let her give evidence in court against the beast who'd harmed her. He hoped the law would hang Jenkins.

SEVENTEEN

Exhausted emotionally and physically, Azmin staggered towards home after midnight, traipsing through the windy streets wrapped in Zane's arms. Cold comfort, indeed, but she would take any relief at this point. She'd lost all confidence in her ability to aid even a single person, and the world was filled with thousands, maybe millions, who needed help like poor Mrs. Jenkins.

They'd paid a neighbor to take her in, warning the Good Samaritan not to let Jenkins find her. They'd have to consult Lady Phoebe about safer shelter in the morning.

Zane kept kissing her, planting brief caresses on her brow and hair and cheek, as if needing reassurance that she was still alive. He'd once been a playful man, one who laughed easily and growled disapprovingly with the same lack of restraint. She thought perhaps his kisses were his way of saying that Zane still existed, hidden behind the stiff and cautious professor he'd become.

Considering the pink bonbon he'd brought home, that could be her wishful thinking.

The house was lit from top to bottom when they arrived. "That's not good," Azmin murmured.

"That means fires are lit and food can be had," he countered, sticking his key in the door.

It opened before he could turn it.

"There you be, sir," Thomson shouted in relief. "And miss, too. They's been all about looking for ye, thinking ye'd been murdered certain sure."

Azmin practically wilted against Zane. "Can we simply vanish?"

He hugged her, but even the all-powerful Dr. Dare could not snap his fingers and fix this. They'd been out all night, together, and the whole world knew. It was a good thing her father was in India or he'd be holding Zane at gunpoint. She might not have much concern for propriety, but the people she loved did.

"Food, Thomson," Zane ordered, even as excited voices sprang to life down the hall. "Fire in my study. Miss Dougall is freezing. Tell everyone to go back to bed, where they belong."

That wasn't happening, of course.

Mr. Blair and Mr. Morgan occupied the study, making lists. Lady Phoebe, Keya, and Louisa rushed in before Azmin could even take a chair. Everyone chattered and exclaimed, but Azmin didn't have it in her to speak a word.

A man had died tonight. So had a baby. And a woman had been left in misery by a man Azmin wished dead in his infant's place. Had she acted quicker on that black shadow in his photograph, could all this have been prevented?

Keya dropped one of Louisa's woolen shawls over Azmin's shoulders. Someone shoved a cup of tea into her hands. She sipped, and it burned all the way down, so she assumed it contained brandy. Nothing would warm the cold place in her heart.

She shivered. Without her flannel, she was thoroughly chilled. She'd have to stand in the fire to be warm enough.

She heard Zane's deep voice explaining, arguing, telling their story. He sounded so very distant. What they'd shared tonight. . . she couldn't quite sort through it all. They hadn't argued. They'd worked together. They'd probably saved a woman's life. Maybe. She wasn't entirely certain that was a good thing, given what lay ahead for Mrs. Jenkins.

Phoebe's aunts, Lady Gertrude and Lady Agnes, descended on the study—Azmin's employers from the School of Malcolms. She wanted to ask if they were so prescient, why hadn't they told everyone where she was? But that wasn't polite. And she was too tired to argue.

A cold meat pie was shoved into her hands—on a china plate, of course. She almost fell face first into it while voices rose and fell in heated argument. Her employers remained calm but adamant. Azmin chewed her way through half the pie and finished the tea.

"Miss White will report to her father. . ."

". . . Azmin is living under your roof. You cannot. . ."

"The university will let you go. . ."

"Really, it's quite simple. If she is your intended. . ."

Zane was a gentleman of the first order. Propriety had been inbred into him. He didn't have a chance. She, on the other hand, had learned to defy society and go her own way.

She was *not* letting him feel obligated to offer marriage and repeat the mistake he'd made in his youth. After their earlier confrontation with the dean, she knew the old bigot would not save Zane's laboratory if he married *her*. He needed Miss White.

Fortified by brandy and food, Azmin set aside her tray and stood. She'd learned military command from the best. "Thank all of you for your concern. I'm going to bed. Keya, would you and Louisa accompany me? Lady Phoebe, Mr. Blair, it's late. Off with you now. If you will excuse us, Dr. Dare. . ." She aimed for the study door.

Lady Agnes and Lady Gertrude immediately protested. Azmin dipped a curtsy, murmured "Good-night, ladies," and departed without hearing their arguments.

She didn't have to listen to anyone. She was an independent woman —one who must stand up for what was right, even if it broke her heart.

ZANE SET OUT BEFORE THE SUN ROSE THE NEXT MORNING WITH NO OTHER goal in mind but to protect his patient and pound Septimus Jenkins into mincemeat and turn him over to the authorities. Once those immediate tasks were out of the way, he might more logically consider all the other problems he faced—like Azmin's employers. And his own. And society in general. And his place in it. And what he owed to Azmin. He might as well ponder the origins of the universe.

Seeking out a church, he caught a vicar at his prayers. A generous donation produced the knowledge of a widow who needed a boarder to help with the rent. The hound dog followed Zane to the widow's home, where he ascertained her willingness to take in an ill woman and prepare her meals, for a sum.

His pockets weren't empty by the time he brokered those deals, but he wouldn't be buying new equipment any time soon. He proceeded on to the tenement, where Dog barked, apparently in recognition of the stench. He left the animal guarding the door and took the stairs two at a time, wishing he could catch Jenkins and grateful he didn't. Murder was messy.

His patient was conscious and bearing up stoically.

"I don't believe you need the hospital, but you will need help while you recover," he told her. She also needed a place to hide from her husband, but he thought that inappropriate to mention. "I've found a widow lady who needs companionship and thought the two of you might manage together. If you're willing, I'll send someone to help you pack and take you to her."

"I'll have to leave a note for Sep," Mrs. Jenkins said worriedly.

Zane thought the top of his head might blow off. Azmin had claimed he didn't *see* people—probably because they were an illogical, idiotic lot of featherheads not worth noticing.

Tamping down his exasperation, he turned to the older woman who had taken in his patient. "I can only fix broken bones, not common sense. Would you make her understand why the man who beat her, caused her to miscarry, then abandoned her, shouldn't be told where she is? I'll have someone come by in an hour. If Mrs. Jenkins is ready, she has a safe place to go. If she's not, I recommend you move her out immediately. Mr. Jenkins is dangerous."

The woman turned to the wan patient in the bed. "Your man don't even live here. He lives with a jade over t'other side of Lawnmarket. He doesn't go off to work at night, he goes to her. Ever'one but ye knows that."

"He brings home his pay faithfully every week," Mrs. Jenkins protested weakly, looking even paler than when Zane had entered. "And he studies all day. He means to be a doctor."

"He never shows up to class," Zane told her coldly. "He'll never be a doctor."

"And he's gambling down at the Green for that coin he brings home. Pays you less than he does his doxy, I wager," the neighbor lady said with scorn. "Don't know what he's selling for the gin and tar."

Tar—opium? Or heroin? That would match what Zane's other student had said about the group experimenting with drugs. What made men rot their brains and their bodies with poisonous substances?

He'd experimented once upon a time. He should know better than most. And then he'd grown up.

"A cart and driver will arrive in an hour, ladies. I leave the decision to you." Zane returned his hat to his head and strode out, no more pleased with the world than he had been earlier.

After hiring a cart for Mrs. Jenkins, he reported to the coroner to confirm Morgan's story of the villain who had fallen down the stairs after attempting to kidnap a lady.

"And I suppose you'll wish to be carving him up to see if he has a heart?" the coroner asked cynically. "From my examination, I'd say he had an abscess in his jaw that must have made the poor fool mad with pain, but his injuries are consistent with your story."

"If you can keep him until this evening, I'd appreciate that. We might learn if the infection from the abscess had any effect on his heart." Zane wondered if Azmin was over at her studio already, setting up the negatives from last night. Maybe her camera was picking up *infections*.

He'd have to kill Jenkins to find out. He'd do it with pleasure, Zane thought grimly as he walked to his laboratory. But it could be he was just in a mood for murder.

He stopped and studied the window of a jeweler. The ladies had made their point last night. He'd abandoned Miss White to seek Azmin and neither of them had returned for dinner. He'd had Azmin out alone until after midnight. She lived in his house. Explanations had not sufficed. Their reputations were in shreds, which wouldn't help either of their positions. He had to offer.

She'd throw a ring back at him.

He didn't know whether to feel relief or regret at that thought as he proceeded onward. Definitely regret that he'd never see her limbs, he decided, and that he would never have a chance to see where her heated kisses led.

Dean Reynolds was waiting for him when he reached the laboratory. Zane sighed.

"I trust there is good explanation for yesterday's destructive behavior." The older man pulled out his pince-nez to examine Zane as if he were an insect. "White is in a rage that you abandoned his daughter to chase after that. . . *foreigner.*"

Zane was no longer a green youth or student. He had alternatives, he reminded himself. Azmin, on the other hand, did not.

He forced a smile that felt like a grimace. "I regret that my disagreement with our guest interrupted the evening. I will send my apologies and regrets to Miss White as soon as I am at my desk. I had hoped to have her aid in choosing students for a dinner I planned, at your suggestion that I socialize more. While I was out, an event occurred requiring my medical skills. The task took longer than I expected."

He'd worked in medicine and education for half his life now. He knew the patter and half-truths he must mouth. By ignoring the reference to the earlier fracas and settling on White's concerns, he'd made the dean's job easier.

Reynolds nodded approvingly. "You're from good stock. I knew there was a sound reason for your behavior. I'll speak to White. He'll understand. I understand you hired a Miss Dougall to teach your niece. Is she any relation to the late earl of Lochmas? He used to hold tenure here."

Zane wickedly wanted to mention that *Miss Dougall* was the lady the dean had insulted, but he wanted his laboratory more, and caution prevailed.

"Yes, I believe so. She was raised by her father's extended family in the marquess's home in Surrey, but her father's home is here in Edinburgh, when he is not in India." He should resent the interrogation, but Zane understood. The dean was being cautious. The university had a reputation to uphold.

Zane could be cautious too. He didn't have to mention that the prior earls of Lochmas had a penchant for India, just as Azmin's father did, to the extent that the colonel had married a Hindu. Her father, however, was not the current earl, only a younger scion of a younger scion who had to make his own way. Azmin was not wealthy enough to fund any of the gleams in the dean's eye.

This time, if Zane married for convenience, it wouldn't be for the money.

It would be for lust.

Could he convince Azmin that was enough? *Did he want to?*

"I WOULD LIKE TO WRITE A NOTE OF APOLOGY TO MISS WHITE," AZMIN declared over the breakfast table. "She should not blame Dr. Dare for his concern for my safety or blame him for saving a woman's life."

It was hard forcing herself to acknowledge that Zane might prefer pink bonbons with mushy insides over chocolate with nuts inside. If he did, then he wasn't the man she thought he was, and she was better off smoothing his way to his happiness and Louisa's.

Louisa wrinkled her nose. "I would not worry too much about her. She was more concerned with her curls than the guest list."

"And with Dr. Dare's wealth than Louisa," Keya added in amusement.

That was somewhat reassuring. If she thought Miss White was unsuitable for Louisa. . . but it truly wasn't her place.

"She was very pretty," Louisa said, her expression brimming with mischief. "I'd love to know her seamstress, and how she curls her hair without burning it. So by all means, write to Miss White."

Azmin studied her student with suspicion. Louisa was a little too clever at times. "I do not know the students, so she is useful. Just because we do not share her interests, does not mean she's wrong. She's simply different." Azmin examined the neatly written guest list the lady had left behind. "We'll need to write invitations and be sure to include Miss White."

She would not judge. She should simply be grateful that Zane hadn't listened to all the nattering in his study last night. She'd been terrified he'd be waiting for her this morning with a ring in hand.

She had one purpose here, and one alone—to help Louisa.

"Can we invite Mr. Dare?" Louisa asked eagerly.

She should have expected that. Azmin practiced a breathing exercise she'd been taught to calm roiling emotion. How much could she tell an innocent child?

"Mr. Dare is *not* Mr. Dare," she said, hoping Louisa would believe her. "He is the reason we were late last night. He beat his wife and left her in the street. His name is Jenkins. We don't know why he told you he was a cousin. Your uncle and his neighbors do not know him except as a student named Jenkins."

There, she'd said it. She waited for the explosion. Louisa frowned in puzzlement. "That does not sound like the same man at all. Perhaps they simply look alike."

"I have a photograph of the man we saw last night outside a tavern. If I bring that to you, will you believe?" Azmin asked, praying Louisa would be sensible.

"Do you still have the flawed one of us together? We can compare them," Louisa agreed, although she still seemed dubious.

Azmin did not press the point. Both images showed him enveloped in evil, but she feared Louisa would see differently.

"Perhaps, under the circumstances, we should ask Dr. Dare if he might accept your teachers as tenants so we may move back to your home?" Keya suggested tentatively.

A very sensible suggestion. Azmin knew Keya would be more comfortable in their colorful nest. And once they were gone, Zane couldn't be accused of living in sin. And yet, she resisted. What was wrong with her?

Thomson barged into the dining room, pushing a skinny lad in rags, with shoes wired to his feet. "This here be the boy Lady Phoebe sent for running your errands, Miss."

Louisa wrinkled her nose at the odor. Azmin searched his toes for chilblains. His skin looked leathery enough to be shoes.

"Good morning, young sir," she said, trying not to look too appalled. "Have you a name?"

"Robby," he said sullenly, not looking up.

"Well, Robby, we need a good strong boy who can run errands for us. Do you think you can do that?"

The boy scuffed his toes on the carpet. "Whasinnit for me?"

"That depends on how well you work, I suppose." Azmin wanted to say *a bath*, but she assumed that wouldn't obtain her objective. Recalling Phoebe's suggestion, she added, "New shoes first, I should think. It would be hard to run errands in cold feet."

His head lifted, and he regarded her through suspicious eyes. "Do I have to dress like *him*?" With a nod, he indicated Thomson.

Thomson did look very fine this morning. He'd acquired a black suit that *almost* fit his broad chest and long arms. His muttonchops had been trimmed. He wore a starched white shirt and not the yellowed one of earlier. His maroon waistcoat was a work of art, embroidered in silver and fastened with carved ebony buttons. Its threadbare satin indicated it had been purchased in a second-hand shop, but it had once been elegant. She'd have to remind Zane to find a tailor for his servants.

"Errand boys don't need to look fancy," Azmin decided. "We could order you a blue uniform like a policeman's, perhaps. With a good warm cap. Would you like that?"

"Gold buttons?" His eyes lit with hope.

So much for not fancy, and Azmin hid her smile. Even Louisa softened enough to assure him he could have all the buttons he liked.

"Louisa, I will leave you in charge of invitations and Thomson in charge of Robby." Azmin rose. "I need to go over to the workshop. Keya, will you join me or would you prefer to stay here?"

"I promised Mr. Morgan I would bring him some of my curry." Keya rose too. "If you have negatives prepared, I can print them for you. You should stay here and write to Miss White."

Keya and Mr. Morgan? A relationship might be very good for both of them, she simply hadn't thought. . .

No judging, she reminded herself sternly. Keya had been married over half her life. And now she was apparently a widow. She wasn't accustomed to being an independent woman.

Being an independent woman was a very lonely business, Azmin decided later that day, as she went about her appointed tasks alone.

She took the hackney over to her new studio to check on the decorating and develop another set of prints for Mrs. Balfour. The friendly draper had done her job and left. The teachers had gone about their business. She didn't need Keya to set up the frames or cut apart the photographs for cards. Mrs. Balfour had been a handsome woman once. She was an imposing one in these images.

When Azmin was done, Wilson waited in his hackney. She was due in her classroom, on the far side of the city, within the hour. Did she want to go to work and confront the ladies after last night?

No, she didn't, but she would.

She recognized the urge to run as she once had when her heart had been broken. It had been a childish heart, admittedly. At the time, she'd been learning to be herself. She had quit attempting to lighten her complexion, given up wearing English attire, and abandoned any hope of an approval she could never attain. And then she'd given up on England completely and fled.

Had she stayed and fought for what she wanted, would things have been different?

She couldn't change the past. But could she change the future, be herself, and. . . fight for what she wanted? She'd have to know what that was.

"There you are!" Lady Gertrude exclaimed irritably as Azmin entered the school parlor. "You will need to arrive earlier if we're to plan your wedding. Have you set a date? I know the bishop. He'll see that you have a church with a minister who understands our ceremonies."

Azmin feared she'd swallowed a stone. Or a boulder. She didn't know how to respond. *Church?* She'd gone occasionally with her

English family, of course, if only to wear a pretty new bonnet. But for vows...? She hadn't even decided what she wanted yet.

"If only dear Max were here, we might have the funds to have an engagement ball. We did used to have such lovely balls," Lady Agnes said wistfully.

She spoke of her son and heir, a man who had taken off to travel the world and had dropped off the face of the map a year ago. Knowing the dangers of travel, Azmin couldn't respond.

"Max will come home when he's ready," Gertrude said curtly. "And the ballroom is a dormitory now. But perhaps a small reception in the parlor, as we did for Phoebe. Once we have a date." She sent Azmin a meaningful glare.

"As far as I am aware, there will be no wedding or reception," Azmin replied, searching for a path through the brambles. "Dr. Dare is a gentleman. We did nothing more than help an injured woman. He shouldn't be punished for performing his duties. I'm grateful you consider me close enough to offer—"

"Pish-tosh. You are as much a lady as he is a gentleman. This may not be London, but I assure you, society has its expectations. Your mother may not be one of us, but your father's family most certainly is. If she were still alive, your grandmother would expect me to look after you. How about June? It is a lovely month." Gertrude sat back in her chair, looking satisfied.

"It's expected, dear," Lady Agnes said. Always the more gracious of the two, she spoke soothingly. "The reputation of our school rests on its staff and students. If we allow lax morals, why we'd lose everything. You understand how it is."

No, she didn't, not really. She was truly grateful to the old ladies for taking her in and treating her as one of her own, making her feel as if she weren't a foreigner. She didn't want to hurt them. But marrying for such a foolish reason... "If my teaching here is a problem," Azmin said, trying to grasp what eluded her, "Then I shall depart. I will be sorry to do so, of course. But I would not cause you or the students harm."

"You have refused him?" Lady Gertrude asked, aghast. "That will not do. That will not do at all. The earl will hear of it. He will withdraw his support, as will all our other relations. No, no, you cannot defy propriety. Dare is a fine young man. The two of you are destined."

If they'd been destined, they'd have married ten years ago.

Lady Agnes interrupted that cynical thought. "I suppose you might take time to discuss it," she said worriedly. "Young people flit about so much these days. He might want to set up practice in London. And you quite rightfully miss your father and your home in India. But it will come about, you'll see. We'll just make the announcements, shall we?"

"Not until he asks me!" Azmin finally retorted in exasperation.

"Oh, well, that can be arranged." Lady Agnes tapped her fingers against her chin as if contemplating the mysteries inside her head. "Once the stars are all aligned, all will be well."

Lady Gertrude looked grim. "It is not the stars we must hold onto, but our funding. If you cannot make the recalcitrant doctor produce a ring, we'll see that he does. We speak for your grandmother."

Azmin had never known her father's parents. They had died of influenza before she'd been old enough to travel from Calcutta. She had no idea if they'd stand on propriety.

But she knew her father's *sisters*. If her aunts chose to descend on her, it would be a dozen times worse than Lady Gertrude and Lady Agnes nagging. Her father's family was large and formidable.

Could the school really close if she didn't obey? That had never been part of her sixteen-year-old fears. Was she being selfish to only consider herself?

EIGHTEEN

AFTER FEEDING THE FAT HOUND THAT HAD BEEN FOLLOWING HIM ALL DAY, Zane left Dog outside and took his own pie to his laboratory to eat.

He was a bloody coward, unable to face the women over the dinner table until he knew what to say.

In his arrogant youth, he'd had all the words he needed to woo and seduce or bargain and banter. He'd had his arrogance knocked out of him since then and learned that the world and the people in it were a little more complicated than he'd assumed.

But he thought he might know Azmin well enough to face her—after dinner and without an audience. Once he was certain the hour was late enough, he left his laboratory and set out through the dark spring night. Only a few workmen scuffled home late to their dinners and a desultory hackney or two clopped down the streets.

After a few blocks, Zane thought he heard footsteps following. Events of late were making him suspicious of everything and everyone. When he still heard them as he approached the park, he stepped into an entryway so he could see whoever passed. Dog growled at his feet. In this more respectable part of town, the streetlights gleamed on a few top hats and walking sticks. No one showed any interest in Zane.

Sticking to the shadows, he returned home without incident.

Thomson took his hat when he entered the foyer. The aroma of a hearty beef soup filled the air. At least he'd had the meat pie for sustenance. But the buzz of conversation came from the back of the house, as expected.

Taking off his gloves, Zane nodded at his study. "Ask Miss Dougall to join me for a moment."

Thomson bowed and popped one of his coat buttons. He casually caught the button, shoved it into his pocket, and hurried down the hall.

If nothing else, coming home was more entertaining than it used to be.

Zane was poking the coals in the grate when Azmin entered, looking pale and anxious. He probably didn't look much better. But he had an offer that he thought she might appreciate more than the platitudes another woman might expect. "I've permission to dissect last night's corpse. Do you wish to photograph it?"

If he'd offered her diamonds, she couldn't have brightened more. "I'll need to go to the workshop for plates and my reflector. Should I meet you there?"

"Over my dead body," he retorted in exasperation. "Were you planning on taking Thomson, Dog, a knife, and two pistols into those streets?"

The Mona Lisa couldn't have produced a more enigmatic smile. A smile like that could smite a man in the heart and rip his guts to shreds before he knew what hit him. Zane jabbed the poker into the coals as he waited for any new abomination she would lower on him.

"You have a new footman," she said politely. "You could order him to follow me about, and I imagine he'd carry the pistols for me, if you provided them."

Zane set aside the poker. "And by that, I deduce he's six-feet tall and looks like Samson."

"Ooh, you're good. I'll fetch my hat and be back in an instant."

Not calling on any damned servant, Zane stuffed a derringer into his pocket, then warily sought his—butler? Under butler? Man of all trades? "Thomson, we have a new footman?"

Thomson scratched his shaggy head. Zane worried about lice.

"There's the new lad, Robby. Want me to fetch him?"

The wicked wench, she almost had him believing in Samson. "How old is the lad?"

"Nine, ten, maybe? Eats like ten men though," Thomson offered genially.

Zane had been in dozens of houses with butlers. Not one had spoken with such familiarity. The women were spoiling the man instead of training him.

Azmin was on her way down the stairs before he could reply. "Are we fetching Samson?" she asked with mischief.

On occasion, she showed signs of maturity. This wasn't one of them. "Dog is probably sufficient, if we can pry his lazy hide from the fire."

He had his doubts about the hound doing anything more than howling, but he didn't wish to take a young boy to the morgue. Along with his medical bag, he picked up his walking stick—just in case.

He diligently tried not to descend into adolescence and think about how delectable Azmin looked as they hurried beneath the streetlights toward Lady Phoebe's workshop. She was enveloped head to toe in a billowing coat with layers of collars, a scarf, and gloves, but he knew the perfect figure beneath that abomination. And her hat was a flowered piece of nothing designed to draw attention to her gorgeous stack of sable hair. Golden earrings dangled against her dusky cheek, and madness lurked just a touch away. What had inspired her to wear earrings again?

His thoughts were a desperate attempt to avoid the discussion they needed to have.

The Green Lion was relatively quiet as they passed. Zane made a mental note to come back some other night to see if he could locate Jenkins, but the corpse wouldn't wait forever, and he'd received word that Mrs. Jenkins was safely ensconced in her new home. So he could wait.

"Thank you for making arrangements for that poor woman," Azmin said, as if reading his mind. "I want to help women in her position, but I have no good idea how to begin. We can't spirit them all away as I did Keya, and you did Mrs. Jenkins."

Unable to determine if that was a sign of her maturity or plain insanity, Zane turned down the unlit alley beside the workshop. Dog ran ahead to familiar grounds. "You cannot save humanity from itself. It's impossible."

"I do not wish to save *all* of humanity. I merely wish to save those I can. What is the point in my recognizing evil, if I cannot act on it?" She unlocked the back gate and swept into the yard.

"First, verify that what you're seeing is actually evil. I agree that your first two examples fit a pattern of criminal behavior, but you'll need far more evidence than that."

"I'll be glad when the days are longer," Azmin complained as they climbed the stairs to her workshop. "In our studio in India, we had so much sunlight, we could develop my photographs almost instantly!"

"Until your new place is ready, you won't have many to take, so your timing seems good to me. Perhaps by next winter, Blair will have developed a lamp that replaces sunlight." Zane waited in the doorway as she gathered her plates.

She laughed at his unrealistic suggestion. "Do we have time for me to finish these plates from last night? I'm rather eager to know if Ulf's spirit left him upon death, or if I have some chance of capturing a better image tonight."

"Will it take long?" Restlessly, he prowled her compact workshop. She'd hung a number of her photographs—striking images of buildings and architecture. But not people, he noticed.

"Long enough for you to tell me why you decided to invite me along tonight." She stepped into the dark closet where she'd left her plates.

Taking down a photograph of an exotic temple of intricate design, Zane examined it more closely in the light of the gas lamp she'd lit. "We need time to talk privately, without a dozen people nattering and telling us what to do." There, he'd said it. He forced himself to exhale while he waited for her response.

"I suppose your dean bent your ear," she called through the door. "I am sorry I brought this trouble down on you. If you ask, I will move out. We can find Louisa a better companion."

"Lady Phoebe's aunts seemed quite determined last night. How did you fare?" He avoided her question about the dean. He had many choices. She didn't.

"About the same as you, I daresay. Everyone is more concerned about their own business than us. I believe I've been threatened with Lochmas. I've never met the earl to my knowledge. My relation to him is quite tenuous."

Zane laughed curtly. "The dean would approve a match between us *because* of Lochmas. The earl was a respected professor before he inherited the title. That practically makes you one of their own."

"All very convenient for everyone else," she replied absently from the closet. "Without even knowing he's met and insulted me, I daresay. Your dean would have an apoplexy should we be introduced. Perhaps it is foolish to dream of hearts and flowers, but I abhor the idea of being trapped into marriage."

"You abhor the idea of being married," he reminded her. "Married women do not gallivant about the city in a derelict hackney, taking photographs of strangers, and hawking their wares."

She shot him a glance as she emerged from the closet with the plate. "*Your* wife might not. You will be an earl someday, a viscount rather sooner. You will be expected to serve in London. Other men do not have those pressing duties. Should I ever feel inclined to marry, I can look among the middling classes who do not mind the extra income I bring home."

Zane felt a rush of fury at her opinion of herself—and him. "You deserve better than that, and I damned well will not allow people to dictate who I marry. They can have their bloody title."

She lifted her eyebrows in surprise but returned to studying her negative. "I do not believe renouncing the title is an option. You can use it to good purpose or let it languish in oblivion or possibly some option in between, but it will be yours—unless you're dead, of course."

She was right, leaving Zane contemplating a dismal future. "I think the mysterious Max has the right idea—take off to Bora Bora and never return."

She laughed. "An intriguing notion, but inconducive to achieving your goals. Is there any chance of finding a cure for Louisa?"

This topic was even more depressing than the marriage one. "Surgery to repair the damage, perhaps, but we do not have the expertise required yet. I had hoped rest and healthy living would help her improve, but she's coughing worse. Research can only do so much, and experimenting on corpses isn't the same as a living human."

"One bleeds. The other does not," she summarized succinctly. She handed him the negative. "The image is reversed and unclear until printed. Does this look as if there's an odd light along Ulf's jaw?"

Rather than contemplate failure, Zane leaned over to study the plate. "I wouldn't have noticed if you hadn't mentioned it. The coroner said he had an abscess. Would a camera pick up such a thing?"

"Not that I can imagine, but then, I shouldn't think it would photograph evil either, but there it is. The light is of a similar quality to that over the man who was stabbed. I don't seem to have any instinct to define it." She pulled on her gloves. "What do you hope to accomplish by staying with a university that doesn't respect your research?"

Forgetting the curious negative, he straightened. "The university doesn't solve our mutual problem," he pointed out.

The notion of never curing Louisa, of his niece never having a normal life... He couldn't accept that failure.

Long years of work stretched before him, brightened only by a vague vision of a woman like Azmin waiting for him at home, wearing bright colors and laughing at him. She'd made her views of marriage clear, so he knew that would never happen.

Unless... he quit being a stodgy professor and wooed her in a way she might accept. And which would most certainly cost him his position at the university.

ZANE WAS UNUSUALLY QUIET AS THEY TRAVERSED THE DARK STREETS TO the morgue. Azmin assumed his mind was on the dissection. He juggled his bag and walking stick to help her carry the various pieces of equipment she needed for the dark cellar. He even helped her set them up when they arrived.

"There are two bodies," she said. "Do I really want to lift a sheet to see which is Ulf's?"

He lifted the nearest cloth and frowned. "I think this is the drunkard who was stabbed in front of the tavern. Apparently the surgeons couldn't save him."

Azmin came over to study his face. "He's the one who assaulted me first. I brought extra plates. I'll take his photograph too. I don't understand why a fight broke out again after we left. . ."

"Unless Jenkins withheld the promised payment for assaulting you. I am not thinking very highly of that young man." Zane checked the other corpse and verified it was Ulf. "I think I'll do both of them too. Let's see what we can find out."

Azmin captured an image of Zane donning his white coat on the other side of Ulf's corpse. She thought Ulf's black shadows might show up better against that white. And then, because she wondered about the odd light she'd seen, she took a second plate of Ulf's jaw before she started on the stranger. She would need to make new plates soon.

Learning about one's gift was difficult enough. Not knowing of its existence until she was full grown complicated matters worse. A child might more easily accept odd occurrences. Adults had enough experience to rationalize and refuse to recognize aberrations as anything useful. How long had she been taking photographs without noticing the odd lights or shadows?

It had taken true evil to shake her out of her complacency.

Had the anomalies been in her paintings, and she'd failed to understand the significance? She knew various ancestors had inexplicably painted prophesies into their art—some of them predicting death. Was it because they had an inner vision that saw what others couldn't? Or was it the paint they used, as she used cameras? She'd be old and gray before she figured it all out!

Rather than go back to the house after she'd packed her equipment away, Azmin waited for Zane. He stood between her and what he was doing, but it was rather hard to ignore the piece of meat he dropped into a jar of formaldehyde.

"Ghoulish," she said as he returned to closing up the last cadaver. "I should be fainting from the sight."

"If I remember rightly," he said, stitching like a seamstress, "one summer when you were very young, one of the boys cut open his head. It bled like a severed artery. You merely smacked some moss over it and wrapped it with handkerchiefs. By the time I swam to shore, I could only lend another handkerchief and order him to hold the compress before leading him home. I was duly impressed that you weren't shrieking and weeping like everyone else."

"I don't remember that particular incident. But we were a rowdy lot, and more often than not, someone managed to hurt themselves." Azmin fastened her pelisse and prepared to return to the cold night wind. "I always felt older than the others and took to carrying extra handker-chiefs. I suppose I was trying to be helpful so I'd be accepted."

"And while others fell out of trees or dived headfirst into shallow ponds, you sat there and sketched their foolishness. Do you have any of those old sketches?" He removed his white coat and reached for his suit coat.

Azmin admired Zane's shirt-sleeved form. For a man who worked behind a desk, he was strikingly well built. "No, I don't believe I took them with me when I left. They may still be at Ives Hall for all I know. More likely, they were thrown out like all our school papers. Why do you ask?"

Why was he thinking along the same lines as she had been?

He fastened his coat buttons and reached for his outer coat. "I'm curious about your gift, I suppose, and also. . . looking for a way to catch your interest." He flashed her an unexpected grin.

Oh heaven help her, there was the Zane of old, the one who had turned her inside out with just that infectious grin.

"I thought we'd agreed that marriage was not on our schedules." She picked up her bag and regarded him with asperity, as a good spinster should.

"I didn't say *I'd* ruled it out," he reminded her, placing his specimen jar in his bag. "I think I've made my interest in you pretty clear. I hope you're not classifying me among the close-minded people you scorn."

She swallowed hard. Zane had never made her feel uncomfortable in her skin. It was as if he had been seeing *her*, not her clothing or color. But that was then and this was now and. . . She still felt comfortable with him, even though she could swear he didn't see *anyone*.

"I don't think you notice people enough to judge them," she countered, heading for the exit.

He caught her elbow and steered her in a different direction. "I need to take the specimens back to my office. It's better if I not carry them through the streets." He lit a lantern and opened a door in the back wall.

She peered into the dark, narrow tunnel. "What is this?"

"A tunnel to the school. We often do dissections on cadavers. Carrying bodies through the streets is a little too ghoulish for most people. And yes, I am aware that people find dissection ghoulish. I simply don't care. Just as I know others judge by skin color or place of origin, but I don't care about that either. You're the one who suffers for the opinions of others, not me."

She'd punch his arm, except her hands were full. "You'd suffer if people called *you* a useless failure. It's easy to not care when someone else is hurt or insulted."

"You misunderstand. I care that *you* suffer. I never want to put you in a place where you might be scorned, if only because it makes me so irrational I want to throttle idiots. I just want you to understand that the problem is theirs, not ours. If they want to call me a failure because I cannot cure Louisa, I will not stop trying. I want you to do whatever you wish to do without caring what others think. And to that end, I believe you should quit thinking of my impending titles and reputation or whatever else is passing behind your gorgeous blue eyes and treat me the way you wish to treat *me*, the man behind the titles."

She mulled that over as they traipsed the clammy tunnel. At least it was out of the wind. "I didn't think I treated you differently from anyone else."

"You told me you could not marry me because I'd have a title and you'd be a handicap, that you have to marry a middling sort where your habits or your color don't matter. I wanted to punch a hole in the wall when you said that."

"I don't recommend punching this wall," she said dryly, too shocked to think.

"Tell me you don't like my kisses, and this conversation will end right here." He halted at what appeared to be another door and turned to face her.

She couldn't read much of his expression in the lantern light, but she knew his tone. This was the dashing Alexander Dare she remembered on a mission.

And that mission was apparently *her*. The notion thrilled her right down to her toes and annoyed and terrified her at the same time.

The rake might be emerging from behind his shell of impassive professor, but the man still didn't understand that physical lust and financial benefit didn't lead to connubial bliss—and were probably death to friendship.

She was no longer young and foolish enough to believe she could change him for what she wanted—someone who would love her despite her many flaws. If she couldn't have his love—did she want to lose him again?

NINETEEN

ZANE STORED HIS JARS WITH THE OTHER SPECIMENS, CLOSED THE CABINET, and feeling as nervous as a green lad, took Azmin's arm to lead her back to the street. She hadn't answered his admittedly odd question about kissing. Perhaps he was more out of practice at seduction than he realized.

Outside, he helped himself to the heavier half of her equipment and enjoyed the gentle sway of her skirts as they walked together. The air was almost soft and fragrant with spring. How long had it been since he'd had the luxury of enjoying the evening, forgetting his burdens, even if just momentarily? He could answer that—ten years.

"I. . ." Azmin stopped and tried again. "*Why* do you want to know such a thing?"

Zane didn't have to give that much thought. "Because I want to seduce you, but I respect you too much to want anything less than your full participation."

"Seduce me," she said in a tone that indicated he might as well have told her he wanted to kiss a frog.

He was becoming a little irritated that she thought so little of herself —or him—that she doubted his intentions.

"If you find the notion distasteful, I will, of course, adhere to your wishes." There was the stodgy professor, and he winced. Maybe she didn't find him interesting, but he wasn't prepared to give up.

He tried for more honesty. "Or I'll argue, at least. I believe you enjoy kissing. Which leads me to believe you might enjoy what follows kissing." This was probably the oddest conversation he'd ever had with a woman, but Azmin wasn't just *any* feather-headed female. He wasn't entirely certain of his motives beyond seduction, but first, he needed to know if she was willing. She was so adamantly against marriage. . . Or marrying *him*. She hadn't been adequately clear on that. Neither was he, for all that mattered. She'd make his life a living hell—when he wasn't enjoying moments like this one.

"I like kissing *you*," she said decisively. "I cannot think that what follows is an idea we should be entertaining."

"Because you're afraid? There are methods to prevent conception, you know," he said casually, feeding her eager mind as he would never dare with another woman.

"There are?" She turned a quizzical glance to him as they walked through the cold spring wind. "And even so, we are already accused of what you're suggesting. Do you really want to prove them right?"

"Again, I don't care what anyone says, if you don't. But I do have some experience in discretion," he added with a hint of his old arrogance. He was well aware that pride went before a fall, but he missed the dizzying heights one needed before falling.

Which was a patently insane thought, but the promise of spring wasn't sanity inducing. Zane supposed the women would say that was his mother's Malcolm heritage calling, but he was pretty certain all men felt the same in the company of a beautiful woman. And he'd long since proved he had no magical gifts—or Louisa would be well by now. He simply wanted a few moments of pleasure before the world crashed down on him again. In her own inimitable way, Azmin gave him pleasure.

"I must admit to enjoying kissing just to hear what you have to say," she said with amusement. "I've never been seduced before."

There was the daring female he remembered.

Their hands were full of equipment, or he'd show her how seduction was done. He had to use his words instead. Those were a trifle rusty. "I've already admitted that you attracted me even when you were too young to consider. So I'm a little wary of the differences in our experience. But you're a beautiful, accomplished woman now, and I cannot resist this time. Will you allow me to come to your room so we might learn if our kisses should go farther?"

"*I'm* beautiful and accomplished?" she asked with a laugh. "Me? You once told me my nose was too large and my eyes were even larger so I should grow into my face."

Zane winced. "Must you remember everything I said? I was a dolt half in love with a filly he couldn't have. I had to push you away somehow. And if it's of any interest, you have very nicely filled into your face. You could bring grown men to their knees with those eyes. But you know that, and you're just looking to get even with me."

She was silent a little too long, and he started to worry. That had been the summer he'd become engaged and she'd run away. He waited a trifle breathlessly to see if he'd failed again.

"I was half in love with you as well," she murmured, slaying him with that knowledge. "I knew you didn't care about my looks, which was why I liked being with you. I believe I called you an arrogant, mutton-headed—"

"—bastard," Zane finished for her. *Love* wasn't a concept he fully embraced, but that the enchanting adolescent he'd known had been impressed with his arrogant stupidity. . . His pulse beat a little too fast. "And then I had to explain to you what a bastard is and you blushed three kinds of purple."

She laughed, a beautiful throaty laugh that carried on the wind and swept his mind of anything but having her. Zane had to physically drag his gaze and his thoughts to their surroundings to assure himself they weren't about to be set upon by hoodlums.

"So, I know a little more now," she admitted. "I've read books *you* would blush to know existed. I will admit interest. But we both have houses filled with people, and I cannot see how you can visit my room without a minister standing at our door in the morning."

"Books!" he scoffed. "With illustrations? I'd like to see them sometime. I can tell you that you cannot learn the art of lovemaking from *books*. And if you promise not to laugh, I can tell you how I learned to enter bedchambers through the window. Yours is particularly easy."

"I'm a flight up!" she protested. "You will break your foolish neck if you attempt such a thing. You're not twenty any longer."

That alone reinforced his intentions. Not twenty anymore! She really did think him a stodgy old man. "You have a small balcony outside your window, if you have not noticed. It's a simple matter to knot a rope on the railing supports. The balcony provides shelter above the back entrance. Unless someone is sneaking out the back door in the middle of the night, no one will notice a dangling rope in the vines." He'd spent half a night working out the placement of her room and the best means of entering. It wasn't as if he'd been sleeping.

Azmin was not impulsive. Her silence didn't mean she was rejecting him, but that she was giving what he said considerable thought. Zane still suffered like a green lad, waiting. This was what happened when he emerged from the security of his professorial guise. He made an idiot of himself. Over a woman. Again.

"You've done this before, I take it?" she said with only a hint of amusement.

"Not something I should admit to, is it?" In his reckless youth, the rope trick had impressed the lonely widows and bored spinsters who'd appreciated his athletic attentions. "I am capable of throwing the rope up to you, but in our case, it's simpler if I leave it under the linens in the upstairs closet. If I see it dangling when I lock up tonight, I'll know you've accepted my suggestion. So you do not need to decide immediately."

"It's an impossibly ridiculous idea," she said crisply.

His spirits plummeted. He hadn't realized how much he'd counted on the reckless Azmin of old. He should be glad that one of them still possessed a modicum of sense.

"Someone will try to find you in the middle of the night," she continued in exasperation. "And you won't be where you should be. The maid will want to bank the fires or some household emergency will find us. It's a terrible example to set for Louisa."

For the first time in a decade, he threw caution to the winds. "And what if any of that happens? Our reputations are already in question. What more can they do to us?"

She halted under a streetlight and curved one lovely eyebrow. "Then, by all means, let's scandalize the family."

~

EVERYONE IN THE HOUSEHOLD HAD SCATTERED TO THEIR ROOMS BY THE time they returned to the house. Zane politely tipped his hat to Azmin as she handed her redingote to Thomson, just as if they'd been out for an evening stroll. Heart pounding, she fled upstairs with her camera and reflector, leaving the lunatic to do whatever insane things he had to do to install rope in a linen closet.

For her to locate.

She was quite barking mad. They *both* were.

Flinging all her equipment in a corner, she strolled down to Keya's room, pretending everything was normal. She knocked softly, and at Keya's call, entered.

"I have plates of two corpses I need to develop tomorrow and another idea to consider. In the one I took right after Ulf died, there appears to be a lighter spot on his jaw. The coroner said he had an infection there. I've tried taking a closer one to see if I can see more. And the other is a man who died of a gut wound. He has that same strange light." She was genuinely excited by the concept, so she didn't need to hide her agitation over Zane's insane proposal.

"An infection? That is intriguing. Are abdominal wounds not particularly subject to infection? Should you re-examine all your portraits for this lightness?" Keya set aside her book.

"I should probably examine *all* my work in this new light. I hope I'm not suffering from an over-active imagination! Are you seeing Mr. Morgan again tomorrow?" Azmin wanted to rush back to her room and prepare, but what was there for her to do? It was too early to change into nightclothes.

"Yes, I am helping him with his books. I am quite good at numbers, and he has so many projects going at once, he's in danger of working himself to death."

Azmin made a moue of worry. "Gopala was there, asking about you. He doesn't understand why you're angry. He is young and could not have had anything to do with your family's decisions."

Keya looked sad as she smoothed the fabric of her gown. "I am hurt more than angry, I think. But I should speak to him, I suppose. I have innocent sisters who might be sold to the wrong men if I say nothing."

"Once all the solicitors have corresponded, maybe you will discover you really are wealthy and can save them!" Azmin wanted to restore the smile to her friend's face—the one she'd worn when speaking of Morgan.

Keya shrugged. "My home is not in Calcutta anymore. I'll check on the workmen in our studio tomorrow also. I have chosen furniture, if you wish to see what I have bought."

"I trust your judgment. You're doing a marvelous job. Will we have furniture by the time Mrs. Balfour returns? I'd like to start slowly, work the snarls out of our methods before we have our grand opening." This was what she should be planning, not wondering how safe the balcony was outside her room—a balcony she had not even noticed.

They discussed plans a little longer, then Azmin said good-night and sauntered to her room. She glanced at the linen closet as she passed. Should she look now? She hadn't heard Zane on the stairs. Really, she should have second and third thoughts about this foolishness.

But she felt like a lovelorn adolescent all over again. Alexander Dare thought her *beautiful*. He desired her as she did him—or he *said* he did. It was a little giddy-making to believe. She would think his words just a rake's seduction, but she had thought he might be interested once before, and he hadn't seduced her then—which had been decent and honorable conduct. Of course, then he'd turned around and betrothed another, so her instincts in these matters weren't reliable. Did she dare believe it had been because he was ready for marriage at the time, and she hadn't been?

She wasn't now, she reminded herself. Was *he*? Which was the real insanity of his proposition—was it possible to enjoy lovemaking without marriage? It opened whole new worlds, if so.

She lifted the draperies to look out her window. She was seldom in here during the day and had never pulled them back. But yes, there was a portico that stuck out over the rear entrance to provide shelter while opening an umbrella. The portico was adorned with a waist-high rail and balusters so that it might be called a balcony, if one wished to be fanciful. For Zane's purposes, the overhang was ideal.

He'd spent time thinking about it. About *her*. The man did know the way to a woman's heart. Or her nether regions, at least. She shivered in anticipation.

She didn't know how to prepare for seduction. Should she call for wine? She almost laughed aloud at that thought. Mary would be very confused by the request. Robby would not even know how to carry a tray. And Thomson. . . would talk all the way down the hall.

So she stirred the embers in the grate and set a kettle of water on to boil. She had the makings for tea, just in case one became thirsty from kissing. Or from politely conversing before leaping into each other's arms.

Did she leave a lamp on? She supposed she should, so if anyone heard noises, they'd think she was up and restless. It wasn't all that late.

Would he expect her to be in dishabille? Not if she was to go exploring linen closets! Perhaps she could remove the bustle and heavier petticoat, though. And put on slippers instead of the high-topped, laced shoes that took forever to unfasten.

Whatever was she thinking? That he'd want to see her naked *foot*?

She wanted to see his. The thought created a blush of heat in unmentionable parts.

She finally heard Zane coming up the stairs, turning off the gaslights. That meant everyone had settled into their rooms for the night. She held her breath as she heard him open the linen closet, then head the other direction down the hall. Wouldn't someone notice if he slipped out again? Was he planning on climbing out his window?

If he'd been teasing her, she'd beat him about the head with his wretched walking stick.

Bracing herself for utter humiliation, she tiptoed down to the linen closet and rummaged under the stacks of sheets. She didn't have to look too hard. The rope was right there at eye level under the second stack she checked.

He'd considerately knotted one end, leaving a loop she could slip the rope through.

The windows! Would they even open? Carrying the rope, she scurried back to her room and slid behind the draperies to test them.

They opened outward. Cold night air rushed in. Hastily, she climbed over the ledge. Choosing a baluster close to the wall, she wrapped the rope around it, slid one end through the loop, and let it drop over the side. It was a little bit like the treehouse the boys had built one long-ago summer. She'd been able to climb the rope by putting her feet against the tree trunk. She wasn't certain the brick wall provided the same traction, but Zane had muscles she didn't.

Praying the knot would hold, thinking she ought to forget this and take the rope back, she climbed back inside, closed the panes, and watched.

He'd done this before? With how many women?

She probably ought to bop him over the head for his male conceit, but she simply wanted this too much. How many nights had she spent imagining Zane holding her in ways supplied by her imagination and books? She'd never lacked courage, and this was an opportunity to know reality.

This was an opportunity to know the real Zane again, not the cautious physician he'd become. She desperately wanted her old friend back, not just the glimpses of him from behind spectacles and cravats.

At last, after she'd worn a path in the rug, she heard a noise outside. Kneeling on the window seat, she pressed her face against the panes. Could she hold the rope if it slipped? Should she go outside? Anxiety ate at her as she watched the knot tighten. . . and hold.

She never wanted to play this game again. It was too fraught with unnecessary risk.

She thought she might expire of fright by the time Zane's head appeared above the rail, but she was so excited she almost laughed aloud. She flung open the window and practically yanked him inside. He was grinning like a schoolboy proud of his accomplishment. Men!

He leaned in and snatched a kiss even before he drew up the rope.

"Risking your neck like this is madness!" she hissed once he'd entered and closed the window. "I almost had failure of the heart half a dozen times, and I wasn't the one out there dangling over nothingness."

He slid his arms around her waist, smelling of crisp night air and shaving soap. He'd shaved for her! His sideburns brushed her cheek as he rubbed his hands up and down her sides for warmth. "You're better than any fire," he murmured, ignoring her protest.

His words and touch burned through her middle. Without thought, she wrapped her arms around his neck and pulled his head down. His lips heated quickly.

This was Zane, a man she'd known since childhood, a gentleman she could trust with her life, if not her heart. Eagerly, she threw herself into his kisses. Who needed words?

He didn't. While he spun her head with glorious kisses, he had her bodice unfastened before she was completely aware of what he did. Releasing her lips, he nipped at her ear and down her jaw. By the time he reached her throat, his hand was inside her gown, caressing her *breast* through her chemise. She gasped and felt a primal tug to her womb.

The need to touch *him* was overwhelming. He'd left his coat and waistcoat unfastened, bless his thoughtfulness! She slid her hand beneath the heavy layers to feel his heart pounding beneath her palm, with only his linen to hinder her. She wanted naked flesh, but she satisfied herself with experiencing the full strength of his hard chest.

"Too many clothes," he muttered, tugging at her corset ties.

Thank goodness she always wore front-fastening corsets. Giddy with sensation, Azmin clung to his muscled shoulders to keep her knees from collapsing as his hand grazed her bare breast. No one had ever touched her so intimately.

Books truly did not describe the excitation.

Shakily, she tried to remove the studs in his shirt so she could return the favor.

Abruptly, Zane lifted her from her feet and set her on the bed's edge while he cast off his jacket and waistcoat. The position left her eye-height with his chest and just a glance downward. . . revealed a hard ridge pushing at the placket of his trousers. She hastily returned to twisting at his shirt studs until she could reach under the linen to caress his naked chest.

Just when she'd found his hard nipple, the professor kneeled between her legs and removed her slipper.

"Slippers, you brilliant woman!" he crowed, tracing his finger down the sole of her foot, through her stocking.

She thrilled as much at his approval as his touch. And then he reached under her skirt to unfasten her garter, and she could no longer think at all except to realize—this was how men seduced women—by erasing their brains with sensation.

TWENTY

Zane had the irrational desire to have never known another woman so he could share equally in Azmin's first sexual experience. But her tentative touches reminded him to be grateful that he didn't need to suffer the nerve-wracking uncertainty of not knowing what to do next.

He stepped away to unfasten his shirt studs and discard them on her night table. He hadn't even let down her hair yet! He really was out of practice. "I want to go slowly," he told her. "I want you to dictate what you want, tell me how you feel, what you need. We don't have to do everything tonight. There's no rush."

His penis protested that insanity by demanding instant gratification. He didn't dare unfasten his trousers.

In the dim light, she resembled a disheveled temptress with her gorgeous dark tresses mussed, her lush lips swollen, and her bodice unfastened to reveal the perfect curves of her bare breasts. But the stunned look in her huge turquoise eyes caused more pressure in his trousers. This was Azmin, the too-clever female who had haunted his nights all one summer.

She was his for the asking, and he needed to do this right. She liked talking. He knew how to do that.

"I want to touch," she said with an air of bewilderment. "I don't want to think."

"That is easily arranged." Throwing aside the last of his studs but leaving on his shirt, Zane placed one knee on the bed beside her and began removing her hairpins—and the katar. He threw that under the bed. "I don't want you stabbing me in the middle of the night."

She laughed a trifle nervously but slid her hands gratifyingly over his chest. "I am not completely ignorant," she reminded him. "I know what emasculation means."

That should have unmanned him right there, but it did quite the opposite. He laughed and threw her pins to join his studs. "This irrationally reassures me. I've never had a virgin before... you are a virgin, aren't you? I only ask so I won't hurt you. It doesn't matter otherwise."

"How very... broadminded of you," she said dryly, growing bold and tweaking his nipples. "But I have never found anyone I wished close enough to smell. You, on the other hand, smell like English soap and manliness, and I find that tantalizing for reasons I don't quite understand."

He dragged his hands through the rich spill of sable he'd unleashed and massaged her head. "You have always smelled of delicious spices, and right now, you smell of feminine sex, and I gather that is how humans are attracted to each other, much as dogs in heat. I hope you didn't expect a romantic response."

She laughed, a rich throaty laugh that destroyed all his defenses. Zane pushed her back against the pillows so he might taste every inch of her bare skin.

Feminine hands encompassed his waist and stroked his back. It had been so damned long...

He rolled her over so she was on top of him. Her eyes widened, but he was too busy unfastening the prison women hid their beauty behind to worry if he'd gone too far.

"I don't know what to do," she whispered.

"Let me see you," he said with the urgency of an adolescent. "Looking is as much an enticement as touching and smelling."

"We do not need darkness?" She sounded excited by that idea. "I had always thought people did this in darkness and under the covers."

"No rules." He yanked down her bodice but it caught on her arms. "Although less clothing would be a good one, if I were dictator."

She finished unfastening her bodice, wiggled, and slithered out of the long sleeves, leaving it hanging at her waist, over layers of petticoats. While she did that, Zane unwrapped her from corset and chemise until finally, at long last, he had her breasts in his palms.

He caressed her sensitized nipples, and she uttered a feminine cry that caused him to fear his trousers would cut off all circulation if he didn't free his erection soon. Using his stomach muscles, he lifted from the mattress to suckle her breast.

Her moan nearly undid him. He rolled her back to the mattress and satiated his need to taste and titillate until he'd driven the princess nearly wild under him, purring and planting kisses anywhere he could reach.

She'd arrived at the state of not thinking. Good. Zane still possessed a little sense, not much. He didn't want to take her tonight. He wanted her to be certain of what they did—because he was not at all certain of what she wanted. But he could take her far enough along this path to make her want him as much as he wanted her.

While she writhed beneath his caress, he hauled acres of skirt and petticoats upward. She'd divested herself of any cages or heavy flannel and left only the gauzy, silky things that tempted his imagination. Her drawers were of a fabric so fine that he could feel her heat as he stroked her thigh. Her legs parted. . .

He was torn. He wanted to go slow. But she was so responsive. . . He rubbed his thumb through the opening in her drawers.

She nearly elevated off the bed.

~

LOST IN A HAZE OF SENSUAL ECSTASY, AZMIN WOKE INSTANTLY TO imminent danger the moment Zane touched her most private part. And even though she knew they'd gone too far, she couldn't stop her reaction to what had become a driving need. Or the moan that escaped her lips when he rubbed her again.

He slid his kisses from her breasts to her throat, and she almost protested to demand he return to what he'd been doing.

"I want you to want this the way I do," he murmured before she could speak. "I don't want you to fear our joining. Just let me touch you. This is something you can do for yourself, so there's no harm."

She was still wearing her gown and petticoats. Surely they couldn't do anything. . . ?

"Don't stop," she managed to whisper, insanely trusting the rake he'd been.

He hummed appreciatively, returned to his delicious kissing, and pushed his talented hand more assertively to parts she gave little thought to—until they came alive under his questing fingers. In moments, she was mindless with need, lifting into him, begging, feeling her insides clench and demand until. . . He curled his fingers inside her and she came apart in spiraling waves of pleasure.

Afterward, he held her while she recovered from awe and shock and caught her breath a little. Then before she could pull away, he caressed her buttocks and limbs with tantalizing strokes while he adjusted her skirt. "There's much more than that," he whispered as he nipped her ear and pleasured her breasts. "Shall I come back tomorrow?"

"How can there be more?" she asked in amazement, and then grew heated as she remembered she hadn't touched him. . . *there.* Experimentally, she ran her fingers down his broad chest, enjoying the tantalizing swell of muscle until she reached his trousers. His belly was hard and ridged and she reached. . . until Zane stopped her hand.

"I don't want to scare you off," he muttered. "I'll take care of myself tonight." He kissed her quickly and stood up.

She ought to protest. She ought to follow him and demand that he teach her everything. But she was curiously lethargic and wanted to relive this experience and understand it more. She didn't know what he meant and only cared that it was cold where he'd been, and she wanted him beside her again.

"Tomorrow?" he asked.

She nodded and watched as he hastily tucked in his shirt and gathered up his studs, waistcoat, and coat, then slipped into the corridor. Zane was the heat she'd been missing since returning to this cold island.

Experience. She had to focus on this as an experience and no more. She had goals and ambitions that did not match his.

But as she stripped off her clothes and prepared for bed, she wondered if she had the strength to resist what Zane had to offer.

There was a reason women were called weak, she realized, stifling a sigh. Knowledge was strength, and men had all the experience.

NEEDING TO STAY BUSY SO SHE DIDN'T WASTE TIME MOONING OVER LAST night, and impatiently waiting for the sensual lessons the evening would bring, Azmin took the hackney across the bridge to the studio the next morning. There was exceedingly little she could do until they opened, but she liked to admire their progress. And it made sense to start moving her supplies from the temporary workshop to her new space.

She'd studied how to use a camera, experimented with artistic images on her own, but not until she'd taken Keya's portrait with her husband had she any inkling of a Malcolm gift. She was eager to acquire more knowledge, but art wouldn't support her research into her possibly psychical gift.

So she'd learned how to organize files and receipts working with other photographers. She had a bookkeeping journal all set up. Keya simply needed to fill in numbers once they opened. She hoped the developing fluids did not create too much of a stench for her tenants, but she needed darkness and couldn't use a room with windows.

While she was there, she processed the plates from the morgue while burning incense to see if that helped. The incense seemed to negate the gaseous fumes, she decided, as she washed the negatives, but her mind kept drifting to last night. Picturing half-naked Zane in her head. . . caused her to squirm in her too-tight corset.

Keya arrived a little later, just ahead of the furniture cart. Azmin pushed aside forbidden images and let excitement of a different sort build as the reception parlor took form.

"Yoo-hoo," a woman's voice called from the open door. "Miss Dougall?"

"Mrs. Balfour," Keya whispered as she directed a table to be placed under the window.

"Footman," Azmin muttered. "Must hire footman to announce callers. I'll go." She left Keya to order the delivery men about and stepped into the foyer.

"I thought you must be here," Mrs. Balfour said triumphantly, still bundled in her fur-lined pelisse, although the day was spring-like. "Do you remember my niece, Mrs. Eleanor Stewart? Ellie, Miss Dougall is now a lady photographer!"

Behind the broad-beamed lady hovered a shadow of a girl. Azmin blinked to be certain the visitor was not a ghost. Even then, she didn't recognize her former schoolmate, but she had a very bad feeling about the pale young woman wrapped in an expensive pelisse and wearing a fashionable hat. If this was her Malcolm gift reacting, it was frightening.

How had she never noticed ghost women before? Possibly because she'd always been surrounded by men and strong Malcolm women. If she walked down the street, would she notice more? Or did she in some way attract these women, as some Malcolms attracted ghosts?

"It's been a long time since school," Mrs. Stewart said in a whisper of protest. "We were very young."

"Ellie hasn't been feeling well, so I thought I'd brighten her up by bringing her here. Is there any chance you might take her photograph today? Or that we could make an appointment for next week? I'm never quite certain when she's able to visit." A trace of worry crossed the older lady's features as she glanced with fondness at her niece.

If Azmin believed in her gift, Mrs. Balfour had reason to worry.

She liked the outspoken lady. Mrs. B was no doubt *nouveau riche* without a clue of how polite society operated, but she was honest and optimistic and that was more fun than polite. Her niece, however. . . Azmin gestured for them to enter.

"It's delightful to see you again, Mrs. Stewart. I have your aunt's *cartes de visite* ready," she said, leading them into the reception parlor. "I'm not prepared for anything more than those yet."

In the brighter light of the front room, she examined her former schoolmate. Shadows lined Eleanor's eyes, as if she did not sleep. Was that a faint bruise on her jaw? Azmin could be imagining that, as she might be imagining the stiff way the young woman walked.

Once, she might have been blind, but now, with experience, she could see.

"Visiting cards would be lovely," the young woman said politely.

"Let me show you Mrs. Balfour's cards, to be certain you both approve." Azmin glanced at Keya, who was already hurrying back to the shelf where the box was stored.

"My aunt says your assistant is Indian," young Mrs. Stewart said. "I heard you returned there. Why have you come back to these cold climes?"

"I wished to make a success of my photography, and I could not do that there, where there is so much poverty and unrest." That explanation sufficed. "Miss Trivedi is Hindu but probably speaks better English than I do," she added as warning that Keya understood what they said.

With a bow, Keya presented the cards to Mrs. Balfour.

"Oh, these are marvelous, thank you! You make me look twenty years younger. I shall have to start knocking on doors just to show these off." The lady passed the box to her niece, who managed an appreciative smile.

"If you can make me look half so good as this, I would be more than happy. My husband wishes me to call on the wives of his colleagues. If I can just send in a handsome card like this. . . That would be perfect."

"Miss Trivedi is good at applying a touch of cosmetics to make your best features shine. Would you like her to do that for you? It will give us a chance to experiment with our new facilities, and your patience would be much appreciated." Azmin tried to speak like a businesswoman, when what she wanted to do was drag the young woman to a physician.

Most women wouldn't talk to a male physician about what troubled them.

Mrs. Stewart smiled wanly and touched her cheek. "A touch of color would be useful. It's been a long winter."

"Mrs. Balfour, if you would like to test one of our new parlor chairs, I'll have a maid bring tea," Keya suggested, indicating an ornate French design chair in blue and silver.

Leaving the older lady to critique the furnishings, they led the younger one to the studio, where they pampered her with tea and rouges, a touch of kohl, and careful conversation.

"You have not been married long, I understand?" Azmin asked, setting up the four-lens camera.

"Since September. Mr. Stewart is a professor at the university and a very busy man," she said diffidently. "I need to learn to help him."

"What department does he teach in?" Azmin kept her talking while she adjusted the lens and Keya added finishing touches to the kohl.

"I don't know much about departments, but he teaches medical students. He wanted to be a physician but he needed to support himself. I had hoped my dowry would be enough for him to return to school, but he insists on earning his way," she said with a little pride.

"That sounds admirable. I know the university can't pay well. Lift your chin and turn slightly to your left," Azmin instructed.

"My parents provided our house, and my dowry is enough to live on." Mrs. Stewart tilted her chin as instructed. "If we live frugally, he really could go back to school."

"Men have their pride. You have a lovely complexion. I think I remember you from an art class. The teacher praised your watercolors, and I was green with jealousy." Azmin snapped the first photo and handed the wet plate to Keya, who hurried it off to the developing room.

"I still dabble a little, but I am no artist, just a copyist, I suppose. I've painted a few scenes for our bedchamber, but I wouldn't dare hang them in the parlor."

"Let me take one more from a different angle. You have such a distinct profile! I'd love to take a full-length photograph of you and your husband for your parlor." Azmin thought she'd reached the limit of her salesmanship here, but her concern for the young wife urged her to more creativity.

"Oh, I'd love that! Mr. Stewart is so handsome. Perhaps we could pose in our wedding attire? Only if he has time, of course," she added hastily. "And if it is not very costly."

"For our inaugural portrait, we will offer a bargain price," Azmin assured her. "Tell him we are not quite open yet, but if he can find time this week, we might even offer a free copy just so we can test our new facilities."

She wanted the man in front of her camera, because she was almost certain the camera would capture the black shadow of evil on his back.

Now that she knew abusive men like Yedhu existed, it was as if she had a second sense for finding them.

She would have to stop at her workshop and find those images of Jenkins. She didn't want Louisa to fall under the spell of a deceptive charmer as this poor woman had.

TWENTY-ONE

"WHAT IF IT'S MY PREFORMED OPINION THAT AFFECTS THE IMAGE?" AZMIN asked anxiously as Zane slipped the hooks from her bodice fastenings that evening. "I let Louisa compare the images of the man she calls Dare and the one you call Jenkins, and she admits the similarity, but she does not see the blackness as ominous. It's just a shadow to her. She has promised to be wary, but she's not convinced."

Zane knew he should be concentrating on her fears, but lust blurred his brain. He'd had the devil of a time teaching class and making research notes while his head was filled with the scent of Azmin and how he would approach her tonight. Recalling her exotic perfume and the musical sounds of her cries had allowed him to satisfy himself last evening. He didn't know if he could be as strong another night. He'd climbed the rope so quickly, he could scarcely recall straining his muscles to do so.

"It could also be your talented instinct, one the rest of us don't possess, that forms the opinion," he suggested, peeling back her ugly brown bodice to admire the gift package within. She wore a corset with so much embroidery, he thought the thread provided stiffening instead of whalebone. "You may have a Second Sight when it comes to abused women."

"That's what I fear, but it's a very odd talent," she said with a sigh, pulling off her sleeves without his aid. "The black shadows I see could be anything, but they *feel* like violence. The fading women feel like dying—or perhaps a lack of hope or life?"

Zane figured she was nervous and concealing it with chatter. While she worked her way out of her bodice, he stripped off his coat and waistcoat and threw them over a chair back. All the layers of clothes delayed the inevitable, he supposed. He knew he *should* delay. He just didn't know if he could—especially after she undid her skirt and petticoat and let the whole contraption fall to the floor.

Wearing only gossamer and lace, his princess rose like a slender nymph from a puddle of heavy fabric. Her brown skin gleamed golden in the lamplight. He practically salivated as he began unfastening his starched shirt.

"Your talent isn't any odder than that of other Malcolm artists. There must be some truth in those old journals that claim our ancestors painted the future or dead people." His patience was rewarded with her admiring stare as he yanked off his linen.

He didn't dare remove his trousers. He was fully engorged just looking at her. They'd yet to exchange more than a few kisses.

"Well, I've never felt compelled to paint a dead person, admittedly." She ran her fingers over his bare chest, playing with the hairs. "Photographing them, yes."

"Let us forget our macabre pastimes for the evening," he suggested, reaching for her corset ties. "I want to see if my memory of your luscious breasts is accurate. I should take notes."

She laughed, as he'd hoped. The translucent silk over her breasts rose and fell with her amusement. He was in danger of reckless behavior.

She leaned over to kiss his chest, and he was lost. Letting her corset fall, Zane tossed her back to her bed and straddled her hips, opening her thin chemise and bending to feast on her breasts while he rubbed his groin into hers. She moaned and started on his trouser placket.

He should have known she'd be a quick and eager student.

"Maybe we ought to talk macabre," he muttered. "Or you'll be ravished in seconds."

"Maybe we should proceed with the ravishing, then talk macabre," she suggested, rubbing her palms over his chest when his trousers defeated her. "Was Ulf's heart as black as his shadow?"

"You captured his spirit in the morgue?" His damned curiosity would be the death of him. He kissed her throat and ran his hand down her cocoon of silk and lace.

"I did. I felt as if the evil was reluctant to depart, but that may be my imagination."

She groaned then and lifted her hips to his as he kissed and lavished her magnificent breasts with the attention they deserved. Zane wanted her legs around him, but he didn't want to frighten her off too quickly.

He pushed aside the chemise and worked at the delicate drawers beneath. Nakedness was his goal tonight.

Azmin pulled his head down and covered his jaw with kisses. He parted her legs with his knee and stroked her until she wept with the same need straining at his trousers.

"Dammit, woman, you're making this impossible," he muttered. Propping up on one arm, he undid his trousers, then groped for the condom in his pocket before he lost all control of his mind.

Her only retort was to test his nipples with her tongue. Zane practically tore himself free of the heavy fabric of his trousers. And while he was at it, he untied her drawers and smoothed them downward, until they caught on her garters.

Only his drawers stood between him and bliss.

She still wore the filmy chemise. He kissed her golden-brown belly beneath it, enjoying the way she writhed in expectation. He used his thumb on her clitoris, until she grabbed the blanket and shoved it between her teeth to silence her moans. He wanted to lick her there, but he feared frightening her. Instead, he kissed her bare thigh and worked off her drawers, leaving the garters in place. He liked garters and stockings.

He left her on the precipice while he opened his drawers and applied the sheath. Then he spread her legs and lay between them, leaning his heavy weight over her. He desperately needed this, but he wanted her to be ready, because once the deed was done, they faced a universe of uncertainty.

Azmin grabbed his arms and rose to kiss his jaw. "Show me," she demanded.

She'd read the books. She wasn't ignorant of what she asked.

As a gentleman, Zane was happy to oblige.

Azmin thought she'd convulse and melt if Zane did not release her from this torture. Her entire body hummed with need just from the proximity of his large, nearly naked body over her. She could see and test the muscles straining in his bare chest. His thighs were like tree trunks pressing into hers. And she couldn't contain her curiosity...

His torso prevented seeing much beyond the outline of his linen drawers against the dark hair curling beneath his navel. But she could feel the pressure of his... what did the books call it? Something ridiculous like horn of passion. Or maybe her translation was weak. But she knew it belonged inside her. Even if she hadn't read about it, she could *feel* the emptiness where he belonged.

He finished unfastening his drawers, distracting her by licking her nipples and caressing her hip. She responded too eagerly, losing herself in sensation until she felt raw hard male pushing at her private place. She was slick. He slid right in, and she had to muffle her screams of pleasure again.

He was huge. How could she possibly...? But babies came from here. Surely a man would fit.

Zane touched her where they joined, stroking, rubbing, until she felt the contractions she'd learned last night. As they broke, he slid deeper, tearing through her maidenhood. And she lifted her hips, driving him deeper, needing more, despite the pain of this impalement.

And in a few strokes, the pain had disappeared, replaced by a driving need to be filled, for a different level of ecstasy.

She throttled her cries as the tide swept them both away into an explosion of stars and pleasure where she floated mindlessly.

She must have dozed off. She barely noticed as Zane lifted himself from her, removing the contrivance he must have donned when she wasn't looking. He kissed her cheek and pulled up the covers. The cold where he'd been was unbearable. She reached for him, but he relentlessly pulled away to gather his scattered clothes.

Now she understood why people married.

TWENTY-TWO

"We've received acceptances from all our guests for the dinner party," Louisa said excitedly as she opened the mail at the breakfast table the next morning. "This is so exciting! Thank you so much for being my companion." She reached over and squeezed Azmin's hand.

The dinner party. She'd quite forgotten the blasted dinner party, the whole reason she was here. Absently, Azmin patted Louisa's hand and tried to tear her thoughts away from last night's bliss and turn them to what one had to do to prepare for a dinner.

Her body practically vibrated. Her corset rubbed in all the wrong—or right—places. Her skin felt as if it were too tight, and she might pop out of a chrysalis at any moment. She wanted to find Zane and drag him into the nearest room and ravish him. She hadn't learned nearly enough last night.

But she had to sit here garbed primly in woolens up to her chin and discuss china. It was a madness of sorts.

The new errand boy carried in a message on a tray as if it were a crown. Bathed, shorn, and garbed in a crisp blue uniform with good leather shoes, he almost looked presentable, until he opened his mouth.

"Dere's summat at da door waitin' fer an answer, mum."

Azmin had a suspicion that this was Robby's imitation of the speech of his betters. It certainly didn't resemble any accent she recognized. "Thank you, Robert."

She opened the note. "Oh dear, Mrs. Stewart says her husband has time this afternoon for a photograph." At least this would distract her from thoughts of ravaging. She glanced at Louisa. "I know you're eager to plan a menu, but this is quite important. Do you mind?"

"Your studio is important," Louisa agreed, hiding any disappointment. "Will you be here for dinner? We can discuss it then."

"Oh, I should be back before that. What you need to do is research cooks, if only to borrow one for an evening. I don't think Mary can handle a dinner this large." Azmin scribbled an acceptance and a time on the note and returned it to Robby, who happily carried it off.

This was no time for her head to be lost in the clouds. If the possibly abusive Mr. Stewart would be at the studio, she needed accompaniment. Keya had planned on working with Hugh Morgan today. Azmin wanted to print out Eleanor Stewart's photographs, but she'd left the plates at the studio.

She feared the image would reflect the same fading as Keya's once had. At least, this time, she had some reason to believe it wasn't her chemicals at fault. Convincing others was the real problem—that, and removing the wife from the husband.

If only she'd been able to take poor Mrs. Jenkins' photograph— might she have saved the baby?

While Louisa sent notes to her vast family asking about cooks, Azmin jotted off ones to Phoebe and the employment agency, asking about a cook and a *proper* footman for the studio. She could probably ask Mrs. Balfour and the aunts as well. With that task out of the way, she went in search of Keya.

"I have photographs from the morgue and Mrs. Stewart to finish," she told her assistant. "I can do that on my own, but I do not wish to meet Mr. Stewart by myself. I've set the time to meet them for after lunch. Will you be able to join me?"

"I'll be there," Keya assured her. "I don't think Mr. Stewart will misbehave in front of others, but one can never be certain."

"Thank you. I may have to give up teaching my art classes in the morning. This rushing back and forth will quickly become inconvenient." Especially once she left Zane's house and returned to her own, which ought to be right after that dinner. Really. She needed to assert her independence before she fell any deeper into his sensual trap.

Wilson drove her over the bridge to her studio and promised to wait. She was wasting a lot of coins by all this driving about instead of walking. But time was of the essence.

She eagerly removed the developed negatives from their frames and washed the sensitized papers, toned them with gold chloride, and fixed them with a solution. After another washing, she hung the papers on the line and turned up the light to better examine the results. The photographs of Eleanor Stewart were small, since they'd been taken with the four-lens camera. Her client appeared to be disappearing into the draperies behind her. Despite all the cosmetics they'd applied and how healthy Keya had made her appear in person, the photograph showed a washed-out image of a ghost—at least to Azmin's eye.

She prayed it didn't look that awful to anyone else. When she'd shown Keya her photograph, Keya hadn't been able to see what Azmin had, so she had reason to hope. The black shadow was the true test, since others apparently could see it.

The ones from the morgue were intriguing. Azmin wished they would dry faster so she could be certain the lighting on moisture wasn't affecting what she saw.

For comparison, she'd brought the fixed image of Ulf right after he died, where the black shadow clung to him. She compared it to the one from the morgue. The shadow seemed to have shrunk, but it was still there—clinging to its human form? Would she ever know or understand?

The morgue photograph of the man who had died in the hospital after the knife fight was even more intriguing. First, it didn't have a black shadow. If the blackness meant a person was about to die, then this man should have lived. He hadn't.

The white light over the abdomen in the morgue image had grown considerably since the one taken at the time of the fight. It just seemed *thicker.*

And then there was her surreptitious photograph of Zane in his white coat, taken as a backdrop as he worked on Ulf's corpse. No white lights or dark shadows—he looked perfectly normal, exceedingly handsome, and engrossed in his project. She smiled at his frown of concentration. Maybe it was good that he'd grown into a man with purpose and dedication, even if it sometimes made him seem like a stodgy professor. He couldn't remain a charming rake forever.

There was nothing stodgy about the man who had climbed through her window and driven her to the heights of ecstasy. She now knew her books hadn't exaggerated. They just had been a little too poetic. Human congress was far grittier than *transcendence*.

After admiring Zane, she started to set the photograph aside—but an anomaly caught her eye.

The black shadow over Ulf had condensed considerably from the one she'd taken just moments before. Had cutting out the heart dissipated the evil? Was Zane endangering himself by working on corpses inhabited by possible demons?

Or was he exorcising them with his knife?

How would she ever understand? She might write the Librarian, but the chance of any other Malcolm having experimented with photography was slim. Science was an Ives affliction. She had Ives on her family tree. It was the reason she'd been taken in by the marquess's family. Interesting.

Zane had Malcolm ancestry, directly through his mother, a famed healer. Perhaps. . . No, she would not believe a knife healed souls. It may have severed this one though.

But Zane's image was so crystal clear, she was certain she'd adequately applied the chemical solutions. The black blur was not from a lack of photography skills or poor paper.

After giving the photographs time to dry, Azmin tucked them in a box and hurried to meet Wilson. She needed to be on time for her art class. The ladies would be upset if she was late again.

Lady Gertrude and Lady Agnes were waiting for her. Before they could quiz her about nuptials—and she had to tell them that Zane still hadn't asked—Azmin produced the photographs.

"Please, tell me what you make of these. I don't want you reading my mind, so I'll run up to my class. Study them and tell me what you think later."

Lady Gertrude's *pince-nez* fell off her nose in surprise. Lady Agnes covered her mouth in shock.

They were studying the photographs and not gaping at Azmin for her audacity. She fled.

Conscious that she didn't have much time before her appointment with the Stewarts, Azmin rushed down after class to find Phoebe's aunts waiting for her.

"These are. . ." Lady Gertrude held out the photographs but lost her words. "Extraordinary," she finally managed. "Can you take another of Dr. Dare cutting on the gentleman with the white pall?"

So she saw it too! "I'm sure the gentleman has been buried by now," Azmin said nervously. "The coroner only holds bodies as a favor, and Dr. Dare has already removed the heart. He wasn't aware that I was catching him at work. Do you think the white—it's not quite a pall, is it? It's in a very specific section as I see it."

"Perhaps you should find out more about the poor man," Lady Agnes suggested. "It. . . feels. . . as if he was not well, but since he is dead. . ."

He was definitely not well. "So it is sometimes difficult for you to inter-pret what you feel too?" Azmin asked in relief. "And you do see the shadows? Not everyone does."

"We were never meant to be gods," Lady Gertrude said severely. "Our gifts are meant to open our eyes and look closer at the world around us. You are doing that. From there, it is up to us to determine what we should and should not do."

"But you feel the black shadow is. . . malevolent, don't you? And that Dr. Dare is excising it?" Azmin slipped the images back into their case.

"Our gifts work better with the living," Agnes admonished. "We're receiving much of what you feel so we cannot interpret without bias. But it is very obvious that the two of you must marry and soon."

Azmin hoped her coloring and her hat concealed her blush. She curtseyed. "Thank you, ladies. I have another appointment. If you think of anything else I should try with my photography, please let me know.

And if you happen to know a reputable cook or footman, we could use that information too."

The ladies were easily distractible. She left them discussing suitable prospects. She didn't need Wilson to take her to the workshop, but he was waiting anyway.

"Dr. Dare says I'm to take you about, miss," Wilson said happily. "He's even paid for my new wheel."

She should object. She really should. But Wilson had been so helpful and courteous, and he needed that wheel. And she was running late. With a sigh of resignation, she climbed in.

Lady Phoebe was waiting in her animal shelter. "I haven't found a formal footman or cook, but I think you ought to take Wolf with you. We trained him when Simon's children were in danger, but now that they're safe at home, Wolf is bored. He'd love to go in your carriage and visit new places."

Simon was their cousin Olivia's new husband. His children had stayed with the Blairs last year. Azmin studied the Irish wolfhound mix with trepidation. She'd had birds and cats as pets, but Wolf. . . Could have been a real wolf. He was intimidating.

"Will he get along with Dog? Thomson is very fond of Dog."

"Oh, they'll be fine. Have you and Zane set a date yet? I want to think of something special as a gift." Phoebe waited eagerly.

Life kept getting more complicated. Lady Phoebe had been kind to her. She didn't like to disappoint, but she couldn't marry because others wanted a party. "We're both so busy. . ." she prevaricated. "You'll be one of the first to know." She glanced down at the guard dog. "I have to go up to my workshop. Do I leave him down here?"

"No, let him follow you about. He needs to learn your habits and your friends. And if Zane doesn't set a date soon, he'll be out of his teaching position as well as his laboratory. Unbusy yourselves." With that warning, the lady returned to feeding. . . a hedgehog?

Azmin conjured obscenities all the way up the stairs, with Wolf on her heels. If Zane lost his position, he'd lose his office and access to the morgue and the laboratory where he learned how to fix human hearts—

Life was unfair as well as complicated.

Keya was waiting for her with boxes of equipment ready to be transported to the new studio. "Mr. Morgan is sending over someone who might act as footman. Our prospect will meet us at the studio in an hour."

After the one o'clock cannon. Sensible for those without timepieces.

"I hope you hugged Mr. Morgan for his helpfulness," Azmin teased.

A smile flitted across Keya's scarred lips, but she did not respond to the jest. Azmin loved the idea that a romance might be developing between these two people who avoided society but not each other. She hoped the problem of Yedhu's death and any inheritance was resolved soon. Having any more mercenary servants turning up on their doorstep would strain Zane's patience.

The mention of Mr. Morgan reminded Azmin of the morgue photographs she carried. She stopped in the investor's office and asked if he could arrange to have them delivered to Zane. Morgan agreed, then rose from his desk to help them carry their boxes.

Wilson was too old and rheumatic to be of much help, so Mr. Morgan's assistance was welcome.

"Is this monstrous animal riding with us?" Keya asked as Wolf followed them to the carriage.

"Phoebe believes we need a guard dog. He's beautiful, isn't he?" She scratched behind Wolf's ears. His tongue lolled in appreciation as he sniffed the hackney, then leaped in to join them. Well-trained, he rode very politely on the floor, leaning over the open footrest, and sniffing the air.

Azmin was starving by the time they reached the studio. She hoped the poor animal had already been fed. "See if Grey can put together a fast lunch," she suggested as she and Keya carried in the last box. "I wonder if she'd know a proper cook?"

"I'll ask. She might like to work with a real cook and learn the profession. Should I suggest it?"

"I'd hate to lose her here, but yes, she should be allowed to advance if she's interested. There should be more schools for servants." Azmin returned to unpacking, giving her thoughts freedom to roam.

If women were educated to support themselves, would they marry abusive men? She couldn't see Eleanor Stewart attending cooking school, but if an inexperienced woman like that left her husband, where would she go? Making a living at watercolor copying wasn't likely. But if Eleanor had her dowry—she'd need a good lawyer to get it back.

She didn't *know* that Mrs. Stewart was being abused, Azmin reminded herself. Mr. Stewart was a teacher at the university. It was more likely her own eagerness to help running away with her. She hadn't thought to ask Zane about him last night, but she should have.

The new footman Mr. Morgan sent over arrived shortly before the Stewarts' appointment. The maid brought him to Azmin's office.

The applicant wasn't tall, but he was broad-shouldered and muscular. His navy tailored suit was elegant enough to be a gentleman's, even if a few years out of style. But she couldn't recollect any gentleman, and certainly, no footman, sporting a pink silk square in his breast pocket. Interesting. He was quite neat, with his brown hair slicked back, and he disdained the thick sideburns of so many young men. He did, however, sport a dapper mustache.

He produced a card from his pocket. "Michael Murdoch, my ladies. Mr. Morgan said you were in need of an experienced footman?"

His voice did not match his sturdy appearance. It wasn't exactly high-pitched, but more. . . soft spoken? With a tendency to sound questioning. Azmin glanced at Keya, who played stoic.

Keya did, however, ask the obvious. "Have you references?"

His expectant expression fell. "My last employer. . . disapproved of my activities on my day off. Mr. Morgan thought that might not be a problem for ladies."

Days off were often used for visiting families. . . or sweethearts. Instinct said the pink handkerchief was a defiant signal. Azmin wondered if her *instincts* told her other things she'd always accepted as normal. It wasn't as if people blatantly signaled their sexuality.

Perhaps she simply had more experience. She had seen and read a great deal more than the average female. She knew English society disapproved of what was a natural inclination elsewhere. Fearing she might be wrong, she glanced at Keya, who simply nodded approval.

"We are an all-female household," Keya stated coolly. "But we will have regular visitors of all sorts. You will be expected to treat them all with deference and respect. What you do with your free time is of no interest to us."

The young man looked relieved. "I am quite good. I was trained in the earl of Lochmas's household, but I had no opportunity to improve my situation. So I took a position in the city. . ."

Lochmas? Azmin was seeing the fine hand of fate, or Lady Phoebe's. But now was not the time to quibble.

"We will need you to help if any of our visitors become troublesome. And do you like dogs? Lady Phoebe has seen fit to gift us with a guard dog." Azmin indicated Wolf, who was lying in the corridor, watching through the open door.

"An earl's household is a busy place. I have experience in all sorts," he said with assurance. "You will not be disappointed in my services, I promise."

"Our housekeeper will show you to your room." Keya gestured toward the door and led the way out.

Before they could descend to the kitchens, the door knocker sounded.

The Stewarts had arrived. Azmin caught her breath and nodded at the door.

Mr. Murdoch immediately marched to the front of the house, prepared for battle or guests, whichever came first.

"I like him," Keya murmured approvingly. "He is ideal for an all-female household."

Azmin snorted. "That's probably what Mr. Morgan thought too."

Humor, while she waited anxiously for her next experiment, one that could affect lives.

TWENTY-THREE

Zane had Ulf's heart sliced and under the microscope when Drew Blair arrived bearing Azmin's photograph box.

Blair studied the laboratory with an experienced eye. "Nice establishment. I don't understand the university wanting to turn it into a classroom."

"Funds. Everything comes down to money." Zane set aside the microscope.

"If I could find a need for slicing hearts, I'd have Morgan look for investors for a laboratory, but as you say, all comes down to money. Investors want to see a return on their investment. Research for edification is up to us with curious minds who don't mind living on beans."

Zane shrugged in acknowledgment and nodded at the package his friend was carrying. "That doesn't look like Lady Phoebe's list of tenants who need positions."

Blair handed over the carton. "Morgan said Azmin left this for you."

Just the mention of her name conjured sweet scents and sensuous curves and eyes the color of the sea, and Zane had to dig his fingers into the rough wood of his worktable to stay focused. He'd sworn never to let women lead him by his cock, but there were days. . .

He opened the package and all pleasant sensation fled. "Morgue photographs." He laid them out on a clean counter.

Blair looked over his shoulder with interest. "Not exactly the occupation of a lady."

"But the occupation of an inquiring mind. You have no business criticizing ladies' behavior." Zane picked up the one showing an odd white light hovering over the fight victim's abdomen. "What do you see on this?" He handed the paper to Blair.

"I am not criticizing anyone, heaven forbid, given Phoebe's propensities. I was simply commenting on your unusual occupation. Azmin doesn't mind being dragged into it?" He held up the photograph to the light, then turned and looked at it in shadow.

"Azmin practically dragged me into the morgue to capture these images. I haven't found a value in them yet, but she seems to think the light and shadows are telling her something." Zane picked up the one showing him cutting on Ulf. He hadn't even realized she'd taken it.

"I don't know what the image is telling us, but the lighting is odd. I can see no good reason for the white to hover over only one part of the body. The reflector should have lit all parts equally. Is she trying to say we carry our spirits in our stomachs?" Blair set that one down and picked up the one of Ulf's sheet-covered body. "And if she used the magnesium lamp on this one too, why is his reflection black and not white?"

Zane returned to looking at the one in white. "Azmin believes it is some combination of the chemicals she uses and her gift. These were taken with an experimental process. She told me she senses malevolence in the black shadows. She's uncertain what to make of the white ones, but the few examples she's found correspond to areas of infection. This one represents a man who died from a knife wound to the bowel. Infections set in early with that type of wound."

He pointed at the photograph with Ulf"s head exposed. "See, in this one? There's a white spot on his jaw. The coroner said he had an infected tooth."

Blake's excitement was palpable. "You need to take her to the hospital, photograph all the patients! If doctors could determine if and when a patient has an infection. . ."

"We could do next to nothing," Zane warned. "A tooth might be pulled, an appendix removed. But an infection of the bowel? Or the heart?" He thought of Louisa and despaired.

"What about broken bones? Do they become infected? Perhaps you could tell. . ."

A knock interrupted. Zane glanced up and grimaced in irritation at the student waving an envelope. "Is this important?"

"Came from the dean's office, sir, a telegram." The student waited uncertainly.

"Telegrams are never good news," Blair said with fatalism.

"If only ignoring them would make the bad news go away. . ." Zane set down the photographs to retrieve the envelope, sliding the student a coin for his trouble—and to send him away.

He had a really bad feeling about a telegram. Blair leaned against the table, studying the images while Zane tore into the envelope.

It was from Edmond House, Norfolk—the Earl of Edmond's residence, Zane's great-great-uncle. *We regret to notify you. . .*

The earl was dead, long live the new earl—his father.

Zane was now a viscount. With a pig farm.

Azmin hated country estates as much as he did.

AFTER CHECKING HER HAIR IN A MIRROR, TIDYING HER COLLAR, AND brushing down her skirts, Azmin took a deep breath and prepared to meet her first real customers. She crossed her fingers and prayed her suspicions were wrong, then, skirt billowing, sailed down the corridor to the studio's reception room.

The gentleman accompanying Eleanor and Mrs. Balfour was slender and not much taller than his fragile wife. He seemed to be younger than thirty, but his face already bristled with sideburns and a cultivated mustache he'd oiled into curls.

Looking displeased, Mr. Stewart rose from his chair at Azmin's arrival. "I thought she was supposed to be aristocracy," he muttered. "She's almost as dark as her servant."

Azmin plastered her smile to her lips. If Keya could take being seen as a servant, she could live with being less than aristocracy. Pretending she was deaf, she offered tea, gesturing for the new footman to fetch a tray from the kitchen.

For the fun of it, Azmin twitched the bigot's feathers, just a little. "We are honored to have Mrs. Balfour as our first customer," she said with a straight face. "We will be sending public announcements of our opening to the society pages in another week or so, but this week's private sessions are exclusive to dear friends and family. My father is still in India with my mother's royal relations. And the earl's family is preparing for the London Season, but Lady Agnes and Lady Gertrude and their niece, Lady Phoebe Blair, will be sitting for us. You're in excellent company."

Appeased by this litany of titles, Mr. Stewart shut up. Perhaps that would prevent him from taking his temper out on his wife later—although he scarcely looked the sort to beat up more than a pillow.

Leaving Mrs. Balfour to her tea, Azmin led the couple to her studio. They both wore what she assumed was their wedding attire. The bride wore a shimmering gray with pearls. The groom hadn't worn a tailed evening suit for his nuptials but a tailored charcoal-gray business suit with a brocaded red waistcoat that he couldn't possibly wear to class without being termed a dandy.

"I want to take a classic studio photo so I can study your best features before doing the *cartes de visite*. You may take it home for free, so it will only cost a little of your time." She had them stand sideways facing each other, theoretically gazing adoringly into each other's eyes. Mr. Stewart looked mostly bored and impatient. Eleanor beamed in delight. She still looked like a ghost.

If her opinion of the gentleman affected the plates, then this experiment would prove nothing. The man was an obnoxious toad.

Trying to think pleasant thoughts, hoping to catch any shadows on Stewart's back, Azmin used both a dry plate and a wet one. Then after handing those to Keya for processing, she positioned the pair in the more formal position facing her. "You will need to stand very still for some seconds, so be certain you're comfortable. Do you need a chair to steady yourselves?"

They declined a prop. She used her four-lens camera this time and took several sets, just in case. She wanted her first studio photos to be perfect.

"You make a lovely couple," she exclaimed after she gave the last plate to Keya. "You should be able to see them the day after tomorrow, if one of you would like to stop by and approve them before I print more."

"Oh, I'd love to come by then, thank you," Eleanor chirruped happily. "I am so glad you're a photographer now!"

"Don't be a fool. A woman taking work from men who have families to support is against the way of things. I should never have let you talk me into this." Stewart caught his wife's elbow and steered her from the studio.

Azmin stuck her tongue out at his departing back.

"An unpleasant person," Keya said softly as they departed. "Did you notice how she favored her right side? That's what one does when a rib is cracked."

"We're wasting our time, aren't we?" Azmin said in despair as the new footman shut the door after the couple and Mrs. Balfour. "Photographs prove nothing, and she will never leave him."

"We have much to learn," Keya agreed. "But we must start somewhere."

"Do you have time to expose the last plates? I can start printing any you've developed, but then I need to leave for Louisa's lesson." Azmin turned back to her studio, hoping work would end her dismals.

If she couldn't help abused women with her limited gifts, what purpose did she have?

She supposed, if the studio started making money, she could go back to art photography. She enjoyed that, even if it wasn't profitable. Or she could experiment more with the dry plates and learn how to use them for journalism. If newspapers would only print photos of abused women. . .

They wouldn't. Men ran newspapers and men read them, and they would have no interest in men who occasionally slapped their wives. The law said a husband had every right to beat a wife until she submitted. Great Britain was no better than India. Perhaps she could interest a woman's society. . .

One step at a time. They took the hackney back to Zane's home, with Wolf lying at their feet. Azmin was torn between wanting to stay in her own cozy nest and not wanting to miss Zane's midnight visits. She was a wanton woman.

Wilson dropped Keya and Wolf off at the workshop so she could finish working with Mr. Morgan. Since it was still daylight, Azmin left the carriage there and walked back to the house.

Louisa greeted her from a blizzard of paper in her sitting room. "I don't know any of these people! How can I create a seating chart? I've all these place cards written, but our guests are almost all male. It shall be a very dull dinner party."

"Why not let them choose their seats and use the place cards simply to let the others at the table know their names? I find I learn a name much faster if I see it in print." Azmin picked up the neatly-written placards. "You have an excellent hand. I could use you for labeling my *cartes de visite*."

"Then I would be able to see all your photographs! That would be fun. Will you make some for me?" Louisa turned up her pale face eagerly.

"I don't have the card camera here, but what if I take a lovely photo for you to send to your father? He'd like that. And I'll try to remember to bring the other camera another time." She'd been meaning to capture a good photograph of Louisa anyway.

"Oh yes, let's do that. I'll need to change and wash off the ink and put my hair up. . ." Coughing as if she might be coming down with a cold, Louisa threw aside her work and pulled herself from her chair.

She looked so wan and fatigued that it broke Azmin's heart. A child that age should be full of energy and bouncing around, eager to explore the world. Louisa, with her limited abilities, was simply happy to have her photograph taken.

Azmin classified that under life-is-unfair while she sought the perfect setting for Louisa's portrait. She didn't have her reflector with her. She thought it was still bright enough outside, but it was too chilly for an invalid. Louisa would want to be in her best gown and not a pelisse. The sitting room it would have to be, with the gauzy draperies providing filtered light.

"Do I pose sitting or standing?" Louisa called as she entered. "I think I should like everyone to see me standing, so they'll know I have grown."

Oh dear, she loved this child so much. Azmin fought back a tear with a smile and set up her tripod. "You look beautiful in that blue. I wish I could do color. I'll add a nice blush to your cheeks, though, and maybe a little to your lips."

"Cosmetics?" Louisa asked with curiosity.

"No, paint. Cosmetics are faster for *cartes de visite*, but for a portrait, I can take my time. I'll add subtle hues, maybe a dash of blue on the gown. Stand so the light falls on your face, like so." She turned Louisa's chin so she seemed to be admiring an object in the distance. "Hold the chair back so you can stay steady."

She took several shots, just in case. She didn't have her chemicals. She had to be satisfied with the dry plates, and Louisa would have to wait.

The front door opened just as they finished. Dog pattered down the hall, so it had to be Zane. From the male voices, she assumed Thomson was taking his coat and hat. The familiarity was almost like home, except Azmin had never experienced this visceral thrill for any visitors to her flat.

The instant Zane entered, she knew something was wrong. One glance at the black armband on his coat sleeve, and she collapsed into the nearest chair. She didn't dare run to him in front of Louisa.

The girl followed Azmin's gaze, saw the black band, and did what Azmin could not, hugged her uncle. "Oh, I'm so sorry, Uncle Zane. Is it the earl?"

He hugged her carefully, then helped her into a chair. "It is. I have no more information than that. His solicitors will be contacting mine and my father's. They've telegraphed my parents. We should be hearing from them soon." He sent Azmin a despairing look that she couldn't interpret. "The journey from the Americas will take a while, so don't expect the new earl and his countess home soon."

Ah, he was seeing a pig farm in his future. Azmin wished she could offer assurances, but she couldn't even file this under life-is-unfair. He was about to be a wealthy viscount. She supposed that came under life-is-complicated.

"What about my dinner?" Louisa asked in dismay. "Must we go into mourning and cancel it?"

Zane looked a little rattled at making etiquette decisions as head of the family. He had never had much use for social customs.

Azmin stepped in for him. "You did not know the earl at all. He was distant family at best. Armbands and mourning clothes, perhaps, until he's been interred and the new earl arrives?"

Zane nodded reluctantly. "He deserves the respect of having his departure noted. But we still have to eat. Canceling the dinner party doesn't seem necessary. It's business, after all."

Louisa smiled in youthful relief. Azmin could hardly blame her for fearing the first party of her life would be denied.

"Maybe there will be funds for your laboratory?" Azmin asked with hope. If Zane had to leave Edinburgh. . . She didn't know if she could bear it. Not yet, not while they were still learning to be around each other again without anyone being killed. Or egged.

"As viscount, my father received an allowance from the estate. That might descend to me. I can't say. I don't think farms are notoriously wealthy these days, though. My father never counted on the allowance. An estate relies on tenants for income, but at the same time, it is also responsible for the upkeep of the properties. A bad storm damaging roofs could disrupt profits for the year." He glanced at Azmin's equipment. "Are we doing photography lessons today?"

"Azmin took my portrait," Louisa said, standing and turning around so he could admire her gown. "Do you think Father will like it?"

"A man would have to be blind not to admire you in your finery. A portrait is a most excellent idea. But you should probably put something warmer on for the evening, while I talk to Miss Dougall."

She pouted but sashayed off—the fastest pace she could manage.

Dog sniffed as she passed but decided to stay in sight of the object of his adoration, big eyes watching hopefully.

Zane held out his arms and Azmin stepped into them, offering what comfort she could. "You knew this day was coming," she reminded him. "We've always known our time together is limited."

"I don't want to give you up," he said gruffly. "I know you want to stay in Edinburgh. I don't have any answers yet. But don't give up on me, please."

"You'll break my heart," she whispered into his coat. "You know you will. You have responsibilities. You need the Miss Whites of the world. I will never be the rosy-cheeked English lady adorning your dinner table. I will stay and help with Louisa's dinner, but you know I have to go home after that."

"No, I don't know any such thing," he growled. "Marry me, make my nights brighter, even if my days are miserable."

Ah, there it was, the proposal they'd both been evading. Even though Azmin had been expecting it—Zane was a gentleman above all—she still hadn't accepted the idea of being shackled to any man. She'd seen too much—and perhaps not enough. She knew better than most that the world was a very large place.

"That is such a thoughtful, romantic proposal, I cannot imagine how I can refuse," she teased, pushing away. "Will I be sharing your miserable days?"

He glared, shoving fingers through his already tousled hair. "Pig farms and London seasons would be in your future, yes. You'd be a viscountess. People would have to respect you."

Azmin tapped her chin as if thinking. "Hmmm, they'd call me Lady Dare and curtsy and not talk behind my back? Can that be arranged? And if I take up photography in London? Will all society flock to my studio?"

"Dammit, Azmin, you know as well as I do what society is like. I can't fix it. Neither can you. Am I so reprehensible that you won't even consider me?" He looked ragged and torn.

He'd just lost a family member and his independence. She should not tease him. She stood on her toes and kissed his cheek. "You need time to consider *me*, which you cannot do while learning your new responsibilities. Let's plan the dinner we promised Louisa and not fret over what we don't know yet."

His mouth set in a grim line. "Right. Dinner. Our priorities always did differ." He stalked away, tearing at his cravat as if it were strangling him.

He tore her heart out as he left. She was thinking of *him*, bless the holy gods and goddesses! Why couldn't men ever see that?

They seriously lacked imagination. And gifts. She should take the carriage back to the studio to see how today's photographs turned out. No one needed her tonight.

TWENTY-FOUR

ZANE SAT DOWN AT A DINNER TABLE SET ONLY FOR HIM AND LOUISA. "Where is everyone?" he asked, not wanting to distinguish Azmin in particular.

Louisa sent him one of her mischievous glances that almost reminded him of a younger Azmin. Adolescent girls were wicked.

"Everyone? Well, let's see, I believe Robby is polishing his new shoes in the kitchen, Thomson is no doubt grooming Dog. . ."

Zane dug into his soup and ignored this foolishness. He was a damned viscount now. Didn't that deserve some respect? He would irascibly leave for his club if he had one. He could return to his lab, but what would be the point? He needed to pull together his notes and leave the compendium for his fellows.

When she didn't get a response, Louisa relented. "Azmin took her first studio portrait today and was anxious to see how it turned out. I assume Miss Trivedi went with her, although she did mention something about seeing her brother, which means she wanted to see Mr. Morgan. Adults are very entertaining when they're pretending to be too busy to speak with each other."

Zane barely heard past the first sentence. "Azmin returned to her studio? Before dinner? In the dark?"

"It is not that far," Louisa said in what sounded like exasperation. "She has a carriage and company and it's her *home*."

All true, and too appalling to contemplate. She was out there riding around in the dark in a carriage that would crumble to dust at any moment, with an octogenarian driver who would faint if attacked. To a place where she might stay the night instead of returning here. . . because she didn't want to marry *him*.

If she left, he had to return to his lonely meals with only Louisa for company and his lonely bed with only his new title for comfort. He'd lived that way for a decade. He could manage until he found someone else. . .

Azmin had brought color and laughter and energy to this damnable house—and into his life. He didn't *want* anyone else.

He threw down his napkin and rose. "That is not acceptable. My apologies, but I need to go out."

"You'll be here in time for our dinner tomorrow, won't you?" Louisa asked in alarm.

"Of course." After he dragged Azmin back by the hair if necessary.

And that was why men beat wives—because they believed their needs came first and women's desires didn't matter. Zane rubbed his nose as the carriage carried him over the bridge and to the townhouse he'd never visited. He knew the studio was important to her, but he'd not once thought about going with her to admire her efforts.

This was what she was telling him—that they couldn't possibly suit because her work was as important to her as his to him, and society simply could not accept that.

Zane wasn't entirely certain *he* could accept that.

Azmin's home was in one of the more established areas of the Georgian side of town. The substantial terrace houses were gradually developing into businesses on the ground floors and probably rentals above. She didn't have a sign installed on the door yet, so it still appeared as a quiet residence, except with lights gleaming on all the floors.

He climbed the stairs and knocked. A stalwart footman in far more fashionable garb than his own answered the door. Wolf was at his heels. At least the damned women had the sense to bring the dog.

Rather than hand over his card, Zane dropped his top hat in the servant's hand and pushed past. Wolf trotted happily at his side. "Azmin?"

Miss Trivedi stepped into the hall from the front room. "Dr. Dare! Is Louisa not well?"

"She's fine and laughing at me. Is Azmin here? I don't want her riding home in the dark in that broken-down derelict of a hackney." He felt like an ass. He was an ass. But curiosity ruled. He glanced surreptitiously at the neatly-appointed entry and wanted to see it all.

He thought Keya's scarred lip turned up in amusement and didn't care. She led the way into the front parlor, where Azmin was showing photographs to a well-padded older woman with feathers in her hair.

Both women looked startled at his arrival, but Azmin recovered quickly.

"Lord Dare, this is Mrs. Balfour, a neighbor and good client. I was just showing her the first photographs we've pulled from her niece's session today." She handed him a stack of stiff paper.

Zane saw what she had instantly, although probably not as clearly or with the same perception. Now he knew why Azmin had been in such a hurry to return to the studio—the man in the photo had a black lump on his back just as in the photo of Jenkins. Zane held the image up to the light. "He looks familiar."

"Mr. Frederick Stewart, my lord," the neighbor lady said eagerly. "My niece's husband. He's a teacher at the medical college."

Zane had heard his father addressed as *my lord*. He'd always thought it ridiculous given the distance of his relationship and the meaningless status. But now his father was *earl*, and Zane was next in line to all that unwanted responsibility.

But Azmin's photos had the potential to be more important than a meaningless title. He needed to pay attention to what she was trying to tell him. He remembered Stewart as a mediocre student who hadn't the perseverance or perception to become a physician. So he'd become an underpaid teacher. He'd rather not mention that.

"I've probably met him." He glanced at the woman next to Stewart in the photo, then raised his eyebrows at Azmin. "It's a nice photo. What are you seeing?"

"Mrs. Stewart disappearing into the draperies," she said curtly.

The woman looked solid to Zane, smiling and weak, perhaps, not to his taste, but just as visible as her husband.

"I was just explaining to Mrs. Balfour that I fear her niece may be married to an abusive man." She sounded defensive.

That might be stretching it, but he wasn't about to take chances after she'd warned him about Jenkins. If she thought this warranted action, he needed to support her—as she did him.

Zane turned to the frowning lady. "Miss Dougall has been correct in these situations before. She has saved my niece from making a disastrous mistake. Have you ever seen any reason to believe that your niece is unhappy? Has she been ill recently?"

Mrs. Balfour seemed to crumple into herself. "I've been denying it," she replied sadly. "Eleanor told me she walked into a lamppost to explain a bruise on her eye. And that she's had a bad cough to explain the way she holds herself lately. I can't believe. . . He's a medical professor! And she loves him. . ."

"She is afraid to leave him," Miss Trivedi said quietly, stroking Wolf's head as the dog kept a watchful eye. "A wife fears she is nothing without her husband. She's ashamed, because he's made her think the fault is all hers. If she would just be a better wife, do things the way he wants them done, then he wouldn't need to beat her. But it is impossible to achieve perfection."

She spoke with the certainty of experience. If Ulf had been one of her husband's servants. . . She'd been a prisoner of brutes. And Azmin had saved her. Zane shuddered and understood a little more of what these women had done and meant to continue doing. He hated the necessity, but he began to understand how difficult it would be for a wife to escape a husband's abuse.

The slender lady in Azmin's photograph would not be as strong as Azmin or Miss Trivedi.

"Is there anywhere you can send Eleanor where her husband would not find her?" Azmin asked gently. "Just taking her to your home will not work. He will follow and beg forgiveness and then when she relents, he'll beat her even worse. It's a cycle we must break."

"I don't know if she'll listen," Mrs. Balfour cried. "I'm only an old lady. I can take her with me to France, but what will she do there? Her home is here. Can we not just speak to Mr. Stewart?" She glanced hopefully to Zane. "Surely you can persuade him to change his ways?"

"Only by beating him up," Zane said coldly, comprehending men like Jenkins and this Stewart better than the women did. Ladies thought men should be empathetic and considerate—like them. Whereas men saw themselves as lords of all they surveyed. Power and empathy seldom went hand in hand. "And there is no guarantee that even a good thrashing will stop his abuse."

Azmin looked properly appalled. Miss Trivedi looked fascinated. Mrs. Balfour managed both shocked and thoughtful at the same time. He ought to drop the stodgy professor persona more often. Beating up Stewart felt right, but he'd end up fighting half the male population if that was the only solution. Despite his murderous mood, logic prevailed.

"Speak with your niece first," Azmin suggested quietly. "Let us not speculate."

"And take Mrs. Stewart to a physician. There could be internal injuries," Zane added curtly. "Men seldom understand the delicacy of a female's physique. A woman cannot withstand blows to. . ." He shifted to politer terms than he normally used, "To her midsection."

Mrs. Balfour paled and bobbed her feathered head as she stood up. "I shall do that, at once, thank you. I don't know how you can see what others cannot, but I've felt something was wrong. I'll confirm it, and then I'll see what I can do."

The footman arrived to help with hat and coat and the older lady stalked out, head high, as if preparing for war.

"Anyone want to wager that she beats Stewart within an inch of his life with a stout umbrella?" Zane mused, falling into the old game he'd once shared with Azmin.

"She's smart enough to use a fire iron," Azmin responded wearily.

"Violence shouldn't have to be the answer." Miss Trivedi retrieved her cloak without aid of the servant.

"When the courts leave us no choice, what else is there?" Azmin signaled for her coat. "But I'd like to believe we can look for alternatives."

Zane didn't like the sound of that, but if Azmin was actually coming home with him instead of staying here, he wouldn't argue. "I brought my carriage and paid your derelict driver to go home."

Azmin shot him a look of irritation. "Wilson is reliable and patient. We are paying him enough to replace his axles and the broken door. You do not need to buy *anything* for us, is that understood?"

No, it wasn't, but again, Zane didn't argue, not as long as she was climbing into the carriage with him. He verified that the lock on her studio door was properly fastened, waited until Wolf was at the ladies' feet, then took the driver's seat and shook the reins.

Debating how long it would take for everyone to fall asleep so he could approach Azmin's room if she refused to set out a rope for him, Zane drove back to George Square and turned down the alley leading to his carriage house. He supposed he could have let the women out in front, but he didn't want them going anywhere at night alone. Azmin wasn't likely to object—

A shot split the chilly night air. Zane felt the impact in his shoulder, but automatically tightened his grip on the reins to control the frightened horse. He shouted "Get down!" at the women behind him.

Wolf leapt silently from the carriage and raced down the alley. Dog's howls reverberated inside the house. Thomson abruptly appeared at the back door, bearing a lantern. The hound ran between his feet, trotting on short legs in the same direction as Wolf.

Before Zane could so much as calm the horse and climb down, Azmin was out of the carriage, staying low and helping Keya to do the same. He sighed in relief as they scurried through the gate and into the house, with Thomson emerging to provide cover.

Zane threw the reins to Thomson. "Take care of this animal first. I'll go after the dog."

He knew his mistake the instant he grabbed the post to swing down. Pain shot through his arm, and he crumpled beneath his weight.

~

WATCHING FROM THE DOOR, AZMIN MUFFLED A SCREAM AND RAN BACK the instant Zane staggered. She dug her fingers into his coat when he protested.

"He has too long a lead," she argued. "Let the dogs scare him off. If you die now, your father will have to find another wife to provide an heir."

She thought he almost laughed at that. She tried to look for blood but it was too dark.

"My mother would poison him if he tried." Sensibly, the annoying doctor put his good arm around her shoulders and allowed her to lead him into the house. "I've had many bad days before, but this one ranks higher than most."

"Personally, I think you arranged the shooter so I'd feel sorry for you and stay," she answered pertly. "It won't work, you know."

"Why the devil would anyone shoot me?" Zane asked in irritation once inside. He released her to shrug off his outer coat and winced. "Do they want my impressive lab coat?"

"Do you think Keya might have been the target?" she asked, puzzled as much as he was. "If she inherited a fortune, perhaps Ulf was not the only one searching for her."

"Gopala said only Ulf accompanied him. I suppose he might not have been aware of others. Where is she anyway?" He helped her with her cloak, hanging it on a peg.

"I sent her to reassure Louisa, if she's still awake. And because I feared she was in danger. I am so sorry. We really should remove ourselves." She didn't want to leave, not while Zane was hurting, but she couldn't let her activities endanger his household.

"It could have been a thief who stole a pistol and thought he'd practice," Zane retorted with a scoff. "The world does not revolve around you."

She didn't think he believed the thief theory any more than she did, but she had no argument to offer. Now that he'd removed his overcoat, she could see blood oozing through a hole in his frock coat.

Thomson was taking care of the horse and dogs. The only other male servant was a child asleep in his bed. It seemed perfectly natural for Azmin to follow Zane to his room. Keya stepped out to offer aid and say that Louisa had slept through the incident.

"Hot water, if you don't mind," Azmin suggested. "I imagine all the fires are banked."

"I've stirred the grate in my room. I'll bring the kettle."

"I am perfectly capable of tending it myself," Zane said in annoyance, sitting on his bed to pry off his coat.

"With one hand. It's a magician you are?" Azmin asked, reduced to mocking a servant from their youth as they once had. They'd been reprehensible brats. She helped him ease off the coat.

The adolescent familiarity eased the tension. Zane grinned ruefully. "Aye, and it's a harpy, you are, and no Florence Nightingale. At least I know I'll not insult your nonexistent maidenly sensibilities if I take off this blamed shirt."

"Inflame, perhaps, not insult," she countered as he removed his cravat with one hand. "Does it hurt much? Shall I cut off the sleeve?"

Red stained the linen covering his shoulder and upper arm. She was crying hysterically inside, but she would not let him see so much as a quiver.

"Shall I tend the wound?" Keya asked from the doorway when she returned with the hot kettle.

"I grew up with the military. It's not anything I haven't done before," Azmin assured her, knowing Keya's modesty was far greater than her own. "If I do it wrong, his mighty lordship will yell at me, not you."

A gleam briefly lit Keya's dark eyes. "By all means, rescue me from his shouts. I'll ask in the morning if we should pack our bags."

"No one is leaving," Zane shouted.

Keya quirked her scarred lips, then slipped away in the direction of her room.

Zane had his shirt off his good arm. Azmin thought she might simply stand there, gaping, as one did before a particularly fine work of art. In the lamplight, shadows sculpted his muscles into jaw-dropping perfection.

His bloodied shirt, on the other hand, was terrifying.

He gestured irritably in the direction of the washbowl. "My bag is in the corner by the wardrobe. There should be carbolic soap in it."

"Carbolic?" She found the bag and set it on his night table after removing medical texts and spectacles so there was room for bag and bowl.

"Lister has discovered carbolic acid forms a layer of protection against infection. Alcohol works to clean but dissipates. Besides, I'm not wasting my good brandy on a scratch." He picked at the linen plastered to his arm.

She dug around until she found an ugly red cake of soap wrapped in newspaper and held it up. "This? Is it something the apothecary might carry? I'd rather have soap in the house than alcohol."

"It's not commercially available, no. I made that formula myself. My father is looking into what it might take to sell it, but the stench alone makes it unmarketable." With a wince, he yanked off the shirtsleeve. "It went through. No bullet to dig out."

"I don't suppose your soap is edible so we could use it to kill infection on the inside." Azmin flung his shirt on the coals and let it go up the chimney in smoke.

He chortled and picked up the washrag in the bowl. "I said it *prevents* infection. We have nothing yet to kill it, unless one counts moldy bread. My mother has cured with herbs and her healing skills, but she cannot advertise her gift."

"Magic," Azmin grumbled, taking the cloth from him and applying it to the soap. "Your mother is magic. I am not. I wish your soap would prevent violence."

"You've only begun to experiment. You don't know what you can do. Do you have any idea how much time Lister and Pasteur have spent developing germ theory and putting it to practical use?"

"If I thought taking photographs might save lives, then it would be worth experimenting," she said in disgruntlement, dabbing at the bloodied mess of his arm. "Do Lister and Pasteur get shot at for their efforts?"

"You don't know who was out there or what they wanted. Don't be foolish. I don't usually use my carriage. He may have thought I was someone else."

"I wish I was Phoebe and could read the mind of dogs. I'd like to see what they saw." Since she heard Thomson calling down the alley, she assumed the animals were on their way home.

"Dogs might recognize a scent, I suppose, but how the devil they can communicate scents to Phoebe is beyond my comprehension." He took the bag off the stand and dug around in it, removing scissors and compresses and bandages. "Hold this gauze to the graze. I'll wrap it. It will be fine in a few days. Quit looking as if I might die tomorrow."

She slapped his good arm. "I am being extraordinarily stalwart and restrained and not running out to retrieve your pistols and stalking the alley looking for villains. Appreciate that."

He offered a muffled chuckle as he used his teeth to hold the bandage he was tying. She took the ends and finished it off.

"Stay with me," he insisted, taking her hand when she was done.

It tore her heart straight from her chest to shake off his hand and gather up his gear. "And shock Louisa and the servants? Unlikely." She stepped from his reach, fighting her desire to hug him and wipe the weariness from his eyes. "Do you have anything in here for the pain?"

"My mother's willow bark concoction. I'll survive," he said grumpily. "I'd sleep better if you were with me."

So would she, but she had no intention of giving him power over her by letting him see her weakness. She kissed his cheek. "Dream of bonbon confections like Miss White. I will see that Thomson has locked the doors and the dogs are guarding the halls."

"I think I'll dream of locking you up until you agree with me." Glaring at her, he stood and began to unfasten his trousers.

"Remember, I wield knives," she retorted. Then swallowing hard, she escaped before she gave into temptation.

TWENTY-FIVE

"Physician, heal thyself," Zane muttered as he applied a fresh bandage to his wound the next morning.

It wasn't as if any of the women had come to tenderly minister to his needs. Of course, that could be because it was still dark and the household still slept.

He hadn't.

He'd had a title dropped on him, proposed marriage, and been shot, all in one day. A day like that would work on the nerves of the steadiest of men, he told himself. He needed his laboratory to find peace.

The laboratory didn't need him. Cursing, he managed to pull clothes on with the use of only one arm. It only took three times longer than usual, and he had to settle for an unstarched shirt with buttons, and his cravat looked like a noose. Maybe he'd have his father hire a valet for him. Viscounts should have valets, right?

That's all he needed, one more voice nagging at him.

He stalked downstairs in the dark to find the boy, Robby, sleeping in the hall with his arm around Wolf. The wolfhound glanced up, studied Zane, then lay his head back down. Fine, then, he wasn't an intruder. Good to know.

Thomson emerged from the servants' stairs before Zane could ring a bell. Blessedly, he carried a tray of coffee.

"In my study." Zane indicated the door. He lit a lamp and stirred the embers while the *footman* lumbered down the hall, doing his best not to tilt the pot and cups.

"Rough night, sir," the garrulous servant offered as he set the tray down. "Couldn't find none aboot to be causin' such a scene. The horse is fine. The lads is taking care of it."

Zane didn't have it in him to explain that servants didn't speak until spoken to. He rather preferred someone else fill in the gaps of silence. He sipped the coffee gratefully. He'd have to take the dogs to Lady Phoebe, see if she could read their feeble minds. He didn't place much faith in that helping.

He worked on his correspondence—thank the powers that be only his left arm was affected. He sent queries about infection in other parts of the body affecting the heart to colleagues working on the same research. He would miss intellectual discussions if reduced to rural pastimes and examining eccentric Malcolm claims for validity. Might as well start now.

A letter from the earl's estate solicitors assured him that the land was entailed and couldn't be sold. They mentioned some elderly widowed relations still living on the grounds, and that the earldom had been given approval to allow the title to pass through the female line. Zane briefly considered performing a disappearing act like Phoebe's cousin Max. But he was too old to be that irresponsible.

The solicitors said they would look into codicils for the future if the new earl didn't wish to limit the inheritance of the land. Their tone strongly disapproved. Zane understood the necessity of keeping the property intact for agricultural development, but there might be better uses for it. He certainly didn't need a wood for deer hunting or a great lake for fishing or whatever the old earl had out there.

He would have to go south and visit at least once. Absentee landlords were a scourge upon the countryside, but he now had some sympathy for their plight.

The dinner was tonight. Would Azmin stay one more night? What did he have to do to make her stay if the dratted woman wouldn't marry him?

He couldn't. He could never force a woman to do what he expected without consideration of what she wanted. He couldn't act like the beasts of prey she stalked.

So, he'd have to settle for pink bonbons if he wanted an heir, he thought miserably. The chance of finding a woman who intrigued him as much as Azmin did was slim. Of course, she irritated and drove him mad and turned his household upside-down, so perhaps that was for the best. If pink bonbons kept an orderly household and stayed out of his way, he could follow his own pursuits and his life would be peaceful again.

Boring and lonely, but peaceful.

Zane recognized Azmin's quick, light step coming down the stairs. Would he ever hear her on those stairs again after today?

Hell, even *he* might not be here to use them in a month or so. What difference did it make? His life was in a spiral spin downward.

He could smell her exotic fragrance before she even entered. Sandal-wood. He'd smelled it in her hair, so she probably used it in her soap.

"You were supposed to wait for me to wrap that bandage," she scolded the instant she entered.

He could feel her studying him, and that irritated him even more. "I'm perfectly capable," he replied disagreeably, finishing his letter.

"Yes, of course." She helped herself to his coffee. "Big manly men need no assistance, I understand. It is we weak women who like to pamper and pet. Forgive me for being a woman."

Unable to resist longer, he looked up. She was garbed in boring blue with a prim white collar and cuffs and not a speck of the jewelry she used to flaunt.

"Unforgivable," he retorted. "Women are menaces to society. I can see why Arabs lock them in harems."

She gurgled with laughter. "I see your humor has improved. Shall I have your breakfast delivered in here so you needn't be subject to our feminine attentions? Personally, I think it better that *men* be kept behind locked doors."

"Dammit." Zane stood and slammed the door, then dragged her against him with his good arm. Her waist was so damned small, and the corset pushed her breasts into perfect mounds against his waistcoat. He kissed her without apology.

She didn't fight him but gave in with alacrity, wrapping her arms around his neck and returning his need with one as strong as his own.

The sound of pattering feet on the stairs pushed them apart.

"Goodness." She tucked straying hairs back into her coiffeur. "That was. . ."

"What we could have every morning if you'd marry me." Feeling surly, he returned to his desk, even though he could barely focus on the words in front of him.

"Yes, well, I'm sure that would wear off in a few weeks. Perhaps you should send Louisa off to her family for a visit until we've worked all that out of our systems." She turned around and marched out, greeting Louisa as if she hadn't a care in the world.

Yes, he definitely understood the need to beat recalcitrant women into submission. Or his head against the desk.

Weeks? He could have weeks?

UNWILLING TO WALK TWO BIG DOGS OVER TO PHOEBE'S ANIMAL SHELTER, Azmin loaded them into Wilson's hackney later that morning. If Zane meant to behave as if nothing had changed, that was his problem. She had a list of things to do so long that she wouldn't have to think about that kiss all day.

Having received Azmin's note, Phoebe was there and waiting, her face a picture of consternation. "Someone *shot* at you?" she asked as she led the dogs inside. "Why on earth would anyone do that?"

"Is Gopala here? Can anyone verify that he was here all evening?" Azmin anxiously glanced about the shelter. After her earlier experience, she feared assassins leaping out of closets. But India was months away and surely there couldn't be two sets of assassins after Keya?

The owl blinked back at her. A black cat peered down at her from atop a cabinet. Other creatures stirred in their various cages. She didn't see any likely hiding places for even someone as slender as Keya's brother.

"I have no idea where he was last night. First, let me find out what Wolf and Dog recall. I don't promise anything." Phoebe sat on a stool with a bowl of dog treats. As if obeying a mental message, Wolf trotted over beside her. Dog remained at Azmin's feet.

Phoebe scratched the wolfhound's ears and fed him a scrap of sausage. "He enjoyed hunting a man who smelled of gunpowder. But the man climbed a wall and didn't come out."

"Would he recognize Gopala?" Azmin asked anxiously. She didn't want Keya's little brother to be an assassin, but she could make no sense of what had happened last night.

"Yes, I believe so. Wolf has been all over this building and Gopala pets him. He should be in front working on some project with Blair right now. We can ask where he was after I talk to Dog."

Phoebe snapped her fingers and Wolf trotted off to a corner with a bone. Dog lumbered up so she could scratch behind his ears. "Oh dear," she said instantly, standing and handing Dog his treat. "He was hunting Jenkins. He didn't just smell gunpowder but the man Zane asked him to follow. He's eager to go back and sniff him out again because Zane feeds him pies."

"Jenkins? Why *Jenkins*?" Appalled, Azmin hurried after Phoebe to the front room. "Could he have discovered that Zane hid Mrs. Jenkins?"

"This started before Zane hid the wife, didn't it?" Phoebe asked before confronting her husband. "We need more guards on Zane. He was shot at last night, and Dog believes Jenkins is responsible."

Mr. Blair glanced up from his worktable where he and Gopala were screwing together pieces of metal. "Has anyone told the police by any chance? Or are we only talking to dogs?"

"The police won't believe I'm talking to dogs," Phoebe said with a dismissive wave. "Zane can tell them he was attacked, but he won't be able to identify the culprit."

"Mr. Dare has been hurt?" Gopala asked in alarm. "And Keya? Is she unharmed?"

"Keya is fine," Azmin said curtly, not entirely convinced he hadn't been involved. After all, he and Ulf had hired Jenkins and his thugs at the tavern to attack *her*. She was disinclined to believe anyone. But if the Blairs allowed him to work here, she had to believe they trusted him. "Lady Phoebe seems to think this has to do with Zane, not Keya, although I cannot grasp the logic."

"You said Jenkins was courting Louisa and calling himself Dare," Phoebe reminded her. "The man is mad. We must catch him before he does harm."

The black shadow indicated *madness*, not malevolence? Or perhaps one related to the other. "I don't think we can persuade Zane to stay home, but he never remembers to carry a weapon. Do I chloroform him and leave him in his lab?"

Mr. Blair snorted. "That might work as well as anything." He set down his screwdriver. "I'll drag him to the police station to make a report. I shouldn't think he'd be attacked during broad daylight."

"I will guard him," Gopala said fiercely. "He protects my sister. I will protect him."

A purported pacifist defending Zane? That should be entertaining. But in the interest of family relations, Azmin suggested, "Perhaps you should stand guard at the house, patrol the alley, things like that. Take Wolf with you."

Gopala looked as if he might object, but Phoebe overrode him. "Dog can follow Zane. He recognizes Jenkins, Wolf doesn't. You're the one who stupidly hired the bully. You'll have to be the one to point him out to Wolf."

Gopala dipped his head in acknowledgment.

"Keya will want to come here to work with Mr. Morgan," Azmin reminded them. "Shall I tell her she must stay with Louisa for now?"

"Yes," Blair said with certainty. "We cannot be guarding half the town. And madmen have been known to use women. You should go back to the house as well. We can guard Zane and the house and that's the limit."

"I'd rather hunt Jenkins," Azmin muttered. "I'll go back to the tene-ment, talk to the neighbors who seem to know where he goes. We can watch for him at the tavern. I'd rather be the one attacking than the one waiting for the battle to happen."

Mr. Blair looked as if he might explode. Again, Phoebe intervened. "You cannot enter those establishments without a man, preferably one with weapons and use of both fists. People here know me and even I wouldn't attempt it. I'll find someone to ask questions. You have a dinner to prepare."

"I might boil the water," Azmin said irritably. "I don't suppose a cook has shown up anywhere? I'll have to bring Grey over and hope she can work with Mary to put something together."

"Boys will eat anything," Blair said dismissively, shrugging out of his work coat and reaching for his good one.

"I can send scullery maids, but they won't be good for serving. I suppose Thomson can manage to set soup on the table without spilling it. I'll tell my aunts you won't be over today. Take Wolf and Gopala back with you. Drew and Dog can find Zane. It won't be difficult finding Jenkins. The problem comes in deciding what to do with him." Phoebe reached for her hat, obviously ready for battle.

Azmin fumed, but she couldn't conceive a better plan. Yet. Refusing to be confined to the house until she'd at least accomplished one task, she ran upstairs to develop Louisa's photographs. And maybe pack chemicals to take back to her new prison.

TWENTY-SIX

AZMIN FUMED AS SHE AND LOUISA CHOSE THE LINEN AND CHINA AND SET the table themselves that afternoon. Everyone else was in the kitchen, preparing whatever they cooked best. Phoebe had sent over scullery maids, but they still had no head cook. Azmin had sent for her maid but that meant they now had Grey, as well as Mary and Keya, all attempting to use the stove at once.

Louisa had tried to help but finally had to be directed away from the chaos of chopping knives and boiling pans. Azmin relented and even called in Gopala from patrolling the house with Wolf so he could lend a hand in the kitchen.

"I could at least be in my workshop developing photos," Azmin complained, polishing the silver to a gleam.

"We should set up a workshop in the attic. Although I suppose if Uncle Zane adds more servants, they might object if you stink up their rooms." Louisa compared napkins and chose the damask ones.

Zane wouldn't be adding servants if he had to leave for the earl's estate.

How would Louisa fare in Norfolk? The fresh air might be good for her, Azmin supposed. Zane was the one likely to chop down trees and slaughter hogs out of sheer frustration.

She had explained her presence to Louisa as preparing for dinner, not being held prisoner in a fortress guarded by a wolfhound and a Hindu terrorist, such as he was. Louisa had been intrigued by Gopala, but not knowing how much he could be trusted, Keya was wisely keeping them far apart. So far, they'd had no word from solicitors verifying Yedhu's death. There was no guarantee a telegram would reach Keya's parents or that she could trust their response. Gopala remained suspect.

Azmin was more interesting in knowing what Zane was doing now.

She had no right to ask.

When Murdoch, her polished new footman—still sporting a pink pocket square—delivered an urgent message from Mrs. Balfour, Azmin couldn't take confinement anymore. Murdoch would make a far better guard for Louisa than she was. And he could help serve dinner!

"Murdoch, how much do you know about setting a dinner table for twelve?" Azmin asked, indicating the task before them.

"Everything, miss," he said stiffly. "I was training to be under butler."

"Most excellent. If you would help Miss Howard set the table, I'll run over and see what Mrs. Balfour needs. Lord Dare's household is a little unusual, but I'm sure you can set everyone right without me." Leaving Louisa admiring the properly attired footman, Azmin introduced Murdoch to Thomson, then grabbed her redingote and escaped.

They'd sent Wilson, their usual driver, away for the day, but she caught a normal hackney down the block, near the university.

When Azmin arrived at the studio, Mrs. Balfour had her niece with her, and Eleanor was hysterical.

Trouble didn't come in ones or threes but in downpours.

"I AM SO EMBARRASSED," ELEANOR CRIED, GRASPING AZMIN'S HANDS AS the carriage carried them down the mews to Zane's home. "I know this is an imposition. I should go home. I'm sure he didn't mean it."

Sporting a large bruise, Eleanor had confessed that her husband had slapped her and knocked her down the stairs—and she thought she might be pregnant. The child was the only reason she'd finally run to her aunt.

"I'm sure Mr. Stewart will regret it," Azmin said. "But your responsibility is to your child. It can't take care of itself. He can. We'll hide you for a little while, just until you decide what to do."

"I feel like a fool," Eleanor whispered.

"You are doing the smartest thing any mother can do. Of course, you may regret your offer to help in the kitchen," Azmin warned. "It is utter chaos. The adage about too many cooks may be painfully true. And a lady in their midst will probably upset the proverbial apple cart." She was so rattled that she couldn't quit thinking in the clichés she'd dutifully learned to fit in with her classmates all those years ago.

"I'm no lady like you," Eleanor said stoically, holding her pelisse around her. "My father is in manufacturing and is now wealthy, but he and my mother are from humble origins. My favorite place growing up was in the kitchen, learning from my mother. Tell them I'm a proper cook, treat me like one, and they might follow my orders. It's the least I can do in return for taking me in."

"We'll have to find somewhere more suitable once the dust settles." There she went again. Her brain was too full to have original thoughts. "But no one will think to look for you in Dare's kitchen!"

The carriage let them out at the back gate, and Azmin sent Eleanor down the kitchen steps, as if she really were a servant. "Wait until I've had time to let them know you're out there. I don't think anyone is watching, but let's take all precautions." Well, Gopala and Wolf should be watching, but they wouldn't know the difference between a lady and a cook.

Eleanor nodded and eased down the cellar stairs while Azmin entered through the back door. Murdoch stepped from the dining room to see if he was needed, but Azmin waved him away, removing her cloak, and hurrying down to the kitchen.

"I've brought you a head cook," she announced. "She should be at the door soon. Take deep breaths and say prayers."

The knock came at the exact right moment, before she could be peppered with questions. "Keya, if you would?" She sent her friend a speaking look, knowing she could trust her not to seem surprised.

Azmin introduced Eleanor as Mrs. Smith. Thomson took her pelisse. Had he been a normal servant, he would have recognized the richness of it, but he was from the slums and had no idea how proper cooks dressed, only that they were very grand and important.

Eleanor quickly determined the eclectic menu simmering on the stove and set to ordering the maids. Azmin gestured for Keya to join her.

"It's late. We need to dress. Do you think this will work?" Azmin hurried up the stairs with Keya on her heels.

"Which *this*?" Keya asked dryly. "As long as no one is shooting, I will count the day a success. You actually have Gopala guarding the house or are we simply keeping him out of trouble?"

"Probably both," Azmin admitted.

Keya rolled her eyes. "I cannot argue with the logic. Have you decided on what you will wear?"

"Unfortunately for Zane, I have," Azmin said in determination as they reached the ground floor and started up to the bedrooms. "This is a party, and I intend to wear my party clothes. Once he sees how unsuitable I am, he will quit fighting me."

"For someone so cynical, you are so naïve," Keya said with a laugh. "You could walk out with nothing on, and he'd find a way to think that normal. Men are very single-minded."

"But this will be in front of Miss White and his students, and *they* will not think me normal. I will be sorry to disrupt Louisa's first dinner, but she needs to have some understanding of the society she expects to move in." There was no reason to delay the inevitable, Azmin thought with resignation. Their time together had been limited. If they parted now, no one would be irreconcilably hurt.

Except her heart, perhaps. Zane had apparently always owned it. No other man had ever compared, even when he was at his stodgiest worst, and she wanted to egg him.

She swallowed hard on that realization and took her time choosing her defiant, flag-waving attire. She had no great desire to freeze in the drafty halls, so she put on her warmest underwear before removing her beloved saris from her trunk.

～

ARM ACHING, EXHAUSTED, DISGUSTED, AND LATE, ZANE ARRIVED AT HIS doorstep just as White's carriage pulled up in front of his house. He checked his pocket watch. Miss White must be very eager. She was early.

Instead of the voluptuous blond bonbon he expected, Director White stepped out, followed by his daughter, who had dressed in trailing silks and lace as if this were a formal dinner party. Was he supposed to wear his evening attire for *students*? He didn't even have time to wash.

Courteously, Zane waited for his guests. He hadn't thought White had been invited, but he'd not been paying much attention to Louisa's chatter.

"Hope it's not too much of an intrusion, Dare, but I heard about last night's incident and didn't want my daughter left unescorted. I would have kept her home, but she insisted. . ." The older man gestured helplessly.

"No problem at all," Zane said through gritted molars, trying to imagine how a thirteenth guest could be added. "I fear I'm running a trifle late and will need to run upstairs to put on my dinner jacket." And find someone to fasten his shirt studs because he couldn't manage with only one good arm.

Zane led them inside. He almost goggled when Azmin's formal footman regally accepted their coats and hats as if he'd always been a fixture in the household.

Recovering, he escorted his guests into the front parlor. "Sherry while you wait, perhaps? I'll let the ladies know you've arrived. The students should make an appearance shortly."

He left them giving Murdoch their drink requests and took the stairs up two at a time. This was the reason he didn't socialize. He didn't have the damned time.

Azmin appeared in the upper hall as Zane raced down it, ripping at his cravat. He almost skidded to a stop and swallowed his tongue.

In the gaslight, she was the vision that haunted his dreams. Earrings dangling, necklaces sparkling, she shimmered in a gauzy gold and turquoise sari, just as she had a decade ago. He supposed she was more shapely and her hair more expertly coiffed, but she was the goddess he carried with him every night after she'd left that long-ago summer.

He'd thought he'd banished her memory. He hadn't.

Recovering his tongue and some of his maturity, he yanked off his cravat and continued at a more sedate pace. "White and his daughter just arrived. He expects to be seated."

"He does, does he?" she asked in amusement. "Let us see how long that lasts. How is your arm? You're favoring it."

"Of course I'm favoring it. It bloody well hurts. Go down and keep the old goat entertained, please. I need to find a clean shirt." Zane halted at his door, all but clenching his fists to keep from reaching for her. He *needed* her right now. He'd never needed anyone before, but his life was coming apart at the seams, and Azmin was the thread who held him together.

She was also the brazen hussy in silks and gold ripping the seams apart. She opened the door for him, gifting him with a whiff of a sensual floral scent he didn't recognize but had him salivating.

"Let me dress your wound before you change. Your guests were rude arriving so early. They can stew for a while." She caught his good arm and steered him inside.

He kicked the door shut and grabbed her. "You are driving me mad. Why?" He drank in her scent as he kissed her throat. Her delicate earrings swung to brush his jaw.

She arched into him, moaning softly, letting him devour her for a brief moment, before stepping back and working his waistcoat buttons, all military efficiency.

His reckless, cynical, gorgeous dream of femininity possessed the soul of a staff sergeant.

"No time," she insisted. "I need to check on Louisa. She must be in a dither. I'll send her down to your guests."

"And leave her unattended when my students arrive? Not a chance. Go down with her. I can manage to dress myself." Zane threw his cravat across the room and struggled with his coat while Azmin determinedly parted his waistcoat and started on his shirt.

"I'll go to her shortly. I only just arrived a little while ago. Mrs. Stewart has left her husband and is now bossing your kitchen staff around."

"What? You have a professor's wife in my *kitchen?*"

"I had no choice. She had nowhere else to go. Did you learn more about Jenkins?"

"He's gone to ground like my life has gone to hell," he growled irascibly. "They haven't seen him at the tavern. His mistress threw him out after his wife's neighbors made sure she had word of his abuse. Dog can't follow cold tracks. I left him with Morgan and Blair, who are hunting through taverns and opium dens, making certain he has nowhere to run."

"And the police?" She helped him shed his coat and waistcoat.

"They're sending an extra patrol and stationing a watchman in the park. If I understood *why* Jenkins hated me, it might make more sense." He was believing a *dog* that it had been Jenkins in the alley. That proved his life had gone straight to hell. He winced as the coat sleeve on his bad arm finally peeled off.

Azmin kissed the pulse at the base of his throat, sending blood rushing southward. A light knock at the door had her drawing away before he could act on impulse. Zane cursed inwardly.

He struggled out of his waistcoat while Azmin answered the knock. Keya stood outside, also in her Indian finery, although hers was considerably more sedate. He had glimpses of gauzy purple and gold threads before his mind fastened on their exchange.

"I didn't see her in the kitchen. I thought she was upstairs dressing," Azmin was saying.

"Her gown is laid out on her bed, but she's not there. I'd hoped you knew where she was. I'll go down and ask." Keya hurried away before Zane could question.

Azmin frowned. "I hope Louisa hasn't tired herself before the evening begins. Let me help you with that shirt, and then I'll tend to her."

He flung off the wilted linen and hastily dragged on a fresh one. "You've lost Louisa?"

"She's been surrounded by people all day. I was just going to seek her out when you arrived. Her photographs turned out lovely, but there's a spot I thought you should—"

Using his aching arm and fastening his shirt studs, Zane pushed past her and opened the door. "Find Louisa. I'll check upstairs. You check down. She may have fainted from overexertion. Let's take no chances."

Looking alarmed, Azmin rushed off. Zane checked all the empty rooms along the corridor. Downstairs, he heard Azmin's voice gradually rising, and he remembered—White was down there.

And Azmin was dressed as the Hindu princess she was.

He didn't need this. Verifying Louisa was nowhere on this floor, Zane jogged down the front stairs, attempting to fasten his cuffs.

Azmin stood at the bottom, her beautiful complexion paled to almost ghostly. "Thomson said Louisa and Gopala left almost an hour ago to fetch flowers from the park. I've sent him over to look."

Director White stood in the parlor doorway, drink in hand, looking disgruntled. "What is the meaning of this, Dare? You can't come down here in worse dishabille than your strange servants."

"My niece is ill and has gone missing." Zane wished the old goat to Hades. Impatient with White's assumptions, he gestured at Azmin. "This is Miss Dougall, my fiancée, *not* a servant."

He brushed past them both and aimed for the door. He was *not* losing Louisa on his watch.

The front door opened before White could speak through his apoplexy.

Thomson stood there, holding Gopala's limp body.

Keya keened a high note that shattered a lamp.

TWENTY-SEVEN

AZMIN UNDERSTOOD WHY OTHER WOMEN HAD HYSTERICS. IT WOULD BE SO much simpler to be Keya and melt into a weeping bundle on the floor and let everyone else handle the chaos.

Unfortunately, she was too much her father's daughter. And probably her mother's, who had recklessly fought tooth and nail to marry beneath her. But it was her father's military precision she channeled. She wouldn't call Zane on his introduction of her as his *fiancée* now.

"Lay Gopala in the parlor," she commanded. "Zane, is he alive? Can he tell us what happened?"

Zane snapped orders for his medical bag and smelling salts, so she assumed that answered both questions.

"Thomson, go back to the park, see if Louisa is hiding in the shrubbery." Azmin pointed at the open front door.

As Thomson ran out, a gangly lad she didn't know arrived, looking bewildered. From his clothes and spectacles, she gathered he was one of the students. "Come in, please. We'll do introductions later. We have a real-life situation and not a philosophical discussion tonight. If you'd gather the other students as they arrive and direct them back to the dining room, I'd appreciate it."

The student nodded speculatively, glanced at the crowd in the foyer, and wisely waited on the doorstep.

"Mr. White, you and Miss White may want to call your carriage. Dinner will be a buffet, at best, while we find out what has happened to Miss Howard." Azmin instructed the wealthy man as she had the student, thinking only of practicalities and not social niceties.

"Who the devil do you think you are telling me what to do?" the director demanded. "I'll handle this. You can go back where you belong and sort out the confounded weeping servants."

Azmin lifted her eyebrows, directed a steady gaze at the old bigot, and with the imperious authority of her ancestors, ignored his orders and brushed wordlessly past him into the parlor. White fell back in astonishment.

If she wasn't near hysteria, that would have felt good.

Zane kneeled beside the sofa, waving smelling salts under Gopala's nose. The boy sputtered and stirred. Zane slapped him lightly on the cheek. "What happened?" he demanded. "Where's Louisa?"

Keya had stopped keening and knelt beside her brother, whispering in Hindi. Azmin clutched her fingers into fists and prayed to every god she knew and a few extras.

"The man from the tavern," Gopala sputtered, struggling to sit up. "He hit me!" His eyes widened. "Miss Howard? Is she here? She was with me—"

"What man?" Zane demanded. "Describe him."

Azmin didn't need to hear Gopala's description. The only men Gopala knew from the tavern were the bullies he'd hired to attack her. And only one of those bullies had any interest in Louisa. Even as Gopala described Jenkins, her mind whirled. She pulled stationery from the writing desk and scribbled a note to Phoebe and another to her aunts.

Thomson returned to report no sign of Louisa. Zane looked as if he'd been condemned to death as he stood and headed for the door.

Gopala would recover. Louisa might not. Azmin sent Keya down to the kitchen with the notes, telling her to send Robby with the messages and to have the meal set on the table for people to grab as they could. They'd need fuel for the night ahead.

She caught up with Zane in the foyer as he tugged on his coat while White nagged at him.

"Wait," she murmured. "I've ideas. Give me time to organize."

Zane dragged his overcoat over his shirtsleeves and reached for his walking stick. Rage boiled in his eyes but he waited.

"We need a signal system. And we need people to know who we're searching for. I have photographs and negatives in my bag upstairs. Let me fetch the photographs so you can show them to everyone here and to the police." She spoke hurriedly.

Another pair of students arrived at the door. Azmin pointed down the hall. Looking confused, they passed by murderous Zane and an outraged director. The pink bonbon simply looked helpless.

Servants began arriving in the rear hall bearing hot food. More students followed their noses.

"Would someone please explain what is happening here?" White demanded. "Did that brown boy hurt Miss Howard? Are the police necessary? They're incompetent at best and scandalous at worst. Surely this can be handled in a more genteel. . ."

"I believe we asked you to leave," Azmin said coldly. "If you can't help us, then take our advice and depart."

"Who the *hell* is she to talk to me like that?" White asked in outrage.

Zane's smile was pure evil, the smile Azmin remembered from all those summers ago, the smile of a man who had reached his limits and was looking for an outlet for all that explosive energy he confined behind cravats and starched shirts.

"Did I forget the proper introductions? Do forgive me," Zane said in a voice dripping with sarcasm. "If you recall, Miss Dougall is my *fiancée*. Her father is Colonel Ronald Dougall, of the earl of Lochmas's clan. Her mother is the daughter of Maharaja Singh. . ."

"Raja," Azmin muttered, but Zane continued her parents' titles without acknowledging the correction. With snotty lack of respect, they used to make up bad poems with their families' many names and titles. She was amazed he still remembered hers.

". . .and her rank and wealth are far above mine," Zane concluded. "She's the general to your foot soldier. If you cannot tolerate Miss

Dougall's orders, then you are in the way. My niece is ill and in danger, and dissension will only make it more difficult for us to organize a search."

Keya returned to the hall. Ignoring male posturing, Azmin gestured for her. "Bring down all the photographs of Louisa and Jenkins, please. I left them on my bed. If you can get away, would you develop more? We may be running low on paper. Do you know anyone who sells them prepared? I don't need my special solution for this purpose, just as many photos of Louisa and Jenkins as we can develop. It could be a long night."

Keya nodded. "I have sent for Wilson. He can show photos to other drivers. I do not believe this Jenkins would carry Louisa through the streets without being noticed."

Remembering how Jenkins had hauled his poor wife over his shoulder, Azmin wasn't certain about that, but having cabbies look for them could only be beneficial.

White marched out in a huff. His daughter lingered, glancing back at the dining room where the students gathered.

White turned around and shouted at his daughter. Miss White looked mutinous. She headed down the corridor toward Azmin and Keya. "May I help?"

Glory hallelujah, the pink bonbon had a spine. Azmin directed her toward the dining room. "Lord Dare will need everyone's help. Explain to our guests what is happening. Some of them may know Mr. Jenkins. We have to scour the streets to see where he's gone."

When White marched back up the outside steps to fetch his daughter, Zane ordered Thomson to shut the door on him.

"Organize," Zane shouted. "And be quick about it!"

"Aye, aye, captain," Azmin murmured, taking a moment to rest her head against his shoulder as she pulled together her scattered thoughts.

He hugged her as if he needed this too.

Inhaling his distressed scent of male sweat and bay rum, she stepped away before she could consider kissing his lordship's scratchy cheek and explained her plan.

He started shouting orders at servants and students as she rolled out each idea.

She meant to create an enormous spectacle, a full-blown, flamboyant circus. Zane didn't even quiver, but catching on, began adding twists of his own.

Everyone in the entire city would be searching for Jenkins before the night was done.

~

"I LOSE ALL RESPECT FOR THE BRITISH ARMY," ZANE MUTTERED AS HE drove his carriage through the crowded streets around Phoebe's shelter.

Everywhere he looked, men marched carrying torches and pikes flying colorful silk flags. Hackneys tied the strips of silk to their horses' collars. Every single one of those people knew about his niece and where to find him if they'd seen her. Until this night, Zane had been invisible to the general populace. Given his position as a mere researcher, he'd been fine with that.

However, *Viscount Dare* was on everyone's tongues tonight—because of this insane woman at his side, clenching her hands and looking as if she'd fly apart at any moment. If making a spectacle of himself brought back Louisa and raging at university directors returned the smile to Azmin's lips, he'd become a circus clown and curmudgeon. Be damned to his pride.

Men shouted and raised their fists in salute as the carriage passed by. Azmin had tied ribbons to his horse, so Zane didn't know if they recognized him personally or just the ribbons.

"The flags work," she insisted. "People notice them. They're signals and symbols of power. An army marching with flags flying is an intimidating sight. A navy using signal flags can communicate. I can't teach all these people how to signal, but they understand that anyone bearing the flag knows Louisa's story. They know there's a reward and where to go if they have information. And if we can pass out enough photographs on the street. . ."

"Someone may have seen them, I understand. And once Jenkins realizes what those flags mean, he'll be terrified and more likely to take our bait." He drove the carriage down the alley behind Blair's workshop. "I should have joined the military instead of becoming a doctor. My knowledge of the human heart is singularly useless, and I despise being helpless."

"Your medical knowledge saved the life of Mrs. Jenkins. And it is not my gift or knowledge aiding us tonight. Anyone can take photographs. If anyone will find Louisa with *knowledge*, it will be Phoebe and her dogs. What matters is that we all bring our separate abilities together and work as one. That is the essence of an army."

"An army of urchins," he sighed, halting his horse in the alley and jumping out.

"And cabbies and students," she added, taking his hand to climb down. "And all of Phoebe's neighbors and tenants. And their families. The more people we can unite, the stronger we are."

She was still wearing her magnificent sari, although she'd covered it in the ugly redingote against the cool evening air. Zane finally had the Azmin he remembered back, but this time, she wasn't running away in his time of need. He should be content with that and not despair.

"If only we could be certain Louisa was unharmed, I'd almost feel hope. She's so very fragile." Mostly, he felt useless. He couldn't beat up a man who couldn't be found.

"That's what prayer is for." She released his hand to pick up her skirts and hurry to the Blairs' back garden gate. "I trust the coroner will not mind us using his morgue."

"I'll pay for any damage if Jenkins does show up." Zane took the key and let them in, then locked the gate behind them. "Is Keya still here?"

"I'll send her back to your house with the last of the photographs. Mr. Morgan has been with her all evening. He can escort her in your carriage. There's no sense in leaving your horse out there all night while we wait for a rat to nibble." She strode through the yard as if discussing tea at four.

The fool woman was counting on Zane and Zane alone to protect her. They were both out of their minds. But he'd gladly die saving

Louisa, so Azmin's trap gave him a purpose beyond gnashing his teeth in frustration. Desperation apparently led to madness.

He was growing fond of the idea of ending his university career in a literal blaze of glory.

Keya was putting away the last of the photographs when they arrived in the workshop. "I do not understand why you ask me to pack the chemicals in your bag. Are we moving to the studio tonight?"

Morgan held the box for the photographic papers and silently questioned them. Zane assumed his web of informers had told him about the circus roaming the streets.

"I mean to take photos of anyone seeking the reward. You need to be at the house when Louisa is found. She will need a woman's understanding." Azmin said, trying to maintain a cheerful face.

"Has anyone reported seeing them?" Morgan asked gruffly.

"We're following dozens of leads," Zane told him. "We think Jenkins may have bought train tickets. The police are canvassing the station and searching all the cars. We suspect he isn't familiar with that side of town, so he may have come back here to hole up until he thinks he's safe. They're checking rooming houses and hotels."

Zane couldn't mention his fear for Louisa. She could have died of fright. She could have been chloroformed. Jenkins was a medical student, after all, and had access to the surgeries. If she was awake. . . He couldn't let his mind dwell there.

"And no idea what he wants?" Morgan assisted Keya into her cloak.

"Not a hint. No ransom note, nothing. We can hunt him down or draw him out. And pray," he added, for Azmin's sake.

The women hugged. The instant Keya and Morgan departed, Azmin began gathering her equipment. She tucked her magnesium reflector under her arm. "And now we set the trap. You are sure he knows of the morgue?"

"The students all sneak through that tunnel at one time or another. He knows all the entrances just as I do." Zane took the heavy valise from her. "If it's money he's after, he'll show up. Word of the reward spread faster than your flags."

"What if he's already waiting for us?" she asked, locking the studio door behind them.

"Then I'll shoot him," he said blood-thirstily. "And leave him for the coroner."

"What if he doesn't bring Louisa?" she demanded.

"Then maybe I'll just wound and torture him until he talks." Zane stalked down the stairs carrying her bags. He knew he'd do no such thing but that didn't prevent him from relishing the thought.

Once on the street again, Zane stopped at Green Tavern. No drunks lingered beneath the streetlight. No merriment poured through the window. A stout policeman swung his baton outside the door. A picture of Louisa and Jenkins was plastered to the wall. Zane nodded. The policeman nodded back.

He'd have to contribute his salary to the policeman's fund.

"Jenkins really will have to be mad to believe I'm willing to meet him at the morgue," Zane muttered as they hurried down the same street they'd traversed that first night he'd run into Azmin in that grim place. Or so drug-addled he couldn't think straight, which was what Zane gambled on.

"It's the safest place I could think of to send people for the reward," Azmin said, sounding tired and uncertain. "If it is really you he wants, he has to know where to find you—and your house can't be it."

"That's presuming madmen are logical. But I have no better idea. I just don't like that you have to be there." He searched the shadows between the streetlights but saw nothing untoward. A boy ran past with one of Azmin's silks wrapped around his filthy neck. She'd sacrificed her entire wardrobe except for the gown she wore. He'd have to order a shipload just for her—provided either of them survived this night.

A gang of torch-bearing, flag-waving students marched down the middle of the street singing some battle cry. One of them had nailed Louisa's photograph to a board. Passers-by stopped to ask questions, just as they'd hoped. Now he'd have to trust the mob didn't start storming tenements and terrifying the innocent in hopes of a reward. They didn't appear that drunk yet.

The university directors were probably already calling an emergency meeting to boot him out.

Zane checked the shadows before he led Azmin down the alley to the morgue's exterior door. With luck, they'd have time to set up before his location spread. Without luck, Jenkins had already had word and was waiting for them.

Recklessly setting himself up as target for a madman almost made sense in his new unscientific universe.

TWENTY-EIGHT

Azmin set the reflector on the opposite wall from the exterior door. That gave them the full length of the morgue for safety and the interior door for escape.

Setting up her collodion bath was more complicated.

"These chemicals can be lethal. What the hell do you do with them?" Zane said grumpily as he examined her bottles.

"I create a fixing solution for my photographs. They haven't killed me yet. It's basically just salt and harmless if one doesn't eat it." Azmin looked for a place to set up the box for her chemical bath. "I shouldn't have wasted all my dry plates. The wet ones require immediate development."

"With chemicals containing *cyanide*. Cyanide may be natural, but it can be lethal." Zane produced a surgical table and set it in a dark corner for her bottles. "It's the reason we don't eat fruit pits."

"Then don't eat my potassium salt."

"Or mix it with acid," he added fatalistically. "I can't think half-blinding him with that lamp will make him talk." He began fastening the special door latch Blair had designed for this purpose.

"For all we know, Jenkins is on a train to Glasgow or York and all we'll see are frauds trying to cheat you out of a reward," she said, setting up her pans. "We have to be prepared for anything."

Louisa might be lost forever. Azmin thought that might just kill Zane. She'd watched him emerge from his stuffy professor suit tonight. He'd burned all his bridges with the university—cliché number forty by now—for a certainty. Slamming a door on a director and turning students loose to riot in the streets was not the work of a studious gentleman.

Zane had been the one to find the torches and poles and encourage marching.

"If I lose Louisa, I might as well retire to a pig farm. I'll have failed in ways I never considered," he said with unusual gloom.

She felt his desperation. Her so-called *gift* may have led to this. Had she not realized Jenkins was a bad man, had they not followed him and saved his wife. . . She would give up photography if only they could bring Louisa back.

If they didn't save Louisa, she'd become a spinster teacher rather than risk one more person. She'd been arrogant thinking she could help anyone.

She understood the depths of Zane's despair only too well.

"It's late," Zane said abruptly, cutting off her dismal thoughts. "I wish you would forget the photograph and go upstairs."

Azmin set her jaw. Argue, she could do. "No. That won't work. Anyone after the reward may be armed. You need me to snap the magnesium light to blind them. And my photographs will serve as evidence if they escape. This is my chance to be useful."

Zane was gripping his walking stick like a bludgeon. He'd probably take Jenkins' head off before he realized what he was doing. Azmin hoped to keep him focused on forcing Jenkins to tell them where Louisa was. *Then* Zane could behead him.

"Is your tripwire in position?" she asked to divert him. "That should give us adequate warning. I'm glad you remembered those sleigh bells."

"Louisa asked for them at Christmas." Zane ran his hand over his hair and grief cracked his voice.

Azmin wanted to hug him, but one thing led to another, and they didn't need to be distracted when inviting a villain to the door. Instead, she positioned herself behind a cabinet with the squeeze bulb connected to the reflector.

Dare flung himself down on the surgical table and yanked a sheet over his head. That would prevent him from being blinded by the light.

They waited for what surely must be eternity before the sleigh bell on the outer door finally tinkled.

Holding her breath, Azmin waited for the door to creak open. Counting to ten, she allowed the intruder to enter the black cellar before she squeezed the bulb. The magnesium exploded, illuminating the room in a bright blue-white light. A shadow froze in the doorway.

Azmin yanked the cord on Blair's latch. The exterior door slammed so their victim couldn't escape.

A GUNSHOT SPLINTERED THE CEILING OVER ZANE'S HEAD, SHOWERING THE sheet with debris. Still blinking and seeing stars from the flash, despite the sheet, he discarded the linen, his gun raised. He disliked pistols, but he had to protect Azmin.

Azmin lit a single oil lamp, revealing the shooter cursing and rubbing his eyes—*Jenkins*.

Louisa wasn't with him.

Zane had to resist returning fire until he knew Louisa's whereabouts. He shoved his gun in his waistband. "Where is she?" he shouted.

Jenkins spun around and raised his pistol in the direction of Zane's voice.

In fury, Zane swung his walking stick, connecting with thin shoulders. Still half-blind in the dark cellar, Jenkins didn't see the blow coming. He dropped his weapon but regained his equilibrium and came forward with fists raised.

Zane's wounded left arm had no force on its own, but the stick gave him leverage. He jabbed it under the man's chin while kicking at his groin. He'd learned to fight dirty to fend off his larger, older Ives' cousins. Besides, the stick and his feet protected the hands he needed to operate.

When his quarry bent over to shield his vulnerable organ, Zane cracked the ebony over his neck. Jenkins went down.

Without being told, Azmin lit another lamp. Unlike the intruder's, her eyes should have been protected from the flash by the cabinet she'd hid behind.

While she performed her photography magic, Zane propped his boot on a skinny neck. The student groaned and tried to squirm away. "Tell me where to find Louisa, and I won't snap your bloody spine."

"You'll kill me even if I tell you," Jenkins taunted. "You'll never find her."

Zane wanted to grind his boot and break the bastard's neck after this confession, but just imagining the damage he could do to all those small bones stifled his murderous rage.

"Oh, we already know where she is," Azmin said unexpectedly. She'd set aside her camera to hand Zane the rope they'd brought for this purpose. "We just thought we'd allow you to do the honorable thing. You should probably hang him with this, Lord Dare. You have a fine hand with a knot."

"*Lord Dare*," Jenkins spat in disgust. "You'll be even worse at the title than your father. You don't care anything about the estate or anyone on it! I bet you don't even care enough about your niece to bring the reward. You should have died last night!"

Well, there was the answer to that question, although the *why* still hung in the air. What did Jenkins care about an earl's legacy?

Zane had a vague recollection of the solicitors mentioning aging widows living on the estate, but he was certain his father wouldn't evict them.

Setting aside his walking stick, Zane handed Azmin his gun and kneeled to tie his prisoner's wrists. "And exactly what good would killing me have done and why should you care?"

This was about his wretched title? He'd have given it away if he'd had a choice.

Jenkins struggled. Azmin shot a hole in the dirt floor near Jenkins' ear. Dirt and stone splattered, bloodying the student's cheek. Zane knotted the rope tighter than he'd originally intended, resisting the need to grind Jenkins' face into the floor. He threw Azmin a disgruntled look. "I hope you know how to load that thing."

"I checked. It has another shot," she said grimly, holding it pointed. "I can put a bullet through the top of his head if you don't mind brain splatter."

"Brain splatter is good." Zane yanked Jenkins up by the rope and flung him against the door. "Tell me Louisa is fine, and I won't let my bloodthirsty companion blow out your brains."

"She's fine," Jenkins yelled, his pallid face infused with fury. "I wouldn't harm my future wife!"

"Oh, dear." Azmin looked at the pistol with regret. "Do you have ammunition on you? I really want to shoot his foot."

Zane almost chortled. No other woman in the world would react with such composure in the face of insanity. "In my overcoat pocket. The gun holds six rounds if you wish to make him dance."

Jenkins gaped at them both. At least the clodpoll wasn't entirely lost to reason. If he'd indulged in drugs or alcohol to build his courage to come here, they should be wearing off soon, but Zane wasn't counting on it. Even though Jenkins' hands were tied, Zane held him against the door with the knob of his walking stick while Azmin intimidated the coward by filling the gun like an expert.

"You were saying?" Zane asked, returning to his prisoner. "And mind you, we've met your *wife*."

Jenkins attempted a sneer, although the dirt specking his face diluted the effect. "She's just a handfast. No English court will accept it, especially once you're dead, and I prove I'm the next heir. Your family will happily accept a viscount as husband for their sickly invalid. You won't find her, and I'll kill you if you try."

"Delusional," Azmin said abstractedly as she finished loading the gun. "Remind him we already know where Louisa is. I don't understand why you simply don't hang him so I can develop my photograph."

She lied so very well. Zane had to wonder how many other lies she'd told and why, but unfortunately, he understood the necessity. "First, I'd like to understand why in blazing hell he thinks he's the heir? I'd hand him the title, if I could, but my father has been heir since the beginning of time. And there's no question that I'm his son and this termite isn't."

"I never saw your father lose his temper the way you do," Azmin said thoughtfully, raising the pistol to aim at Jenkins' heart. "Although that's scarcely proof that you're not his son. I suppose you both have the same scientific mind."

Jenkins tried to twitch away, but Zane wasn't done with him. He jammed his stick more forcefully against a skinny chest. "Enough. How did you intend to convince the world that you're heir to an earldom when you have scoundrel written on every thick hair on your face?"

Jenkins spat at Zane's boots. "Because with you out of the way, I *am* heir. While you and your father pretended the old man and the estate didn't exist, my mother found a way to ensure our future. We just kept hoping you or your father would die before the earl."

Even Azmin shut up and waited with interest for that explanation.

When neither of them spoke, Jenkins continued defiantly. "My grandmother is the earl's sister. Didn't know you had a great-great aunt, did you? She had the old earl sign a codicil to the title. His solicitors presented it to parliament. It allows the title to pass through a maternal line if no direct male heir can be found."

"Oh, charming," Azmin said. "See, my lord, if you died, you wouldn't have to inherit after all."

Her byzantine comment served to puzzle addled Jenkins enough to make Zane smile. "Not a laughing matter," Zane told her, wincing as he recalled the solicitor's letter mentioning the codicil. Jenkins could be a distant cousin. The thought appalled. "I'm not dying for anyone's convenience, but if anything has happened to Louisa, my one and only heir will hang. What a blot on the family escutcheon that will be."

The thought that this turnip might be his *heir* turned Zane's stomach. He'd definitely tarried too long in finding a wife.

"I told you, she's fine," Jenkins spat out. "She thinks I've rescued her from kidnappers."

Zane suffered a frisson of alarm as Azmin closed in, murderous intent on her usually serene visage. Not knowing what conclusion she'd drawn from Jenkins' declaration, he waited. Maybe Jenkins would believe they knew where Louisa was and reveal her location if they kept him talking.

"You knocked Gopala over the head and told her he was a *kidnapper?*" Azmin asked in a deceptively pleasant voice.

Ah, Zane understood her ire. Of course, the man with the brown skin would be labeled a villain.

"He hired me to kidnap his sister. It wasn't a difficult leap." Jenkins shrugged. "She trusts a gentleman like me, not a filthy lackey."

A lackey. Before Azmin could shoot off Jenkins' face, Zane rammed the knob of his stick up under the imbecile's chin again. Jenkins quivered and shrank back. The alcohol bravado wearing off?

Amazingly, Azmin's fury faded to a hint of amusement. "I like to believe it's justice when a bigot's prejudice works against him. As long as she doesn't exert herself, Louisa probably *is* fine. You didn't bind her, did you?"

"Of course not," Jenkins said, indignant. "I put her in a carriage and took her to a nice hotel. I have tickets to York. We'll be married right and proper with my family as witness."

Zane couldn't let himself believe Louisa was fine. She was too delicate, too sheltered, she'd be paralyzed with fright. Azmin apparently had other ideas.

"The poor delusional idiot thinks Louisa went with him willingly," she explained. "But Louisa knows he beat his wife almost to death. She knows Gopala is Keya's brother and not a kidnapper. And she's been warned all her life not to overexert herself. So she wisely didn't attempt to run. Your niece is smart. She simply placated this imbecile and waited for him to leave. The hotel will have already found her a carriage, and if Wilson has done his job, she's on her way home in a glorious parade of hackneys. Can we kill him now or must we wait for authorities?"

"Noooo, you're wrong!" In a fit of fury, Jenkins twisted away from the walking stick and slammed his shoulder into Zane.

Zane kicked the bastard's knee out from under him.

Jenkins stumbled over the developing table—overturning the container of acid. Azmin grabbed at it to prevent it from spilling. Too late, the acid splashed onto the salt—and cyanide gas hissed.

Hit directly by the fumes, Azmin swayed, dropping the gun.

Zane caught her. To his horror, she collapsed as a dead weight in his arms. Coughing on the gas, terrified Azmin would stop breathing, Zane used his boot to roll Jenkins through the closest door, then kicked it shut. Leaving the bastard to run on his own two feet, Zane carried Azmin through the dark tunnel leading to the school.

Let the bastard escape. Azmin was more important than killing a cretin.

TWENTY-NINE

"She's been exposed to the chemicals too often," a male voice expostulated over Azmin's head. "Females are weak and cannot tolerate the harsher elements as men can. They shouldn't be allowed to dabble in chemicals."

A strong stench of astringent, vinegar, and carbolic almost choked her raw nostrils. She shifted uncomfortably on a hard mattress, wanting to protest that *women* had no doubt used those harsh chemicals to clean wherever she was.

"The damned man *died* without attempting to save himself. Miss Dougall is still alive. Which one is the weaker?" A familiar angry voice shouted what her throat hurt too much to say.

Azmin would have smiled in recognition of this outrage, except what he said was troubling. She had to gather her wits. Was she in the hospital? It certainly didn't smell of home.

"Opium smokers have weak minds and lungs," the unfamiliar voice argued. "He passed out instead of escaping. The lady was fortunate you were there to help her."

"I don't call being poisoned *fortunate*," Zane roared. "Can't you wake her? Will she recover?"

"Louisa?" Azmin rasped anxiously.

Deathly silence. A moment later, strong arms hauled her up to almost sitting, and she was embraced by the familiar awareness of a furious Dr. Dare—because this was Zane at his officious best. She was weak, she told herself. It was all right to succumb to this welcome embrace while she was weak. Once she had her strength back, she'd shove him away, as she must.

"Louisa is fine. She did just as you said, and she's home sound asleep," Zane said soothingly, as if singing a lullaby.

"Lungs," Azmin rasped, remembering the discovery she needed to tell Zane.

"Yes, the gas affected your lungs. You just need fresh air. I've ordered them to open the windows but the dolts fear nocturnal miasmas."

"*Louisa's* lungs," she corrected, although her voice sounded hoarse. "Photographs—the ones I took and developed."

"The patient is hysterical," the unfamiliar voice said. "We'll give her some laudanum, let her rest."

"Tell whoever that is to shut up and go away," she grumbled irritably.

"Shut up and go away, doctor," Zane repeated with more authority. "Miss Dougall doesn't possess an hysterical bone in her body."

"Make a joke about my lacking a humerus bone, and I'll bite you," she murmured, snuggling against his strong chest, which smelled distinctly of more chemicals.

"Princess Azmin is back," Zane said with a laugh, kissing her hair. "You terrified us."

She liked this far too much. She struggled to sit up. He wouldn't release her. Fine then, she was still weak. She snuggled closer again. "I need my original photograph of Louisa. I still don't know if I need to develop it myself..."

"Shhhhh. You've burned your throat. Give it a rest. Keya is out there. And half the city, or maybe just your family, is roaming the halls. They'll find the photograph."

She could feel him turn slightly and order the other doctor around. Dr. Lord Dare was becoming a little too confident in this commanding authority business. He'd be a good viscount. But probably a lousy husband, she told herself, drifting off on the clouds of whatever they'd given her now that she knew Louisa was safe.

ZANE REFUSED TO LEAVE AZMIN'S BEDSIDE. HE GROWLED AT PHOEBE AND her aunts, ordered Keya to go home, and slept with his feet on the cot so he'd know the instant his patient stirred. He knew Azmin's habits. She'd flee to the far ends of the earth if he let her out of his sight.

His medical degree allowed him to get away with this behavior. She was *his* patient now. Maybe he hadn't completely wasted his youth by becoming a physician.

He'd already told the police what happened. The coroner confirmed his testimony. Louisa had given witness of her ordeal. The rest of the night evaporated like an opium smoker's dream.

By the time Keya returned in the morning with fresh clothing, Zane thought he had himself in control. His university position was gone of a certainty. He'd have to move out of his monstrous large house. Saving Louisa was more important than the university and a house. He could take up a position at the hospital, he supposed. The pig farm still loomed.

Azmin was the big question mark left unresolved.

She blinked at him in surprise when she woke, but Keya threw him out. Zane leaned against the wall outside her cubicle. If he had to tie her up and carry her, Azmin was going home with him.

She emerged wearing a plain gray gown that made her look as if she were in mourning. He should have torn up *those* abominations for flags instead of her colorful silks. He pushed himself off the wall and offered his arm.

"Have you seen the photograph?" was the first thing she asked of him.

Zane tilted his head and considered all the better subjects they could discuss, but she was walking beside him without argument, so he refrained. "I haven't been home yet. The prints I saw were lovely. Louisa probably has offers of marriage piling up at the door."

Keya snorted but wisely didn't comment.

"You haven't been home? It's not as if I was dying, my lord. You could have just left Keya here if you worried about hospital care." She sounded indignant. Her back was stiff and straight, and she strode like a woman with a purpose.

So much for pampering the invalid. "And give you time to abscond so I have to chase you to the ends of the earth? It's beneath my dignity. This is simpler."

The carriage was waiting at the door as he'd requested. He lifted her into it before she could protest. Keya climbed in on her own. Zane went around to the other side and blocked Azmin from escape by sitting beside her.

She narrowed her eyes at him and clasped her hands in her lap. "I am not going anywhere until I show you Louisa's photo. Then I shall pack my bags and go home. The teachers in my house will simply have to return to the school—unless you wish to let them use your home. That would be an exceedingly thoughtful thing to do, but you are under no obligation to have your life disrupted because of a few women you don't know."

"My life disrupted?" Zane asked rhetorically, sprawling his legs across the limited carriage space as the horse turned toward his home. "Heaven forefend that we should *disrupt* my life. Oh, and in case the gas has erased your memory, my father wired to say my parents are sailing today. They'll be back by summer. I'm sure that won't be a *disruption* either."

"There are journalists watching the house," Keya said quietly. "You might want to take the alley. Louisa has been feeding them."

Zane laughed. He couldn't help it. "Pet journalists?"

Azmin grinned, just a little. "Shall we call Phoebe once they're trained to the leash?"

Even Keya smiled as Zane directed the driver to take the mews and run over anyone who got in the way.

He was a viscount with journalists on his doorstep and a pig farm in his future and no surety that he could keep the woman he wanted more than gold. Laughing seemed the only possible response because grown men didn't weep.

Once inside, Azmin discarded her cloak and gloves and strode straight for the sound of voices, without his aid. Zane shoved his hands in his pockets and followed after her. What else did he have to do? Dean Reynolds could hunt him down if he wished to shout about his behavior.

With a knowing look, Keya abandoned them at the stairway and escaped upstairs, presumably to pack their bags. Zane was having none of that. He had a word with Thomson.

Then he leaned against the door jamb as Louisa and Azmin hugged in the formal parlor. He should send Louisa back to his parents when they returned. He wasn't doing her any good. Her ordeal had brought roses to his niece's cheeks, but that was probably more a result of the flowers decorating every shelf and the gentlemen she entertained under the watchful eye of—who the hell was that?

Azmin hugged the stranger too. "Eleanor! I'm so glad you're still here. Zane, have you met Mrs. Stewart? Only we're calling her Mrs. Smith these days. Oops, sorry. Eleanor, this is Lord Dare, our host. Eleanor organized our dinner last night."

"Such as it was," the wisp of a woman said shyly. "You didn't have to worry after all. Your servants are all good people."

Zane searched his memory banks and concluded this was the abused spouse Azmin had rescued and deposited in his kitchen. He'd need to keep the house if she insisted on saving every stray she photographed. "Pleased to make your acquaintance, Mrs. Stewart-Smith. I thank you for stepping into the breach, as it were."

She curtseyed. "I promised your maid that I'd show her how to make *blancmange*. If you'll excuse me?"

Zane stepped aside so she could pass, then narrowed his eyes at the students littering his sofa. They hastily rose, made their excuses, and escaped. He smiled in satisfaction as the room cleared of all but the women in his life.

"I saved the original photograph as you asked," Louisa said, handing the print to Azmin. "It's so beautiful. I'm amazed anyone recognized me last night, but I'm grateful they did."

Azmin held the print up to the light, driving Zane mad with curiosity. But he wasn't leaving his position guarding the doorway.

"You look just like this," Azmin admonished. "Of course they recognized you. I hope you didn't exert yourself too much in making your escape."

Louisa giggled, then returned to solemnity. "I am sorry to hear that Mr. Jenkins died before he could learn the error of his ways. He really was most polite. But why on earth would he think I'd believe him? I simply waited until he left and called for help. The maid unlocked the door, and the hackney driver recognized me. I didn't have to lift a finger."

She turned to Zane. "Was Mr. Jenkins your heir?"

Damn. He shrugged uncomfortably inside his dirty waistcoat. No one had thought to bring *him* clean clothes. "He was delusional, but there may have been truth behind the delusion. If the title is allowed a matrilineal line, providing an heir will be one less obligation I must fulfill immediately. But I never knew Jenkins as other than a student. The earl never offered our branch of the family invitations to meet his immediate family. I'll have the solicitors investigate and draw up a family tree."

"We should visit his wife," Azmin said. "And perhaps help with the funeral expenses."

"He tried to *kill* me," Zane growled. "And he could have frightened Louisa to death and killed *you* in his addict's insanity. Just because we lived and he didn't doesn't mean I'll forgive the termite."

Azmin frowned, and Zane sighed. If he didn't want his hands on that damned photograph she held, he'd drag her into his study and fight this out right now. Thomson should have had time to fill his request.

"Fine then, we'll visit Mrs. Jenkins and pay expenses. If he was some kind of heir to the estate, perhaps there is an allowance that should go to her. Now, what was it that you wanted to show me that you almost wore your throat out ordering me about?" Zane waited expectantly.

Azmin finally relented and brought the portrait to him. "Tell me what you see."

He was expecting black shadows or unearthly wisps of light. He saw only Louisa, looking beautiful and healthy and smiling as if the whole world was hers for the asking. Louisa was right. The photograph showed her as far healthier than she was.

A prediction, like one of the family's fortune-telling paintings?

"I've not had time to touch up the negatives as I intended, although really, she looks so lovely this way, she doesn't need paint. But don't you see it?" Azmin clasped her hands nervously.

This wasn't a jest. She saw something here that he. . . Zane frowned and traced a small white spot under Louisa's breast. "The chemicals weren't distributed evenly?"

"I'll have to take another photograph to be certain," she said uncertainly. "But I don't think it's a flaw in the process. I *feel*. . ." She hesitated then added hurriedly, "I feel as if that might be an infection, like we saw in those men. I'm not a physician. I don't know what is there—"

Zane gripped the photograph harder. "It's the wrong side for her heart. We don't know if the white shows only the front or reflects the back as well. You'll need to take a photograph of her back. It could be lungs, liver, gall bladder. . ."

Lungs. An infection of the lungs, like consumption or pneumonia. The symptoms were similar to those Louisa suffered, if the disease had only just started. Maybe she had been recovering until she caught this new infection. If they'd recognized it early. . .

Zane stifled the urge to shout in excitement and demand Louisa submit to an examination—and more photographs.

His mother had cured his father of just such an infection. She had healing skills medical science didn't.

"We don't know that it means anything," he concluded stiffly. "But it's possible an infectious disease could cause her to run fevers and tire easily. We would not be able to differentiate from her earlier weakness. If it can be cured. . ."

"I might be well again?" Louisa asked quietly, hopefully.

"No promises," he said, causing her lips to turn down. "But your grandmother's healing skills have cured lung infections, although even she cannot heal scars. Still, if you are healthy, the muscles in your heart may eventually grow stronger. It's something we can look at."

Tears rolled down Azmin's cheeks as she took the photograph from him. "I would so much like my gift to bring hope instead of pain. I don't dare expect it."

"You have given Mrs. Stewart hope," Zane reminded her. "And Mrs. Jenkins. They have second chances, if they take what you have given them. And look at Keya. She is flourishing. Morgan said he's found solicitors who are verifying her husband's death as we speak."

And because Azmin's tears caused him to come undone, Zane relinquished his patience and dragged his princess out of the parlor and across the hall, into his study, where they could settle matters between them once and for all.

He noted with satisfaction that Thomson had carried his message about the eggs to the kitchen.

The basket sat on the corner of his desk.

THIRTY

STUDYING LOUISA'S PHOTOGRAPH THROUGH TEAR-BLURRED EYES, AZMIN didn't resist Zane's tug. She felt like the mushy confection she'd labeled Miss White. Could her photographs predict abuse and illness? And possibly malevolence. It didn't seem credible, but she so wanted to be useful. . .

"Miss Dougall, I believe I have suggested this before, but I've been remiss in not asking properly." Zane intruded on her reverie as he closed the study door behind them.

Her pulse beat a little harder at the seriousness of his tone. She set the photograph aside, clasped her hands, and tried to spool back his exact words, but he apparently didn't expect an answer and continued speaking.

"I think we know each other well enough to know we'll suit. We work together well. I daresay I've lost my university position, but I have an income, and we won't starve. If you'll give me permission, I'll write to your father and formally ask for your hand. Or perhaps now that we know the telegraph to India works, we could wire him. I'd like to settle matters between us quickly."

Azmin stared at Zane in disbelief. He was leaning against his desk, garbed in yesterday's dusty, wrinkled shirt and waistcoat, his jaw unshaven and black with whiskers—while sounding like a stodgy professor. What was *wrong* with him?

"Is that a formal proposal?" she asked quizzically. "Or a sermon?"

"A proposal," he said stiffly. "I've tried not frightening you off by asking too soon, but after last night—" He took a deep breath. "I don't want to lose you. I will try my damn. . . my best to give you everything you need and make you happy."

"I've explained why we can't marry," she said, still puzzled, although her reckless heart insisted on racing in excitement. "You have lost your position because of me. Any moment now, you'll have an angry husband pounding on the door. Once I open my studio, there will be more. Should you ever become earl, parliament will most likely ostracize you once they realize I'm foreign. You'll never accomplish anything without a wife who can handle. . ."

An egg flew at her from out of nowhere. Astonished, Azmin caught it. She had excellent reflexes, although she lacked understanding of what had just happened.

"Let's not worry about parliament when *you're* the bigot!" Zane shouted—inexplicably. "You don't like men with whiskers. You won't marry a *respectable* man. You know perfectly well I don't care if you paint yourself blue and wear circus costumes, just as long as I know you'll not leave me. It's not me, but *you* who calls yourself unsuitable. And for the life of me, I cannot understand why!"

She didn't mind *his* beard, she wanted to tell him. In fact, there was something amazingly appealing about his day-old scruff, but admitting that wouldn't aid her cause. Irritably, she flung the egg back at him. He caught it and tossed it dangerously in his palm. Why did he have a basket of eggs on his desk? But she reacted to his words and not eggs.

"I can't be a viscount's wife," she tried to explain rationally. "I can't be the little woman who sits home planning dinners while you bury your-self in research. I know my photography may not seem much to you, but it's the only gift I have, and I need to explore it. And sometimes that means I'll smuggle women into the house or not be home for dinner or I'll call the police and have my name in the papers, and it will reflect on you."

He flung the egg again. Azmin caught it. The shell cracked—*boiled*. The kitchen kept boiled eggs on hand—although maybe not quite so many as in that basket. She refrained from flinging this one.

Zane reached in the basket for another. "After last night, you still think I'm a stodgy professor? *You're* the stiff neck who believes a blamed *title* disqualifies me as your husband. You're the chauvinist who thinks wives only sit at home knitting! Are you afraid a professor will ruin your artistic reputation? Or maybe—just maybe—you don't want someone who tells you when you're frigging wrong!"

Azmin flung the egg back, this time with force and direction. It should have cracked on his fat head, but he caught it as deftly as she had. "I'm protecting *you*, you. . . cretin! You could be the Count of Monte Cristo for all I care. The King of Siam! But you're a medical professor who wants to do research. You need a university and a laboratory and the intellectual stimulation of your colleagues. The Mr. Whites and Dean Reynolds of your world will not allow that if I'm your. . . *frigging*. . . wife!"

Zane shrugged off his overcoat and wound his arm in circles, loosening up his damaged muscle. Azmin couldn't help gaping—just a little —at the sight of his shoulders straining at his wrinkled linen, and the taut slim waist emphasized by his maroon waistcoat. She truly loved that particular garment.

While she was distracted, Zane flung two eggs at her. One hit her shoulder and cracked. She caught the other and flung it waspishly. Unfortunately, Thomson had mixed fresh eggs with the boiled. The flung one smashed nicely on Dr. Lord Dare's middle—ruining the pretty waistcoat.

Preparing his next volley, he didn't even notice. "I don't need a university to build a lab. My *colleagues* are scattered around the world and care nothing of your existence. What I *need* is a woman who shouts back, a woman who throws eggs when I deserve it. I don't want treacle bonbons who would melt if I kept formaldehyde hearts in my bag! And I damned well don't need a woman to *protect* me!" He flung another egg.

This one connected, leaving a streak of yolk down her bosom. Azmin snatched up the overcoat he'd discarded and dragged it on backward over her front so he'd only egg himself. It smelled deliciously of Zane and bay rum. If he had some idiot notion that she'd strip off her clothes as she had in her youth, he was seriously mistaken.

"I cannot be less than I am," she asserted. "If I see something that must be done, no matter how reckless, I will do it! I won't change. I can't stop helping people who can't help themselves, even if that means I must sometimes act hastily, without thinking." She caught the egg he flung this time. "You're the one who wastes time pondering every single possibility."

Zane started to grin, making her insides feel funny and liquid, like the egg.

"Then marry me without thinking, save me from a life of stodginess!"

Azmin reeled at this outrageous declaration.

A knock rapped at the door. It opened before either of them could respond.

The epitome of boring, respectable academia stood in the entrance, adjusting his spectacles in bewilderment at their disarray. Azmin considered flinging an egg but refrained for once in her life.

ZANE REACHED FOR ANOTHER EGG AND OFFERED FAIR WARNING. "CATCH!" He threw the egg at the dean. There was something refreshing about immaturity.

Reynolds caught it.

Fair enough. Zane crossed his arms and leaned against the desk, prepared to listen to his chewing out. He'd earned it after all. "Azmin, you remember Dean Reynolds. He reports to the directors. If you'll recall, sir, my fiancée, Miss Dougall."

He waited in satisfaction as the old bigot swallowed that bit of news and examined Azmin garbed in a ridiculous apron of an overcoat. Zane thought she looked gorgeous with her cheeks pink, her gorgeous sable hair coming undone, and her eyes sparkling like sapphires. He damned well didn't care what bigots thought.

"I believe we've met," Reynolds said stiffly, apparently recognizing her name. "I need a word with you, Dare, if you have a minute."

"Can it wait? As you can see, my fiancée and I are having a slight disagreement, and I don't like to lose my momentum when I'm winning."

He'd lost track of the eggs. One flew straight at his head. Zane ducked and let it crack against his desk chair. His beloved had a strong arm and wisely held her tongue at his crass lies.

Reynolds tugged at his cravat. "There are reporters outside."

Even Azmin turned to study the dean with interest.

"Louisa is feeding them," Zane offered, a grin tugging at his mouth. It felt damned good to be free of restrictions at last.

"I thought we could give them an announcement, something more appropriate than this." Reynolds threw a folded newspaper on the desk.

Zane examined the front page. "Nice photograph of Louisa. You do good work, Az."

Out of eggs, she flung a lump of coal from the bucket at him. He dodged and scanned the article. "I'm no journalist, but I understand they enjoy sensationalism. I think they've achieved the right note. It only lacks white knights on gallant steeds." He tossed the paper to Azmin to admire and to give her hands better things to do than fling coal.

"Yes, well, sensationalism is effective," Reynolds said with a harrumph. "I've had telegrams from Lochmas, half our alumni, and any director not currently in town."

Azmin chuckled as she read the column. "Apparently, you have single-handedly executed a villain, saved a maiden in distress, and rescued me with your medical expertise and knowledge of explosive chemicals. I only rate a line about being a well-known female photographer. I think I'll help Louisa feed the journalists. You're more notorious than I'll ever be."

She started to rise, but Zane pointed her down. "Stay. We're not done here."

She stuck her tongue out but didn't grab an egg.

"And does Lochmas, et al, want my head on a pike?" Zane asked, his tone silky. He was still primed for battle.

Reynolds looked uncomfortable as he gently set his egg in the basket. "Lochmas demands your presence, along with his great-nephew's daughter." He bowed in Azmin's direction.

"I'm not leaving Louisa alone while we travel across half Scotland so he can complain," Zane responded mulishly.

"He's old," Azmin reminded him. "If he's inviting me, I can go for you, although I'm sure you're the one he wants to shout at."

"He doesn't want to shout," Reynolds said with a heavy sigh. "He believes in Sir Walter Scott's tales of heraldry and heroism. He wants to raise funds for a research facility—" Here he hesitated and gave an even larger sigh.

Zane prepared himself. Here it came. Lochmas would fund the facility if Zane got pitched out. He'd been expecting the last part anyway.

Reynolds worked his hat brim with both hands and unclenched his teeth. "He wants you, Dare, to direct it."

Momentarily panicked at this unexpected turn, Zane glanced at Azmin. She grinned and reached for the egg basket. Zane swiped it and put it out of her reach. Did that mean she'd run if he accepted?

All this time the featherbrain had been protecting *him*, his career, his position—from *her* behavior. Or existence. He was a little unclear on that. Surely that meant she liked him just a little. Only it was *his* behavior that had brought Lochmas down on them. . .

He didn't want to lose Azmin because she had some crackbrain notion that she was holding him back because the university was riddled with bigots. Ergo, either the university or the bigots had to go if he meant to keep her.

What was the quote about beginning as you meant to go on?

"I can't accept," Zane said flatly, not regretting the decision in the least if it meant he had his mad princess to keep his life interesting. "I would need to have the power to hire and sack. I would need a director's seat so I could oversee the funds and ascertain that such a facility would meet the donors' high standards. And I fully understand that's not possible under the current administration."

Reynolds tugged at his hat brim some more. "White resigned in a pique of temper when I told him I was accepting the earl's offer and giving you the position. Lochmas is not as wealthy as White, but the earl wields considerable influence with men who have wealth. The directors will accept you." He glanced at Azmin. "And your fiancée."

Azmin chortled. "*Malcolms.* The earl's wife, her sisters, and daughters and probably granddaughters are all married to men of position and wealth. I do believe at this point, every peer in the kingdom is married to a Malcolm. Every intelligent one," she amended.

"I am not acquainted with most of the peerage," Reynolds admitted grudgingly. "I believe a man should be respected for his contributions to society." He hesitated, then added, "Lochmas has contributed generously of his time and knowledge and continues to do so even after his retirement. I must respect his opinion. Will you take on the task, Dare, if I give you what you ask?"

Zane began juggling eggs. "Respectfully, sir, that will depend on my discussion with Miss Dougall. I will talk to you later this day, after I've had time to clean up."

Glancing at his egged dishabille, the dean nodded. "That's all I ask. Good day to you and to your lovely fiancée." He bowed to Azmin and departed, closing the door after him.

Zane flung his eggs at the coat she was wearing. "Now, where were we?" he asked as a yolk ruined the fabric.

THIRTY-ONE

"You were considering undertaking a monumental task and calling me a bigot," Azmin said pertly, rising from her chair and flinging the egged coat back at him.

"Ah yes, a monumental task that will keep me in Edinburgh and justify not being reduced to pig farmer." Zane flung the coat over his chair. "A home a certain pig-headed bigot might appreciate if we marry. I believe I was challenging you to take a chance on me."

Heart pounding, Azmin began unfastening her egg-soaked bodice. "Responsibility limits risk-taking," she informed him with hauteur. "Marriage means being tied to one man, to his fortunes, his work, and his children. That is a risk so enormous that even I won't consider it unless assured of suitable recompense. So far, I've heard nothing to give me that assurance." She opened the bodice and untied her skirt, wriggling out of the ugly gray to reveal the delicate silk beneath.

Zane grinned and started on the buttons of his waistcoat. "Actions speak louder than words. Men speak promises all the time. I'm willing to *show* you my sincerity when I say I love you to the point of utter madness."

He *loved* her? That was the first she'd heard of it.

With more confidence, she laughed and dropped her petticoat. "As if last night didn't prove you are utterly mad without my aid. I am to assume that proves your love?"

Zane cast aside his waistcoat, revealing a half-unbuttoned wrinkled shirt, which he yanked open. Azmin stopped what she was doing to admire the muscled flesh revealed. The bandage on his shoulder was starting to come undone. He hadn't taken time to tend himself while watching over her. Her middle melted a little more. Lord Alexander Dare was a very focused gentleman.

And that intensity was completely on her. The heat of his gaze sizzled her skin.

"I have loved you since you first egged me years ago," he declared, catching her waist and dragging her into his arms. "I love your ability to be yourself, to defy society, and go your own way."

"To challenge you and tell you when you're being a stiff-necked prig?" she suggested.

"Your defiance is far more interesting than simpering sheep who agree to anything I say, but I can see where your audacity might be a hindrance for you in finding another man in a world that prefers simpering sheep." He began unlacing her corset. "Admit that you need me to keep you from becoming a bitter spinster who despises men and society and turns her back on those who love her, despite your prickliness."

"That sounds like fun," she said, laughing at his cajoling tone. "The bitter spinster and the dull curmudgeon walking into the sunset together." Azmin attempted the fastenings of Zane's trousers, but the bulge beneath the fabric made it difficult. "I fear if I tell you that I love you, that I have always loved you, it will swell your head as much as your masculinity, and you will be even more impossible."

He roared in laughter, and she joined in, simply because she so loved hearing him laugh again.

Apparently, so did all the household. Someone knocked. Voices whispered outside the door. Zane shouted at them to go away.

She rubbed his bulging placket suggestively and kissed his bristled jaw. "And we're not doing this again until you've telegraphed my father with *my* demands for my dowry."

She grabbed an egg, crushed it against his bare chest, and yanking on his coat, ran for the door.

Laughing uncontrollably, Dare threw her over his shoulder before she could turn the latch.

Not caring that the entire household watched in amazement, he carried her up the stairs and completely ruined her reputation forever and all time.

EPILOGUE

"Is your pig farm near the sea?" Azmin asked, leaning out the carriage window as it rolled down a perfectly civilized macadam road. "I smell salt air."

She looked too luscious to ignore any longer. Giving up on reading the presentations various architects had made for the new research facility, Zane glanced out the window. "I was here only once, during a great fog. I doubt I saw more than the roadside. Does the sea make a difference?"

She cast him an incredulous glance, then grinned. "City boy. Now put that medical degree to work and think about Louisa for just a moment."

Zane took that moment to appreciate that his bride was even more beautiful than the day they'd exchanged vows to love, honor, and take each other in equality. That day, she'd worn a silver-blue sari to match her eyes—a garment which peeled off to reveal next to nothing when he'd taken her to bed. Today, she wore the new pelisse he'd given her, in the same silver-blue. He'd ordered it lined with soft shearling so she could wear her flimsy silks anytime she liked. Today, though, she'd worn a long-sleeved gown of russet and gold, adorned with sufficient flounces to be declared fashionable enough for a viscountess—and colorful enough to be all Azmin.

Zane dragged his thoughts away from peeling off those flounces and back to his niece. "Rural air and sunshine are always better for any form of lung infection than city air," he acknowledged. "We lack the ability to tell if an infection is pneumococcal or tubercular, but either way, clean air, fresh food, and healthy exercise will alleviate the symptoms and slow the infection. Once my mother arrives, she'll be able to use her healing talent to cure whatever it is your photograph shows us. Louisa's prognosis is far better than it was. I fail to see how sea air factors in."

"Salt," she reminded him. "Salt is a strong element that can scrub her lungs or that of anyone else suffering from lung infection. I hope this estate isn't crumbling to the ground. I have so many ideas. . ."

Zane laughed and tugged her into his arms. "I believe you'll send ideas from heaven long after you're gone."

"I love hearing you laugh again." She snuggled against his chest and her hat feathers brushed his chin. "Even if the building is falling apart, it will be a safe place for Mrs. Jenkins and Mrs. Stewart and any other women who need to hide and regroup."

Both women were traveling more slowly behind them, accompanying Louisa, who insisted on seeing an earl's estate.

"My father will particularly appreciate a sanatorium for Louisa and others like her," Zane said with relish, knowing his father would now have to take up the responsibility he shirked. "He might even condescend to visit his own estate, since he lives considerably closer than we do."

"And your mother won't be able to stay away if there is healing to be done. And you called it a *pig farm*," she said in amusement. "I almost told the aunts that they might consider it for their school." She frowned a bit in worry. "They're afraid if Max doesn't return, his cousin will declare him dead and cut off their allowances."

"Don't you have a 'finder' relation out searching for him?" Zane knew he'd embroiled himself even deeper in the Malcolm family weirdness with his marriage, but every positive had a negative side.

"Not yet. It's an expensive search, and the aunts aren't wealthy. For now, we're relying on a network of friends and relations. Now that Keya's inheritance is confirmed, she's helping a bit, along with Mr. Morgan. But she wants to invest her funds for her family."

"Not the second wife, I trust, not after your father verified she was related to Ulf," Zane said warily. Mail and telegrams had been flying fast and furious these last weeks, and he never knew when the women would strike him with some new revelation.

"Keya's family has been informed that no funds are to go to her," she said loftily. "They are currently handling the estate per her instructions."

"We'll see how long that lasts. I think Morgan has bought Keya a ring, but he's too terrified to ask." Zane chortled.

Azmin swelled with hope that Keya might someday share the joy of a good man's love as she did. Still, she punched Zane's arm at his unromantic attitude and sat up again to watch out the window. "It's such a glorious day! Look at those trees blossoming."

"An orchard of some sort, I surmise." Zane studied the landscape they passed. "It looks well-tended."

The carriage horses trotted around a curve and the house came into view.

Both of them had lived in larger mansions, but Edmond House extended impressively along a hilltop, with two large wings off a tall central edifice. As the carriage rolled up the drive, servants poured through the front door and formed a double line down the stairs.

"I think that answers a few questions," Azmin said dryly. "You need only sign checks to pay the staff, and they'll manage from there."

"I've been corresponding with the estate steward. He takes care of pay and rents and has for years. The solicitors audit his accounts. All seems well. Whether they'll accept our plans is another story entirely. We'll need nurses for a sanatorium. Teachers if you mean to bring in abused women of every class. Instead of housing earls and countesses, we'll be housing commoners. The servants may rebel. Bigotry isn't limited to the upper classes, you know." Zane almost bit off his tongue when he realized what he'd just said.

But Azmin seemed perfectly cognizant of the criticism she faced.

She beamed even more brightly. "I give you permission to sack anyone who insults a viscountess. Power has gone to my head."

Zane laughed, kissed her, and mussed her hair as the carriage pulled up to the stairs and the waiting staff. "You're a mean woman, but Mr. Stewart needed to be sacked. He was a rotten teacher and did not treat the college's new female students with respect."

"Now that she is seeing more clearly and has some support, Eleanor has hired a very good solicitor," Azmin said in satisfaction, studying the lines of neatly uniformed servants. "Divorce is only possible for adultery or desertion, so she's only filing for separation for cruelty. She's feeling protective of other women at the moment. She doesn't want the blackguard marrying anyone else."

Zane stepped out and offered his hand up to help her descend. "She has an infant to think of for the moment. She may change her mind later. Maybe the laws will change by then. Smile, they're watching every movement."

Azmin laughed, shook out her new pelisse so it revealed only glimpses of her russet and gold skirt, and took his arm to face their future.

Having been prepared for this moment by the steward, and his consultation with the earl of Lochmas, Zane stood still for a moment, letting his bride absorb the staff his eccentric relation had gathered—from all over the world.

Azmin beamed at the colorful array of faces. "Your uncle traveled widely, I take it?"

"No, he was crippled by a stroke decades ago and decided to bring the world to him." He nodded at several young Asian maids bobbing curtsies. "Your wandering relations aided his cause. Had I not been so obsessed with saving Louisa, I might have met the rather extraordinary old man. My horizons need widening," Zane admitted as a solemn black man opened the door.

"Then we shall travel to meet my father and explore the world as soon as your other obligations are satisfactorily completed. I'm so glad I brought my equipment. I'll have some extraordinary photographs by the time we leave here." Azmin lifted her skirt and followed him, greeting each disparate servant with delight.

Zane did not argue with his wife's need to carry on her photography. He planned on giving her a studio in his new research building—so they might explore the use of photography in determining infections and disease. It was a long shot, but research had to begin somewhere.

"I am the world's happiest woman," Azmin whispered as Zane led her into a grand foyer stocked with curiosity cabinets crammed with exotic ornaments. "I'm so glad you threw eggs at me."

The halls echoed with Zane's laughter.

CHARACTERS

Dr. Alexander Dare (Zane)—doctor, professor

Azmin Dougall—photographer

Keya Trivedi—Azmin's friend; **Yedhu**—her husband

Gopala Trivedi—Keya's younger brother

Hugh Morgan—accountant; investor

Louisa Howard—Zane's invalid niece

Septimus Dare Jenkins— student

Jane Jenkins—wife of Septimus Jenkins

Lady Agnes—one of the heads of the School of Magic

Lady Gertrude—sister to Lady Agnes; the other owner of the School of Magic

Wilson—disabled hackney driver

Mary—Zane's housemaid

Dean Reynolds—head of Zane's university department

Thomson—Zane's untrained butler

Mary Belkin—Zane's untrained maid

Grey—Azenor's housemaid

Mrs. Balfour—Azmin's neighbor

Eleanor Stewart—Mrs. Balfour's niece, married to Frederick Stewart

Miss Rose White—daughter of university director
Ulf—Indian servant
Robby—errand boy
Earl of Lochmas—part of Azmin's extended family
Colonel Ronald Dougall—Azmin's father
Michael Murdoch—Azmin's new footman

AUTHOR'S NOTE

When I started this book, Covid-19 or Corona Virus was not even on the periphery of my vision. I wrote about a fever familiar to the Victorian era that struck my hero's family because it suited my story. Infectious diseases have always swept through human populations, killing and maiming. I had no idea one would soon be affecting us. As I prepare this book for publication, I know thousands have died and many more are in danger. I do not know the outcome. My heart is with everyone affected by the disease and the crisis brought on by it. I can only hope this book is a temporary distraction from problems and that someday, this will be read with only a vague memory or a few scars from this terrible time. Virtual hugs and elbow bumps to anyone reading this.

My original concern was about writing a non-white character. In today's current environment, there is always an audience that cries racist if any of my characters do or say anything of which they, personally, in their 21st-century sensitivity, do not approve. In fact, the word *racist* didn't come into use until the 1930s. Our collective social consciousness did not develop until much, *much* later, and is still a work in progress. So may I gently remind the reader that my characters live in the 19th century, in a world with very distinct, however racist, ideas of skin color.

A world where the cut of your shirt indicated your place in society certainly reeked of bigotry beyond our present comprehension. But we don't object to the classist behavior of our characters because we know these are romances and that the characters are flawed and in need of improvement. And as they learn to respect each other, they see through different eyes. Heroes *learn* from their errors.

Every single solitary one of us harbors prejudices, if only in attitude. Reading is one way to widen our perspectives, learn to overcome preconceptions—and one hopes, alleviates our need to be judgmental. Which means readers are heroes too! (and I did not say heroine, because if you think about it, why should *hero* be divided by gender? Glad to get that off my mind. <G>)

I write to show that love really does make the world go around. Communication, coming to know each other, are how we humans learn to live with our differences, not by throwing insults and accusations. I apologize if I offend anyone in my attempt to achieve that objective and ask you to look through the characters' eyes, not mine or your own. Thank you!

ACKNOWLEDGMENTS

Here is where I usually acknowledge everyone in my immediate sphere for their kindness, helpfulness, and willingness not to kill me when I'm writing and researching. This time, I would also like to acknowledge all the wonderful photographers who have spent time blogging, videoing, and producing brilliant essays on the various methods of Victorian photography. For a concise but detailed video, I recommend https://www.khanacademy.org/humanities/becoming-modern/early-photography/v/wet-collodion-process

I had no idea how difficult it would be for me to grasp all the various photographic processes when I began this book or I probably never would have begun it in the first place. I wasted immense amounts of time worrying about timing and length of sun time in an Edinburgh spring and other idiocies because I didn't understand development. I have a very bad habit of diving into characters and plot and researching as I go—which was nearly disastrous in this case.

So, yes, I know I've goofed up the details in places. Please forgive me and call it authorial license. I have, when possible, gone back and corrected as many errors as I could make work with a little delete button and a lot of imagination!

And just for the visual among you, if you'd like a map of Old Town Edinburgh, there's a truly brilliant one with zoom capabilities here: https://maps.nls.uk/view/74400070#zoom=5&lat=4745&lon=4785&layers=BT

SCHOOL OF MAGIC SERIES

Lessons in Enchantment
Book 1 of School of Magic

Can a straitlaced engineer, three psychic children, and a lonely witch find love?

The daughter of an earl, Lady Phoebe Malcolm Duncan has the ability to talk to animals. She longs to be a veterinarian, but education requires more coin than she possesses. When the walls of her home come tumbling down, she has to take two steps back —to servitude.

Inventor Andrew Blair keeps his nose to the grindstone, knowing his friends and family depend on his talent for turning machines into money. He is about to embark on his biggest investment yet—rebuilding crumbling tenements in Old Town Edinburgh— until his beleaguered cousin begs him to hide his precocious children from a killer.

When the School of Malcolms sends Lady Phoebe as governess for his wards, Drew's well-ordered beliefs are upended. Ladies don't live in slum housing like the one he's about to tear down, nor do they command ravens or encourage children to talk to dead mothers. It might take a vengeful ghost to show the disparate pair how to join forces, fight their fears and their enemies, and reveal a path to love.

～

A Bewitching Governess
Book 2 of School of Magic

She's the mistress of illusion; How can he trust her lessons on love?

Lady Olivia Malcolm Hargreaves is a viscountess, a widow, a governess, the adopted mother of a disabled toddler—but above all else, she is a survivor. When the father of the young children she's been caring for arrives on Christmas Eve, drunk and ranting, his aura and her own sad experience tell her he's dangerous.

Heart hardened after the murder of his beloved wife, Simon Blair is an industrialist who has no use for another psychic Malcolm. His late wife's weird family is more than enough interference. But his twin daughters are talking to their mother's ghost, his son and heir is floating objects that shouldn't float, and he's beleaguered by aristocrats who refuse to acknowledge his plebeian existence.

When Simon learns that Lady Olivia is in a position to help him obtain the land he needs for his business, and she recognizes that by helping him, she might regain the home she's lost, they must fight their respective prejudices and forge an uneasy alliance. It might take a ghost, an army of children, and a criminal gang to force them to recognize that they want far more than real estate.

ABOUT THE AUTHOR

With several million books in print and *New York Times* and *USA Today's* bestseller lists under her belt, former CPA Patricia Rice is one of romance's hottest authors. Her emotionally-charged contemporary and historical romances have won numerous awards, including the *RT Book Reviews* Reviewers Choice and Career Achievement Awards. Her books have been honored as Romance Writers of America RITA® finalists in the historical, regency and contemporary categories.

A firm believer in happily-ever-after, Patricia Rice is married to her high school sweetheart and has two children. A native of Kentucky and New York, a past resident of North Carolina and Missouri, she currently resides in Southern California, and now does accounting only for herself.

ALSO BY PATRICIA RICE

Moonlight and Memories

Shelter from the Storm

Wayward Angel

Denim and Lace

Cheyennes Lady

Dark Lords and Dangerous Ladies Series

Love Forever After

Silver Enchantress

Devil's Lady

Dash of Enchantment

Indigo Moon

Too Hard to Handle

Texas Lily

Texas Rose

Texas Tiger

Texas Moon

Mystic Isle Series

Mystic Isle

Mystic Guardian

Mystic Rider

Mystic Warrior

Mysteries:

Family Genius Series

Evil Genius

Undercover Genius

Cyber Genius

Twin Genius

Twisted Genius

Tales of Love and Mystery

ABOUT BOOK VIEW CAFÉ

Book View Café Publishing Cooperative (BVC) is an author-owned cooperative of over fifty professional writers, publishing in a variety of genres including fantasy, romance, mystery, and science fiction. Since its debut in 2008, BVC has gained a reputation for producing high-quality ebooks. BVC's ebooks are DRM-free and are distributed around the world. The cooperative is now bringing that same quality to its print editions.

BVC authors include New York Times and USA Today bestsellers as well as winners and nominees of many prestigious awards, including:

Agatha Award
Campbell Award
Hugo Award
Lambda Award
Locus Award
Nebula Award
Nicholl Fellowship
PEN/Malamud Award
Philip K. Dick Award

RITA Award
World Fantasy Award
Writers of the Future Award